A STUNNING SEQUEL TO *STAR TREK® VI: THE UNDISCOVERED COUNTRY* BY ONE OF THE WRITERS OF THE FILM! #74

STAR TREK®

THE FEARFUL SUMMONS

POCKET
BOOKS
STAR TREK®

DENNY MARTIN FLINN

$5.50 U.S.
$6.99 CAN.

A novel by
William Shatner

ASHES OF EDEN

**Available from
Pocket Books Hardcover**

In the apparent
twilight of his carreer,
Kirk's path takes an
unexpected turn that
forces him to choose
between conquering
the gravest challenge
of his career,
or surrendering to
the greatest passion
of his life.

ISBN 0-671-89007-7

9 780671 890070

50550

EAN

"GREAT. ANOTHER KLINGON JAIL . . ." DR. McCOY SAID.

"Maybe this time they should just skip the trial," the doctor added as he and James Kirk were hustled along, Klingon disruptors prodding them in the back. "I don't think reasonable doubt is part of their judicial system anyway."

"Bones," Kirk whispered, "when we get to the next corner, I'm going to trip this guard next to me; we'll head for the crowd on the street. Maybe they won't attempt to fire with so many Prometheans around."

"Relying on a Klingon's humanity? Excellent plan," McCoy groused.

A few feet farther, the Klingon leader stepped off the sidewalk. A few moments later, Kirk and McCoy reached the same spot. As Kirk began to step down, he shot his foot out in front of the guard next to him. With the help of a strong push in the back, the big Klingon stumbled off the sidewalk.

At once, Kirk and McCoy turned the corner at a run and sprinted several yards ahead and into the crowd.

"Scotty!" Kirk shouted into his communicator. "Where the hell are you?"

Look for STAR TREK Fiction from Pocket Books

Star Trek: The Original Series

Star Trek: The Next Generation

Star Trek: Deep Space Nine

Star Trek: Voyager

STAR TREK®

THE FEARFUL SUMMONS

DENNY MARTIN FLINN

POCKET BOOKS

New York   London   Toronto   Sydney   Tokyo   Singapore

An *Original* Publication of POCKET BOOKS

POCKET BOOKS, a division of Simon & Schuster Inc.
1230 Avenue of the Americas, New York, NY 10020

This book is published by Pocket Books, a division of Simon & Schuster Inc., under exclusive license from Paramount Pictures.

ISBN: 0-671-89007-7

First Pocket Books printing June 1995

10 9 8 7 6 5 4 3 2 1

POCKET and colophon are registered trademarks of Simon & Schuster Inc.

Printed in the U.S.A.

Thanks to Deborah Schneider, Dave Stern and Kevin Ryan for their continuing support of this project, Nick Meyer for introducing me to the world of STAR TREK, and Barbara, Brook and Dylan for their patience.

THE FEARFUL SUMMONS

Day One

"THERE IS A SAYING in the Book of Muharbar," Maldari said to the Steersman behind him. "Things belong to those who desire them most."

Maldari stood in front of his viewscreen, staring at the enormous, sleek *U.S.S. Excelsior,* its white hull gleaming, its observation ports shining, its huge twin nacelles' engines silent as it floated in black space.

"I have heard they are capable of a cruising speed of warp eight," the Steersman said. "And that they can stay in space for five years at a time, without returning to their port."

"You have heard more than that," Maldari said, knowing the young Steersman was out of his planetary system for the first time. "You have heard that Federation Starships are invincible. You tremble at the thought of their power, their swiftness. You believe they have magical abilities to be everywhere, hear everything, see everything. But they do not."

"They have defeated Klingon Birds-of-Prey in interstellar combat."

"Perhaps. Or perhaps the Klingons defeated themselves." Maldari twisted to see his Sightsman. "Have they scanned us?"

"Not yet," the third Beta Promethean on the bridge answered.

Maldari turned back to the young Steersman. "Then put that dead moon between us at once."

Maldari watched the sparkling Starship disappear behind a great gray lusterless globe, pockmarked with craters.

"You don't want the Federation ship to see us?" the Steersman asked. "Are we going to—"

"Patience, Barush. I don't know what we are going to do. When I do"—he turned away from the screen, and his sharp, crooked teeth flashed in a sarcastic smile—"you will be the first I will confide in, of course." Maldari's pear-shaped body, which rested on four short legs, scuttled behind the two crewmen and ducked under the archway. The young Steersman's mottled gray face darkened with embarrassment.

Maldari continued along the corridor joining the bridge to the *Sundew*'s central hull. *In the meantime,* he thought, *it will be best if they are unaware of us. Perhaps it can be to our advantage. It has been an unrewarding voyage. We have boarded an ancient starship that turned out to be virtually empty but for a few scientists. No valuable commodities, not even any women to take to the slave markets. We landed on a planet that had no use for dilithium, or any other goods, for it had no technology. We have searched whole systems and found little of value. Our holds are practically empty, after nearly a year away from port. Our permit for star travel will be rescinded if we do not bring home something valuable, and if I cannot tithe a sufficient amount to the Shrewdest Ones, they will mark my ship as undesirable, and I will have difficulty enlisting a crew for another voyage.*

Frustrated and dismayed, Maldari entered the central cabin. His foul mood further darkened when he found both Kornish and Dramin there.

2

The *U.S.S. Excelsior*
Somewhere beyond the frontier
Spring, 2294 A.D.

The planet floated serenely in black space, three-quarters of its surface shimmering in blue, the rest islands of brown and green. Puffy white clouds hugged it and a single barren moon drifted in close orbit. *How like Earth,* Sulu thought as he watched it on the forward viewscreen, and for just a moment he was back there, wandering the pleasant streets of San Francisco, where, almost three decades earlier, he had reported to Headquarters for his first assignment for Starfleet and the United Federation of Planets.

It was quiet on the bridge of the *Excelsior.* Low voices percolated around him. Lights had dimmed automatically when the science officer put the illuminated celestial body on the monitor. Most of the crew were staring at it, as Sulu was, transfixed by its beauty.

"In actual fact, it is not a bit like your home planet," Science Officer Sencus said in a low voice to Sulu from behind him, guessing his thoughts. "According to our scans, the atmosphere is entirely free of pollution, the soil is without chemicals of any kind, and the water is pure H_2O. There are eighty million species, all fairly abundant, from insects to fish to mammals, some of which have developed a fairly complex form of communication. But nothing humanoid. From volcanic substances we can estimate the age of the planet to be one hundred fifty billion years, somewhat older than the Earth, in fact. It has abundant vegetation and no carnivorous species. Surface storms are short-lived and mild. Because it is equidistant from two suns, the temperature only varies approximately ten degrees in either direction from a mean of fifty degrees Celsius."

"In short, it's a paradise." Sulu smiled. "Lucky us."

"None of the species has made any attempt to leave the planet," the Vulcan went on without acknowledging Sulu's comment. "Nor have they yet attempted to communicate with other sentient beings."

"We could be in stationary orbit in one hour, Captain,"

3

Sulu's navigator said. "I'd be glad to lead a landing party." The young officer had turned around and was smiling at Sulu.

The conversation had attracted half a dozen of the officers on the bridge. They were clustered around the captain's chair, trying to appear casual. But Sulu knew perfectly well what they were hoping. It had been several months since they had last set foot on land, and their most recent visit to a foul and frigid planet inhabited only by massive swarms of watermelon-sized animals resembling cockroaches could hardly be called rest and relaxation. They were hoping for a chance to make a closer examination of the pristine mass that floated on the monitor in front of them.

"Unfortunately"—Sulu raised his voice for the benefit of his eavesdroppers—"we will have to pass it by. If we reveal ourselves to them at this time, the knowledge of our existence alone could alter the course of their history. Suddenly aware of artificial technology and other civilizations, they might be forced to respond. And as you all know, it is against the Prime Directive of Starfleet that we should interfere in any way with the development of another civilization. Sorry, ladies and gentlemen."

The little body of officers drifted away amid some groans and muttering.

"A logical decision, Captain," the Vulcan science officer said. "Though apparently an unpopular one," he added.

Sulu looked up at Commander Sencus. When his original science officer, Masoud Valtane, had been transferred to another assignment, Sulu requested the old Vulcan as his replacement because of the Vulcan character. Although it was sometimes a strain to continually be confronted with a man who lacked emotion entirely, he knew from observing the relationship between the captain and the science officer on his first starship assignment that it was worthwhile. A Vulcan's ability to meet every situation, no matter how urgent or complex, with crystal-clear logic, could be an excellent balance for a commander with human emotions and sometimes all too human failings.

"They had hoped to spend a few days on a nice, habitable planet," Sulu explained.

"Why?" Sencus asked.

"Because—well—because it's a new environment. They could have taken a walk, or a swim."

"They can do that on the rec deck," Sencus answered.

"Well, they could have had a meal that wasn't from the synthesizers. Perhaps even held a conversation with an alien. You know, just a little change from routine. Something different from our starship. Just for the variety. For the pleasure of it."

"The pleasure of it . . . I see." Sencus nodded, then returned to his customary station at the science console.

Clearly he doesn't, Sulu thought. *He doesn't see at all.*

"A Federation Starship would be a great prize," Dramin said carefully. "It must be full of freight. Valuable commodities from all over the galaxy."

"And a crew," Kornish said warningly. "For a ship that size . . . how many, Maldari?"

"I have no idea," Maldari answered, wishing he hadn't run into these two—the political officer and the religious officer—and then deriding himself for casually informing them that they had come across a large, modern Starship. "It could be a few dozen. Or hundreds. I've never seen one inside."

"It's large enough for hundreds," Kornish followed up quickly. "Many of them soldiers, no doubt."

"Disbelievers, all of them," Dramin said.

Maldari watched Dramin sip thick, steaming liquid from his cup. *It's that thick sludge they all drink,* he thought. *Must be addictive. Makes them fanatics.*

"I heard once they allow beliefs of every description," Maldari suggested.

"There, you see. How absurd. They do not belong in the universe."

"It's a big universe," Kornish said. "We have to be realistic."

Maldari couldn't tell which way Kornish was leaning. It was always the same. Every time members of the Ruling Family are aboard, they serve only to confuse the issue. They are here purely as spies. If Kornish made no commit-

5

ment, he was free to claim support for a success, and able to distance himself from failure. *Members of the Ruling Family must be taught hypocrisy at the cradle,* Maldari thought.

"Does this mean," Maldari said politely to Kornish, peevishly deciding to put him on the spot, "that you favor turning toward home? Shall we return to port with only what we have managed to secure so far?"

"Your holds are practically empty," Kornish said equivocally, emphasizing the pronominal adjective as if it were entirely Maldari's fault and responsibility. Which, come to think of it, it was.

"I can't put a Federation Starship in them," Maldari answered sarcastically. Next he listened to Dramin, though he knew that fanatic wouldn't have Maldari's fortunes in mind.

"The Book of Muharbar," Dramin pontificated, "divides the universe quite clearly into those who follow the Only Way and those who do not."

Convenient to call it the Only Way, then, Maldari thought.

"Those who do not, stand against those who do, and we have the obligation to remove them."

"When the holy war begins, Dramin, you must inform me," Maldari said. "I will be first to enlist. Provided, of course, that it is sanctioned by the Ruling Family." He nodded at Kornish. "In the meantime, as captain of this starship, I must decide what is worth dying for and what is not. It's certain they have shields. And even if we could catch them with their shields down, it's unlikely we have the firepower to knock them out at once. They could be a formidable foe."

"You are afraid of a Federation Starship," Dramin said.

"I am not," Maldari said proudly. "I am only careful. Perhaps you are willing to commit suicide if the Book of Muharbar says so. But the crew to which I am responsible may not all feel the same way. For them, piracy is merely an occupation. There are no cowards aboard my ship, there are only brave men. But neither are they stupid. If I do not bring the majority of them home with a large profit, I will not be a captain they will fly with another time."

"You are going to pass them by then?" Kornish asked.

"I didn't say that. But that Starship is not a lightly armed freighter with a crew of five sleepy starmen. Ramming and boarding them will gain us nothing for our holds, and the *Sundew* will be renowned for its fool of a captain."

"What you need," Dramin said, his fanatic's eyes shining, "is a plan."

"Thank you, Dramin," Maldari said. "I'm so glad I ran into you while I was considering my options. Whatever Conclave gets you for their Shrewdest One will be lucky indeed." He scuttled out of the lounge, once more feeling that he had been less than diplomatic with his political and religious officers. He hoped that his sarcasm had been over their heads, but he doubted it.

In the corridor again, he thought over how Kornish and Dramin seemed to be always together. They couldn't possibly like each other. And they certainly couldn't trust each other. Then he realized why. It was only because all the ordinary crew members stayed away from them both.

Sulu sat with his science officers in the conference room off the main bridge and chaired a discussion on the planet, since dubbed "the Mirage" by the crew, because they would not get to visit it in person. More scans had been run and several probes had been sent to the surface camouflaged as rocks. The communications team had recorded and decoded several languages used by the cetaceans. Geologists had mapped the planet's landmass down to the core, and constructed a natural history of the planet. Meteorologists had charted its weather patterns, and chaostaticians had projected them one hundred years into the future, identifying what sort of effect the climate would impose on the inhabitants. Microbiologists had mapped the genetic structure of the principal species and projected their evolutionary development for the near future. Short of visiting the surface, it was the consensus of the scientists that little more could be learned.

"Although there are no cities or complex structures of any kind," Sencus was saying when Sulu's mind settled on the conference, "each species fits into the biosystem in a benign and comfortable fashion. And while they have consistently adapted to gradual changes in the environment, there is no sign that any of the species has ever attempted to adapt the environment to itself. Thus the planet is entirely uncorrupted. Finally, I have monitored a very advanced degree of mental activity. Many of the species seem to exhibit an intelligence that is quite advanced in the psychic sense, not unlike your dolphins. It is an almost perfect laboratory. They are a perfect example of millions of years of evolution without aggression." Sencus completed his presentation and turned to the biologist Sandra Pastur.

"In fact," Pastur took up the discussion, "most of the species have adapted so well to their environment—they have not dammed their rivers, interfered with migratory patterns, or cut down their rain forests—that long-range projections for evolutionary development in their physical structure indicate very little change. Here is an example of their most advanced species."

The biologist moved her hands over the console. A holograph took shape in the center of the conference table. It was a pleasant-looking creature with the face of a dolphin and an eel-like body approximately four feet long.

"For convenience' sake we have dubbed it a dolpheel. It is comfortable on both land and sea, either swimming or moving along land effortlessly, something like a snake. It mates for life and lives in family units within larger communities of several hundred. There is no identifiable antagonism either between the dolpheel and any other species, or between dolpheels themselves. They travel extensively, but not owing to either weather or food-chain patterns, since they can survive anywhere on the planet. They are simply nomadic and restless for no discernible reason. What sets them ahead of so many other species we've studied here is their thought patterns. They are apparently developing a higher consciousness, and doing so at a fairly rapid rate."

"They can read each other's thoughts, then?" Sulu asked.

"It's more like they all share many of the same thoughts. They function mentally both individually, and as a group. They do this for practical reasons—something like the way birds migrate back on Earth, where the leader's flight pattern seems to be understood so instantly by the others that they fly as one—and they do it for fun as well. They seem to play many mental games with each other, games that are very highly advanced. And they are intensely spiritual, though of course they have no religion in the institutional sense. These mental exercises seem to have a purpose. Some kind of exploration of the soul you might say. It seems a bit silly to say that they are searching for the meaning of life. They're aware already of the extremely chaotic and random nature of the universe, and even of the concept of infinity, though they have not traveled in space as you know. Rather than developing any technical skills, they are developing the mental skills that will enable them to *transcend* time and space. If that's possible. If they reach an impasse, there is no way of knowing which way they will turn. I don't think we're ever going to find them in starships traveling the galaxies like us. But in less than a hundred years we will almost surely hear from them."

"How could they contact us if they don't build subspace transmitters?" a communications officer asked.

The biologist smiled. "One of these days, they'll begin to communicate with offworlders. They'll probably begin with telepaths. Then we're going to find them inside our own heads."

There was a moment of silence around the polished conference table. The senior crew of the *U.S.S. Excelsior* looked at the figure floating in front of them curiously.

"They respect the privacy of other species, however," the biologist said in anticipation. "It is highly unlikely that they will arrive without some warning and an invitation."

The officers breathed a group sigh of relief. Sulu looked over at Dr. Bernard Hans, at eighty-three years old the oldest of the crew of the *Excelsior*.

"Dr. Hans," Sulu said. "Please give us a brief overview of your observations today."

The doctor spoke in a quiet voice, accented slightly by languages from the European continent of Earth.

"These dolpheels, and for all practical purposes every other species on the planet, have fit themselves to their environment so well that, at this point in their evolution at any rate, they are virtually untroubled with sickness or disease of any kind. I could not detect any inhabitant of the planet which was, or had ever been, sick as we know it. Of course, a few of these species are part of the larger food chain, and do fall prey to other species, but all the principal species—certainly all with any intellectual development at all—survive on the planet's vegetation. They do not have, because they do not need, an immune system. Nothing causes illness or premature death. The oldest of each species is by far the most advanced, for they never seem to slow down in their development. At some point, at approximately one hundred and fifty years old for the dolpheels, for example, they simply go off and die peacefully. Like elephants on Earth. They are neither sick nor senile in any earthly sense, but they seem to realize that their natural life span has ended. When they reach their own burying ground, their heart stops and, well, that's it. I am not often given to characterizations outside of the purely scientific, but I must say I find these creatures rather noble. I for one look forward to the time they are ready and able to introduce themselves into the community of the universe. They may have much to teach us."

The doctor's report had closed out the round of talks on the planet with a humane touch.

"I think, then," Sulu took over the discussion, "that we've done just about as much as we can here from a distance. And if we move any closer they're likely to see us. I want to thank you all for your hard work and your very impressive and complete reports. Please see that everything is stored in the ship's memory bank. We will inform the Federation of our discovery upon our return, and at that time transfer the information into Alpha Memory in the Federation library. I expect to be moving to our next assignment by 1900 hours. That's all, ladies and gentlemen."

Before the officers could rise, however, the holograph of the dolpheel drifted toward Sulu. Sulu looked at the biologist controlling the device. He was running his fingers rapidly over the console in front of him.

"Ms. Pastur, I appreciate your competence with the

projectors. If you'd like to make a film for the crew's enjoyment—"

"I'm sorry, sir, it's not me. I seem to have lost control of the holograph." She was fiddling with the console and staring at the dolpheel as it swam through the air and hovered in front of Sulu. "It seems to have taken on a life of its own."

"That is highly improbable for a holographic image," Sencus said.

"Really, I—"

Before anyone could respond, however, the animal made a quick tour of the conference table, past each officer's face, its eyes lit and its mouth twisted up in an ever-present smile. Then it returned to the center of the table, and faded away.

"Got it," the controlling biologist said. "Sorry, sir, I wasn't doing that on purpose. I guess I crossed my signals for a moment there."

The whole event took less than thirty seconds, and when it was over the crew rose and began to leave the room. Only Sencus lingered, his own elegant hands playing over the console in front of him. Sulu noticed this and walked up behind him. He glanced around, but they were the only two officers left in the conference room.

"What is it, Mr. Sencus?" Sulu asked.

"I was just checking the ship's principal memory banks, Captain."

"And . . ."

"And it seems that they have been accessed from an outside source."

"That's not possible. The computer isn't available to anyone beyond the *Excelsior,* and it's completely secure. It requires voice identification and only recognizes the senior officers."

"Nevertheless, there is evidence that the ship's basic library and internal instruction data have been scanned quite recently."

"What are you suggesting . . . old-fashioned hackers in space?"

"The memory banks have been accessed, but not directly. It's almost as if they were simply read in place."

"No one can mind-meld with a computer, Sencus."

"No one we know of, Captain," Sencus said. He rose from the table and began to leave the room.

"Wait a minute. You can't leave it like this. What are you thinking?"

"While we were studying that planet today, Captain, someone or something was studying us. That is all I know. They did not do us any harm at all, which they probably could have if they so desired. I am afraid they left no evidence of who or what they are."

"Well, what's your guess, Sencus?"

"I never guess, Captain. You know that perfectly well." He left the room.

Sulu stood alone for a minute, staring out the observation windows at the vast panorama of space. The planet was not visible to the naked eye from their current distance, since the *Excelsior* had stationed itself well beyond the range of reasonable vision for every species. In the corner of the screen was only a gray, cratered moon, without life.

Maldari stood behind his Sightsman on the bridge.

"They haven't seen us?" he questioned.

"No. They have been in orbit around that planet for nearly twelve hours."

"And you kept us hidden behind this moon?"

"Always."

"Put their image on the viewscreen."

The *U.S.S. Excelsior* appeared in black space in front of them, but its image was not as clear as it had been in the morning. Maldari looked at it again. It was the largest starship he had ever seen. And the most modern. Its great holds must be filled with treasure, he thought. Why else build such an enormous ship, if not to carry great cargo.

"Can you read an interior plan?" he asked.

"No, Captain," the Sightsman said. "We didn't have them in sight long enough. This is only from the memory banks and—"

"All right, I understand. Still, that must be the bridge, on top."

"Captain, do you think we can take her?" Barush asked.

"Barush, you are a fool much too anxious to rush in and have your *picades* cut off. To go into battle with a Federation Starship would gain us nothing but scorched hide."

"We could sneak up on them."

"You are mistaking this ancient bucket for a Klingon warship with a cloaking device. They could blow us out of the galaxy with a single photon torpedo. Little fish that want to survive hunt only littler fish, not sharks."

"Then we're going to run?" Dramin said. Maldari turned around and saw that the religious officer had entered the bridge, closely followed by the political officer.

"The *Sundew* has never run from anything in her entire career in space," Maldari said using his most guttural voice. "Not when my grandfather captained her, and not when my father captained her. And she will not run on my watch either."

"Then you have a plan?" Dramin said. "If you return with the bounty of a Federation Starship, the Shrewdest Ones would be very impressed."

"And what shall be my excuse to board her?" Maldari asked. "She may be a disbeliever to you, but she's a Starship in open space to me."

"Actually," Kornish said quietly "We've been talking about that, and I pointed out that, technically, she could be in Beta Promethean star space. We're not a signatory to their Federation. And therefore . . . Well, you see the situation."

Maldari looked at his Sightsman. *"Are* they trespassing in Beta Promethean star space?" he said harshly.

The man didn't answer at once, but his hands stumbled over his console. While they did, he kept his head down.

"Of course," Kornish went on, "it depends on your definition of star space. I'm not an expert on that, but . . ." The political officer shuffled his feet, and whatever was left of his thoughts he didn't express.

"Sightsman, are we in Beta Promethean star space?" Maldari asked again. The Sightsman looked up.

Maldari was sure that the Sightsman looked at Dramin

13

before he answered, and though Maldari wasn't looking at Dramin, he was willing to bet that Dramin nodded.

"Yes," the Sightsman said. "We are."

"Well," Maldari sighed. "It would be suicide to attempt to subdue a Federation Starship the way we deal with independent freighters. But if we could board her somehow, and control the bridge . . ."

Maldari realized that he had committed himself to a course that, a few minutes earlier, he had evaluated as extremely risky. He couldn't decide whether he had let Dramin talk him into it, or if he just couldn't resist the prize. Certainly there would be goods aboard a Federation Starship that would make his year in space the most lucrative one any Beta Promethean space trader ever had.

After the conference, Sulu visited the bridge and set the *Excelsior* on course to a Federation starbase, where they were expected to arrive within two twenty-four-hour cycles. Then he returned to his cabin. He was sitting at his desk in his white tunic carefully carving a piece of ivory when a chime sounded.

"Come in," he called without breaking his concentration on the delicate swirls of white sculpture. The hatch slid open, exposing a young Starfleet officer with a thick thatch of gray hair shading a round and eager face.

"Commander," Lieutenant Russel Roose said, "I think you might want to hear—"

"Come in, Lieutenant," Sulu called. "Look at this."

The lieutenant walked up behind him.

"Have you ever seen one of these?"

"I don't think so, sir."

"It's ivory. Synthetic, of course. But it's an exact duplicate. Real ivory only comes from the tusks of elephants, and isn't harvested anymore. You're from Africa, aren't you?"

"Yes, sir. Mandelaport, South Africa. But I don't think I've ever seen ivory that wasn't connected to its owner."

"Centuries ago ivory was a prized commodity. It was thought to be an aphrodisiac when it was ground up. It was used to make the keys for a musical instrument called the piano. And it was a medium for artwork. Before we could duplicate raw materials precisely, poachers killed elephants just for their tusks. These tusks were carved into elaborate statues and trinkets. Using these long thin razors, artisans often carved a series of ivory balls, one inside the other. The effect was truly magnificent. You can see many of these balls in the Chinatown museum in San Francisco. I'm attempting to duplicate the art—a new hobby. This will be a model of our own solar system, and I'm working on a model of the *Starship Excelsior* that will float here just between the seventh and eighth planets."

"I see . . ." Roose knew that his commander was well known by his penchant for trying to interest the many junior officers aboard the *Excelsior* in one obscure subject or another.

"Do you have a hobby, Lieutenant?"

"No, sir. I guess not." Roose was only four years out of the Academy, and his whole world was the *Excelsior.*

"You'll enjoy this. It is very calming and satisfying. Here, you take this piece and a knife."

"Thank you, but—"

"Go ahead. You try to carve something. You're going to love this. Bring it to me when you've finished."

"All right. Thank you, sir."

"Everybody should have a hobby," Sulu said with a smile. "Maybe we could start a club for ivory carvers. Meet once a week."

"Maybe so, sir."

"Be sure to show me the results. Good day, Lieutenant."

"Good day, sir."

The lieutenant lingered in the doorway, a shapeless chunk of ivory in one hand and a dangerous-looking knife in the other. Never having held a weapon that couldn't be disabled, he looked at it curiously, and handled it gingerly. Suddenly he remembered the reason for his visit.

"Uh . . . sir?"

"Yes, Lieutenant?"

"We've had a kind of mysterious communication. I thought you might want to listen to it."

Quickly Sulu put his knives neatly down on the workbench and turned to Roose. "Mysterious communication? What kind? Linguacode?"

"No, sir. A fairly ancient system of transferring information through space."

"Not on one of our normal subspace channels?"

"No. A radio transmission, actually. That is, something broadcast within the old electromagnetic frequency range."

"That is odd. Why didn't you tell me, Lieutenant?"

"I meant to, sir."

"What does Sencus have to say about it?" Sulu asked.

"He hasn't heard it yet, either, sir. He was off the bridge when it came in."

"Let's go up to the bridge. I'd like to give a listen to this myself."

"That's what I came to suggest, sir."

Sulu grabbed his jacket and hurried out the door. The lieutenant, trailing him, smiled inwardly. You could always catch the captain's full-spirited attention with an anomaly, he thought.

On the bridge Sulu went directly to the communications station, where Janice Rand was working. The blond officer looked up at Sulu and the lieutenant.

"Could you replay that message for us," the lieutenant requested.

Together they listened to thirty seconds of static. In the background Sulu faintly heard a dozen varying beeps that seemed to be repeating over and over.

"I've checked it against all known languages, sir. Everything that's in the ship's computer. If it is a language, then it's from a civilization unknown to us."

"It is not a language, exactly, it is a code," Sencus said, having walked onto the bridge just then.

"You can understand it, sir?"

"I cannot. But I can identify it for you. It is the original code used when the telegraph was invented. It is called Morse code, after the inventor of the telegraph, Samuel Morse. Six centuries ago it was utilized frequently on Earth.

But it died out as soon as voice transmission became possible." Sencus strolled over and stood behind Sulu.

"Identify it as a code and let's see if the ship's computer still has the morse vocabulary in its memory," Sulu said.

Lieutenant Rand's hands flew over the console.

"I have it," she said. "I'll put it up on the screen in English."

They looked at the forward viewscreen. One at a time, a three-letter series appeared, and repeated over and over again. Marching across the screen in block letters, it read: "SOS . . . SOS . . . SOS . . . SOS . . ."

"SOS," Lieutenant Roose mused. "That's all it says. SOS. What does that mean?"

"It means," Sulu answered quietly as he stared at the monitor, "Save Our Ship. Now, I wonder who would be broadcasting such a thing . . . ?" Sulu stepped away from the communications console and stood by himself just above the main command console. He appeared to be deep in thought. The lieutenant followed him.

"Save our ship?" the lieutenant echoed. "What kind of a message is that? I'm afraid—"

Sulu turned to the lieutenant. Any evidence of his casual nature was gone.

"It is an ancient distress signal, Lieutenant," he said sharply. "I haven't ever heard it actually used, but I can tell you it is quite serious. It's a Mayday message, an urgent appeal for the nearest Starship in the sector to provide aid at once. Back in the nineteenth century, when sailing ships actually floated on the water to cross oceans and seas, if they had capsized or were crippled for any reason, they broadcast an SOS as an immediate request for help. According to maritime law of the period, the nearest ship was required to go to its aid. In fact that is still true. Regardless of the ancient form of communication, this is a distress signal, and we are obligated to respond. Have you located the origin of the message?"

"Yes, sir, we have the coordinates of the source. It isn't far from here, though it is in the wrong direction. If we're going to make Starbase 499 by—"

"We're not. Send them a message that we're going to be late. Tell them we have answered a call for help and give them the coordinates as well, so they'll know where we'll be. Helmsman!" Sulu moved close to the center of the bridge and stood behind the conn. "The lieutenant will give you new coordinates. Alter your course at once, and increase our speed to warp eight."

"Yes, sir."

"ETA?"

The navigator swiftly calculated their speed and distance on the console. "Approximately one hour, sir."

"Let me know when we are within visual range." Sulu walked over to the science station.

"Sencus?"

"I have been listening, Captain. You will want to know exactly who is broadcasting this archaic message."

"Exactly."

"Unidentifiable at this time. No energy fields are detectable. If it is a starship, it is not under power. In fact, it is stationary."

"Orbiting?"

"No. Simply sitting in space."

"Lieutenant," Sulu called. "Send a message on all frequencies in all known languages, including morse code: 'The *Starship Excelsior* is coming to your assistance.' Sencus, ask the computer for any information on abandoned vessels or ancient ships that might have been lost in the area. And let's put the entire crew on standby."

The bridge hummed with activity as the great Starship changed directions and increased its speed. Sulu took his seat in the command chair. Everyone awaited the uncertain rendezvous.

An hour later the *Excelsior* dropped from warp eight and cruised quietly in space at vessel speed. The navigator turned to Sulu.

"I have them in range, sir."

"Visual," Sulu answered.

The forward viewscreen lit up. In the far distance they could see a ship.

"Magnify."

The ship loomed up. It was an ancient design by Starfleet standards, dirigible-shaped, gunmetal gray with few viewing ports. The material it was coated with was corroded and dented in places, as if it had collided with small asteroids or space debris and never been repaired. There were few markings, but a faded identification could be made out on the nose cone.

"Scan the markings."

The monitor jumped again, and quickly featured the nose of the old starship. It was painted with odd hieroglyphics. Sulu turned to his science officer.

"Sencus, can you translate?"

"It is the language of the Prometheans from the Beta Prometheus star system. The name of the starship roughly translates as *Sundew,* out of Archnos.' That is the largest city in their civilization."

"Give me hailing frequency."

"Channels open, sir."

"This is Captain Sulu of the *U.S.S. Excelsior.* We have received your distress signal and are prepared to assist you. Do you read me, *Sundew?*"

"I'm getting an answer of some sort, Captain," the communications officer said. "I'll run it through translation. Here you are."

The bridge was silent. The entire crew listened. Then a gruff voice came over the speakers.

"This is Maldari of the *Sundew.* Your assistance is required at once. Please transport my crew to your ship."

"Captain Maldari, this is Captain Sulu. I'm going to put you on the monitor."

The forward viewscreen crackled with static and then an unusual figure came into view. The Promethean looked humanoid, but his skin was mottled gray and wrinkled, and scaled like the belly of a snake. Short spikes of hair radiated outward from his cranium. More spikes filled his upper lip and dropped down around his mouth, reminding the crew of a fierce Mongolian warrior. His teeth appeared razor sharp and jutted out at various angles, and his eyes were black pools without pupils. Sulu felt uneasy looking at the stern visage and unbending glare. He resolved not to be ungraciously suspicious. Knowing that his own image would appear before the Promethean, he smiled and addressed the screen directly.

"Can you tell us what your trouble is, Captain?"

"We've lost all power. My engineer says it can't be restored in space. Emergency power is rapidly running out, and our life-support systems are going down now. We have less than an hour of air. We haven't had food for several days. We have a large supply of dilithium and can pay handsomely for your help."

"That will not be necessary. We will be glad to provide assistance. Please—"

"Thank you. We'll assemble in the main deck and you can transport us over at once. There are about fifty of us."

There was a short pause. The crew looked at Sulu. Then Sulu spoke to the screen.

"I'm afraid it will take us a few minutes to prepare. Please stand by, and we'll be with you shortly."

Then Sulu nodded to the communications console, and Lieutenant Rand, understanding, shut down the communication temporarily. The Promethean's vision disappeared from the screen. Ensign Violet Bays stood up from her post at the conn.

"Captain Sulu, we are capable of transporting their crew in two shifts at once. If their life-support systems are failing, shouldn't we—"

"Thank you, Ensign. Though I've never seen a Beta Promethean before, I must say that Captain Maldari didn't look like he was dying. He didn't even look hungry for that matter. And he did say that they had almost an hour of life support left. I think they can wait just a few minutes. I want to think about this for a moment."

Never be hasty, Sulu thought. *Particularly where haste seems to be desired by others.* He smiled at the sudden memory of his first commander, standing like a rock amid chaos. *Nobody pushed him around.*

Sulu turned calmly toward the science station. "Sencus, what do we have on Beta Prometheus?"

"They are not a member of the Federation, and have

never sent envoys to galactic conferences. Of their three planets, only BP 1 supports life. Although we could tolerate their atmosphere, temperatures vary from eighty degrees Celsius to below freezing at night. Something like your Earth desert."

Sencus's hands played over his computer, and he drew up a holograph of the race. All the officers on the bridge saw that a Promethean's large, squat body spread out like a pear, and four leglike tentacles were attached at the bottom. Their two arms were the portion of their anatomy closest to human: short and hairy and intensely muscular. They were slightly shorter in height and broader in girth than humans.

"Because of their extensive deposits of dilithium crystals, they are quite rich. This has turned them into space traders primarily. They create almost nothing, preferring to travel the galaxy trading their dilithium crystals for everything they need or want. Even food production has almost disappeared from their planet. Thus the ship we have before us is probably a cargo ship."

"Thank you, Sencus." Traders, Sulu thought. Nothing wrong with that. An ancient and noble profession. But not people to be taken always at face value, either.

"Ms. Bays, how far are we from Beta Prometheus?"

The seven-foot woman looked over at Sulu from her seat at the navigator's console.

"Almost eleven light-years, Captain. To return them to their home port would place us several days beyond our original schedule for rendezvous at the starbase. Travel time would depend on whether or not we were towing their ship."

Sulu sat for thirty seconds more, a dozen possible circumstances racing through his mind. His officers waited in silence. Then he stood up.

"Sulu to Engineering."

"Svenson here." The rich voice came over the intercom and everyone on the bridge heard him.

"Mr. Svenson, do you think your crew could repair their ship and send them on their way?"

"Ya, but I'd have to take a look to be sure."

"All right, prepare your crew to beam aboard the *Sundew*. I'll meet you in the transporter room. We'll take a portable energy converter and get their life-support systems working at once. Then we can investigate the necessary repairs to their ship."

Sulu turned to his bridge crew.

"I'm going aboard with Engineering. Lieutenant Roose, Ensign Bays, I'd like you to accompany me. Mr. Sencus, you will remain here as the senior officer in charge."

"You are not intending to beam them aboard then, Captain?" Lieutenant Roose asked.

"I don't think that will be necessary, Lieutenant. Besides, have you ever heard of the ancient story of the Trojan horse?"

"I don't think so, sir."

"It was an enormous wooden horse that was left at the gates of Troy as a gift. The Trojans brought it inside their walls. But it was a trick. It was filled with Greek soldiers, and that night they came out and conquered Troy. It is the myth upon which is based the old saying, 'Beware of Greeks bearing gifts.' No offense meant, Spiros. Why don't you come with us as well, in case their navigation systems need attention?"

The young cadet turned around from his post and smiled, his dazzling white teeth set off by his long black hair.

"None taken, Captain. A wise decision." He rose eagerly out of his seat.

"All right, then," Sulu said. "Put me on with this Maldari fellow again."

The forward viewscreen came to life. The Promethean scowled at them from the screen.

"Captain Maldari, I believe we can help you more efficiently without having to beam your whole crew aboard the *Excelsior*. We have sufficient equipment to power your life-support systems and will bring it aboard. Our engineers can then assist you in making the necessary repairs to your power source. We have an excellent chief engineer. He and his crew and I will beam aboard the *Sundew,* with your permission."

"We are going to die here, Sulu, if something isn't done."

"I understand the emergency nature of your situation.

Please reassure yourselves that you are in no danger. The *Excelsior* has outstanding resources for full repair work in space. We will bring a portable food synthesizer as well, and can provide nourishment for your entire crew while we get your problems straightened out."

"Very well, Sulu."

The monitor went dark.

At that moment, Sulu became aware that Dr. Bernard Hans had come onto the bridge and was watching the exchange.

"Dr. Hans," Sulu said. "Would you mind coming with us? There may be some injuries or illness due to the failure of their power source. We don't know what kind of medical care they have, and you might be of some assistance to them."

"You couldn't keep me away. I came up from sickbay for exactly that. Besides, they may be an interesting species for observation as well. I've never seen humanoids with such bad teeth."

Maldari had to think quickly. It didn't help that Dramin walked up beside him.

"What will you tell them when they discover our engines are functioning?"

Maldari left the question unanswered. But after a moment of thought, he turned to the Steersman.

"Set a course for Beta Promethean star space. Put us inside the boundaries. *By everyone's definition.*" He looked up at Dramin and Kornish. Both of them were expressionless. "We are to leave as soon as they are aboard. Barush, raise our shields as soon as they all step off the platform."

"Shields or not, you said they could blast us out of the galaxy with one photon torpedo, Captain."

"As long as we are holding some of them, we will be safe. Humans are like that. They are ridiculously loyal, and will not endanger each other. We will then be able to trade our prisoners for an enormous amount of goods. It will be the greatest swap in Promethean history. I am going below to assist in their arrival."

Maldari flashed his crooked smile, then scuttled across the deck and disappeared into the corridor.

Five men and women from the engineering section, led by Chief Engineer Norquist Svenson, were already waiting with several large crates of equipment when Sulu, Lieutenant Russel Roose, Ensign Violet Bays, Dr. Bernard Hans, and Cadet Spiros Focus arrived at the transporter. The engineers had loaded the transport crates onto the platform already.

Sencus appeared in the doorway.

"Captain, I think it would be wise if I went with you. This is an alien race with an eccentric background and their experience in dealing with others has been largely confined to trading. I might be of some assistance."

"You would be of enormous assistance, I'm sure. Unfortunately, our first responsibility is to the *Excelsior,* and you are first officer. It's important that I leave you in command of our Starship. We will be in constant communication with you, and will probably be able to return and continue on our own way within a few hours. Svenson could build a working engine out of Popsicle sticks if he had to. Repairing this old bucket won't be any trouble at all for him. Carry on."

"As you request, Captain Sulu." Sencus, tall and thin and with the aristocratic bearing of all Vulcans, turned and left the transporter room at once.

"Logic," Sulu said quietly to Lieutenant Roose at his elbow, "would have dictated that as second-in-command he remain aboard the *Excelsior.* His desire to come with us was probably nothing more than pure curiosity and a sense of adventure. Don't ever let a Vulcan tell you they are entirely without emotions. Somewhere in the Vulcan genetic code there is a hidden warm spot."

"Yes, sir. I'll remember that."

"You have it on good authority. I knew one who was half human, and yet he was constantly denying that side of his own character. You can trust them to act with an absolute clarity of logic. On the other hand, you can always trust them, period. That is a reliable characteristic which goes well beyond logic, and gives them the ability to form great friendships. I'm hoping for one with Sencus," Sulu whispered. "But he's all Vulcan, and it's going to take a lot of time." Sulu changed his tone, but continued speaking to Lieutenant Roose. "Are we ready?"

"I think so, sir," Roose said, then he handed a small disk to Sulu. "I've programmed these Universal Translators for the Beta Prometheus language. They will fasten to our uniforms here." He touched a point high up in the center of his chest, just below his throat. "They will enable us to be understood, and will turn their language into English."

Sulu took one and put it on. His crew did the same.

"Well now, let's see what a Promethean is like, shall we?" Sulu said. He smiled at the lieutenant and stepped up onto the transporter platform. The others followed quickly. Then Chief Engineer Svenson signaled to an officer at the console, and the transporter beams buzzed and flickered. As the eleven Starfleet officers and their cargo dematerialized, Sulu thought how attractive an assignment in deep space was. You had the opportunity to encounter so many interesting new civilizations.

Acting Captain's Log, Stardate 9621.8

While Commander Sulu is aboard the *Sundew*, a trading ship to whose assistance we have come, I am responsible for the *Excelsior*. It is odd that the crippled starship was not able to receive help from someone in their own fleet. Surely they must have other Promethean starships in the sector, closer than we were. And while it may be impolite to judge aliens by their appearance, Prometheans seem to me to be a sinister-looking lot. Circumstances here are not as simple as they appear to be, and should be monitored closely. Science officer and acting Captain Sencus.

As the boarding party dematerialized on the *Sundew*'s transporter platform, Sulu immediately felt that something was wrong. Then it hit him: *The transporter room is illuminated, which means that the ship cannot have lost all its power.* With an uneasy feeling he stepped off the platform, his hand instinctively resting on his phaser.

But as he did, several dozen Prometheans scuttled into the transporter room from several corridors. They aimed a formidable if motley array of weapons at the crew of the *Excelsior*. Maldari scuttled in behind them. He pushed his way to the front and stood several feet from Sulu.

"You are under arrest for spying in a Promethean sector. Take your hand away from your phaser or your crew will be killed."

Sulu's face turned red with anger.

"The *U.S.S. Excelsior* has not been spying. We have arrived here at your request for assistance. We are not in violation of anyone's star space, least of all Beta Prometheus. Your hospitality leaves a great deal to be desired, Captain Maldari."

"You are spies from the Federation. You have been caught red-handed, and now you are prisoners of the People of Light." Maldari spat out the words angrily, and acted as if he believed them. "You will put all your weapons down at once. Also your communicators. Come this way."

Sulu looked at the weapons aimed at him and his crew. They were varied and ancient, but they all looked as if they could do serious damage to humans, and the aliens who held them looked experienced in their use.

"Don't resist. Do as they say." Sulu tried to keep his voice even. Inside he was seething, as much at himself as he was for the behavior of the Prometheans.

At his instructions the crew stepped off the platform and, surrounded by Prometheans, followed Maldari out of the transporter room, leaving their phasers, boxes of equipment, translators, and tricorders on the floor behind them.

I should have foreseen this, Sulu thought. *I should have been more careful. Now I have endangered my crew.* It was absurd, he couldn't help thinking, to think that this fifth-rate space pirate Captain Maldari could get away with kidnapping officers of a Starfleet ship of the line. Shields or not, the small space freighter they were on wouldn't withstand a minor hit by *Excelsior*'s phasers. And the United Federation of Planets had a starbase less than three light-days away, with powerful ships on call. In fact, this was ridiculous, was the principal thought in Sulu's mind. It was patently absurd.

Spiros Focus was shoved by one of his captors. He turned around instinctively and quickly swung his hand against the bridge of the man's nose. Everyone in the corridor heard the bone crack. Green blood spurted out from the man's face. His gun went off, and a thin laser beam shot forward and went through Spiros's upper arm. He staggered backward. It all happened in a moment.

"Stop it," Sulu yelled out to his officers.

And Maldari raised his hand sharply.

There was a brief minute, almost frozen in time, when the two sides were poised to do battle. The crew of the *Excelsior,* without weapons, would surely have gotten the worst of it. Sulu feared there would be a bloodbath.

"Spiros, do as they request. That goes for all of you. Do not oppose them. Their outrageous conduct will very shortly be subject to intergalactic scrutiny. In the meantime, we will all have to do as they say."

Sulu said this without his Universal Translator, and Maldari listened without understanding. When Sulu's crew turned away from their guards and relaxed their aggressive stances, Maldari waved for them all to continue.

In the corridor Dr. Hans caught up with Spiros and gave his arm a cursory examination.

"I'm all right, Dr. Hans," Spiros said.

"It's just a scratch. But there is no telling what kind of infection might set in from these primitive weapons. Maldari," he said to the Promethean walking several feet in front of him. "I've got to have my medical equipment. I've got a scanner and—"

But the man only shouted something unintelligible and turned his attention away.

"This is outrageous, Captain Sulu," Dr. Hans said.

"Nevertheless," Sulu said quietly, "I'm afraid we are at their mercy for the time being. As soon as I can, I'll try to talk with Captain Maldari again."

At that moment the glorious unpredictability of deep space, its inhabitants and its phenomena, did not seem so attractive to Sulu. Even the pleasure of having his own command seemed dulled just now. As he rapidly began to run over the various permutations and possibilities in his mind, Sulu resisted the impulse to ask himself what his old commander would do.

Casually scanning the *Sundew* with a sensor he had sent to orbit the craft, Sencus noticed a level of activity in the energy fields that belied the fact that the *Sundew* was without power. He read the scans and turned to the helmsman.

"Lieutenant Henrey," Sencus said quietly. "Do you read shields on the *Sundew?*"

"They just went up this minute, sir. I thought that their power was—"

"Yes, precisely. Yet they can raise their shields. And why have they done so just now? It seems a peculiarly rude thing to do." He turned to the communications station. "Get me Sulu."

"Sir, I've been monitoring the team's whereabouts continually and a few minutes ago I lost track of them." Lieutenant Rand, at the communications console, looked puzzled and harried. She was rapidly trying out different frequencies. "The fact is, I can't seem to raise him. Or anyone else on the team. It's as if their communicators had all failed at the same time. I've never—"

"Raise the *Sundew,* then."

"I have them, sir."

"Captain Maldari, this is Captain Sencus, acting commander of the *U.S.S. Excelsior.* Come in, please."

Everyone on the bridge looked at the main viewscreen. It remained black.

"Sundew, do you read me? This is the *U.S.S. Excelsior."*

The screen flashed with static, but nothing appeared.

"They're accelerating, sir," the navigator said quickly.

There was an uproar on the bridge. Sencus called for quiet. He ordered Rand to keep track of the *Sundew*'s course and whereabouts.

Sencus was sure that Svenson and his team of *Excelsior*

engineers couldn't possibly have gotten the *Sundew*'s power systems up and operational in just those few moments. And he knew that Sulu wouldn't have allowed their propulsion systems to be tested without warning the *Excelsior* that they were going to use their engines.

"Lieutenant, follow the *Sundew*."

"Yes, sir!" Henrey moved his hands expertly over the conn, and Sencus felt the *Excelsior* surge forward.

"Don't scare them, stay at least a sector away and travel no faster than they do, so they do not think we are going to attack. If they alter course radically, let me know at once."

"Yes, sir."

"Rand, are they still within range of our sensors?"

"Yes, sir."

"I want their ship mapped at once. Before they are out of range. Get me the layout of the *Sundew* as quickly as you can."

"Yes, sir."

"And call Commander Garvin to the bridge at once," Sencus said as an afterthought.

"What do you think is happening, sir?" one of the younger officers asked.

"The *Sundew* is moving away from us with eleven of our officers on board," Sencus said crisply. The experienced officers on the bridge smiled inwardly at the incredulous look of the young cadet who had asked the Vulcan science officer for what was, in essence, a guess.

Maldari saw his prisoners secured in one of the empty holds of his starship, then hurried up through the corridors and ramps to his bridge. He noted that two of the Starfleet officers were women, and that the taller one was voluptuous by many standards. *If there are as few imperfections on her dark peach body as there are on her silky smooth cranium,* he thought, *she alone will be worth a small fortune in certain markets. I'll deal with the men first. The* Excelsior *ought to be more than willing to give up some of their cargo for these officers. They won't care about the two women; we'll sell them off on the way home.*

29

When he arrived on the bridge, his star freighter was just dropping its speed and coming to a floating orbit. He noted that Kornish and Dramin were still present. They didn't appear on the bridge often, knowing that as captain of the *Sundew* Maldari had the psychological advantage there. He ignored them.

"Were we followed?" he asked the Sightsman.

"I think so," came the answer.

Maldari, about to trade for the most valuable haul with which he had ever returned home, and buoyed by the feeling that he had, on the spur of the moment, turned the whole situation to his advantage, was not in a mood to play politics with his bridge crew.

"Garith, you miserable toady, surely you can spot one of the largest starships in the galaxy. If you have to consult with your religious leader to answer a simple navigational question, then do so, but if you cannot do your duty as Sightsman, I will have you relieved, and your share of our profits for the entire voyage will be reduced accordingly. Where is the *Excelsior?*"

The young Beta Promethean's gray skin darkened on the back of his neck. He didn't look at Maldari or around at anyone else on the bridge when he answered.

"Sir, the *Excelsior* has remained out of visual range, but I believe our sensors show that it has followed us. She slowed to cruising speed when we did, and now sits approximately two light-years farther out from our position on a direct line from Beta Prometheus."

"Send this message: 'The *Excelsior* has been caught spying within restricted Beta Promethean star space. Eleven spies have been taken prisoner. Unless a satisfactory arrangement can be made, they will be tried by the Court of the People of Light. Punishment is death.' That should bring a response from their ship."

"The value of the spies is directly related to their flagrant abuse of our star space," Kornish said, stepping forward from the dark-shadowed edges of the bridge. "And thus it is the People of Light themselves who ought to receive the majority of their payment."

"As disbelievers, they ought to be executed at once," Dramin said, following him quickly.

"If I execute them here," Maldari said to Dramin testily, "the men who remain on that Starship will have no reason not to blow us out of the galaxy, which a Starship of their size could surely do. As for the Ruling Family's share"— Maldari turned to Kornish—"which I know you will use assiduously for the benefit of the People, you can be sure that we will pay our appropriate fees when we return."

Commander Peter Garvin, the *Excelsior*'s chief of security, hurried onto the bridge from the turbolift. Sencus turned to the tall, square-shouldered man with silky black hair cut short.

"The captain and the boarding party have been taken hostage by the Beta Promethean ship, Mr. Garvin. I am afraid the situation is very dangerous. The Prometheans have threatened to kill them."

"I have a team standing by right now in the transporter room. We can beam aboard and—"

"Not just yet."

"But Captain—"

"I know you are anxious. I am as well. It would only complicate matters to move precipitously, however."

"The sooner the better, I say. The quicker we act, the more likely we are to have the element of surprise on our side. We can't let them get away with this, Sencus," Garvin urged.

"We will not, I assure you. We will have a map of their ship shortly. I want you to draw up a plan of attack."

"Yes, sir." The security chief hurried off.

Sencus turned to communications again. "Are we within range?"

"We are now," Rand said.

"Put them up."

The viewscreen crackled and Maldari's face appeared. Sencus stood in the center of the bridge.

"Captain Maldari, what in Hades do you mean by 'satisfactory arrangements'?"

Sencus spoke evenly and calmly, but the Starfleet officers on the bridge had not in the four years of their expedition heard him use language like that.

Maldari smiled his crooked smile.

"The People of Light are quite poor," he began carefully. "Aside from dilithium, we have very little, and need much. The Federation is rich with resources of all kinds. If you are carrying goods that would be valuable to us, I am sure that our political officer would be disposed to accept them as a penalty for your transgressions."

"The *Excelsior* is a research and exploration Starship. We are carrying scientific equipment and little else."

"Surely the great holds of a ship such as yours are filled with freight. Perhaps if you would care to tell us what your cargo consists of . . ."

"I told you, we are not carrying freight."

"Then perhaps you can suggest something else."

"I can suggest that you return our officers at once." Sencus stared evenly at the viewscreen.

Maldari began to sweat. He had assumed the Starship was staffed only by species from the planet Earth. But this Sencus was a Vulcan, judging by his ears. He had often heard that they were not as predictable as humans. He pressed on sternly.

"Unless you can suggest substantial quantities of valuable resources, I doubt if I can get our political officer to back down. If I return to Beta Prometheus with the officers"— that was something Maldari had no intention of doing, for the Federation Starfleet officers could be extremely hard to sell—"they will have to undergo a trial for trespassing and spying. I cannot guarantee their safety in that case. I suggest you send us your Starship's manifest, and perhaps—"

"We are not paying a ransom," Sencus said, an imperceptible rise in the volume of his voice. "That would be strictly against Federation and Starfleet regulations. I could not do it if I wanted to."

Silence.

Maldari turned to his Sightsman and made a curt motion, and the screens on both ships went dark. He scuttled to his stool but hovered over it, wishing he could think clearly.

"We have heard that the Federation values its officers highly," Kornish said. "That the humans who staff the Starships do not even believe in the Higher Calling, and fear death. How could they put their cargo ahead of their people?"

Maldari didn't answer. His mind was a miasma of apprehension. *That Sencus is a Vulcan,* he thought. *I can hardly read him. His impassive face, his even voice. Is he bluffing? How do I call his bluff? What will happen if I execute one of the prisoners? How many soldiers are they carrying? Dammit. I expected to make a clean trade for a rich cargo, and hightail it home.*

"Bring their captain up," Maldari ordered. Two Promethean pirates on the bridge scuttled back down the corridor.

"We should put them on trial at home," Dramin spoke up for the first time. "It will give the people great satisfaction to see Federation species executed."

"I'm sure," Maldari agreed, thinking that the people couldn't care less about Federation species. "But it is our mission to buy and sell on behalf of the families in our Conclave, and I would prefer to honor that mission, even if it means passing up the glory of returning with spies from the Federation."

"If you give them to me," Dramin said, "I'll make good use of them at home."

"Perhaps I should," Maldari said, thinking that it would be a relief to put the whole mess in Dramin's hands. "But it would be cowardly of me to ask you to take on what is my responsibility."

Besides that, he thought, *they're my only way out of here.*

The two Prometheans returned, pushing Sulu between them. Maldari signaled for them to bring him to the center of the bridge, where he stood beside the Starfleet officer.

"Bring up the transmission," he snapped. The viewscreen came on. The Vulcan appeared to be waiting patiently.

"Commander Sencus, I wanted you to see that we have no intention of harming your officers. It is a long way back to Beta Prometheus, and in spite of the fact that they have been caught red-handed, we will return them to you if you could supply us with a respectable penalty fee for—"

"Captain, are you all right?" Sencus spoke past Maldari.

"None of our officers have been badly hurt," Sulu said carefully. "One has a superficial wound."

Maldari turned to Sulu. "You have been caught spying in the Beta Prometheus star system. As I have explained to your comrade, we should transport you back to our city, and hand you over to the Court of the People of Light. But should the *Excelsior* be able to pay a significant fine in useful resources and goods—"

"Sencus," Sulu said, startling Maldari. "No ransom. You may not offer these pirates anything. Under no circumstances should you negotiate with—"

The screen went black as Maldari shoved Sulu out of range and nodded angrily at the Sightsman. He waved at his two men and they dragged Sulu off the bridge. Then he turned to Kornish and Dramin.

"It seems," Maldari said, sighing, "that we are returning to our planet with human cargo." Then he scuttled off the bridge after Sulu, feeling as if he were caught between a titanium wall and a Rakatan volcano, and wondering how exactly he had gotten there.

Sencus sat down for the first time, assuming the captain's chair. He sat quietly for a moment, staring at his console, though nothing was illuminated there. The bridge was quiet and none of the officers moved from their stations. A knot of people had arrived on the bridge, and stood uncertainly near the turbolift. Sencus knew that everyone was staring at him.

"Put the ship on Red Alert. You may as well return to your stations. There is nothing you can do here." The group drifted off.

"Now, Lieutenant Rand, let me speak to the entire crew."

"Communication channel open, sir."

"This is Commander Sencus. This is an urgent priority report. Captain Sulu and a team of officers beamed aboard a Promethean ship a few minutes ago in order to assist them. Apparently the request for help was in fact a ruse, and the team has been taken hostage." He paused for a second, knowing that four hundred people aboard the *Excelsior* were going to be startled and upset. There would certainly be friends and even relatives of some of the hostages aboard hearing the news for the first time. "As you can guess, this is a totally unexpected and rather delicate situation. Beta Prometheus has no formal agreements with the Federation and this is an act of aggression tantamount to war. There is nothing, however, that we can do at the moment. We are following them, we are preparing several contingency plans, and we have notified Starfleet Headquarters. I can assure you that everything is going to be done to secure the safety of the captain and our fellow crew members. In the meantime, I ask for your patience. All communication monitors aboard the *Excelsior* will be immediately sent any new information as it arises. Thank you."

Sencus nodded to Lieutenant Rand at the communications console and she gave the bridge privacy once again. Then he laced his elegant fingers together, and began to silently project for himself all possible permutations of the circumstances.

"Put the *Sundew* on the main viewscreen."

The screen lit up with the ship's profile as it glided through space many kilometers ahead of the *Excelsior.*

"This is hypothetical, sir," Henrey said. "I'm keeping us out of visual range."

"Good. Just keep her within the range of our sensors."

Then Sencus joined Peter Garvin and Janice Rand at the cartographic projection console just as the *Sundew*'s skeleton frame was forming.

"The bridge is here." Rand pointed to the blueprints that were projected on the monitor in front of them. "A single corridor connects it directly to a central room, probably some kind of assembly area, or lounge."

"Is that corridor the only access to the bridge?" Garvin asked.

"Yes," Rand confirmed. "The bridge is almost like a self-contained pod. The corridor is like a round tube that connects it to the body of the ship. It's narrow; you and your men might have to bend over to go along it."

"Prometheans are seldom more than five feet tall," Sencus explained. Then he lapsed into silence as Rand gave them a quick tour of the alien starship, pointing out the four levels. Sencus noticed that Garvin listened with intense concentration.

"Scans show that they have approximately sixty humanoid forms aboard," Rand said briskly. "Eleven would be ours. So we're guessing they have a crew of no more than fifty, as Maldari said."

"That is a lot. They are probably all armed, since they are clearly some kind of pirate ship. What do you think, Garvin?" Sencus looked at the big man.

"We'll have to search the ship for the hostages?" Garvin asked Rand.

"I'm afraid so. Heat scans indicate that there are warm bodies all over the ship. Without their communicators we just can't identify Sulu and the others. And they might be split up by now."

Now that they were actually discussing a direct attack, Sencus knew it would face pretty strong obstacles.

"This is not going to be a simple operation," Sencus said.

"The longer we wait, the more difficult it will be," Garvin said quickly.

"It seems very difficult as it is," Sencus said. "In hand-to-hand combat, we lose the advantage of superior power. They will be fighting on familiar ground. We do not even know where the hostages are." Sencus stared at the ship's plan. Finally he turned to Garvin. "All right, what is your proposal?"

Garvin only hesitated for a moment. Sencus knew Garvin was anxious to go forward, but only the ship's acting commander had the authority to initiate an operation of this kind. Federation standards dictated that force was always a last resort.

"Three teams of six men each," the big man began. "We'll use a directed phaser to open a hole in their shields just long enough to transport us through. You'll transport us at once, here, here and here." He pointed to the bridge, the main assembly room, and a cargo hold on the third level. "A helmsman will go with my first team. They'll take and hold the bridge. We'll shut down all their systems, leaving only auxiliary power for life support aboard. Then we'll control the helm and lower their shields. At the same time, the second team will work their way down from the top deck, and the third team will work their way down from the third level, both searching for the hostages. It shouldn't take more than twenty minutes to cover the whole ship."

"And anyone aboard who is not hostile?"

"We have to assume everyone aboard is," Garvin said.

"Can you go in with your phasers on stun?"

"We'd be at a disadvantage. Teams sweeping forward shouldn't leave living hostiles behind them," Garvin said firmly.

"We cannot start killing Beta Prometheans haphazardly."

"They've committed an act of war."

"Acts of war are not so easily defined," Sencus said quietly.

"I'd hate to send my team in with a handicap. If these Beta Promethean pirates fire on us, we must be able to fire back with full capacity. There may be casualties. It's my job to see that the casualties are all on their side."

Sencus thought through the logical alternatives in seconds. He was aware that a number of officers stood around the little group, listening. He raised his voice slightly. "We will initiate this action at once." He looked right at Garvin. "With the appropriate amount of force dictated by the situation as you find it."

Maldari warned the Sightsman to set the shields and transporter alarms carefully, then left the younger Prometheans in charge of the bridge and headed out the corridor.

"Where are you going, Captain?" Dramin asked.

"To interview the prisoners," Maldari said. "I want to know what their ship is carrying."

"I think I should be present, don't you? As religious officer."

Maldari didn't. But he knew it was futile to object. In such a delicate situation, he should be careful to keep both Kornish and Dramin on his side.

"Good idea. Kornish, you should be present also," he said, knowing that the other man was lurking in the shadows as well. He scuttled through the corridor and down several ramps, leading the two men, until he was on the bottom deck of his ship.

Once there they began to make their way to the rear of the ship. They had only gotten a few paces when a siren blared. Maldari stopped, swearing a guttural oath.

"What's that?" Kornish said over the din.

"Something has breached our shields." Maldari drew his laser weapon.

"They're firing at us?" Dramin shouted.

"Yes. We may have to defend the ship." Maldari shouted in front of him, where a dozen of his men were stationed. "They are trying to board us! Repel the invaders!" He turned around and started back, adding for Dramin's benefit, with less enthusiasm than cynicism, "The infidel invaders." He was scuttling up the ramp to the next level, when Starfleet soldiers appeared at the top. Maldari fired quickly. Several Starfleet officers fired at once, hitting Kornish, who stumbled and fell. Maldari scuttled back along the main corridor until he came to his men. He ordered a dozen of them to go to the foot of the ramp and make a stand, then led a few of the others to the rear of the ship, where the prisoners were locked in the largest hold. Behind him Dramin was terrified.

"I can't believe they would engage us in battle like this. When all they had to do was pay for—" An explosion covered the rest of his words. Smoke filled the corridor.

"Follow me," he shouted. He pushed through the smoke until he reached the first turn in the corridor. Then he felt along the wall until he came to a cabinet. Prying it open, he pushed the flat of his hand against a glass panel. A red ray flashed, reading the peculiar handprint. A rumble started in the wall.

"Now what?" Dramin shouted as the smoke and explosions rose around them.

"This way," Maldari said. He led the small group down a tangential corridor and into a room with consoles rising from the floors. "Everyone strap in to a seat. If you don't have one, hold on." He scuttled to the central panel and his hands flew over the controls. Suddenly the room they were in tilted and dropped away.

"Oh, my God," Janice Rand said.

As the *Excelsior*'s bridge officers watched the *Sundew* on the main viewscreen, the rear half of the bottom level of the starship hinged away from the main body.

"Their shuttle is built into the ship." Sencus thought quickly. Then he asked Rand to patch him through to Garvin.

"Commander Garvin, this is *Excelsior*. Report at once." There was a crackle and Garvin's rough voice came on.

"We have secured the bridge of the *Sundew*. All systems under our control. Teams B and C have searched levels one and three and are moving down—"

"Level four is a shuttle," Sencus said. "I repeat, level four is a shuttle. It is leaving the *Sundew*." Even as they watched, small explosions along the hinged side blew puffs of smoke into the galaxy, and the shuttle completed its separation. Then it shot into space.

"Track it," Sencus said to the officers beside him. "Garvin, subdue the crew and search every inch of that freighter." But even as he said it, he knew what the result would be. If they had not found the hostages yet, they were on the fourth level. The pirate Maldari had outwitted them again.

Maldari didn't feel so clever. Around him the crew members that were knocked to the floor by the disengagement were climbing back on their feet.

"Where are we?" Dramin asked.

"In our shuttle," Maldari said.

"And the prisoners?"

"In the hold behind us. They're coming along for the ride."

"And everyone else?"

Maldari saw in his mind the fallen Kornish. "They are battling the disbelievers, I suppose," he said. His men took up positions in the small shuttle, and began to bring the little ship's systems under control.

Great, Maldari thought. *I'm locked in a shuttle with a religious fanatic, and the only thing I have to show for a year in space is eleven Federation officers.*

"What do you propose to do now?" Dramin demanded.

"I wish I knew," Maldari said to Dramin, figuring he had nothing to lose with a little honesty.

"But where are we going?" Dramin insisted.

Maldari looked over at the Promethean crewman who had settled into the seat next to him. The Promethean brought his controls alive, and lights danced across the glass table he sat behind. Then he looked over at Maldari. Maldari sighed.

"No Where," he said.

Aboard the *Excelsior,* Sencus paced the bridge. The turbolift opened and Commander Garvin stepped out, his uniform muddied with Beta Promethean blood. Sencus spoke to him quietly.

"Report?"

Garvin didn't answer at once.

"It is not logical to blame yourself, Commander," Sencus said. "We did not know about the shuttle. What happened after that?"

"They fought us anyway. I don't think most of them knew that the others had escaped. The starship is under our control. Most of the pirates are dead. A few are injured."

"Medical," Sencus said out loud. "Board the ship. See what you can do." He turned to Garvin. "Our personnel?"

"No casualties."

"Good."

"But we didn't find a single hostage."

"Undoubtedly, they were all held on the fourth level. Re-arm your team."

Garvin turned heavily and went back toward the turbolift.

"I'm losing the shuttle," Lieutenant Henrey called.

"Follow it with all due speed," Sencus said.

The *Excelsior* shot through the galaxy. The ancient little shuttle was no match for the speed of the great Starship, but Sencus couldn't fire on it for fear of endangering the hostages.

"Course heading?" Sencus requested.

"Somewhere in the Beta system, I think," Henrey said.

"Archnos? They're returning home . . ." Sencus mused.

"No, they're not heading for BP 1. They're—" Suddenly a noise boomed outside, the bridge lights flashed off and on again, and the ship rocked.

"Asteroid," Henrey said. "A fairly large one."

"Evasive action," Sencus said.

"I'm trying, sir, but we seem to have entered a fairly large field of asteroids. And they're emitting some kind of radioactivity that's interfering with our guidance systems."

"Viewscreen."

On the main viewscreen, hundreds of barren rocks ranging from tiny to nearly the size of the *Excelsior* herself were raining against the ship's shields.

"Maldari's shuttle came this way?" Sencus asked.

"Yes, sir. She's still ahead of us. She seems to know the way."

"Then follow her."

"She's slipping through spots too small for us."

"Are we tracking her?" Sencus said to Rand.

"The sensor we fired is attached to her hull."

"Then she will not lose us. In the meantime—"

Another boom and the ship rocked unsteadily.

"—more power to the shields," Sencus said.

On the screen, the density of the barrage increased.

"The radioactive anomaly is interfering with our navigational instruments," Henrey called over the increasing noise. "I'm having trouble keeping her level."

"Open all viewscreens. Maximum visibility. We will fly on the stick."

"Sir?"

"An ancient expression," Sencus said. "Try to pilot her through. This rock storm cannot last forever." He was determined not to lose the shuttle.

"The shields are draining power from thruster capacity!" an engineer said.

"We don't need much speed," another voice shouted.

"We won't have any at all if this keeps up," came an answer from the engine room.

The ship was rocked and buffeted by the huge boulders slamming against the shields.

"Navigation, map this asteroid belt."

Sencus knew he'd have to make a decision soon. The *Excelsior* couldn't fly much longer without strengthening its shields with further power, and that would cripple their capacity to leave the area.

"Sir," an officer shouted over the din. "Heavy concentrations of asteroids surround us. The field ranges from one hundred to two hundred kilometers in almost all directions. Above us it thins, and disappears completely within thirty-five kilometers."

The *Excelsior* slowed to a crawl.

"It's no use, sir. I can't take the *Excelsior* much farther without pushing through these rocks. Our shields need additional power."

"Reduce speed to cruising."

"The asteroids are emitting some kind of radiation that is interfering with our sensors, and my controls are malfunctioning."

"Go to backup systems."

Henrey's hands flew over his console, but even as Sencus watched, he knew it was useless.

"They're not much better, sir. These asteroids are hot enough to cause interference with guidance sensors, and even interior electrical systems." The ship's lights blinked and went out, and the red backup lights gave a ghostly illumination to the deck.

The ship rocked and bucked erratically, and the constant booming of the asteroids against the shields echoed on the bridge.

"Stop following the shuttle, Lieutenant. Pull her up.

42

Engine room, allocate all remaining power to thrusters. We will push the ship out through the top of this obstacle course."

Sencus knew that the great *Excelsior* was rising up, asteroids slamming off her shields. Little by little she steadied herself, and on the viewscreens Sencus saw the number of asteroids diminish, until the ship was steady and once more the black space around them was an infinity of emptiness. In the sudden quiet, Sencus turned to Rand.

"Where did she go?"

"Deeper into the asteroids, sir. The radioactivity is interfering with our ability to read the sensors. I don't understand how she could have navigated right through that belt."

Sencus sat down at his science station.

"They had a much smaller ship," he explained. "And an older one. If their guidance systems are relatively primitive, the radioactivity would not have interfered as much. Their willingness to enter the belt indicates a familiarity with the area."

"I don't think I've ever experienced so much radiation. If those planets were all dead, where was it coming from?" Henrey asked.

Sencus had already been wondering the same thing. His hands played over his science console.

"Perhaps they were not always dead," he postulated.

"Then . . ." Henrey thought of something he had learned years before at the Academy about radioactive isotopes and their origin.

"Yes. A civilization that misused nuclear power may have suffered an atomic accident of some sort," Sencus finished the young helmsman's thoughts for him. "On an enormous planet. It was not uncommon centuries ago. With a radioactive half-life of literally thousands of years, those rocks will remain barren and hot forever."

"But then Maldari couldn't have a base there."

"No, but we can postulate that he uses it when he wants to go undetected. Yet he will have to come out the other side soon. We will orbit the belt and attempt to pick up his trace."

"And if we can't?" Lieutenant Rand asked.

"Then we will continue to search the quadrant for eleven Starfleet officers," Sencus said quietly. "Have we heard from Starfleet Command yet?"

"Starbase 499 has acknowledged our message sent and passed it on. Nothing from San Francisco as yet."

Day Two

Somewhere in the Beta Prometheus star system

FOG WRAPPED THE GRAVEYARD of ancient starships when Maldari set down the shuttle in its midst. Pushed by a light wind, it drifted around the detritus. The wind also made the rotting hulks creak, and a light symphony of straining metal played on the desert junkyard. Maldari instructed the remnants of his crew to guard the prisoners, and then descended the outside ramp of his shuttle. Dramin was at his side before he even put his boots on the cracked dry ground.

"Where are we?" Dramin asked.

"In the desert," Maldari answered.

"What's all this?"

"Starships. Ancient, broken beyond repair. Parts here are free, you just have to take them."

"You need to repair the shuttle?"

"No."

"Then why did we put down here?"

"Would you rather land on an official freight dock, and when the authorities ask for our manifest, tell them we have eleven Starfleet officers kidnapped from a Federation Starship?"

Dramin paused. Maldari scuttled off the ramp and set out across the junkyard. Rusting walls of starships dumped at

45

every angle created a near-maze. As Maldari threaded his way through, Dramin followed.

"Where are we going, then?" Dramin insisted.

"Dramin," Maldari said, stopping in the shadows and looking at him for the first time. "There are a number of things which freight brokers in Archnos do not take under consignment. I haven't read the regulations lately, but I'm certain that a human cargo is probably one of them." *Dramin,* Maldari thought, *is probably something of an innocent where trading is concerned.* "Let me spell this out, and then when we go inside, you keep your mouth shut."

Dramin was startled by Maldari's sudden lack of deference. Maldari turned and walked on. He spoke to Dramin over his shoulder.

"We're going to find out what the market might be for these humans. From brokers who do not operate under the oppressive eyes of the Archnos authorities."

"And why would such brokers be here?" Dramin asked, staring about him at the outsized junkyard.

"Because, Dramin," Maldari said as he climbed over a twisted piece of metal and scuttled out into the open, "this is the No Where cantina." Maldari nodded ahead of them, and Dramin saw a large starship, upside down, its nose buried in the ground apparently where it crashed. Modifications had turned it into a ramshackle building. Violet lights glowed out of various windows, and in the center there was a rusted metal door.

"There are disbelievers here?" Dramin asked.

"There are all kinds of species here. Many offworlders as well as Beta Prometheans. Here their worship revolves around a slightly different set of principles than yours. Namely, profits. Just have a drink. You can probably get some of that sludge you like. I have some inquiries to make."

Maldari scuttled across the open space and went inside, where the fog was replaced with an even thicker smoke, and the creaking of the wind in the ghostly starships was buried by the clink of copperware, multiple voices, and electronic noise. He searched the faces of the denizens spread about the loftlike space as he made his way along the floor to the bar.

"Maldari, I can't say it's good to see you." The Beta Promethean bartender was the first to speak to him.

"Isn't my credit good?" Maldari said.

"Your credit is, but your cargo isn't," the bartender said in a low voice.

"Picades," Maldari swore. "Who knows?"

"Everybody. Although I think there is a settlement of offworlders three systems from here who forswear subspace communications. They may not have heard yet."

"Very humorous."

"You're here to trade?" the bartender said, scratching his thick eyebrow.

"I have to talk to a few aliens first. Is Licus around?"

"I think so. You have humanoids, then?"

But Maldari took a steaming cup in his hands and turned his back on the bartender without answering. He scuttled slowly through the customers. In the corner, he spotted a lizardlike male with narrow eyes and a snake's head, his scaly body draped with leather. He was sitting at a table with his back to the wall, talking with half a dozen aliens from various systems. As Maldari approached, Licus looked up at him and smiled.

He knows already, Maldari thought. *Then he knows I'm in a corner. But the females will still be worth a fortune, if we move quickly.*

"Maldari, I've been expecting you," Licus hissed.

"I don't know why," Maldari said, sitting on an empty stool across from him without acknowledging the other offworlders around the table. Licus nodded at them, and they disappeared into the smoke of the establishment.

"It could be because I am the only one in this system who deals in living species."

"There are others," Maldari noted. "Trafficking in sentient species other than Betas is not illegal."

"Perhaps not. But even I have never tried to sell a Federation Starfleet officer."

"If they disappear quickly into a far galaxy, they will soon be forgotten."

"You don't know humans."

"Two of them are women. One is a magnificent specimen, worth a small fortune."

Licus's heavy-lidded eyes sparkled for the first time. "And the other?" he asked.

"Older, but also good."

"Only two women . . ."

"Licus, let's get down to business. Seventy thousand kerns."

Licus's placid face lit up.

"You mean you have them here?"

"They are well guarded."

"Picades! You must have brought the whole starfleet with you."

"They didn't follow us. They couldn't. A Starship that size couldn't navigate through the Kitarian Cloud Rocks. Listen, there are eleven altogether. Seventy thousand kerns is a bargain."

"Let's go see," Licus hissed. Maldari got up and scuttled toward the door. He looked around for Dramin, but the fanatic had disappeared. *Good riddance,* he thought.

Lieutenant Roose sat on the hard floor, leaned his back against the bulwark, and listened idly to the two men next to him.

"I hope," Dr. Bernard Hans said to Spiros Focus, "this isn't going to be the ignominious end to a glorious career."

"The *Excelsior* is my first assignment, and I only joined her two months ago," Spiros answered glumly. "That is hardly a career."

"I was referring to my own," Hans said, smiling at the young man. "I have served as ship's surgeon aboard Federation Starships for four decades now, and was only just the other morning contemplating retirement. Stuck in the hold of an unreliable shuttle in an obscure corner of a far galaxy at the mercy of absurd characters from a comic-opera civilization is hardly what I had planned for my retirement."

The young cadet looked at him sympathetically.

Hans went on, primarily out of the conviction that idle chatter was better than silence for morale.

"I had in mind something a good deal more bucolic. Fishing the canals of Mars, reading mystery novels under warm Venusian skies, perhaps a visit to the famous gardens of Orgon. Why, I might even take up a hobby. The commander is always recommending one or another."

Roose was galvanized by the old man's remarks. As the officers spoke in low voices, his hand went down to his boot. He pretended to scratch his ankle, and there felt the imprint of the long knife Sulu had handed him. Too busy to return it to his cabin, and worried that if he left it anywhere it might hurt someone, he had slid it into the leather of his boot as he rode the turbolift to the bridge with Sulu. In all the excitement since, he had forgotten about it. He started to pull it out, then hesitated. *What if they are monitoring us in here?* he thought. Instead, he stood up and walked casually over to Sulu, who was standing with Svenson nearer the door.

"Captain, uh, how are you doing on your hobby? You know, the ivory carving?"

Sulu looked at him curiously.

"Fine, when I can get to it. Right now—"

"I've taken it up too. Just like you suggested." Roose smiled, feeling like an idiot.

"That's interesting, Lieutenant Roose. Perhaps if we can get back to the *Excelsior* in the near future, we can—"

"With the tool you gave me. Remember?"

"Lieutenant, right now ivory carving doesn't—"

"In fact, *I couldn't put it down.*"

Roose saw Sulu's face lose the look of bemusement at last, and stare penetratingly at him.

"The tool I gave you?" Sulu asked.

"Yes." He raised his foot and adjusted his boot. "I thought it might come in handy."

Sulu looked at Roose's feet. Then he looked up at Roose.

"And you've still got what I loaned you?"

"Yes," Roose nodded.

"You're right, it might come in handy. Be cautious."

"Yes, sir."

The door opened as Roose was crossing back to his uncomfortable seat near the bulwark. Half a dozen Beta Prometheans came in with their weapons drawn. Maldari came in behind them, followed by a tall, thin, agile alien Roose didn't recognize, but whose home system must have featured a blistering sun, for the alien had leathery, scaled skin.

The pirate crew moved forward and prodded the officers with their weapons, moving them back against the far wall. Maldari gave instructions in his guttural sounds, but the Starfleet officers, without their Universal Translators, didn't understand them. Maldari and the lizardlike fellow seemed to be discussing something. And then Maldari pointed to Violet Bays. He gestured for her to come forward. She held her ground.

He gave more instructions, and two of his men pulled her away from the others and brought her to the center of the cargo hold. As the other hostages moved forward, the pirates raised their weapons threateningly.

"Maldari," Sulu shouted and moved between Maldari and the woman. "If you harm any Starfleet officer—" Sulu suddenly felt the immense strength of the Beta's upper body as Maldari shoved him back. He sprawled on the floor.

Maldari said something to Violet Bays. Roose and the others were listening carefully, but the Beta Promethean language was impossible to fathom. Maldari raised his weapon and pointed it at her. He shouted something in a harsh voice. Roose wanted to reach for his knife, but in the tense room, any kind of movement would have attracted the attention of the well-armed pirates. Everybody waited. Maldari shook his weapon. The alien put his hand over Maldari's and gently pushed the weapon down.

"I don't want damaged goods," he said to Maldari in the Beta Promethean language. He looked at the tall woman. "We want you," he said in a halting, lisped English, "to take off your clothes."

"Up yours," Bays said in a forceful tone. Maldari didn't

understand her at all, and the lizard-man puzzled over the meaning of the phrase.

On the way back to the bar, Maldari tried to reassure Licus. "Probably female humans are allowed more modesty than our females are accustomed to. I doubt if she was hiding any significant blemishes."

"You should have insisted. Your men could have stripped her," Licus said.

"When I have been paid, you can do what you like with her. In the meantime, the others looked like they may have caused trouble. I can't start shooting them, they're valuable."

"Not to me," Licus said. They had crossed through the junkyard and come to the clearing. "The men aren't worth much at all and, considering the belligerence of the United Federation of Planets, will probably be too hot to handle. But I'll take the women off your hands. Forty thousand kerns for the two of them." He pushed through the steel doors of the bar and left Maldari standing outside in the gloom and fog.

Maldari swore a Promethean oath to himself. He was going to be stuck with nine male humans if he wasn't quick about it. He hurried inside after Licus and followed him to the table in the corner.

"I am anxious to get back into space. I'll throw in the men for just ten thousand kerns. Surely you can sell them on a slave planet somewhere."

"It isn't so easy." Licus frowned. "Human females are well known throughout the universe for their durability, their adaptability, and their common sense. But the men will be obstinate and argumentative. As servants they'll be truculent and moody. And they will breed not for intelligence or even strength, but for valueless commodities such as beauty. Besides, the whole Starfleet will be looking for them. Slave planets don't want trouble from Federation Starships. I'll tell you what. I'll give you fifty thousand kerns for the two women. That's my best offer. Make up your mind, because I want to transport them quickly."

Maldari sat on the stool and rubbed his face with his open hand.

"All right," he said. "All right. The women are yours. Now what in Hades am I going to do with nine males?"

"I can help you with that," a familiar voice said.

Maldari swiveled around and found that Dramin was standing behind him. There were two more Clerics with him, one of them much older. *Great,* Maldari thought, *more fanatics to deal with.* But the figure that made him most suspicious stood just next to the Clerics. He was tall and powerful-looking, and had an angry visage. Though Maldari had seen many of them on his home planet, there were few in this low-life establishment in a barren spot in the far corner of the Beta Promethean star system. And this one was well dressed in a military-style uniform. He was a Klingon.

"Dramin, I don't know if I want to get involved with Klingons," Maldari said, after he had moved aside with his religious officer. *And I don't know if I want to get involved with you Clerics either,* he thought. "Besides, they don't subscribe to the Only Way, do they?"

"Sometimes we have to work with disbelievers," Dramin said. "You've lost your ship. Your shuttle will be easily spotted, is unarmed, and is much too slow. They are willing to transport you, your crew, and your freight back to Archnos. They have a B'rel-class Bird-of-Prey right here on this moon. It is commonly used to carry cargo in and out of Archnos. As they have their own freight warehouses and facilities, no one will question its manifest. The spaceport there is full of opportunity."

"And what do they want for this help, exactly?"

"Only to use the Starfleet officers for a few days. After that, you can do whatever you want with them."

"I can't sell dead Starfleet officers, Dramin."

"You can't sell live ones either, Maldari," the Cleric said.

So Dramin understood the situation. Maldari reminded himself to stop thinking of Clerics as quite so unworldly.

Maldari glanced around the bar. He ran his eye over a number of offworlders. Few were traders in species, he knew. If Licus wouldn't take the men, no one would. What did he have to lose?

Then he spotted a Beta Promethean he knew. The odd figure sat alone at a table, but was staring straight at Maldari. His Beta Promethean features were ugly, smooth, with straight white teeth and even skin. His hair was silky, his eyes blue. Maldari remembered that he was a half-breed. If the other half was descended from any of the Federation species, then . . . Maldari told Dramin to meet him outside the shuttle with the Klingons. After they left, Maldari went straight over to the curious Beta Promethean.

Before Maldari could introduce himself, the man rose on his four short legs. "Please, sit down." He smiled, and the milky white teeth annoyed Maldari. "My name is Taras Tarquin. We've traded once before, some years ago. You probably don't remember. It doesn't matter."

"No, I remember. Vaguely." Maldari wanted to recall whether he had gotten the best of the swap or not.

"I can imagine you are having a bit of trouble getting rid of your current cargo," Tarquin said.

"Sometimes the market is good, sometimes not," Maldari said evasively.

"Perhaps I should explain. You're wondering about my heritage. My mother was Beta Promethean. But my father was a human. He was part of an early colony in a neighboring system."

"I'm not a bigot," Maldari said. "I leave that to the Clerics."

"Your cargo. I may be able to help you."

"I don't need any help," Maldari said.

"In placing it," Tarquin went on politely. "I have a number of contacts among the people, probably the only people, who would buy. Or trade. Or, say, even if you just wanted to give it back without causing an intergalactic incident. Which might be the best thing."

"You represent the Federation?"

"No, not at all. I am merely a trader, like yourself. But because of my, shall we say, unattractiveness, I am more welcome outside the Beta system than in it, and I am in the habit of traveling freely in Federation space. I often visit their starbases. That's why interspecies trading has become something of a specialty with me."

"I've already unloaded the women. I'm transporting the men back to—to somewhere else. But I haven't made a deal for them yet."

Tarquin shrugged. He let Maldari think.

"In a few days, the men might be available," Maldari said. "Where can I reach you?"

"Here," Tarquin said. "I'm here often. Or you can leave a message with the bartender. An ancient but useful alternative."

"And you could find a buyer for nine human males? Even if they were Starfleet officers?"

"I can find a buyer for anything." Tarquin smiled, his straight teeth once more reminding Maldari he was dealing with a perversion of the Beta Promethean species. "It is a special talent of mine," he appended, looking at Maldari.

Caught staring at the odd half-alien, Maldari was not embarrassed.

As soon as the pirates locked them in again, Sulu hurried to reassure Violet Bays that she would be safe.

"We'll be out of here soon," he said to her. "In the meantime, we'll all stand together."

"Something has to happen," Lieutenant Roose added. "They could have killed us by now if that's what they wanted to do."

"Somehow that doesn't give me a lot of hope. They look like a murderous bunch of thugs to me," Bays said.

"You mustn't judge aliens by their cosmetology," Dr. Hans put in. "What do you really think our situation is, Sulu? What do these villains want from us?"

"I wish I could answer that," Sulu said seriously.

Roose spoke up. "If these pirates want to call themselves traders, I hope they'll trade us for something."

"A ransom?" Sulu said. "That would be difficult for the Federation to swallow. Think what it would open up. I'm sure Sencus is moving forward on some front or another. We can count on him to do his very best. He's enormously resourceful. We can trust him with our lives."

"At this point," Dr. Hans said simply, "I believe we are."

The little group broke up. Dr. Hans waited until he could join Sulu in the corner of the hold.

"Can we really expect to be rescued?" Hans said.

"That depends," Sulu said, measuring his own thoughts. "I can imagine that Starfleet cannot move on this without authorization from the Federation Council. They may be unwilling to trigger any kind of military action. There could be political delays, negotiations. Then too, the Starfleet is spread very thin around an infinite universe. We pay a certain price in exchange for the almost limitless autonomy that an Excelsior-class cruiser has so many million light-years from headquarters. I think we're paying that price now. We are, functionally if not theoretically, on our own, as is usually the case."

"In other words, we're expendable."

"Surely you knew that," Sulu said as calmly as he could.

"It wasn't exactly in the Basic Orders." Hans smiled and put his hand on Sulu's shoulder.

On the other side of the room Lieutenant Roose looked closely at Ensign Bays. He had always liked her. She was efficient on the bridge, dedicated and anxious to learn off it, and eternally ebullient socially. Now he saw for the first time the strain starting to show in her pale face. He tried to reassure her.

"Don't worry, we're going to be all right. It's just a matter of a few days' patience."

"I may not have a few days," the young woman answered. "I'm sure there's a reason Maldari brought that man to look at me."

"Listen," Roose said, feeling protective. "We wouldn't let you become separated from us. If it comes to that—"

"If it comes to that, Lieutenant Roose," Bays said, her confidence returning, "I can take care of myself. It would not help for any of you to get yourselves hurt or killed, on my account. Don't try to do anything foolishly gallant."

"Tell you what," Roose said, bending down as if to rebuckle his boot, then straightening up. "You take this. Put it in your pocket or something. Just in case." He slid the sharp knife into her hand. Her face showed surprise. "I happened to have it on me when we were ambushed."

Sulu saw the maneuver, and knew at once that the lieutenant had given Bays his knife. If it came to hand-to-hand combat, Sulu thought, this crew could take these pirates, and the idea gave him some relief—a feeling that faded as quickly as it came. The Prometheans had murderous weapons. He'd need a better idea than that. He looked around at the hold, and saw that there were numerous panels and tubes holding the controls. He approached Svenson.

"Sven," Sulu said in a low voice. "Look at the walls. They're loaded with systems."

"I've noticed that," the taciturn Norwegian said. "We could probably disable this ship from here. Disrupt all of the power. But then what?"

"What about communications?" Sulu said.

"What do you mean?"

"What do you think you could fashion out of some of these wires and things? There must be a power source in the walls somewhere."

The tall blond man stood up. "You mean, could I contact the *Excelsior?* Probably not without a voice sensor. But I'll bet I could fashion a simple signal transmitter. By tapping into the shuttle's own power source, I could broadcast our coordinates on the *Excelsior's* coded emergency frequency."

"Give it a try."

"If I start tearing up the facilities, the ship might not function."

"Let them worry about that."

Svenson scouted the walls. He opened a number of ducts and found an archaic amount of wiring, a few sensors, and some hardwired boards. Then he found the subspace receiver the ship would depend on for long-range communication. In less than half an hour he had a signal-transmission device ready. He called Sulu over.

"Just press this, and a low-frequency signal on *Excelsior's* emergency band will go out from it. If they're listening, they will be able to identify our coordinates by tracing the source."

"They're listening," Sulu said. "Ship's regulations require constant monitoring of the emergency frequency if anyone is missing." Some of the other officers had gathered around and were admiring Svenson's handiwork.

"Hey, Sven," Spiros Focus said jovially. "Why don't you build us a transporter and beam us the heck out of here?"

"What's the matter, Spiros, don't you like the frontier life?" another officer said.

"To be honest, I have yet to see anything up here that compares with my islands. I think when my tour of duty is over, I will go back and sit on my hillside, watch the starships land in the Mediterranean ports, and be glad the only aliens I deal with are fish from the sea."

"Just one thing," Svenson said to Sulu. "I'm fairly certain that this will be a one-time-only transmission. By diverting the main power source on the shuttle, I'm fairly certain I've got enough range to reach the *Excelsior,* provided she hasn't left the region."

"She hasn't," Sulu said quietly.

"But when the surge of power needed is monitored by the shuttle's main onboard computer, it will recognize a renegade and unauthorized use of its propulsion boost by the electromagnetic field, and probably—if their systems resemble ours even slightly—shut down automatically until it defines the loss of power as necessary. Since the main communications in the control cell do the same thing, the computer will probably either reroute the power on its own, or at least sound a warning on the main control panel that our captors might see or hear."

"In other words," Sulu said thoughtfully, "let's hope it works the first time. All right, Sven, give it a try."

Svenson touched a couple of loose wires together, then pushed a small metallic button he had rigged. Nothing happened.

"Well, that was pretty anticlimactic," Spiros said.

"It's only a subspace transmission, Spiros," Sulu said. "It wasn't supposed to be bells and whistles." He turned to Svenson. "Think it worked?"

The tall Norwegian shrugged. "Hope so," he said.

Silently all the officers agreed with him.

Sounds outside caused the men to break up. The door opened. A dozen men came in, half of Maldari's pirate crew, the other half versions of the lizard-man who had visited earlier. They prodded the crew back again, and this time without words pulled both the women forward. Holding them by the arms, they turned to go out the door.

Instinctively several of the officers jumped toward the guards. A scuffle broke out. The guards hit two of them hard with the butt of their weapons. Sulu hurried up and tried to insert himself between the women and the door. He reached for Bays.

"Wait a minute," he yelled. "We are Federation citizens. I demand—" A blast from Maldari's weapon knocked him backward. The last thing he saw before he blacked out was the door closing after the two women were pushed out.

Violet Bays had never much liked reptiles, and these half-humanoids bore far too much a resemblance to that particular species. She thought of them as the lizard-men. They were escorting her and Nora Schmidt from Engineering through a yard that seemed to be the repository of intergalactic junk, primarily shuttles and even starships too ancient or busted up to be of any use. The rotting hulks lay haphazardly scattered around and some of the larger ones towered above them, but the lizard-men seemed to know the path, and their leader quickly led them through the twisted carnage. One of them held Bays' forearm tightly, and she could feel the cold-blooded hand, clammy and scaly on her skin.

"Why do you think we've been separated?" Bays said to Nora. Nora looked over at Bays as one of the lizard-men pulled her along the path.

"I'd rather not speculate," she said. "Though perhaps we are being released, in some sort of goodwill political gesture." Bays recognized Nora's gift for sarcasm. She glanced at the lizard-man pulling her along, but he didn't seem to care that the two women were conversing.

"But you don't think so?" Bays said.

"Societies out here," Nora answered. "Or perhaps that's unfair—let's say, underdeveloped societies have a lesser

58

regard for women than the societies of our sun. The fact that their leader up there tried to get you to disrobe, well . . ." Nora let the thought go unfinished. But Bays found the conversation comforting.

"Then too, they're pirates," she said.

"I don't think we'll have to walk a plank," Nora said. "If that's what you're worried about."

After another few yards, Bays looked at the man guarding her. "Go to hell, lizard breath," she said pleasantly. He didn't react. She turned to Nora.

"I'd say they aren't translating us just now."

Nora smiled, and turned to her own escort. "Hey, scale skin. How would you like a swift kick in the balls?"

She got no answer.

"In that case," Violet said in a noncommittal tone, "you'll want to know we aren't without resources. I've got a very sharp knife in my boot."

Nora tried not to be startled.

"You are a clever girl," she said. "I think we'll be able to take on these Jurassic types after all. Maybe we should hold off a bit, however. Until we get settled somewhere."

"All right. But if their leader wants me to take off my clothes again, I can't be responsible for my actions."

"That's certainly up to you. When I was your age, I would have done the same thing. Now I think I'm jealous that they asked you and not me." Nora smiled sideways, and Violet decided that if she was going to find herself in a tight situation, there was no one she'd rather be in it with than the frank and imperturbable Nora.

The lizard-men hurried Violet and Nora through the junkyard and across an open space of desert. Violet noticed that the ships around them changed in character and seemed to be reasonably intact. They were all small shuttles parked in the open desert, and some were attended by species from outside the Federation planets. But the lizard in the lead, whom Violet had heard Maldari refer to as Licus, ignored them and hurried the small group onward. Then Violet saw their obvious destination.

Ahead of her in the open desert sat a series of cages, each containing one or more individuals of an alien species.

Violet noticed a pair of Berengaria dragons, which she knew were a protected species under Federation environmental regulations. Nora, however, was looking in the other direction.

Violet followed her gaze. A shudder ran through her. A number of the cages held humanoids. Although she saw no races from Earth, several were known to her as sentient beings.

"You think this is some kind of zoo? I've heard of those," Violet said.

"It's possible, since we're outside Federation territory. Federation treaties allow only for wilderness parks, not zoos. But the care and feeding of the species trapped here doesn't seem to be their keeper's highest priority."

Violet and Nora were pushed into an empty cage, and the gate was shut behind them. Violet looked around. They were in an open pen no more than eight feet square, with wire enclosing the ceiling. The walls were contiguous with other walls, and over a hundred pens were linked together in the clearing. Although they were locked in, and the grid of wire fencing was too narrow to slip through, construction seemed rather flimsy. Violet wondered how sturdy it was. But when she went to grab the wire mesh, Nora pulled her back. Then Nora searched the ground, and came back with a bit of twisted metal. She tossed it against the wire, and a spark sizzled in the air.

"I'd say about eighty volts," Nora said. "Don't touch it or lean against it."

"So that's it," Violet said. "I thought some of these species looked pretty strong."

"Even a zoo wouldn't have boundaries as inhumane as these," Nora pointed out.

The dry desert dust blew up, and a shuttle cruised in and stopped in a clearing in front of the cages. The species around them became agitated.

Two Klingons climbed out of the shuttle, strode to a squat building at the edge of the cages, and disappeared inside. After a minute or two, Licus and several other lizard-men came out with the Klingons. The group strode toward Violet and Nora. They paused in front of the women's cage. Their translators taken, Violet and Nora couldn't understand the exchange. The Klingons seemed intrigued, but eventually shook their heads and moved on. Violet watched them walk along the cages and stop in front of another pair of females, whom Violet recognized as Caltarian. They were humanoid, tall and lithe, without any hair, wearing only loincloths. They backed away from the front of the cage as Licus began a conversation with the two Klingons. The Klingons nodded. Licus turned and waved back toward the building he had come out of, and one of his guards threw a switch on the wall. Then two lizard-men opened the cage and went inside.

The Caltarians resisted. They slipped to the back corners of their cage. When the lizard-men approached them, they kicked furiously, and one of the guards went down. Licus hissed out a few orders, and the rest of the guards rushed in and subdued the two. Long poles were brought in, and the Caltarians' wrists and ankles were tied to them. Then the lizard-men hoisted the poles on their shoulders and carried the struggling Caltarians out of the cage and across the clearing. Violet watched them disappear into the Klingon shuttle, and the two Klingons followed them in.

"Caltarians are a highly intelligent species," Violet said quietly to Nora.

Violet watched the shuttle power up, then dash out of the clearing and disappear into the clouds. She watched as Licus and his men returned to the building, leaving only three guards roaming the perimeter of the stockade. The guards paid little attention to the species trapped inside.

"Some say superior to humans," Nora answered. "I sure hope that signal Norquist rigged up went out okay, and someone knows where we are."

Lieutenant Janice Rand stood up suddenly.

"I'm getting a signal on the emergency channel!" she said. Everyone on the bridge looked over. Sencus walked to her side.

"It's a Mayday code."

"Anything else?" Sencus said.

"No. No message. But it's on our coded emergency channel. No one could have transmitted on it except Captain Sulu or his people."

"And it is nothing more than that?"

"Yes. It's stopped."

"Already?" Sencus said.

"It was a one-time-only transmission."

"Can you pinpoint it?"

"Yes."

"Lieutenant Henrey?" Sencus turned to the helmsman he knew was tired. They were all tired. Not one officer had left the bridge since the *Sundew*'s shuttle had disappeared ahead of them in the asteroid belt.

"Sir," the young man said quietly.

"Wherever it is, take us there. Right now. Fast as we can travel."

"Yes, sir."

The bridge came alive at once as the *Excelsior* shot into space.

"We'll have to go the long way. Around the asteroid belt," Henrey reported.

"Sir," another officer said from his console. "I have confirmation on the location. We'll be well within the Beta Prometheus star system."

"Their home planet?"

"No, sir. On the outskirts of the system. An uninhabited moon."

"Lieutenant Rand, send a message to Starbase 499 for transmission to Starfleet Headquarters at once. Tell them we are entering the BP system in search of the missing Starfleet officers. Tell them we can expect a confrontation with their abductors, and we request permission to use all available force if necessary. Henrey, ETA?"

"Within minutes now, sir."

"Forward monitor," Sencus said, raising his voice.

The monitor came alive with black space. A dark planet floated in the far distance.

"Enhance."

The planet grew larger.

"Is that it?" Sencus asked.

"That's where the transmission came from, sir," an officer said.

"Scan it."

All the officers on the bridge were glad to have something to do at last.

"Sir, this side is deserted. No life-forms."

"And the other side?"

"I haven't scanned it yet, sir."

"Well, as long as no one is home on this side, let us go around and look for ourselves."

A few moments later the *Excelsior* had identified the small community on the dark side of the barren planet and hovered in space above it.

"Report, Mr. Cavanaugh," Sencus said.

"Our scans show only three basic areas in use, the rest is desert." The officer was bent over his console, his craggy face intent on the readings. He pushed back a shock of gray hair in an unconscious gesture. "There's a great many starships and shuttles, or parts of them. None of the ships have a power source of any kind aboard. For that matter, most of them don't have all their walls intact. It seems to be a junkyard or salvage yard of some kind. But there are two areas that are filled with life-forms."

"What kind? Beta Prometheans?"

"Yes, sir, but many others as well. It looks like an intergalactic crossroads."

"What is the nature of the two areas?" Sencus said.

"It's hard to say, sir. We'll need to take a closer look."

Sencus turned around. Commander Garvin stood a few feet away, waiting for an order.

"Proceed there at once."

Even as Sencus was saying it, Garvin turned swiftly and headed for the turbolift.

"Two teams," Sencus said to his back. "One for each encampment. Garvin!" Sencus said just before the turbolift doors closed on the security chief. The big man turned around.

"Phasers on stun only. We have no idea what species are down there, or why."

"Yes, sir," Garvin said grudgingly as the turbolift doors closed around him.

When Commander Garvin and twenty-four of his best people had been transported down to the surface, he divided them up into two teams. He studied his tricorder.

"According to the navigator, we're in the middle of a junkyard," he told them, his deep voice rumbling in the deserted yard. "Alpha team, you'll find life-forms in that direction. Zeta team, we'll go this way. Teams are on your own. When you need to pull out, notify *Excelsior*. You know what we're looking for. Let's go."

Both teams hurried through the aisles of rotting metal fuselages. There were no straight paths, but by using sound-reflection, they were able to follow their tricorders until they made their way to the edge of the junkyard.

It was just as the Alpha team was crossing the open space that Maldari glanced out the window of the No Where and saw them coming. He said a few words to Dramin, who looked out the window. Maldari nodded to the Klingons with them, and the four of them got up and hurried across the bar.

The Alpha team entered the No Where cautiously. Its denizens were surprised to see Starfleet officers, and nervous when the intruders were recognized as not ordinary flight officers but a security team. But the traders who patronized the place were not easily intimidated. Most of them merely watched as the soldiers spread out and went through the large open area, searching the faces of any Beta Prometheans there. After that they moved into the back rooms, where smaller groups of species were gathered. They didn't find any sign of the hostages.

By that time Maldari and his cohorts had slipped out the back way.

Nora saw them first. Two Starfleet security soldiers were moving cautiously out of the junkyard into the clearing. She knew there would be more. They were scanning the area, but hadn't seen the women yet. Nora shouted to Violet, and the two women waved. The officers saw them, but as they ran across the clearing toward the cage, a guard near the cage spotted them and fired. One of the soldiers was hit, but the other rolled to the side and shot the guard, who was knocked backward and rendered helpless. The noise must have warned the others, and a dozen lizard-men poured out of the building.

Before they could fire, a dozen more Starfleet officers poured out of the junkyard and spread out in the clearing, and a furious firefight ensued. In the chaos, the original soldier reached Violet and Nora.

"Don't touch the fence!" Nora shouted. "It's electrified! There's a switch over by the wall!" Violet pointed out the controls she had seen the lizard-man work when the Caltarians' cage was opened. The soldier ran toward the building, firing ahead of him. Violet saw him blast the little panel. She looked around the dirt at her feet for something to test the wire with, but saw only bare dust. She quickly slipped her knife out of her boot and threw it against the gate. The wire was silent.

"It's off!" Nora said. Violet picked up the knife. A soldier appeared out of the rising dust in the clearing and fired his phaser at the latch. Then he kicked the gate and it swung open. Violet and Nora hurried through the gate and into the clearing, where a rising cloud of dust cut their visibility, and the noise of phaser fire exploded around them.

Just as the soldier stepped back to let the women through, Licus appeared behind him. The lizard leader fired a weapon and the soldier went down. Licus reached out and grabbed Violet Bays's hand and yanked her toward him. He held his phaser to her head and twisted one arm behind her back. Then he moved out into the clearing.

"Cease firing!" Commander Garvin's deep voice boomed in the clearing. The soldiers had stunned most of the lizard-men and the others had run away. But Licus moved forward, using Violet as a shield, and worked his way toward a shuttle parked next to the low building.

Violet thought she wouldn't be able to do it. Although she had received weapons training at the Academy, she had served only on the bridge for almost five years. She had never had to kill a member of another species in her life.

Licus was forcing her across the clearing. The shuttle was coming closer. Garvin and his people were stationary. They had their weapons raised, but wouldn't be able to fire. In a short time she and Licus would have reached the safety of the shuttle.

"Violet!" she heard Nora's voice shout. "Violet, now!"

Ensign Bays thrust the knife with all her might behind her, plunging it into the thick reptilian skin pressed against her.

Licus stopped. He dropped his phaser. His webbed feet tried to find a balance in the dirt, but he swayed and dropped to the ground, where he twitched, the knife deep in his side. Violet stood over him, her hand still extended.

"First-rate use of ancient weapons," Nora said to her as she reached her side. "I never liked this guy. He wanted to see you naked, and couldn't care less about me." She smiled at Violet.

Violet realized she was shaking. She felt Nora put her arms around her. "I never killed anything before," she said to Nora.

"If it makes you feel better, and it should," Nora said quietly, holding her, "this guy was scum."

"Zeta team to *Excelsior*." Garvin had touched his communicator. "We have secured our area. Two hostages are safe. No sign of the others. We will continue to search."

"They're probably still aboard the shuttle," Nora said to Garvin. "That's where they were when we were separated. It's this way."

The two women retraced their path back across the junkyard maze. They came to the original landing site. They hurried across the clearing to the *Sundew* shuttle. The door hung open. The Starfleet security team searched the small shuttle, but it was deserted. An officer with a tricorder stepped up to Garvin.

"No life-forms here, sir," he said. "They must have been taken somewhere else."

As soon as the team was back aboard the *Excelsior*, Garvin reported to the bridge. Sencus listened to a brief account of the events at the stockade, and the Alpha team leader reported finding nothing at the No Where. Both teams had searched the small inhabited areas of the planet, and found no sign of the Starfleet hostages, nor of Maldari and his men.

"They must have been taken off the planet," Sencus said. "Lieutenant Rand, what kind of activity has there been since we arrived?"

"A single starship left the vicinity, sir. It's heading across the system toward BP1."

"Identification?"

"Yes, sir. It's a Klingon ship. A Bird-of-Prey."

"Klingons. Wouldn't you know it," Sencus said. "But what would the Klingons be doing in all this?" he said more to himself than the officers on the bridge.

"Sir," Rand spoke up. "We are receiving a subspace transmission from Starfleet Command."

"Finally. What do they have to say?"

"Admiral Belzie, Starfleet Command Headquarters, United Federation of Planets to *U.S.S. Excelsior,*" Janice said aloud on the quiet bridge, one hand holding her earpiece in tightly. "Situation acknowledged. *Excelsior* will report immediately to Starbase 499. Do not, repeat, do not enter Beta Promethean star system."

Sencus stood silently for a long time. The bridge officers watched him. Finally the helmsman spoke to him.

"Course heading, sir?" Henrey said.

"Hmmm?" Sencus was stirred out of his thoughts. "Yes, course heading. We will cease pursuit of the hostages, and report to the nearest Federation starbase."

"But sir—" Henrey said. "We could catch that Bird-of-Prey in a matter of—"

"Starbase 499," Sencus said abruptly, and returned to his own science station, from where he was most comfortable commanding the Starship. "At once. Those are our orders."

Day Three

Starfleet Headquarters, San Francisco Bay

THE ORIGINAL MESSAGE from *Excelsior*—a simple statement that eleven *Excelsior* officers had been taken hostage aboard the *Sundew,* a star freighter presumed to be from the city of Archnos in the Beta Promethean star system—had flashed to Starbase 499 on an Urgent, Highest Priority channel. It was read by the commander of the starbase and immediately passed on to Starfleet Communication Headquarters on Earth, where it arrived in San Francisco via subspace radio seconds later. It spilled across the chief of communications' monitor automatically as it came in coded Highest Priority. He read it at once, then reached out to his console and entered his personal password. He rerouted the message directly to the central office of Starfleet Command.

The commander in chief of Starfleet heard the warning beep and looked up at the screen from his seat in the conversation pit, where he had been conducting a meeting. He read it over to himself twice.

"Oh, shit."

The other officers present had also read the brief message.

"The Beta Prometheans are not members of the Federation," the admiral said.

One of the younger officers spoke up.

"No, sir. They don't belong to any political entity, they're entirely on their own. They're principally traders. We get a good deal of our dilithium crystals from them, but they trade it through intermediaries, or on our starbases, and they have never allowed Federation Starships to visit their planets."

"Why the hell would they do something like this?"

There was no answer. Finally one officer ventured a suggestion. "They are not very stable politically. This Maldari might be a renegade ship of some sort."

"Do they have an ambassador to the Federation?"

"I don't think so, sir."

"All right, never mind. See that at least three Starships are at the nearest starbase as soon as you can get them there. This is one for the politicians, I'm afraid."

He stood up, and the other officers hurried to their own offices. The admiral walked to his desk and touched his computer. It read his fingerprint. He asked to be connected with Federation Headquarters on the mainland.

"The President's Office," a voice intoned.

"This is Admiral Belzie. Where is he?"

"He's just down the hall in the cabinet room, sir."

"Tell him I'll be in his office in five minutes. Tell him it's Federation security. He'll probably want his team there too. Tell him there's a problem outside Federation space, on the frontier."

The admiral turned away. Then he walked across his office and through glass doors that opened automatically. He walked onto his private terrace. The shuttlecraft navigator snapped to attention.

"The President's Office."

"Yes, sir."

They stepped into the small craft and almost at once floated up to local traffic level. The commander in chief relaxed back into his seat and gazed out the window at the waters beneath him.

This is going to be a serious problem, he thought. *This could be anything from a strategic assault to a full scale war on the frontier. The Federation hasn't fought a war since the Romulans in 2160. They don't want one now.*

* * *

Thirty minutes after the meeting in which the Starfleet commander in chief briefed the president of the Federation on the message from *Excelsior,* a press release left the President's Office on all public transceiver channels. That evening monitors throughout the Federation carried the brief story. Activities beyond the borders in far space did not concern too many of the Federation citizens.

But right there on Earth, in San Francisco, in living quarters high on Telegraph Hill, one communication monitor had been set to sound an alarm when certain information appeared in the daily news stories. The name Sulu, as captain of the *Excelsior,* had been given a priority warning flag, and when it appeared in the file story, that monitor beeped throughout the apartment's rooms.

James Tiberius Kirk, who happened to be home that evening, heard it.

He walked to his monitor and uploaded the story that contained the names Sulu and *Excelsior.* He read it through twice, to be sure of what he was receiving. He attempted to call up more information, but there was nothing else on the wire that night.

Walking to his bookcase, he took down a disk, and inserted it into his computer. He called up Beta Prometheus and read a short essay on the unfamiliar civilization. They were space traders and smugglers, they had refused an offer to join the Federation half a century earlier, and their record on humanoid rights was abysmal.

Kirk walked to the big picture window that faced the bay. A full moon lit up the night and sparkled off the waters. Shuttlecraft of all sizes—small taxis, buses, freighters—flew back and forth, servicing the twenty-four-hour spaceport city. He stared across the water to where the gleaming towers of Starfleet Headquarters rose above the pine-tree-covered hills. Moonlight bounced off the mirrored one-way walls. In the illuminated reflection he could see the hills of the city and the shuttlecraft floating by. He stared at the thirty-seventh floor where, six months earlier, he had been toasted, roasted, and retired by a handful of officers in the commander in chief's private conference room.

I don't miss the place, he thought. *The byzantine bureauc-*

racy, the by-the-book bureaucrats, the hours at the computer monitor, the staff meetings where officers droned on about supplies, requisitions, promotions, and discipline, officers whose entire experience of the galaxy amounted to a few trips to the Earth's moon for weekend seminars in management training, and a year stationed on a Starbase well within the Sol system. The gleaming desks and the cushy armchairs and the Starfleet gossip. I don't miss that at all.

But I miss the *Enterprise. I miss the company of the Starship crew, the eccentric men and women who spent their lives traveling deep space together. I miss the galaxy, the starfield just outside the observation ports. I miss the alien civilizations, the emergencies in space. I ought not to admit it, but I miss the danger. I miss Spock, and Scotty. And Sulu.*

Sulu. He was the best helmsman Kirk had ever known. He had stayed with the *Enterprise* loyally, long beyond the time he had a right to be promoted. He had, at last, reluctantly left the *Enterprise* and advanced to his own command. As captain of his own Starship, he had stayed in space when Kirk and the others had been sent down. And now he was a prisoner of some alien pirates. *What,* Kirk wanted to know, *was Starfleet Command doing about that?*

Kirk knew that if he visited Starfleet Headquarters in the morning, he would be treated politely. He would be welcomed at the security gate, given an ensign escort to the admiral's floor, and Starfleet admirals, even the C in C himself, would stop what they were doing and shake his hand warmly. They would ask him how he was doing, bring up all the old complaints about Starfleet bureaucracy, pretend to envy him in private life. But after twenty minutes he would wear out his welcome. They would be alerted to a meeting, told by their assistants that someone was waiting, or called back to their monitors for priority messages. The business of Starfleet would grind inexorably on all around him, and he would not be a part of it. He would feel awkward, as people hustled by and shouted "Good to see you, Commander," and kept on their busy way.

And if he reported to the public-relations section, they would be glad to give him a private briefing. They would roll out the red carpet and fill him in on the situation at Beta

Prometheus. Which would tell him nothing more than exactly what he had just read about on the news.

Not only did he not relish the feeling of being a white elephant, a grand old man on display, but he was impatient for news and did not want to wait until the next morning to find out what Starfleet was going to do. And he wanted to know what they were *really* going to do.

So he spun away from the window, walked to his closet, put on his jacket, and left his apartment to go drinking.

The Flag and Grog was a Starfleet officers' hangout on Kirk's side of the Bay, tucked away among the shuttlecraft docks, freight warehouses, and administration offices on Starship's Wharf. By this hour at night it would be packed.

Kirk walked along the waterfront and, as always, admired the small starcrafts that hung gracefully in the air just above their titanium docks. Although the big starships, like Sulu's *Excelsior* and Kirk's old *Enterprise,* docked in space, the freight carriers and the huge variety of smaller shuttlecraft that could pass through the atmosphere and land on the Earth's surface were equally as beautiful to him. They were trim and taut and graceful, and they spoke to him of the space they had navigated. But Kirk hadn't left the ground since his retirement. Climbing into a small Starship or shuttle would be like trotting on a pony after he'd had a thoroughbred to race.

A revolving yellow light pierced the dense night fog in the distance. As he drew closer he recognized the insignia of Starfleet, which the bar had appropriated, modified, and turned into its logo. He smiled at the small sign in laser lights that glowed next to the front door: HUMANOIDS AND ALIENS MUST WEAR SHOES AND SHIRTS. He swung the door open, stepped into the turbolift, and ascended to the second-floor establishment. The doors parted and he walked into a steamy loft, packed to the walls with a combination of off-duty Starfleet personnel, and the riffraff of the galaxy.

An electronic wall of music washed over the scene, and the inhabitants had to shout at each other to be heard. Barrel-shaped robotic devices rolled around with trays of exotic drinks. An Octoan perched its squat body on a stool behind the bar, its twelve three-fingered tentacles rapidly filling drink orders. It was a busy scene. Even the ferns that decorated the bar were roaming around the room on their root tentacles.

Kirk went to the bar and ordered a glass of Saurian brandy. The Octoan bartender nodded, and delivered it. Kirk turned away from the bar to survey the room.

He spotted several tables of Starfleet personnel. Not wanting to appear anxious, he waved and smiled at a few acquaintances who spotted him, but stayed where he was for the time being. He saw that Admiral Caius Fesidas was sitting with a much younger Starfleet bureaucrat he didn't recognize, and decided to try them for information. But not just yet. The admiral and his friend only had one drink in front of them. Kirk was patient. He had all night. And the Flag and Grog was not an inhospitable place to wait.

A burst of starlight and red, white, and blue lasers flashed in the giant mirror above the bar. It reflected activity throughout the large room. Low tones thundered out of speakers overhead. The surface of the mirror turned to glass, and behind it Kirk could see two humanoid forms. Then the glass turned to smoke, lights dimmed throughout the bar, and the smoke began to clear, leaving the two figures standing on a mirrored stage floor, bathed in a red-orange glow.

They made a handsome couple. The woman wore only a white satin G-string featuring the Starfleet insignia, spike-heeled glass shoes, and a string of Martian pearls around her neck. The man wore a black G-string pouch in the same shape, and knee-high leather boots. Both were Deltan, Kirk knew. The most erotic people in the galaxy. They were six feet tall, with long muscular legs. The female's breasts were firm and round and small, her nipples erect. The male was lithe and muscular. Both were completely hairless. They held hands as they faced their audience. Their bodies undulated slowly to a primitive beat set at precisely the normal pulse rate of a resting heart.

A Kartoan dwarf appeared at the side of the stage, his

sleek bald head glistening with sweat, his large round eyes sparkling. His mouth split in a wide grin and he shouted over the intense music.

"Males and females, Vulcans, Tellarites, Andorians and Centaurians, Denebian slime devils and Aldebaran Shellmouths, Betazoids, Chemizoids and Humans! Welcome! Tonight the Flag and Grog is proud to present, for the first time on any stage on Earth, from the distant Delta Triciatu system, dancing to music by the Trendoids, please welcome: Silky Way and Puss-in-Boots!"

The music pounded and the couple began to dance. They separated, worked their way down a short flight of stairs on either side of the stage, and began working different parts of the room. They slid in and out of the tables, gyrating for the males, the females, and the androgynous equally. A husky reptilian bouncer followed them discreetly, making sure that none of the rowdier customers touched the couple. The female passed directly in front of Kirk. She smiled at him. He could feel her powerful pheromones wash over him and felt a fire building inside. He had to remind himself that it was purely a chemical phenomenon.

The Deltans returned to the stage. They danced with each other erotically, until they were wrapped around each other like mating boa constrictors. Suddenly Kirk realized that the couple was no longer performing for their audience. They had eyes only for each other. The heretofore noisy room quieted down. Everyone felt the effects of the rich Deltan pheromones that lingered in the room like a perfume cloud.

The electronic beat increased its tempo, drawing the pulse rates of the bar's inhabitants along with it. The dancers moved faster and faster. Finally the sound reached an enormous crescendo, the beats coming on top of each other so fast as to preclude distinction. The couple posed in a series of positions, the last of which saw them pressed together so tightly that Kirk doubted if even the music could pass between them. They kissed. The lasers burst off their bodies in kaleidoscopic patterns. Sweat poured down their glistening bodies. Finally they broke, and turned toward the audience.

"Yowee! Supernova! Let's hear it for the Deltan Duo!" the Kartoan shouted, as he hustled back onto the stage. "Whoa! Was that as hot as a supergiant blue star or what! Thank you, Deltans! See you later! And me a unisexual."

The stage disappeared behind a mirrored wall and conversations resumed. Kirk looked over at the table where Admiral Fesidas and his fellow officer sat. The admiral had a second drink in front of him. One more and he'd make his move.

Suddenly Kirk felt a hand on his thigh. Not a hand, exactly, more like a length of steamed asparagus. He looked down and saw a damp green Phylosian tentacle curl around his upper thigh. A vegetable, he thought. He followed it and found that it was connected to a plantlike alien in roughly humanoid shape. The head had no features beyond the leafy green foliage, but Kirk assumed the thing was looking at him. Then he knew the alien's opening thought.

Come here often? the Phylosian seemed to be saying.

Oh, great, a telepath, Kirk thought.

I'm sorry, I didn't mean to intrude. You looked a little lonely.

I'm about to join a couple of old friends across the room, Kirk thought.

Maybe we could meet up later?

I don't even know if this thing is male or female.

If you don't know, what difference will it make in the dark?

Kirk tried not to think. He tried to frame a polite response. *You're very sweet, but I'm afraid I've taken a vow. I can't have a relationship with anything I might have had for dinner.*

Very funny. You Earthlings are so provincial. Loosen up.

The plant wandered off. Kirk breathed a sigh of relief. It was his own fault, he shouldn't be standing alone at the bar. Better to join some friends.

He strolled across the room. He shook hands with a young officer from the southern hemisphere he had sponsored to the Academy, and was introduced to several recent graduates.

"This is Admiral Kirk, everyone," the young man said. "He was my mentor at the Academy."

"Admiral *James T.* Kirk?" a young woman with black hair and pale blue eyes said, her eyebrows going up. "This is a very great pleasure."

"Captain. Thank you," Kirk said, smiling and shaking hands.

"I'm only a cadet, sir." The girl had a firm handshake.

"I meant that *I'm* a captain. Retired, actually. I was an admiral once. I didn't like it at all. Too much administrative work. The pay was a good deal better though."

"You're still a hero at the Academy, sir. If I may say so."

"At the Academy they teach navigation, astronomy, and Starship etiquette. In Starfleet they teach politics. I wasn't very good at that. That's why I ended up back at the rank of captain."

"Your short-circuiting of the *Kobayashi Maru* scenario is a legend at the Academy. But you must know that."

"I'm afraid I do. It's come to haunt me, as a matter of fact."

"And your escape from Rura Penthe, and then the *Enterprise* as a renegade ship until you—"

"Now, look, I don't know what you've all heard, but disobeying Starfleet Command orders is most definitely not a smart thing to do. Not if you want to survive in Starfleet. Everything by the book, that's what I recommend."

"And what if you want to survive on the frontier?" the Latin officer he had sponsored asked. "Where the book hasn't been written yet."

"Well . . ." Kirk smiled. He enjoyed his reputation, though he hated to admit it. "Look, I don't want to turn this nice evening into an Academy seminar, but I'll tell you this. Alien civilizations can't be judged by Federation standards and practices. And our job is exploration, not confrontation. If you just stay out of alien affairs, you won't get into trouble. And when you can't avoid interaction with the natives, remember that you're thousands of light-years from headquarters. There isn't often time for consultation. I hope the Academy is still teaching you to think for yourselves . . . within, of course, the strict limits of the General Orders. . . . How's that for a politic answer?"

They all laughed.

"Now, if you'll all excuse me . . ."

"I hope you'll be around for a while, Admiral Kirk," the dark-haired girl said. "We'd really like to hear about your voyages."

"The old man's memoirs?" Kirk said ruefully. "Sure. Just let me do a little brown-nosing with an admiral I know over there."

"I thought you were retired?"

"I am. I guess old habits die hard." Kirk touched his friend on the shoulder and headed through the crush of customers to the table where he had last seen Admiral Caius Fesidas.

The admiral was three sheets to the wind when Kirk finally arrived at his table. The young officer, who introduced himself to Kirk as Lieutenant Eugene Marasco from the Press Liaison section, was still nursing his first beer. When Kirk shook hands with the admiral, Marasco pulled out a chair and signaled the waitress so quickly, it was clear to Kirk that the lieutenant was desperate for company. Kirk sat down genially.

"This is an honor," the lieutenant said. "You're the best known Starship commander in the history of the Fleet. You captained the *Enterprise* on a five year mission, didn't you?"

"I did. I had the honor of captaining her after Commanders Robert April and Christopher Pike. She was a sweet ship."

"When you came back, I was part of a team that promoted your image to the public. I used to do advance work for your lectures around the system."

"So you're responsible for all that hype surrounding my reputation. I don't know whether to thank you or not."

"I hope you don't mind too much. Starfleet Command wanted a hero, and ordered us to make you a star."

"Frankly, I'm a little uncomfortable with all that malarkey. The *Enterprise* was a great assignment, and I'm grateful, but I'm not a hero. I had some great adventures, and thanks mostly to an outstanding crew, I lived through them. Not everybody did. If there are any heroes, they're the ones we left behind."

"A drink to fallen comrades." Caius lifted his glass toward the center of the table. Kirk looked at it, and a rush of memories flooded into his mind. He raised his tankard and touched the admiral's glass. The lieutenant, a little startled by the sudden, sobering theme, hurriedly joined them. They drank in silence for a moment.

"Speaking of heroes," Kirk said quietly, hoping to introduce the subject as unobtrusively as possible, "one member of my crew is still out there. And I understand that he's in a hell of a predicament. His name is Hikaru Sulu. He commands his own starship now, the *Excelsior*. And apparently he and some members of his crew have been taken hostage by a bunch of pirates from a bizarre out-of-the-way planet. I hope he's all right."

"We don't know," Marasco said somberly. "The Beta Prometheans captured our officers from the *Excelsior*, claiming they were spying, and invading Promethean star space. The *Excelsior* was able to get the two female officers back, but nine males are still missing, including their captain."

"Spying?" Kirk said. "That's absurd. The Federation doesn't engage in spying. Unless I'm misinformed"—Kirk left the opening for Caius and the lieutenant as gracefully as he could—"the mission of the *Excelsior* is the same as every other Starship's. Exploration."

Neither of the two men contradicted him.

"Anyway," he went on, "haven't we been trading with Prometheans for years? What is it they want?"

"Don't know yet," Caius said. "The fact is, we haven't even been able to communicate with the bastards."

"The Promethean civilization is—in spite of all our technical information—quite a mystery to us," Marasco said. The lieutenant was happy to talk with Kirk. For the last hour he had been listening to the admiral's complaints about Starfleet politics, about his wife. His principal theme seemed to be that he was only getting from the former what he should have been getting, but wasn't, from the latter.

"They are deeply religious for one thing," Marasco continued. "I mean in a political way. Their government is not as powerful as their clergy, or whatever they call themselves.

So, for one thing, if you can imagine this, their belief system dictates their policies, both domestic and foreign. They consider most members of the Federation to be the enemy because our societies operate independent of religious beliefs, specifically theirs."

"But that's absurd," Kirk said. "The Federation alone contains some tens of thousands of belief systems for spiritual strength and guidance. If these organizations were political in any way, we'd be divided into hundreds and hundreds of splinter groups clashing with each other all the time."

"It is absurd to us, but not to Prometheans. I can assure you they take themselves very seriously. And as a consequence of their opinions of outsiders as the moral, spiritual, and physical enemy, trading with them has been a headache, I can tell you. It's the reason we don't have facilities on their inhabited planet. For just one thing, they wouldn't allow either women, or many of our races, equal access, and the Federation, as you know, refuses to create crews or staff Starships based on physical or spiritual identities, even to bow to local conditions. We've been trading either in space, on our own starbases, or through other planets, but never on their terrain, ever since they have been offering dilithium on the intergalactic market."

"In other words," Caius broke in, "we've brought the bastards out of their stinking, primitive, undeveloped past and into the future. We've given them resources beyond their wildest dreams, just because their primitive planets happen to be sitting on dilithium-crystal mines. And still we've had to kowtow to their demands, and play patty-cake with their leaders. When what we really ought to do is fly up with a shitload of Federation Starships and take the pious bastards over."

"That's not the official position of the Federation, of course," the lieutenant appended. "We have invited them to become members of the Federation, but so far they have declined."

"I see," Kirk said thoughtfully. "But we've dealt with primitive, belligerent societies before. Shouldn't we retrieve Sulu and his crew at once?"

"At this point, we don't know exactly where they are," Marasco said, again lowering his voice.

Kirk was chilled by the admission. In order to appear nonchalant, he interrupted himself, waved to a passing waitress, and ordered another brandy. Then he pretended an interest in the Deltan Duo, who had entered the club clothed and were sitting at a table near them. He winked at the aging admiral.

"You know, Caius, interspecies marriage is the latest thing. I wonder what it would be like, married to a Deltan female."

"Oh, you think you're in love, and it's only those Deltan pheromones. Causes all kinds of trouble among the younger officers."

Kirk laughed in spite of himself. Then he said to the lieutenant, "Sorry, what were we talking about?"

"The situation on Beta Prometheus," Marasco went on, lowering his voice. "We're putting Starships in the area now, and creating contingency plans for going in. That's highly classified, I'm sure you know. But, frankly, I doubt if this is going to be a Starfleet operation. The Federation president has sent a special envoy, and the politicians will try to effect a release of the hostages. Until then it's a stand-off, I'm afraid, and Captain Sulu and his crew are stuck dead in the middle."

"Let's hope that's not literal," Caius intoned.

"Damn," Kirk said, and took a drink of his brandy to disguise his feelings.

"Did you—sorry, do you—know this Sulu well?" Marasco asked.

"Hmmm?—Oh, fairly well." Kirk shrugged. "He is a good officer."

Like family, Kirk thought. *He is the best helmsman and one of the most loyal men I have ever known. And I'll be Goddamned if Federation politics and Starfleet bureaucracies are going to let him rot in a Beta Promethean prison.*

Two hours later the population of the bar had thinned out, closing time was approaching, and Kirk hadn't really learned much more.

Admiral Caius Fesidas pushed off in a sluggish state, ably supported by Lieutenant Eugene Marasco, whose job, he hinted to Kirk privately, was to see that the admiral got home to bed safely, without causing himself or Starfleet Command any embarrassment. Kirk watched them weave through the room and disappear into the turbolift. He didn't think he was going to learn anything more useful. Most of the Starfleet executive officers he had spotted earlier were gone and the bar was only inhabited by nocturnal aliens and some younger cadets. But he didn't feel like going home either. He spotted the table of Academy graduates he had spoken to earlier, and walked over to them.

"Mind if I join you?"

"Captain Kirk," his protégé said. "Sit down, please." The young men and one woman at the table stood to salute.

"I'm retired," Kirk said, and waved them down. "Please. In fact, though loath I am to admit it, I'm a civilian pure and simple. Call me Jim."

"That," the young woman with pale blue eyes said, "will be very hard to do. You will be Captain Kirk forever."

"I don't know that I'm going to like that." Kirk smiled. He was used to being treated deferentially in the halls of Starfleet Headquarters owing to his rank, but this was something new altogether. He found himself in the role of Grand Old Man, and it made him feel old. He thought about Caius, who years ago had given up a Starship command in favor of steady promotions within the Starfleet bureaucracy, and had risen steadily in the ranks since. And now look at him: a boozy, bemedaled, overweight ghost of an officer.

"You seem preoccupied, Captain," a voice called him back.

"Oh, sorry. A Starfleet crew has been taken hostage beyond Federation airspace. Have you heard? I knew one of the men."

"I'm sorry," the girl said.

"I heard about that late this afternoon," the Latin officer said. "I guess I've always known that a Starship assignment is dangerous, but this really brings it home. I don't know if I want to serve on the frontier."

"If you have to think about it, you probably don't," the

girl said. "There are going to be too many sacrifices for anyone with second thoughts. Isn't that right, Captain?"

"Well, I'm not the best one to give advice about career moves, as you know." He shrugged in his civilian jacket. "But, yes, I'd say that getting posted to a Starship that serves at the frontier is a special calling. If you want a family, for instance, you won't see them for years at a time. You won't have any regular home except your cabin, and if you want to rise in Starfleet, your record is going to have to reflect more prestigious—need I say political?—assignments than drudging around in deep space. Not to mention that it is dangerous. And disorienting."

"What do you mean?" the girl asked.

"When you've been away that long, things change. You come home—if you even have a home—and there are a lot of things to get used to. I don't know how to define that better, and maybe this is only me, but I've never been really comfortable on the ground. Too many years aboard Starships, I suppose."

"What about the adventure? The excitement?" the girl pressed. "Isn't it worth it?"

"Oh yes, for me it was. But then, I never had much attachment to terra firma anyway. Couldn't wait to finish up at the Academy and get out into deep space. I was glad to get away from the theories and statistics and management side of Starfleet Operations. Where are you headed?" He looked at the girl.

"I'm in Biological Records right now. It's a bore. But I've requested a Starship assignment. I'm hoping for deep-space exploration. I'm a helmswoman by study, and I've taken a second in navigation in the hopes of getting an outward-bound assignment."

"How about you?" Kirk said to the Latin officer.

"Frankly, I didn't put in a request. There were so many things to think about. I've been assigned to a facility port, but it's just here off Jupiter. In fact, I leave in the morning. That's what this little gathering is all about."

"Well, congratulations and bon voyage." Kirk toasted him with his remaining ale and the others chimed in with some "here, heres."

"Your first time in space?"

"Yes. I was born on Earth."

"Good luck. And how about you?" Kirk said to another cadet at the table.

"I'm a little embarrassed to admit this," the boy said, "with all this talk about the glories of space, but I was raised on an asteroid colony and traveled around a lot with my parents, who were teachers. I was looking for something really steady, and I've applied to the Political Liaison section. I suppose I'll be assigned some diplomatic post, and I'm hoping it's an advanced civilization filled with humanoids, rec decks, and all the comforts of home. Sorry."

"Don't apologize. Get what you want out of life while you can. There's a lot of paradise in the galaxy; why freeze your butt off on a subzero planet or risk your life in a Starship? Maybe I gave up too many good years of my life . . . or maybe I'm just getting old and regretting some of the things I missed." *Or maybe I'm getting maudlin about this boring retirement,* he thought. *Because I've had too much Saurian brandy tonight.*

The table was quiet. So, they all noticed, was the bar now. There was a final round of good-luck wishes to the officer who was shuttling to Jupiter in the morning, and then the little party broke up.

Kirk went down in the turbolift with the young people, then shook hands all around, and watched them climb into a tram for the trip back to the Starfleet dormitory. When they were gone, he zipped up his jacket and turned to start his walk back toward his apartment. It was then that he realized the girl with shiny black hair and pale blue eyes had not gotten into the tram with the others.

"Can I get you a shuttle? You're not living at the Academy?" Kirk said politely.

"I am. I just didn't feel like going home right away." She didn't move. Kirk suddenly thought she must be trying to tell him something. *Don't,* he thought to himself, *misinterpret this young woman's actions. You could be her father.*

"We could get a bite somewhere, if you like," he offered, equally reluctant to go to bed with so much on his mind.

"There won't be anything decent open at this hour."

"No, I suppose not. Well . . ."

"I just wanted to talk to you some more. You really are a hero to a lot of young people at the Academy. Including me."

"And here I am, tired and slightly inebriated, and even a little overweight. So much for heroes. Feet of clay." Kirk smiled.

"You're very concerned about the *Excelsior,* aren't you?"

"Yes."

"There is a special camaraderie among the Starfleet officers who have served in deep space, isn't there?"

"You're very perceptive. Yes, I think there is." The two of them began walking slowly along the deserted space dock streets. "It's not something that's easy to explain. You couldn't tell a civilian, and I've found a lot of Starfleet officers who have never served in the frontier who don't get it either. You just have to have been there. You'll get your chance, don't worry. Then you'll feel it too. It's a little like a private club. There's nothing like it in the solar system. And nothing like the men and women who work out there. I'll tell you the truth, this Captain Sulu is a very close friend. We were aboard the *Enterprise* together for twenty-five years. That's why I'm so concerned. He served under me."

They walked along the fog-shrouded streets in silence for a while. Then the girl stopped and turned her face up to his. It was, he realized, a very pretty face. Smooth young skin and rich lips. Soft hair, eager eyes. She pulled a scarf around her neck in the damp air, and in spite of himself he saw her breasts push against her form-fitting uniform. *I don't know,* he thought. *It can't be. I've been in space too long. Is she really trying to tell me something?*

"I'd like to serve under you," she said, her face breaking into a wide smile as she took a step closer.

Son of a gun, Kirk thought. *I guess I got that right.*

Day Four

Kirk had been too preoccupied the night before to turn the large windows in his bedroom opaque, and the morning sun flooded in and woke him up much too early. He blinked and groaned. His head felt heavy and stuffy. His tongue tasted of Saurian brandy, which had a lingering aftertaste he had forgotten. Pulling himself up onto one elbow, he looked out the window. The sight of the blue-green San Francisco Bay always cheered him. There was no fog this morning, and the sun shone brightly just above the East Bay hills. He peered around his bedroom to the glowing display set in the wall. It read 0600. *Damn.* He slumped back down and tried to relax his neck and head. Then he felt her move beside him.

Kirk looked over and saw the girl sprawled across the middle of the big bed. For a moment he was almost startled.

Of course I remember, he thought. *We met at the* Flag and Grog *last night. I wasn't that drunk. She's a recent graduate of the Academy and works at Headquarters while she's awaiting a deep-space posting. Her name is . . . her name is . . . Uh-oh.*

He pulled himself up on one elbow again, this time with his back to the big windows, facing the center of the bed, where the girl lay peacefully. He glanced around the room.

Her clothes were scattered along with his across the floor. He looked back at the girl. She was entirely naked, only a thin translucent sheet thrown loosely over her. Her body was muscled, pale, attractive.

And I must look like hell, he thought. *I think I'll take a sonic shower before she wakes up. And a face steam. But first her name.* He spotted her cadet purse on the other side of the bed. He reached across slowly. She breathed easily, her pale skin unwrinkled from the night's sleep.

His fingers were within an inch of the purse when she opened her eyes. She smiled up at him and he froze.

"Good morning," she said.

"Good morning."

She looked at his arm. He smiled.

He moved his hand a few inches and set the fingers down lightly on her exposed breast. Now he remembered a good deal more of the previous night.

"You are . . . very beautiful," he said as he stroked her breast. "In case I didn't tell you last night."

"You didn't. But actions speak louder than words. You were wonderful. Thank you."

"Thank *you*. I hope you don't think . . . that is, I mean, I didn't mean to take advantage of you."

"We took advantage of each other. By my invitation. I was only afraid you wouldn't accept. But don't worry, I don't expect a proposal. It was a pleasure serving under you, Captain." Her smile was broad and genuine and infectious.

She reached out and stroked his face. She pulled his head down and kissed him. Then she pushed on his chest and rolled him onto his back. She rose up to her knees and straddled him. She leaned forward slightly and her black hair dangled on his bare chest.

"Then again, you're not the only officer here, even if you do outrank me. You can serve under *me* this time."

He looked up at her face, which she was lowering toward him. Just before her pretty face disappeared behind a wave of flesh, he thought, *How did I get so lucky?*

Two hours later she had showered, eaten a huge breakfast of ground-grown food foraged from his refrigerator, and was going out the door in her Starfleet uniform. He wore a Vulcan robe that had been a retirement gift from his science officer.

"Thanks for making that coffee," she said. "It was the best I've ever had. Really."

"It's the water. It's imported from Mars. And it's handmade from real grounds, not from the synthesizer. Sometimes the old ways are the best."

"Yeah, that's just what I thought about last night."

"Oh, stabbed." He clutched his heart.

"I didn't mean—"

"That's all right." Kirk smiled. "You know what I got from Starfleet when I retired? A gold chronometer. This was much better."

"This wasn't entirely a question of hero worship, Captain. You're an attractive man." She encircled his stomach with her arms and laced her fingers behind his back. "You might be a little out of shape, but you're a very attractive man."

"I'm not sure I can stand any more of your compliments, but I'd like to see you again."

"You don't have to say that. I'm a big girl."

"You're an extraordinary girl. And honest. How about tonight. Dinner."

"All right, where?"

"Let's see—" Kirk realized he hadn't taken a woman out on a formal date in a while.

"I'll tell you what," she said. "While you were in the shower I put my terminal address in your computer. You can send me a message. Just look under my name."

"Oh, fine. Uh, that is, well, I, uh—"

"And my name"—her face crinkled up with her big smile again—"is Barbara O'Marla. You can call me Babs."

"I'll be in touch. I will. Babs."

"Have a good day. Jim."

She kissed him and stepped out into the apartment corridor. She walked down the hall to the turbolift. He watched her wait for the car. Then he heard the latch click on another front door just across the hall. He stepped back into his apartment feeling embarrassed, and closed the door.

As he walked toward his kitchen he passed a mirror. *I think I'll go to the gym today,* he said to himself.

Kirk spent the morning at his club, Sutro Selestial Baths, where he rowed several kilometers in the hydroplane, boxed with a machine set at intermediate level, and relaxed in the steamy, invigorating Mercury Room. Afterward he went shopping, and watched as a hologram of himself materialized in a number of new tunics. He picked out two that he thought made him look young, and had them sent to his apartment.

By late morning he was idly walking along the beach and gazing out over the crystal blue Pacific Ocean. He watched children skim along the waves on space boards. He admired the sand artisans. But it was the toy Starships that put him into a contemplative and nostalgic mood he couldn't shake off. He sat on a bench for half an hour and watched elaborate model starships as they were piloted by remote control in a dazzling series of races and maneuvers in the air over the breaking waves.

He wandered idly through the pine trees and down to the shuttle docks. There he watched uniformed personnel depart for the big Starships that would take them to the uncharted frontiers.

Instead of living great adventures, I'm talking about the old days. Instead of facing Klingons, I'm wandering around spacedocks, mooning over the sleek Starships that are under somebody else's command.

He walked slowly across the city, through the lush green park, up and down hills, past habitats, and through the downtown area teeming with shops carrying exotic goods from all over the galaxy. He reentered his apartment just after noon. He went to his computer terminal and turned it on. Before he could read a summary of the day's news, however, the screen lit up with a bright red facsimile of a bouquet of roses. They started as tiny buds, burst open, and bloomed. They settled their green stems in a beautiful, ancient Asian vase. Cursive writing curled across the bottom of the monitor: "All best, Babs." He smiled to himself. He looked at the pretty graphic for a minute before he waved his fingers over the console built into his desk, and left her a message, asking her to meet him at 1930 hours at a romantic restaurant. Then he called up the Intergalactic News Network.

A list of keywords he had placed in his computer's memory ran instantly against the stories on the public frequency channels that day. An updated report on the *Excelsior* crew trapped in Beta Prometheus flashed across his screen.

Starfleet Command "deplored the actions" of the Prometheans. The Office of the President of the Federation Council said that everything was being done to "insure the safe return of the nine Federation citizens." All diplomatic channels were being employed. There were sidebar pieces on the Promethean civilization and the history of dilithium crystal trading. Sulu and his team were named and profiled.

Nothing new, and nothing was being done.

Kirk paced his apartment, worrying. He settled into his commander's chair, a gift from his old crew of the *Enterprise,* which was bolted to the floor in front of his window, and tried to put the story out of his mind by reading fiction from late-nineteenth-century England. Usually he found that to be entirely absorbing, but not this afternoon. Finally he fell into a short, troubled sleep. In his dreams he saw jumbled images of deep space, the young Barbara O'Marla, and the face of his old comrade, Sulu.

When Kirk awoke from his nap, he felt the sluggishness he associated with . . . what? Old age. Impossible. He ran two kilometers on his treadmill, changed his clothes, and went out to meet Barbara O'Marla at the restaurant Nebulae, where they dined together. He was glad to have somebody to talk to. His restlessness had increased as further news of the Sulu hostage incident was not forthcoming.

"No news is bad news in a case like this," Kirk said. "I've been reading up on these Beta Prometheans. They're not trustworthy. As long as Sulu and his crew are at their mercy, they're in grave danger."

"You're very loyal, aren't you?" she asked.

"Loyal? I hadn't thought about it that way. Sulu was

certainly loyal. He had several chances to transfer off the *Enterprise* to other assignments that might have advanced his career faster, but he never did. He got us out of hot water more than once with his skills as a helmsman. When he finally took up his own command, we all missed him. I'm worried about him. Apparently the Federation isn't," Kirk finished with a touch of anger.

"You're becoming obsessed with this, James," Barbara said quietly.

"I suppose I am. Maybe I should get my mind off it."

"What about your memoirs? You told me you were writing them. I think they would make a hell of a book. It would become required reading at the Academy."

"I started on a memoir once. I wrote 'These were the voyages of the *Starship Enterprise* . . .' Then I stalled. I think they call it writer's block. Anyway, trying to do that made me feel as if it was over. I didn't like that feeling."

Afterward, they walked back to Kirk's apartment. Barbara took her coat off and walked over to his desk, where a large model was under construction.

"You've taken up a hobby," she said, indicating the work.

"This is the original *Enterprise,* the ship my first command was named after. It's a sailing ship, built during the nineteenth century for trading and sailing the Atlantic ocean. It predates man's ability to fly. I'm building a fairly exact model. Then maybe I'll take it out to the Bay and try it out."

"Where's the engine?"

"It doesn't have an engine. The wind takes her."

"The wind?"

"You see these? They're sails. They're raised and lowered to catch the natural wind. That's the only power she has. If there's no wind, she's becalmed. When there is, she runs in front of it. She must have been beautiful to captain."

Barbara watched Kirk's face as he explained the details of the great sailing ship to her. "You must miss traveling."

"You can't imagine what it's like, cruising through a cloud of gas, illuminated by a nearby star, all pink and purple, brilliant colors. Or the uncertainty of traveling to an uncharted planet. And then there's warp speed," he said to her, his tone changing. "You're racing faster than light, covering enormous distances in microseconds. Sometimes the old Starships rattled a bit, vibrating under your feet."

He had unconsciously wandered to his big window and looked up at the night sky. She came over behind him and put her arms around his waist, leaning her head against his broad back.

"You're a man of dreams, James."

They made love, slower and more tenderly than they had their first night, and he tried hard to be attentive to her needs. *She's a fragile gift,* he thought. *A gift a man my age doesn't usually come across. I have to take this relationship slowly and carefully.*

He was distracted by the view outside. More than once he looked over her shoulder and thought about the darkening sky, as the stars came on like lights, one after the other, until they were twinkling in the millions and millions and millions, their light racing through the Earth's atmosphere, right to his window.

"You're going to do something, aren't you?" Barbara said to him while they lay back, side by side, in the middle of the night.

"Yes," he said, hearing his own voice echo in the bedroom. "Yes I am."

How did she know? he thought. *How did she know, when I didn't know myself, not until this very minute?*

Kirk laid awake the rest of the night while Barbara slept at his side. He watched her breathe easily, ran his eyes over her white skin, her smooth muscles, her black hair. She aroused him even in her sleep, even after the night of lovemaking, even in his distraction. He felt the yearning and the energy again. He stared at the stars beyond his window. It was no coincidence that Starships were thought of in the female gender, he mused. Women and Starships had a great deal in common. They were sleek, mothering, energizing. They were exotic and erotic. They were temperamental, transitory.

And you could ride them into forever, he thought.

Day Five

He waited until she had left for work. Then he went to his closet, and stared at his clothes.

If he wore civilian clothes he would be stopped by any security personnel who didn't recognize him. Yet he hadn't worn his uniform in almost a year.

Starfleet never actually mustered anyone out of the service, or even officially retired anyone. All officers were placed on inactive status, allowed to pursue their own interests, and kept in reserve against the day their talents might be needed. As, officially, a reserve officer, Kirk could have worn his uniform when he held a seminar at the Academy, or attended an official function. He never did. It felt somehow fraudulent now that he was no longer the captain of a Starship. And he didn't want young cadets to call him sir. Nevertheless, he had the right to wear it, and it might just come in handy today. On that small excuse, he pulled it out and put it on. Then he traveled across the Bay to Starfleet Headquarters.

There he strolled across the great grassy field around which the giant bureaucracy of Starfleet centered. It was crisscrossed with officers, but he saw no one he recognized and no one glanced at him a second time. *So far so good,* he thought. He passed under the great glass arch topped with the Fleet's insignia and walked into the fifty-story atrium that was lined with offices on either side. Starfleet personnel were everywhere. Kirk remembered when, as a young cadet, the hallways of operations were continually deserted because all communications took place electronically. Now they were busy. It was rumored that the Fleet's Department of Humanoid Resources began some years ago to encourage face-to-face meetings where possible. The department apparently now felt that the failure of electronic dialogue to carry useful nuances and improvised content was a factor in inhibiting the quality of collaborative decision making.

Kirk was halfway across the great space when he realized he had never felt comfortable at Starfleet Headquarters. He knew and loved every inch of the ships that had been under his command, but the labyrinthine village represented a bureaucracy from which he had been happy to escape. He was not sure how much of his reason for being there he wanted to divulge, and found himself hoping he wouldn't run into anyone he knew. Something deep inside him, a vague instinct for what could happen, cautioned him to avoid drawing attention to himself. He strolled over to a bespectacled young cadet sitting behind a console, and said quietly, "I'm looking for an old friend. He's a science officer. But he's on leave, and he's probably gone back home. Which department do you think could help me?"

"You probably want Humanoid Resource Records, sir. That's right here in this building. Level thirty-two. Unless he prefers to be unlisted, then we won't be able to help you unless you have a class-triple-A security clearance."

"I do," Kirk said, not having the faintest idea what that was. "Records," Kirk repeated. He looked up at the towering glass shaft that held the turbolift, and walked toward it, feigning casualness. "Thank you," he said over his shoulder.

He got off the turbolift at level thirty-two. He headed down the main hallway, reading the holographic signs next to the doors as he strolled along. COMMSATTRAC, ALLANGTRANS, GALVEGRE, RESTROOMS. Communications Satellite Tracking, Alien Language Translation, Galaxy Vegetation Research, thought Kirk. Then he saw large letters floating in double glass doors at the end of the hall. RECORDS, it said, in a startlingly simple statement. Kirk went through the doors.

Inside he found only a series of cubicles, each with a chair and a computer. Some of them were occupied with Starfleet personnel, but most were empty. He sat down at one and read:

> Welcome to the Starfleet database.
> Please enter your password.

He hadn't used his Starfleet password in all the years he had been in space, and was momentarily stymied. When he recalled it, he was surprised to find that the simple seven-letter word he had chosen as an idealistic and passionate youth still suited his self-image. He leaned over and said quietly to the console, "Voyager."

"Password and voice identification confirmed," a flat and mechanical voice said. "You are cleared for full access. State nature of inquiry."

It should have been discontinued six months earlier when he retired, but it worked. *One thing about bureaucracies,* Kirk thought, *they're always months behind.*

He paused for a moment. Suppose he couldn't find them? Suppose they didn't want to come with him? Was it putting them in an awkward position even to ask? Each would have his or her own life now. He had a right to ask. Each would make his or her own decision.

Who first? he thought. *Of course.*

"Locate," he said. "Spock. Captain. Science officer."

The terminal flickered and read:

> SPOCK
> Rank: Commander (inactive)
> Contact:
> Vulcan Science Academy
> Shikar
> T'Khasi
> 40 Eridani A (19.5, 60.0 -0.6)

Kirk downloaded the information to his own handheld tricorder, then requested another entry, and another. When he had uncovered all their whereabouts, he exited from the database.

Then he connected to a database for travel information. He asked it to plot a course for him, starting at once. When the arrangements had been confirmed on his tricorder, Kirk left Starfleet Headquarters.

His visit had not gone unnoticed. The young cadet who steered him to the correct department had been too polite, or perhaps too startled, to let on that he had recognized Kirk, but as he had only recently come through the Academy, and as Kirk's holographic image was used to teach the *Kobayashi Maru* scenario—not to mention that Captain Kirk himself was something of a legend—he had in fact recognized the officer immediately. And gossip being what it was, especially in the hothouse environment of the Academy, the cadet was well aware that a friend of his was having an affair with the captain. The young cadet couldn't resist, and he communicated Kirk's presence in the building with Barbara O'Marla.

If he isn't here to visit me, she thought, *I won't seek him out.* When he left the building without looking in on her, she felt a pang of sadness, and realized that she felt much stronger about him than she had admitted to herself. Now she could only sit back and wonder why he made an impromptu visit to the Records department, when he was almost stubborn about not having anything to do with Starfleet these days.

In a sleek office overlooking the bay, high in Starfleet Command Headquarters, someone else was thinking about Kirk's short visit. Admiral Caius Fesidas had been apprised of it when his own terminal flashed a message that the password "Voyager" had entered the data-management web. He watched as the password was cleared, knowing it would be, because only the day before he had reattached the highest security clearance to the retired password. He tracked it to the thirty-second-floor Records department. He saw the five locations flicker across his own screen. He didn't have to match their service records; he could guess who they were. And if he knew his man, he could guess why Kirk was tracing them. He wasn't the type to organize a reunion, and it was months before holiday greeting cards were due.

The admiral spoke briefly to an aide, then returned to his previous business.

In the Neutral Zone

"Sarek." The 129-year-old Vulcan nodded after he gave his name. "I have been asked to represent the United Federation of Planets."

"Kannish," the figure that sat across from him at the huge black onyx table said. "I represent Beta Prometheus."

Sarek knew the Beta Promethean had not been elected, was born into the Ruling Family. The representative looked tired and old. But Sarek knew that it took an iron will to maintain leadership in an aristocracy, and Kannish was one of the principal family members.

"My son was an officer on the *Sundew* when the Federation Starship attacked it."

Long experienced in negotiating with non-Federation civilizations, Sarek kept his face still at the sudden statement.

"Then," Sarek began carefully, "you have heard a first-hand account of the incident."

"No, I haven't." Sarek saw the mottled dark gray skin lighten imperceptibly. "My son Kornish was killed during the . . . in what you call an incident."

This is not going to be easy, Sarek thought.

"My apologies. And may I express the Federation's deep regret over the loss of your son."

"Regret? You can't imagine what it feels like to lose a son. He was twenty-five years old, my oldest. Only halfway through a Beta Promethean life. He was destined to sit on the Inner Council after I am gone."

Sarek thought for a moment why he could very well know how it felt to lose a son. And how grateful he had been when his own son's regenerated body and spirit were reunited in the *fal-tor-pan* ceremony. Careful not to insult Kannish by discussing his own personal experiences, however, Sarek simply nodded slowly.

"We must," he began, "insure that no such thing should ever happen again. The Federation has every hope that a peaceful and productive relationship between it and the Beta Promethean people can continue. If the *Starship Excelsior* had drifted into Beta Promethean star space without prior permission, I want to assure you that it was an accident, and that our Starfleet will be most careful not to do so again until a working treaty for your area of the galaxy can be defined between us. Many of your people are traders, and certainly know how important it is that intergalactic travel go unrestricted. I must ask, however, that before we discuss such broad issues, we discuss the incarceration of nine of our Starfleet officers. The Federation wants to assure you that they were not spying. What can we do to effect their safe return?"

Kannish glowered across the table. The two Beta Prometheans that sat near him seemed to fidget on their stools. Sarek's own aides, two young humans newly posted to the diplomatic corps, sat as still as they could.

Kannish waved his muscled hand as if to dismiss the issue. "No, no, this is not productive at all. The important issues first. Surely in the great scheme of things, the Starfleet officers hardly matter. But the dilithium prices, which have until now—"

"To us," Sarek broke in as politely as he could, "the matter of the officers is of the utmost importance. Perhaps you could assure me that they are all healthy?"

"I don't understand the Federation's concern with a few officers." Kannish shook his head. "The Federation itself should be of paramount importance. The lives of the officers are a small price to pay."

"The Federation *is* the lives of the officers. Each one is of great value to the Federation."

"Then your worlds will not progress very far in this universe. Surely you can see how unimportant individual lives are in the vast spaces of the galaxy and in the creator's vision."

"Indeed, the single life is dwarfed by the time and space of our universe. Yet it is the very sanctity of that life that gives our society strength. . . ."

Kannish and Sarek spoke on into the night, Kannish laying out demands—a new, higher dilithium price and a commitment to buy dilithium only from the Beta Prometheans, a guarantee of noninterference in the political workings of their planet, and fees paid to the Beta Prometheans for travel within their system—while Sarek continually tried to steer the conversation back to the officers somewhere in a Beta Promethean prison. And away from the discourse on the inefficiency of a democracy, which Kannish appeared to be anxious to expound on. When he noticed that his counterpart's energy was wearing down, Sarek remembered that a Beta Promethean was old at fifty. He begged his own exhaustion—in truth he wasn't the least bit tired—and the group broke up, with assurances that they would meet again the next day.

In the hallway outside, he walked back to the shuttle that would take him back to Starbase 499 while talking quietly with his aides.

"This is going to be a difficult one," Sarek said, as much to himself as for the education of the young diplomats. "You notice he was fairly obtuse about the health of our Starfleet officers, and did not really want to discuss them at all."

"They don't take the individual life very seriously here," the young man on his left said.

"No, they do not," Sarek agreed. "But divergent philosophies are not our central problem. We have to get them to spell out a working timetable for the return of the men. And that may be difficult. All this 'for good of the system' talk aside, the traders here seem to go their own way a good deal of the time. I do not believe the Ruling Family controls the hostages. Or even knows exactly where they are."

When they were seated inside their shuttle, the young man turned to the ambassador.

"I know you also have a son, sir," he said. "Isn't he serving in the Starfleet?"

"He was. He is on an extended leave," Sarek said. "I believe just now he is at the Vulcan Science Academy pursuing a complex problem to its logical conclusion."

The Planet Vulcan

Kirk stepped out of the shuttle onto the Vulcan planet surface and immediately felt the increased gravity and searing heat. He threaded his way through the terminal and boarded a tram that took him to the Science Academy. There he looked up an acquaintance in an obscure office. Although the Vulcan did not know where Mr. Spock was living just then, he knew where he could be found that evening. Kirk thanked the scientist for the directions, and walked leisurely through the city.

It was extraordinarily peaceful after the streets of San Francisco. The buildings were bleached from the constant desert climate, and the landscape was sparse and simple. The air was close and warm. The sister planet was enormous in the sky, its dust storms and volcanoes visible to the naked eye. No one hurried. Long-robed Vulcans walked calmly in small groups. Many pedestrians appeared to be deep in meditation. Handfuls of alien visitors roamed the streets like tourists.

Kirk found the small Globe Theatre at the bottom of a narrow alley. Posters flanking the box office announced the Melpomene Players' production of William Shakespeare's *Hamlet*. The lobby was deserted, the performance had already begun. Kirk walked around the building until he found the stage door. He opened it quietly and stepped into an empty corridor. Following it, he found himself in the semidarkness of backstage. Then he heard the voice of the man he was looking for, speaking in bombastic tones.

"He will come straight," he heard Mr. Spock intone. *"Look you lay home to him: Tell him his pranks have been too broad to bear with, And that your Grace hath screen'd and stood between much heat and him. I'll sconce me even here. Pray you, be round with him."*

Kirk walked closer to the sound until he was standing behind the set. Bright lights flooded the stage and he could see through a crack in the ersatz stone wall that Spock and a woman were playing a scene. Then a handsome young Deltan male walked up, stood right next to Kirk in the shadows, and shouted toward the stage.

"Mother, mother, mother?"

The female human's voice came from the stage.

"I'll warrant you; fear me not:—withdraw, I hear him coming."

Kirk watched as Spock stepped through a curtain in the set. Then the young man walked past Kirk and went onto the stage.

"Now, mother, what's the matter?" Kirk heard him ask the actress.

"Hamlet, thou hast thy father much offended."

"Mother, you have my father much offended."

"Come, come, you answer with an idle tongue."

"Go, go, you question with a wicked tongue."

As the voices continued, becoming increasingly agitated, Kirk walked around the braces that held up the flats and came up beside Mr. Spock, who was standing just offstage behind a curtain. Spock turned and saw him.

"Captain Kirk," Spock whispered. "This is an unexpected surprise. If you have come to see our production, you would enjoy it much better from a seat in the front of the house."

"Spock, what the hell are you doing?"

"I am playing Polonius. Surely you recognized *Hamlet,* Captain."

"I can see that. I mean, since when have you gone in for acting?"

"Oh. That is quite recent actually. And primarily because of you."

"Me?"

"You often told me that I should get more in touch with the human side of my nature."

"Your emotions. I said you should get in touch with your emotions, Spock."

"Precisely. I took an acting class which promised exactly that. One thing led to another, and here I am."

"I see. The roar of the greasepaint."

The onstage voices continued to float over the scenery to them.

"Why, how now, Hamlet!"

"What's the matter now?"

"Have you forgot me?"

"No, by the rood, not so: You are the queen, your husband's brother's wife; And—would it were not so!—you are my mother."

"Nay, then, I'll set those to you that can speak."

"Come, come, and sit you down; you shall not budge; You go not till I set you up a glass where you may see the inmost part of you."

Kirk was about to speak when Spock tilted his head toward the stage.

"One moment," Spock said to Kirk. "I have a line coming up. . . ."

"What wilt thou do? Thou wilt not murder me?—Help, help, ho!" the young man onstage yelled.

"What, ho! Help, help, help!" Spock shouted through the curtain.

"How now, a rat? Dead for a ducat, dead!"

Kirk watched, amazed, as a sword ripped through the curtain. Spock wrapped his arm around it, shouted *"O, I am slain!"* then fell to the ground, dragging the curtain with him. It tore off its moorings, and wrapped around Spock as he slumped to the ground. Kirk stepped back just in time to keep from being seen by the audience. There was more dialogue, and finally the lights dimmed onstage. In the shadows Kirk saw Spock jump nimbly to his feet and walk by him.

"That is all for my character. Come to my dressing room. We can speak before the calls."

Kirk followed Spock down a staircase to a basement, and into a low-ceilinged room with Spock's name on the door. Obviously, Kirk noted, the Vulcans had taken pains to re-create a human theater environment. Spock sat in a chair before a large mirror and began removing his stage makeup.

"Captain. I am aware of your interest in culture, but surely, even in your retirement, you have not come so far simply to view a Vulcan production of *Hamlet?*"

"I might have. I think your death scene was marvelous."

"Thank you. We have not had adequate rehearsal time and, between you and me, the director is handicapped by a large ego and self-absorbed personality that precludes him from recognizing and acknowledging the genius of William Shakespeare. Thus our production has been saddled with artificial notions that cloud the fundamental issues. The producer was impressed by his résumé, and imported him from somewhere in the galaxy."

"I'm sorry."

"On the other hand, his inadequate direction has united the cast against him, and I have benefited from a wonderful camaraderie I have not before experienced. Not since our voyages aboard the *Enterprise,* that is."

Kirk stared at Spock for a moment, then decided to plunge ahead.

"I'll bet you'd like to know why I've come to see you."

"I assumed you would tell me when it suited you."

"I will. I am. That is, well, how should I put this . . .?"

"Let us 'cut the cackle and get down to the horses.' I would be glad to accompany you to Beta Prometheus."

Kirk stopped. "How did you guess?"

"I, too, have been following the news. Our old helmsman is in a difficult situation. For two days now, Starfleet has not moved to assist the hostages, and the Federation is mired in politics. You are a captain with intense loyalties to your crew, which you have demonstrated on more than one occasion. You have come to visit me suddenly and without warning, although I have not heard from you since our last voyage together over nine months ago. It is only logical that you have come to recruit me for a mission."

"I sent you a postcard just last Christmas."

"It said only, 'Winter Solstice Greetings.' In standard print."

"Okay, I admit I was never much for writing. Will you come with me?"

"I will."

"You understand, Spock, that this is entirely on our own. I haven't been reactivated by Starfleet."

"As you are wearing civilian clothes and not your uniform, I had assumed that to be the case, Captain."

"I can't stand waiting around doing nothing, and I thought I'd go out there and, you know, get a little closer to the situation. In case I can be of some assistance. But what about the play? Do you have an understudy?"

"I was informed earlier that tonight we are giving our last performance," Spock answered with some finality. "The principal critic is Vulcan and found the play to be illogical."

"Great. I mean, I'm sorry about the play, but I'm glad you're available. I thought we would get together at my apartment in San Francisco tomorrow. We can make plans then."

"Logical. How many of the others have you recruited?"

"So far . . . let me think. None."

"I am the first?"

"You're the first."

"I am flattered, Captain."

"By the way, there's no need to call me 'Captain' any longer, Spock. I'm a civilian now."

"I am aware of that, Captain."

"So you can call me Jim."

"Thank you, Captain."

"I guess old habits die hard."

A stage manager stuck his head in and announced the calls. Spock and Kirk went up the staircase, and Kirk found himself milling about with dozens of actors, hushed and waiting. From the stage he heard a solemn voice.

"Take up the bodies. Such a sight as this becomes the field, but here shows much amiss. Go, bid the soldiers shoot."

There was silence, the lights dimmed out, and Kirk was standing in pitch darkness. He heard applause, and bright lights came up. The actors poured onto the stage. Kirk watched from the wings as they smiled and bowed.

Later Kirk and Spock walked up the alley together, the noise from the carousing actors dimming behind them.

"I hate to take you away from all this," Kirk apologized.

"It was going to be my last foray into the theater in any case. As an experiment it held out some remarkably interesting events, but I shall return soon to my research at the Academy. There is altogether too much Sturm und Drang in theatrical production for me. I prefer a more logical approach to problems."

"But that's what Shakespeare is noted for, the Sturm and Drang as you call it."

"I was referring to the backstage atmosphere. Actors and actresses from the more emotional races having affairs, arguments, and nervous breakdowns. And all the shouting, crying, yelling. No, the theatre life is not for a Vulcan, or even a half-Vulcan. I will be glad to get back to my studies."

"What, and quit show business?" Kirk said wryly.

Spock simply said, "I will see you in San Francisco." He waved and turned down the street. Kirk watched the tall figure disappear into the balmy night, then turned and headed back toward the terminal.

The Eurosphere, Earth

Kirk came down to Earth at London Intergalactic, and shuttled immediately up-country. There was no public tram beyond the foot of the mountains, so he hired a private shuttle and gave his driver the name of the small hamlet.

The heather-covered hills flashed beneath the taxi. Small towns and country manors grew farther and farther apart until they reached the Highlands. There was no landing dock in the little village, so the driver hovered onto a grassy field behind the single street of small shops. Sheep bleated and scurried out of the way as the space van stopped a foot above the ground and its single engine stopped humming.

Kirk made arrangements for the driver to return in several hours. Then he jumped down and walked across the field toward a handful of low buildings. He stepped onto the village's only carbonized road. Spotting several open shops, he chose the local pub. The last time he had seen senior engineering officer Montgomery Scott, the man suggested he had a lot of idle endeavors to catch up on, and planned a good deal of them in his retirement.

The doors of Pluto's Inn slid open and Kirk stepped inside a brightly skylit room, the far wall lined from bar to roof with bottles from every brand of fermented and distilled drink known in the immediate solar system. The ceiling was laced with a unique collection of laser signs featuring the names of the most popular brands, and the floor was a jumble of tables and chairs made from highly polished natural woods. At this hour in the midafternoon, Kirk was the only customer. He approached a burly woman who was wiping glasses behind the bar.

"I don't think I've ever seen such a fine collection of natural wood furniture."

"Then you're a stranger to the Highlands," she said in a musical burr. "We get everything we kin from Mother Earth. As long as we replace it, she does na mind. Who are ye seeking?"

"Montgomery Scott. An old friend. How did you . . .?"

"Strangers do na come here for the entertainment. We do na have Alien Parks or Environpods or Fantasy Stimulators."

"You have the greenest earth and the bluest sky I've ever seen."

"Aye, and lakes and rivers so clear you can count the scales on the fish at the bottom. But regulations have nay permitted hunting nor fishing for some centuries now. You're from the city, I can see by your clothes."

"And I thought I was blending right in."

"They're the right style, but they're artificial. They come from the synthesizers. Feel this. It comes from the sheep." She held out the tunic she was wearing. He politely felt the material.

"Ye kin tell, can't ye?"

"Uh, yes, it's quite remarkable." Kirk did not go on to say that he didn't understand how the woman could wear something so rough next to her skin all day, just for the sake of avoiding synthetics. Then he realized that she was probably a Gaian, a follower of a native religion he had heard about in which the principal Goddess was the Earth herself. They tended to congregate in the country, away from the megalopolises, and were committed to self-sufficiency and natural products.

"Do you think you could help me. Mr. Scott is about six feet tall and—"

"—almost as round, since he retired. Ye'll find Scotty at the end of the third path in the second vale if ye leave the village walking north. But if you just sit here, he'll come walking through that door in a coupla hours, calling for his pint o' bitter, and ready to tell the tallest tales ye've ever haird tell of."

"Tales?"

"About quare places all over the universe. About people that kin read your mind from standing across the room, and others that kin put strange thoughts into your own head. About trees that kin walk, and machines that kin take you back in time. All nonsense if ye ask me. People kin nay be that different just because they do na live on Earth. It's only hoo-man."

"Well, Scotty always did have a vivid imagination." Kirk smiled. "I don't think I'd take him too seriously. Thank you for your help. I don't think I'll wait though, if you don't think it's too far a walk?"

"I do nay think it is, but then, I do nay go flyin' round the heavens in machinery, either. Ye look like ye could use the exercise anyways."

"Yes, you're right, I'm afraid. Too much city living. North two vales and three paths, then? All right, thank you. Good afternoon."

Kirk spent a pleasant thirty minutes walking north along the Scottish roads. He calculated the two valleys and three small paths as best he could. Most of the area was uninhabited, though he could see the tops of habitats nestled back among the trees here and there. Finally he turned up a slim path and followed it as it wound through trees, then paralleled a creek for a few hundred yards. Coming out of the woods he saw a simple geodesic dome tucked into a clearing, a perfect glass hemisphere, the green trees and blue sky reflected in the glassy walls. The exquisite, utterly simple technology was impressive, particularly so far from the nearest urban center. He knew at once he had come to the right place.

The end of the path stopped in front of one of the dome's panels, but it was indistinguishable from the others. He could find no way of announcing himself except by knocking on the thin, opaque glass, which he was reluctant to do. Then he noticed a sliver of red light cutting the path at knee level. He walked through it and heard a metallic voice announce "Visitor at the main entrance" from inside the dwelling. He waited. The voice repeated the message. After a few minutes he gave up, and began to circle the dome.

Behind the building he found a large, grassy patio. At the far end hung a hammock of reeds hung between two enormous trees, well shaded by their foliage. Lying on his back on the hammock, his loud snoring keeping the birds away, was Kirk's old friend, Montgomery Scott.

Kirk tiptoed over to the sleeping engineer, looked straight down into his face. He noted the three-day beard, the jowly cheeks, the red nose.

"Engineering!" Kirk shouted.

Scotty's eyes shot open and he looked directly into the bright sun. The dark shadow of a man stood next to him.

"Huh, whazzat?" he said, bringing his hand up to shade his eyes and knocking himself in the forehead with it. "Ooch," he complained, and closed his eyes again.

Kirk moved slightly to block the sun and throw a shadow on Scotty's face. Scotty opened his eyes tentatively. This time he saw James Kirk.

His face jumped, his eyebrows arched, his mouth twisted up into an enormous grin.

"Captain Kirk!" he shouted. He tried to raise himself up, but the hammock swayed with the change in gravity, and Scotty lost his balance, flopped over the side, and landed facedown in the grass.

"Oof!" he muttered.

"Commander Scott, what in God's name have you been doing with yourself?" Kirk said to his back.

Scott rolled over and propped himself up on his elbows. He smiled up at Kirk.

"Not a damn thing." He grinned. "Not a goddam thing. Aye, Captain, it's a glorious life."

A few minutes later they were seated in the shade of the dome on two comfortable cushions of air that rose from vents in the grass.

"Scotty, you amaze me," Kirk said as he glanced worriedly at the ground beneath him. He tried to put his hand on whatever it was that he was sitting on, but his hand only passed through air. "What the heck is this thing?"

"It's not but a wee thing I've been tinkering with. The column of air adjusts itself to your weight, and the heat to your body temperature. When you get up it goes off. It's quite safe, I can assure you."

"Amazing."

"It's got one small bug, however. Because you can't see it, my guests are stumbling over it all the time."

"I guess you'll have to work on it a bit more."

"That I will. Though between my naps and visits to the pubs, I dinna have much time." Scotty chuckled. "Now, what is it that brings you so far away from civilization?"

"Have you heard about Sulu?"

"Nae, I have not. What's wrong?" Scotty's face clouded over. "Is he not still captain of the *Excelsior?*"

"He is. But he and his crew have been taken hostage."

"What! Klingons? Why, I knew those——"

"Not Klingons, Scotty. Some two-bit space pirates operating out of a small, obscure planetary system called Beta Prometheus. They've taken nine of the *Excelsior's* officers hostage, including Captain Sulu. The Federation is negotiating for their return, but as yet it isn't even clear exactly what they want. It's possible that their government isn't even really in control of the situation. There's very little news coming out of the sector, and I'm getting worried that they're going to rot there for a long time unless something is done. But Starfleet can't act without a directive from the Federation, and for complicated reasons, the Federation is being ultracautious."

"How far is this Beta Prometheus?"

"Far. In the frontier. Sulu was exploring deep space beyond the border."

"So . . ." Scotty's face broke into a sly grin. "The only way to get there is by Starship at warp speed. And you're thinkin' it might be friendly-like to go up and see for yourself what's happening?"

"Exactly."

"And ye'll need a good engineer."

"I will." Kirk grinned.

"Would you accept me as a volunteer?" Scotty said.

"I certainly would, Mr. Scott."

"Then I'll join you."

"And leave this idyllic life behind? You looked like you were enjoying yourself enormously."

"I'll tell you a secret, Captain Kirk. This easy life isn't all that it's cracked up to be. I'm not complainin', mind you. After all the running around the universe I've done, it's a pleasure to have your feet on your own hammock, an ale in your hand, and all the time in the world. But . . ."

"But what?"

"It can get a little boring, if you know what I mean."

"I do, Mr. Scott. Indeed I do. How long do you think it will take you to get ready?"

Scotty looked down at the paunch overhanging his belt. He put his hand on his stomach, and frowned.

"Oh, three or four days, sir."

"I'll need you in one. We meet in San Francisco on the morrow."

Scotty struggled to his feet and drew himself up straight.

"I'll do it, sir."

Kirk smiled. "You always do, Mr. Scott. You always do." He returned the salute, and walked back around the path that would take him to his waiting shuttle.

New York

"I'm afraid I can't find a thing wrong with you, madame."

"But, Doctor, I'm sure there must be something you can

do. I've been feeling faint for several days now, and my stomach growls at the oddest times."

"Do you get any exercise?"

"Well, no . . ."

"What do you eat?"

"Actually I'm rather fond of the cuisine of Gamon VII. It's wonderfully rich and meaty."

"You're a cholesterol factory."

"You needn't be so blunt, Doctor."

"Good nutrition and exercise. That's my prescription. Pull yourself together and come back in thirty days."

The doctor left the woman sitting on the table in her white gown, and sauntered out into the hall. He wandered over to the nurses' station. A young woman at the desk looked up.

"Mrs. Melgood can get dressed." He lowered his voice and spoke to his new nurse in a plaintive tone. "Isn't there anybody really sick waiting for me?"

"I'm afraid not, Doctor."

"A case of Debellium brain rot disease? Aphasia and disorientation from passing through the Guardian of Forever? Bitten by the two-headed toad from Rangoren?"

"No, sir. As a matter of fact, I've never heard of any of those problems. Are you sure—"

"Never mind. They're not from around here." McCoy tapped his fingers on the desk between them and gazed over her head up into the skylight. She had seen him gaze out the window into the sky more and more lately. And always with a faraway look in his eyes.

"Mr. Zieglar is coming in at four o'clock. He wants to know if you can artificially lengthen his ankle tendons to improve his tennis. And there's a Mr. Akara who needs some immunizations. He's going on vacation in the Vornok System, and is afraid of, well, you know. . . ."

"Yes." McCoy made a noise that clearly indicated his displeasure. "A bunch of spoiled, idle people."

"I beg your pardon, Doctor?"

"My patients. Nobody is ever really sick. Well, how could they be? They all live right here on terra firma. There hasn't been any rogue bacteria in centuries. They all have their predispositions mapped at birth, and are correcting them before they even start to appear. It's disgusting."

"Actually, Doctor, New York is considered something of a paradise. Even most aliens prefer to live here when they can. I don't quite see—"

"It's boring! I'd even welcome seeing some Klingon blood! Oh, you should see it, nurse. It's pink. God knows what its biological compositry is, they won't let us screen it. You know, once I had to work on a Klingon. He was dying, right in front of me! My anabolic protoplaser did nothing. So I leaped up and tried to resuscitate him by hand! What a fool, to think that a Klingon's heart was in the same place as ours. Or that they would have one at all." He chuckled. "But that's another issue altogether."

"Did you save him?" The nurse looked at McCoy, but he was apparently thinking of something else, and staring out the skylight behind her with a vague expression once again.

"Dr. McCoy?"

"Hmmm? Oh, sorry. What?"

"Did you save him? The Klingon?"

"Oh. No. I'm afraid I didn't. And he was our last best hope."

"I don't understand."

McCoy shook his head, and stood up. "Never mind. That all seems like a long time ago now. Well, if there's no more patients, I suppose I'll go over to the Star Club and start my infusions."

"Infusions? I didn't know you were sick, Doctor."

"Of wine."

"Oh. There is one thing more. A man is waiting in your office. Not a regular patient. He said he was a friend of yours."

"A friend of mine? That's funny. I don't remember making any plans. . . ."

"He said it was a surprise visit. But he said you would know him."

"All right. I suppose someone I once met on the golf course wants some free advice. I've got to stop giving out my card." McCoy wandered down the hall. The nurse looked after him. Then she began to close down her own workstation for the day.

McCoy opened his office door.

"Now, what's wrong with—" But he stopped when he saw the smiling figure relaxed in the armchair. "Kirk! James Kirk! James T. Kirk! Well, you're a sight for sore eyes!"

Kirk smiled and stood up. They embraced, then shook hands. McCoy—who in twenty-five years of service had seldom shown much enthusiasm at all—astonished Kirk with the warmth of his welcome. He stepped back, and pumped Kirk's hand. Then they embraced again.

"My God, it's good to see you. How the hell are you? Don't tell me something's wrong with old Stone Constitution Kirk?"

"No, I'm fine, Bones. How are you?"

"Fine, Jim, just fine."

"Good."

"Well, I'm all right."

"Just all right?"

"I'm . . . oh, I don't know . . . things lately have been a little . . . how should I put it . . ."

"You're not sick, are you? You never would think about yourself. You never once looked after yourself."

"No, no. I'm healthy."

"You're in private practice, I see."

"Yep. Ministering to dowagers who want lipolifts. Prescribing for old men who've heard about the latest aphrodisiac. Once in a while I give a lecture over at the Health Science Center."

"I've done that. At the Starfleet Academy."

"You too?"

"Makes me feel old."

"Exactly! I find myself telling young kids about this or that alien physiognomy, and it makes me . . . oh, never mind."

"What?"

"I suppose it's silly."

"You can tell me."

"Well . . ." McCoy looked around, and whispered. "It

makes me wish I were back in space again. It's ridiculous. Why would a man my age, after decades of bumming around the galaxy, want to go back up there."

"Wanderlust?"

McCoy looked at Kirk. "I'm afraid that's true, Jim. I've got it bad."

"I'm sorry, Bones." Kirk suppressed a smile.

"Bones! I haven't been called Bones, since . . . well . . ."

"Yes." Kirk let the silence between them stand, and McCoy looked toward his office window.

"I suppose I'll get used to it." McCoy sighed. Kirk let more silence gather. Then he said, "You don't have to."

"Don't I?" McCoy came back to Kirk. "There's not much I can do about it now."

"I think there is, Bones."

McCoy looked at Kirk suspiciously. Kirk smiled. He began telling McCoy a story in a whisper. McCoy leaned in, listening. He didn't ask any questions, and he didn't respond. But halfway through Kirk's story, he held up his hand.

"Say no more, Jim."

"We could use a good doctor. You never know what can happen, so far away from terra firma."

"You couldn't keep me away. When do we get our orders?"

"Orders?"

"From Starfleet. Aren't they going to recommission us? Are the uniforms still—"

"Bones, Starfleet didn't send me here."

"No? But then . . ."

"I just got tired of waiting."

Bones began to understand. "You never were any good at waiting, Jim."

"No."

"Neither was I." The doctor shook his head.

"We'll be meeting up with some old comrades tomorrow at my apartment in San Francisco. We ought to talk things over. And I don't mean old times."

"I'll be there."

Kirk stood up. McCoy stood up behind his desk. Kirk reached across the desk, and they shook hands.

"Tomorrow then. At noon," Kirk said.

"Tomorrow," McCoy smiled, and Kirk left the room.

McCoy stared at the door that shut behind Kirk for a minute, then touched his intercom.

"Mrs. Vegune?"

"Yes, Doctor? I was just leaving."

"Cancel all my future appointments. Something of an emergency has come up. Call Dr. Reiss, and ask him to take over my cases for me. There isn't much to do, he won't mind."

"Yes, Doctor. Where will you be?"

McCoy smiled. "A very long way away."

"How long will you be gone?"

"I'm not sure."

"Through the weekend, then?"

"Yes, Mrs. Vegune, through the weekend at least." McCoy turned off his intercom. *Or through century's end,* he thought. *Who knows?* He opened a bottom drawer and took out his portable medical tricorder, heartbeat reader, spray applicator, medical scanner, anabolic protoplaser, and surgical scalpels, and packed them in the antique black bag which was his parting gift from the crew of the *Enterprise.*

Then he danced around his desk and out the door.

The Siberian continent, Earth

Kirk disembarked from the *Shanghai Expresscraft* and asked directions at a nearby InfoPort. The computer quickly transferred brief instructions into Kirk's datapadd. As he strolled through the snow-locked Ukrainian freighter port megalopolis, the air was frigid and few citizens were on the street, but inside the enormous environpods he knew the city was bustling.

The streets became narrower and narrower as he followed the directions on his monitor, until he found himself walking among the long shadows of ten-story freight wharves. He made another turn down a tiny alley and came to a door with a round mirror at eye level. In the mirror floated a hologram featuring dice in green smoke, and the words ASIAN PARADOX. It was where Kirk's former navigator could be found, according to his landlady.

Inside, the club was filled with thick smoke. Kirk squinted into the distance, but the room was long and disappeared into the fog of Cobanian cigars. He looked up. The upper floors, platforms really, were made of antigravity plasticine and floated overhead, connected to each other and the ground by suspension bridges.

A short, hunched-over alien with huge ears and bad teeth was dispensing liquids at a long bar crowded with humans and aliens of all races. Not wanting to appear out of place, Kirk managed to secure some iced Mongolian tea and held it in his hand as he worked his way among the tables. He passed the Pan Gow tables, the roulette spinning disks, the long green pits within which floated combinations of numbers changing positions and dice bouncing on horizontal energy waves. He passed tables where small groups of individuals—some whose home planet he recognized and some he didn't—played ancient and modern games of cards. In front of all the denizens of this club were personal velvet bowls filled with silver and titanium chips, gems in dazzling colors from throughout the galaxy, chunks of gold. Kirk watched the frenzied activity through the blue haze of smoke. But he knew he wouldn't find his navigator among the gaming tables. He saw the section he wanted above him, and climbed the floating stairs to the third level. Above them the great loft's windows were opaque, and the club was lit by halogen sprinkler lights, affecting a perpetual sense of nighttime.

Kirk walked by a long line of tridimensional chessboards, with rows of players faced against each other. Behind them stood various humans and aliens kibitzing quietly. No one looked up as he passed. Everyone stared intently at the boards. Up here there was none of the shouting, in hundreds of languages, or the energetic body language of the games below, only the occasional shifting in chairs and a languid arm moving a piece. After a player moved, he touched a clock between them, and sat back. But the concentration, Kirk sensed, was intense.

Finally Kirk stood behind the man he had sought out. He watched as Pavel Chekov puzzled over a move, then reached for a bishop. A female Betazoid sat facing him. She was blond, with dazzling eyes, and she looked up at Chekov before making an answering move.

Chekov made another move, and again the female looked at Chekov before answering. There was a long pause. Kirk was tempted to interrupt, but he knew it would be rude, and in any case he had no good advice to give for Chekov's next play. Finally Chekov sighed, and moved his king. Quickly the female picked up her knight with long, delicate fingers and deployed it. Then she looked up at Chekov and smiled faintly.

"Checkmate," she said.

Chekov frowned. He studied the board. "You're right." He pushed his king over on its side with a snort. "I hope you won't mind payment in—"

"Any currency will do." She smiled. He reached into his pocket and pulled out a number of multicolored, exquisitely etched bills, and handed them over. She rose as she took them.

"Thank you," she said. Then she walked away. Kirk watched her as she gracefully disappeared into the crowd. Chekov was staring at the tridimensional playing field. Then he sat back and gave a long sigh.

"Boje moi," Kirk heard him curse under his breath.

"Mr. Chekov," he said quietly, "she knew perfectly well you were playing the Kolchinsky gambit."

Chekov turned at the voice. He leapt up from his chair.

"Captain Kirk! Captain Kirk, vhat in the galaxy are you doing here? How are you?"

"Fine, Mr. Chekov. How are you?" Kirk looked at the chessboard.

Chekov followed Kirk's look, then smiled with embarrassment and shook his head.

"Well . . ." he said, "I thought I played this game better. But . . ."

"Is this what you've been doing with your life since I saw you last?"

"Only between assignments."

"Then you're still navigating starships around the universe?"

"I am. I vork for Trans-Universal Shipping. Sometimes ve transport materials, sometimes ve take tourists out for a spin around the solar system. Sometimes ve even dock on habitable planets." Chekov shrugged. "It keeps me busy."

"Not busy enough, I suspect," Kirk said as he motioned to the fallen king. "Do you gamble often?"

"Too often, I am afraid. Perhaps it is in my Russian blood. But Captain, vhat are you doing here? I thought you vere living hafvay around the vorld, in San Francisco."

"I am. Just now I am in need of a good navigator, and I thought I would look you up."

"Excellent. Just let me get my charts from my apartment."

"I can't promise what you'll get out of this trip. If you're trying to keep up with your gambling debts . . ."

"Captain, you insult me. I would be glad to take a Starfleet assignment. Just because I stepped down to inactive status after twenty-five years in space doesn't mean I don't vant to serve the Federation."

"I appreciate your loyalty. But I'm afraid this isn't a Starfleet assignment, and it isn't the Federation you'll be serving. Let's sit down in that booth over there, and order some food and drink. I'll fill you in."

Half an hour later Chekov sat back in the booth and stared at Kirk.

"If Sulu is in danger, ve must transport ourselves there at vonce."

"We don't have a ship. Or much of a crew. But Mr. Spock has agreed to go, and the good doctor too. And I've tracked down Scotty. We're all meeting at my apartment tomorrow to talk things over. I thought you'd like to be there."

"I vould not miss it, Captain."

"Great. Then I'll see you there." They rose and started back through the club. Chekov checked his chronometer and looked around the club.

"Tomorrow, you say? That gives me a few hours to try and get back vhat I haf lost here. You go ahead, and I vill see you in San Francisco."

Kirk stopped and looked at Chekov.

"All right. But don't lose your shirt."

"My shirt?" Chekov was puzzled. "Vhy vould I bet an article of clothing? Who vould take such a thing as valuable?" He looked at the denizens of the club, a motley assemblage of aliens in all sizes and shapes. "And vhat possible good could it do them if they von it?"

"It's just an ancient expression, Chekov. Never mind."

"Ah, still interested in Earth history, are you, Captain?"

"Right now I'm interested in getting up to Beta Prometheus. Think you can find it, navigator?"

"If it exists in the cosmos, Captain, I can figure the co-ordinates."

Kirk waved. Chekov turned toward the chess tables as Kirk headed back through the crowd of aliens toward the front door. Then Chekov turned and called after him.

"Captain?"

Kirk stopped and looked back at him.

"Yes?"

"Vhy did you say she knew I vas playing the Kolchinsky gambit?"

"Mr. Chekov. Never play chess with a Betazoid. Don't you know? They're all telepaths. She was reading your mind."

Chekov stared at Kirk as the realization hit him. "I vas robbed!" he said.

Kirk waved and disappeared.

In orbit between Earth and Mars

High in the infrastructure of a black-glassed satellite-sphere as large as a small city, Uhura sat at the head of a huge polished table, her left hand holding a small monitor firmly in her ear, her right hand floating over a panel in front of her. Around the table, where other chairs might have been, a wall of monitors faced her. On each screen a face blinked out at her, some of them human, some not, all babbling in their native tongue. Uhura deftly held a number of conversations at once, in several different languages.

"The Orion Nebula is undergoing firestorms and we can't get through," she said in a sweet voice. "However, let me assure you that deliveries will only be delayed one and one half of your orbits." She smiled and touched another part of her console, then spoke again in a much stronger voice. "Mr. Singh, there are over two million Federation citizens in that colony, and they are counting on you to complete the order before the rainy season, after which there will be a half-year delay before another shuttle can land there. If you are unable to meet the deadline, tell me now and I will subcontract with another company to take the load off your shoulders. . . . Yes, I thought you could. Always good to do business with you, Mr. Singh. Good afternoon."

When she saw a familiar face pop onto a monitor, she changed frequencies again. "Harrison, I've sent you a private message on our coded subspace channel. It will be waiting when your planet reappears from the eclipse, which is half an hour from now. It includes the details you requested, but if this leaks to any of our competitors before the prototype is ready, I'm going to take it out on you, and your next assignment will be very close to the frontier." She saw the man nod, and she smiled. "On the other hand, if your product reaches the market first, I.G.S. will be most grateful, and you'll be promoted to the planet of your choice. I'll talk to you tomorrow."

Uhura went efficiently on, dealing with requests and problems from far-flung regions of the galaxy, until she was startled by a tap on her shoulder. The office was off limits to I.G.S. personnel without top security clearance. When Uhura turned around, she was even more surprised. Behind her stood the tall figure of James Kirk, for whom she had been chief communications officer for twenty-five years.

"Captain!"

"Uhura. Still fluent in an awful lot of languages, I see."

"Oh, the Universal Translator can do most of the work. But I like to keep in practice. Wait a second." She touched the console in front of her and the monitors went dark. "David?" she said.

"Yes, ma'am," a young male voice said.

"No calls for a few minutes."

"Yes, ma'am."

Uhura swiveled toward Kirk.

"All right, now, what in the world are you doing here? And while you're at it, how did you get in? This is a highly secure area."

"Is it? No one stopped me. Come to think of it, there was some sort of sign on the door about Authorized Personnel. I couldn't think who was authorized, however, so I ignored it." Kirk was looking around the room, impressed by the luxurious furnishings, the floor-to-ceiling windows that held a view of the galaxy, the enormous desk. "This isn't a Starfleet operation, is it?"

"Oh, no, it's far more confidential than that. It's I.G.S. Headquarters."

"I.G.S.?"

"Inter-Galactic Systems. I'm Senior Vice President in charge of Procurement and Delivery."

"Why all the secrecy?"

"Industrial espionage. There are very sensitive issues coming through my desk."

"Really? Such as?"

"Some of our subsidiaries are on the cutting edge of technology. If another corporation even guessed at the nature of a new product, it could mean years of research and development down the drain."

"But technology patents are only good temporarily. Then they become the property of the Federation anyway."

"Trillions in value can be earned in that time. Additionally, we want a new product to be identified with us. It's good for company moral, and good for business."

"I didn't realize. I don't suppose I ever knew much about business. Maybe I ought to start thinking along those lines, now that I'm a civilian."

"I noticed that, Captain. You're not wearing your uniform. And here I thought you'd have made admiral again by now."

"I left active service when the *Enterprise* was decommed, same as you. Came here on a private starship, as a matter of fact. Sat in the back and hoped the crew knew how to handle her. It was an unusual experience, I can tell you. I haven't actually been off Earth since returning. Until today, anyway. So, this is what you do, huh? At a desk all day." Kirk looked around.

"It's an enormous responsibility," Uhura said with a touch of pride. "Many colonies depend on us for their very survival."

"Oh, sure, sure. I didn't mean—"

"Never mind, Captain. Tact was never your strong suit. I'm a bit busy here just now," Uhura said as she gestured at her video screens. "I've been monitoring the press reports. Why don't you just tell me what's up with Sulu?" Is he in real danger?"

"Could be. A few old friends and I are going out there to see if we can be of any use."

"What friends?"

"Oh, Mr. Spock, for one. And Dr. McCoy. And I just enlisted a navigator . . ."

"Chekov?"

"How did you know?"

"I think I hear something taking shape in all this. You'll need an engineer."

"Oh, yes. Well, Montgomery Scott said he wouldn't mind helping out. So . . ."

"And a communications specialist, of course."

"Of course."

Uhura smiled. She pulled out the little ear monitor she had been wearing and set it down on the console. She touched the desk. The monitor screens in front of them lit up with the words PLEASE STAND BY.

"Okay, let's go," she said.

"What about your new career? I don't want to inhibit you from taking your rightful place in the business world."

"I'll take a sabbatical. Out of loyalty to Sulu, of course."

"Of course."

As they headed for the door, Uhura said to Kirk, "Just how far away is this Beta Prometheus?"

"Very far. It's in the frontier. It was just being charted when all this happened."

"Uncharted, eh? I wonder what language they speak? I expect it will need decoding."

"I'm sure it will," Kirk said, as he hurried ahead. A metallic voice chimed in the room just as they were leaving.

"The Vice President is in a meeting. Please leave your message, and your call will be returned."

Day Six

San Francisco

THE NEXT MORNING was Sunday. Kirk woke up early and went directly to his communications monitor, where he had flagged any news items that contained the words Beta Prometheus, Sulu, or the *U.S.S. Excelsior*. There wasn't anything new. In fact, there wasn't anything at all. Kirk suspected that, probably for diplomatic reasons, a shroud of privacy was descending slowly over the issue. Even the nonpublic Starfleet channels to which he still had access did not have any updated information on the status of the "incident" on Beta Prometheus.

Turning to his personal channel, Kirk found only a note from Barbara O'Marla, asking him to meet her at Poseidon, an upscale bar overlooking the starcraft wharves, at 1800 hours that night, when she got off work from Starfleet Headquarters. He knew his visitors were arriving during the day, and didn't want to make a commitment he would have to cancel, but when he tried to call to speak with her she was not in her office or her room. In the end he had to leave a message for her on her monitor. He hoped she wouldn't show up at the destination without some confirmation. He took a long shower while he thought over what he would say to the four men and one woman who would be gathering that afternoon, then made himself some authentic coffee.

He sat in the comfortable captain's chair that faced the great window overlooking San Francisco Bay and did what he had often done in the last few months when he found himself restless and with time on his hands. He idly watched sleek starcraft dock and depart from the port below his window. Sometimes, looking through his televiewscope, he looked at the great Starships hovering just beyond Earth's atmosphere, waiting for the smaller ships to ferry them a crew.

After an hour or so, and a breakfast Kirk fixed himself, the door chime sounded for the first of six times.

By noon, everyone was assembled. They were all enmeshed in exchanging stories of civilian life, when Kirk spoke up.

"I know everyone is happy to see old friends," Kirk said. "But maybe we'd better begin. I believe I've told you most of it already. Captain Sulu was taken hostage just under a week ago by a group of thugs from a star system known as Beta Prometheus. They have fabricated a spying charge. The Federation is engaged in diplomatic conversations with the leaders, but the facts are that nothing is happening, and from what little bits of information about the Prometheans I have been able to unearth, I am not at all sanguine about the position Sulu and his comrades are probably in."

"Sanguine?" Scotty frowned.

"He's pissed," Uhura decoded.

"Extremely," Kirk appended. "Sulu is rotting in these pirates' jail, under who knows what kind of conditions, and Starfleet will not get him out."

"In fact their hands are tied," Spock said from his position by the window. Everyone turned to look at him. "They cannot engage in an act of aggression unless it is sanctioned by the United Federation of Planets. And the Federation prefers to negotiate. At least for the time being."

"Diplomats!" Kirk snorted.

With that a silence overcame the room. Finally Spock spoke again.

"In any case, as I understand it, you propose to go and, shall we say, take a look?"

"Exactly."

"Sounds like a very good thing to me," Scotty said. "We should fire up our engines at once."

"Count me in," Chekov said.

"And me," Uhura said.

"I don't," McCoy said, "want to be a wet blanket, Jim. I am packed and prepared to volunteer my services. I know we are all anxious to help out Sulu. But as *I* understand it"—here McCoy nodded toward Mr. Spock—"this is not a Starfleet mission. That poses all sorts of problems. What sort of actions can we take out there on our own? Is the Federation going to sanction our mission, or stand in our way? We are all, remember, inactive. We could find ourselves with the welcome of ants at a picnic. Finally, and I ask this in a spirit of optimism of course, how in hell are we going to travel several sectors into deep space? Federation Starships with warp-drive capacity are not given away as door prizes. And they require a large crew. As I look around myself, I see a number of trustworthy if ancient comrades from the *Enterprise*. But only six in all. What in God's name can we do?"

Having come all this way on a wave of enthusiasm, they were brought up short by the pessimism expressed by the doctor. They sat in silence for a while. Kirk then got up out of his chair and faced them all.

"I don't know. I don't know what we can do. I guess I gathered you all together more out of frustration than a specific plan. But I simply can't stand by and do nothing. Let's take it one step at a time. Here's what I propose. Scotty, you and Mr. Spock will spend the afternoon looking for transport. Bones, you and I will see if we can dig up the latest on the situation. I know a young press relations officer who might be willing to bring us up to date. Chekov and Uhura, you get the navigational charts we'll need, and any background you can dig up on the Beta Prometheus star system and that part of the galaxy. We'll all meet back here at 1900 hours. We'll discuss our options then. Would that be all right?"

He looked around the room. Everyone nodded. In a few moments the apartment was empty.

Chekov and Uhura strolled along Starship's Wharf on their way to the Maritime Museum where, in a private attic room upstairs to which Chekov's membership gave him access, there was an outstanding collection of navigational maps and guides. There was also a port on-line to the Central Reference Library of the Navigational Research Division at Starfleet Headquarters. But it was the private collection that made Chekov choose this particular location to access the information they would need. More than one official constellation map had mistakes in it, and often vast amounts of galactic space were uncharted altogether. Although Starfleet had been organizing information for almost two centuries, only a small portion of the vast galaxy had been explored as yet. Information poured in to Headquarters daily, but even the true size of the universe had yet to be identified, and vast amounts of space, hundreds of galaxies, and millions of planets had yet to be properly classified, or in some cases even identified. Chekov often found that in the collections of small, private organizations there were ancient logbooks and archaic essays by early galactic travelers that gave him information he might otherwise never see. And in the wisdom of the early Starship captains he often came across minor remarks that helped him with the eccentric and eclectic pathways of travel, especially those beyond Federation boundaries. For all the streamlined efficiency of the Starfleet Central Reference and its vaunted Memory Alpha, the fact remained that, not unlike the early days of covered-wagon travel across the original United States, each Starship was mostly on its own in uncharted routes through the vast universe.

And there was the question of anonymity. This tiny private museum was unlikely to be visited, particularly on a Sunday afternoon, by any Starfleet personnel. Had they gone to Starfleet Headquarters, they might have run into any number of officers, some of whom would know them. Then there would be an awkward moment when Chekov had to explain why he and Uhura were rummaging around the library, and what they were looking for, and Chekov knew from experience that he was not good at dissembling. They had all agreed to keep their trip a secret between themselves until the last possible minute, against the possibility that Federation diplomacy might prohibit such a trip and Starfleet bureaucracy would consider it interference.

Thus he and Uhura were headed for one of the coziest places in the universe to Chekov's mind: the attic room, for members only, of the centuries-old Maritime Museum, a tiny three-story building right on the beach, tucked into the shadows of the huge commercial environpods of the port city. They walked quietly, enjoying the clean salt air of the headquarters city. Then Uhura broke the silence.

"Why do you think Captain Kirk has organized this expedition, Pavel?"

"To see vhat can be done about the situation, as he said."

"Do you think there's anything the six of us could do to help that Federation diplomats and Starfleet Starships can't?"

Chekov didn't answer that right away. Finally he spoke.

"Probably not."

"Then why?"

"The captain is restless. I as vell. I admit it. There's nothing like a deep-space voyage."

"He didn't have to ask the old crew. He doesn't have to go to Beta Prometheus. He could hire himself out as captain in private industry and pilot a star freighter almost anywhere he wants. Or he could request active duty. Starfleet would find something interesting for him."

"He is concerned about Sulu. Ve all are."

"Yes. But, again, the question is, if Starfleet and the Federation can't solve the impasse, what could we do?"

"What are you getting at, Uhura?"

"The captain has been known to be impatient at times. Hotheaded."

"He vould prefer to call it self-directed, I think."

"Whatever. I'm not a young cadet any longer. Excuse me, but you're not either. Are we going to have to do battle? I'm not sure I want to be fired on by Klingon battlecruisers any more in my life. Or trapped by alien unintelligences. Or bounced around the skies while I'm trying to decipher static. I don't know about you, Pavel, but I was sort of enjoying a quiet life."

"Then vhy did you come?"

Uhura sighed. She didn't answer. They walked a few more yards and stopped in front of the entrance to the museum. Then Chekov spoke again.

"Me too," he said. "Because he asked." And he led the way up the stairs to the reception desk.

Kirk and McCoy strolled across the grassy quad on their way to a lunch with Lieutenant Eugene Marasco, the young press officer Kirk had met at the Flag and Grog on his first hunt for news. They arrived at Heaven's Hearth a few minutes late. The neon archway was filled with Starfleet and civilian personnel on their lunch hour. Marasco had particularly picked this eatery because it was populated more by lower-echelon workers and civilians.

Not that Kirk expected Marasco to be much of a source. He would be selective about the classified information he passed to Kirk. That was his job. But Kirk hoped there might be more to the story, and trying to find out kept this worry in check.

Kirk and McCoy threaded their way past waiting groups to a corner Marasco had already commandeered in the rear of the restaurant.

"Captain Kirk, it's good to see you." Marasco stood and shook hands.

"This is Dr. Leonard McCoy. Bones, Lieutenant Marasco." They sat down.

"I hope you don't mind this place," Marasco said as Kirk arrived at the table. "It's devoted to macrobiotic food."

"I'm always interested in something new. What is that?" Kirk said.

"Well, for one thing, it's not new. Macrobiotics has been around for centuries. It's extremely healthy and energy-oriented. I've taken the liberty of ordering for us."

"Great."

"In the meantime, I'm sure you'd like to know about the hostage problem."

Kirk dropped his casual pose.

"You've caught me. I did want to pick your brain. I'm very worried about Sulu and his crew. How did you guess?"

"It wasn't difficult, Captain Kirk," Marasco said. "You are one of the legends of the Starfleet, and your crew is not far behind. In fact, it's my guess that your running into old Caius two nights ago was not entirely an accident. The Flag and Grog is where I would go if I wanted to tune in to the Starfleet grapevine." Marasco leaned in and lowered his voice a bit. "The truth is, Starfleet has been restrained from taking action on this—some kind of military action, I mean—by the Federation. They don't want a war, an invasion, an incursion, a police action, or even a strategic incident. Of course they want the hostages returned. How they expect to effect that, nobody knows just yet."

"Those are Federation citizens," Kirk said with some urgency. "Whether the politicians like to admit it or not, what has happened is an act of war."

"They're Starfleet officers, too, and if we don't take care of our own, we're not going to get many volunteers in the future."

"And the future," Kirk intoned, "is our business."

Marasco laughed. "All right, touché. I suppose I've been in press relations too long. Let me try to stop talking like an advertising executive. Most of the Starfleet brass are impatient and angry too. You're not alone. It's still a top priority, but we haven't gotten permission to move, and, frankly, I don't think we will."

"Well, then, what *is* being done?" McCoy asked bluntly.

"A diplomatic mission has been sent. They are attempting to talk with the Ruling Family. The problem is that the *Excelsior* officers were captured by some pirates from a strata of the Beta Promethean civilization the government doesn't really control. The government says they deplore the situation, and they probably do; any interruption in dilithium trading affects their profits. But these pirate-traders are a large part of their society, and keep them in power by refusing to align themselves with the Spiritual Leaders. If they were antagonized, they might throw their weight behind the Conclaves and the Spiritual Leaders would rule entirely. The society could become wholly theologic, which would put the Ruling Family out of business. The Federation wants the balance of power maintained as well. We have agreements with the Ruling Family about the dilithium that keeps the supply going and the price reasonable. So everybody is happy. If the Spiritual Leaders took over, they might change the rules. They have what they call a Higher Calling, and they don't seem to care if the dilithium gets mined or not."

A waiter arrived with two plates piled high with green rice, moldy water chestnuts, and tough bamboo shoots. Marasco's face lit up.

"You'll love this. Pure protein."

McCoy looked at it cautiously.

"This is, ah . . . what exactly?"

"It's real. Not from a synthesizer," Marasco mumbled through a mouthful of rice. "You can't get this just anywhere. It has to be grown. Takes enormous quantities of land and water. An entirely inefficient method of agriculture. But you can taste the difference."

"I can see the difference," McCoy said glumly as he looked down at his plate. "There aren't any worms in here, are there? I've heard they're a delicacy, but I've never . . ."

"No, no worms. Nothing that moves. That's part of the macrobiotic creed."

"Well, that's a relief," McCoy said as he picked up his utensils. Kirk went on. "So what you're saying is, the Federation is simply not going to allow the Starfleet to take any kind of aggressive action."

"That's probably true. It's going to be a political show all the way. It will just take time. We've cordoned off their system. We're not allowing them out of their own immediate space. We're allowing a bare minimum of humanitarian supplies through, but nothing military."

"And how long do you think the Prometheans can withstand being isolated like that?" Kirk asked.

"No more than a few decades."

"Oh, great," McCoy said sarcastically. "Sulu will be home free in no time."

As they finished, Marasco asked Kirk and McCoy about

their years in deep space, and they accommodated him with a few stories. They all left the restaurant together, and separated just outside. As Kirk and McCoy headed off, Marasco thoughtfully watched them go.

They walked back in silence. Kirk was thinking about the next day. He was taking the responsibility of dragging his old crew into uncharted areas in the frontier on a mission, the precise nature of which was not really clear. Was this a vainglorious attempt to recapture old feelings of leadership and adventure, or a genuine mission of loyalty to an old friend and comrade? Suddenly Kirk had his doubts, but he kept them to himself. They turned the corner and hiked up the last hill to Kirk's apartment.

"I did not want to be a wet blanket myself with the others present," Scotty was saying to Mr. Spock, "but unless we can get Starfleet to work with us on this, I do not see how we're going to travel hundreds of millions of light-years into deep space. It is not like goin' to Mars for a vacation."

"I have been to Mars for a vacation."

"Really?" Scotty said. "What was it like?"

Mr. Spock paused to remember. "They lost my luggage," he said.

"I'm sorry."

Spock shrugged. "I have not been on vacation since."

With that Mr. Spock set resolutely out to visit the docks and offices along the port, and Scotty followed cheerfully.

Two hours later Scotty was losing his ability to maintain a jaunty attitude. They had hiked what seemed like several kilometers. They had walked throughout the spaceport, talking to numbers of starship captains and freight operators, transportation specialists and port chiefs, engineers and cadets, and even some humans and aliens who appeared to be simply lounging around the docks which held the smaller starcraft. Scotty turned to the tall Vulcan.

"Mr. Spock, we're not getting anywhere. Starships do not just rent out like hovercraft. The big ones are not even here, they're in spacedock above the planet. Do ya think—"

"It would not be logical to give up before we had traversed the entire port." Mr. Spock had hiked through the area at a pace so steady that Scotty, his human anatomy sometimes causing him to fall behind and sometimes to hurry ahead, had become frustrated. He had felt at home climbing in and out of the spacedocks, talking to the men and women who ran the transportation for various intergalactic enterprises. But he had to admit failure so far. They had not found a starship available for their purposes. As he had warned the others before they started out from Kirk's apartment, ships capable of speeds up to warp ten "do not grow on trees."

They hiked on. They had almost reached the limit of the port when, high up on a steep cliff overlooking China Beach, Mr. Spock stopped.

"What's that?" he asked Scotty. He was staring at a small but sleek white star yacht floating twenty yards above the edge of the high cliff, just off the terrace of a mansion on the bluff.

"A very small starcraft," Scotty answered. "It could not hold more than a dozen personnel. And by the looks of it, it could not last the first asteroid storm. She's built for looks and for luxury, Mr. Spock. I do not have to visit her engines to see that."

"Nevertheless, she is worth a visit."

"She's not even correctly docked."

"It looks as if she belongs to that private environpod on the cliff there. Let us go see."

Spock set off at a rapid gait toward the path that led through a front garden to the home. Scotty sighed, flexed his toes in a vain attempt to relieve what he was sure were soon-to-be-blisters, and followed glumly. *Another toy bucket,* he thought, *that could not take me home, halfway across this little planet, much less into deep space.*

Spock knocked on the door, while Scotty attempted to smooth the rumples in his clothes caused from several hours of hiking around the port. It was a large mansion overlooking the Pacific Ocean, all sleek titanium and opaque glass. Colorful flowers at its base were well tended. Thick fog slid off the angular roof.

The door was opened by a tall furry humanoid, and when Spock asked if he could interview the owner of the star yacht moored in the air off the terrace, the alien turned around and headed into the house. Spock and Scotty followed. They were ushered into a large room with rich upholstering and a huge picture window that overlooked the Pacific Ocean. The yacht could be seen floating outside, just above the window. The alien left the room.

As they stood admiring its sleek lines, a short, stout man with no hair on his glistening head walked in. He was dressed in a casual jumpsuit, and his age was difficult to assess, but his joviality was not. He was clearly proud of the star yacht and eager to show it off.

"Hello," the little man boomed. "My name's Thaylor. Rockefeller Thaylor. You like my starship, I understand? If you're from one of those databanks, she's all yours."

"Databanks?" Spock said, not sure if he should introduce himself until he got the full picture.

"Star Yachts. Interior Architecture. Luxury Worlds. They've all been here. Doing holographic essays. The Plush Princess has been featured in all of them."

"The Plush Princess?" Scotty asked.

"My baby," Thaylor purred. "Commissioned her two years ago. She's fitted with the best there is from all over the galaxy."

"Twin nacelles engines?" Scotty asked, his interest rising. "Matter-antimatter cones? Gravitational and life-support backup systems?"

"Huh? Oh sure, I suppose so. I don't know anything about that stuff. I meant the furnishings. There aren't many hotels on Mars that have this kind of luxury. She sleeps eight in four cabins. The galley can synthesize the most complex gourmet meals. The control deck has an enormous main viewscreen, and is custom-fitted with genuine leather chairs. Why, wait until you see the aft space lounge."

"Oh. Well, that sounds outstanding," Scott said, casting a glance at Spock. "It sounds like just what we are looking for."

"Great," the enthusiastic man said. "You can scan her any time, just give me a day's notice to inform the cleaning crew."

"In actual fact," Spock said, "we had her in mind for something a little different."

"Oh? What?" Thaylor smiled pleasantly.

Spock was about to explain, when he heard Scotty speak.

"For a holodoc!" Scotty said.

"A holodoc?"

"In a documentary style," Scotty appended, hoping it sounded important.

"A documentary holodoc? That sounds interesting. About star yachts? You won't find one better outfitted than mine."

"Not exactly," Scotty said. "About . . . travel in deep space."

"Deep space? I haven't been out of the solar system myself. Too many aliens out there."

"Yes, well, that's just where we're going. Deep space. Can she travel at warp speed?"

"Of course. She can do it all. Her designer said she was the fastest ship in her class. Said I could go to the end of the galaxy if I wanted. She's in peak form. My private pilot sees to that."

"She must have warp speed, then," Scotty said to Mr. Spock.

"Presumably," Spock said, unsure of where Scotty was going with this.

"But I don't think—" Thaylor frowned.

"Imagine how famous she'll become," Scotty said quickly.

"Famous?"

"Of course. As the star of a holodoc on alien worlds. Have ye never heard of the *Calypso?*"

"That's a kind of dance, isn't it?"

"It's also the most famous oceangoing ship of its time!"

"Oceangoing? What time was that? Why would anyone want to travel on water?" The man was becoming more puzzled, and rapidly losing his booming personality, while simultaneously Scotty was taking on the personality of a used-hovercraft salesman.

"Why, the twentieth century, of course," Scotty said.

"I'm afraid I'm not much on history," Thaylor said lamely.

"Captain Jacques Cousteau. The greatest explorer of our oceans the world has ever known. He took the *Calypso* to every corner of the globe. And Captain Spock here, who is a metaphorical descendant of that stalwart breed of intrepid explorer"—he nodded at Spock, who stared back stoically—"would like to take the . . . what's she called again?"

"The *Plush Princess.*"

"Aye, the *Plush Princess* . . . to an obscure, unexplored corner of the galaxy. She'll become as famous as the *Calypso*. Famouser." Scotty slowed down, realizing he was getting too carried away. "Captain Spock you've heard of, I expect."

"Well . . ."

"He's made any number of discoveries in space. The Tholian Web. The asteroid Yonada. The Murasaki 312. All his discoveries."

"I'm afraid science isn't my strong suit, either."

"Well, he's really going for it this time," Scotty said in a confidential voice.

"I am?" Spock said.

"For what?" Thaylor asked.

"The greatest discovery in history. He's going into a black hole. I forgot to introduce myself. I'm Montgomery Scott, the documentary producer. My crew and I are making the holodoc, so that children everywhere and always will have a firsthand look at Captain Spock's amazing adventure. And we thought that your starship would be just right for the voyage. Imagine. One month from now, the *Plum Princess*—"

"The *Plush Princess.*"

"—the *Plush Princess* will be the most famous starship ever built. You'll be equally well known as its owner, of course."

"This sounds exciting."

"That's exactly the word."

"But I don't think I could let my baby fly right into a black hole. As I said, I don't know much about science, but isn't that dangerous? Has anybody ever done that before?"

"Did I say *into* a black hole? My mistake. We're just going to scan one up close."

"Still . . ."

"But not that close. A safe distance. Your baby will be completely secure in his hands. Mr. Spock is the best pilot flying today. Also the safest. Wouldn't risk a hair on the head of his crew. Those that have hair. What we were hoping, is that you might be willing to supply that beautiful starship for the holodoc. She'll be the principal character, just like the galactically famous *Calypso.*"

"The ship that Cousteau fellow was on?"

"Exactly."

"Well, it does sound important. How long would you need her for?"

"A week, only. Two at the outside."

"I suppose I could do without her for a week. I don't often charter her, but I have on occasion. What would you consider to be a fair price?"

"Did I mention that the captain here donates any and all profits to the Starship Historical Preservation Society and Intergalactic Geographic Museum? Our holodoc is, what d'ye call it, nonprofit?" Scotty lowered his voice, and tried to be as humble as he could. "Frankly we were hoping you would volunteer the use of the starship. As a philanthropic gesture." Scott looked over the man's shoulder and studied a series of holographs that were set on the marble mantel over the fireplace. "Other contributions have been made by some prominent people you might be familiar with. The Zone Governor. The North American president . . ." He hoped he had identified the men in the pictures with their arms around Thaylor correctly.

"Really?" Thaylor said. "I know them!"

"They want to remain anonymous, of course," Scott said rapidly. "Because of their public positions. So right now we're looking for someone who does not mind the notoriety. To name the expedition after."

"Name the—?"

"The Thaylor Expedition, for example. If you would allow us. Public relations needs this sort of thing. Of course, by the time we get back the holodoc will be released

Federation-wide, and she'll be terribly famous. You'll probably have people coming from all over the cosmos to take her picture. I hope you would not mind the intrusions."

"I suppose I could loan her for such a good cause."

"Excellent. You'll have the gratitude of the entire scientific community. Our crew will be back first thing in the morning."

Scotty managed to steer the conversation away from the star yacht before the little man could change his mind. He inquired about paintings of ancient lineage that lined the walls of the hallway as they walked back to the front door. At last they were in front of the house again.

"Good afternoon," Scotty said. "And thank you again for your generosity. We'll take good care of her. And of course, I'll see that you get an advance copy of the holodoc."

"Hadn't we better sign a contract or something?" Thaylor said.

"If you like, I'll be glad to." Scotty glanced at Mr. Spock, who was standing patiently if sternly at the edge of the footpath. He drew Thaylor aside. "You do recognize that Mr. Spock is a Vulcan?"

"Of course. I know they are extremely trustworthy and honest. I was not suggesting anything else. But——"

"They are sensitive too. A Vulcan's word is better than a contract."

"Well, yes, all right. I suppose, if you promise to bring her back in good condition, Mr. Spock."

Scotty saw Spock hesitate for a fraction of a second.

"Absolutely, Mr. Thaylor. I can promise you that," Spock said.

Scotty let out his breath. He shook hands with Thaylor, then indicated to him the Vulcan salute. Thaylor understood, and raised his right hand toward Spock, separating his middle and ring fingers. "Ah, live long and prosper," he said.

Spock returned the greeting, and the men separated.

As Spock and Scotty walked back down the front path, Thaylor stood in the doorway. He seemed to be thinking of something.

"Spock . . . Spock . . . Wait a minute . . . Mr. Spock?

You know, I believe I have heard of you. You're quite famous for your documentaries, aren't you?"

"Me?" Spock said. "Oh, no, I do not believe so."

"He's an extremely modest man, is Mr. Spock," Scotty jumped in. "Likes the crew to get most of the credit. Well, we'll be back first thing in the morning. Good day." As they walked briskly away down the front path, he turned and waved goodbye to the round man in the doorway of the house.

"I trust," Mr. Spock said thoughtfully as they strode back along Starship's Wharf, "we have not presented too large a falsehood to that man."

"We haven't," Scotty said with an avuncular smile. *"I* have, I'm afraid. I was worried if we told him the truth, he'd never loan us his yacht. And as we were at the very end of our hopes for finding something suitable, I thought I had no choice. I hope that's all right. I know that Vulcans never lie. But I do not believe you did."

"I could hardly get a word in," Spock said.

"There you are then. Your conscience is clear. As for mine, I'll just have to undertake to bring the *Princess* back soon in good condition."

They walked on in silence, Mr. Spock considering the ethics of the situation, and Scotty wondering just what he would find when he went aboard the craft he had managed to borrow. He looked over his shoulder at the *Plush Princess*. The sun was deep in the sky and an orange glow lit the city.

"Do ye think she'll actually fly?" Scotty said finally. "She looks a mite fancy for deep space."

"I put my faith in you, Engineer Scott," Spock said. "If it is any kind of a starship, you can coax it into space. Besides, you heard what the man said: the best of everything."

"I think he was referring to the seat cushions," Scotty said glumly. "I do not expect a starship like that to have much real power."

"Well, it is a beginning," Spock said.

For his part, Scotty was worrying about that tiny starship and how she would handle in deep space. But then, Scotty was used to worrying. And now that he had a starship to worry about, he felt a glow of pride he hadn't felt since he left the *Enterprise*.

When the door chime sounded, Kirk wondered who it could be. He looked around his living room, but his crew had reassembled and were all present. He went over and opened the door.

Barbara O'Marla stood in the doorway. She looked crisp and young in her Starfleet uniform. Before he could speak, she did.

"I'm going with you."

"Come in."

"When you couldn't meet me tonight, I knew you had decided. You can't really intend to go alone. Oh, don't worry. It's not because of our relationship. It's the trip. I've always wanted to go into deep space. I'm not going to miss this chance."

"Don't stand in the hall. Come in."

She entered and went into the living area, where she stopped. Kirk's friends were all busy in the room, going over charts and talking quietly but urgently among themselves. Everyone turned and looked at her. There was a considerable silence, and Barbara realized she had assumed that Kirk would be alone in his apartment. She looked around at the curious faces staring at her.

Kirk closed the door and came in behind her.

"This is Barbara O'Marla, everybody. A friend of mine. Barbara, this is Mr. Spock. That's Montgomery Scott by the window. This is Mr. Chekov, and that's Uhura." Uhura smiled and waved. "And this old pile of bones is Bones. Dr. McCoy. Don't get too close to him, he's still lethal."

Everyone said hello. There was another pause. Kirk attempted to fill it.

"We were just, uh, talking about our mutual friend, Sulu." Another pause. Then it dawned on Barbara.

"You're the senior crew of the *Enterprise,*" she said to them, and she felt herself blush.

"That's us, lassie," Scotty chimed.

"The crew of the *Enterprise,*" she said again, this time, almost in awe. "Wow. Mr. Spock, the science officer. You're half Vulcan. Dr. McCoy, medical officer. Mr. Chekov, you were the navigator. Uhura, communications. And you must be Scotty. I can't believe I'm meeting you all."

"She's a very bright lassie, Captain," Scotty said from his chair. "Who is she?"

"I'm sorry for sounding so insipid. It's just that I'm so impressed. Mr. Scott, I was at your lecture on the Klingon Bird-of-Prey warship. It was terrific."

"I'm very glad someone was listening."

"I wasn't expecting, I mean, I didn't realize Jim would have company. Excuse me for bursting in."

"The pleasure is all ours," McCoy said, moving closer. "I was at the Academy only six months ago. Were you at my seminar on alien physiognomy? I don't think so. I would have remembered."

"You'd have been lucky to remember your lecture," Scotty said to him. "Now stand back and give the lassie some room. We were just opening a rare, if illegal, bottle of Romulan ale. Part of the loot from years of traveling in space. Perhaps you'd join us in a glass. Or maybe you'd better not. It's contraband, and I see you are in uniform."

"You better sit over here with me, honey," Uhura said. "They're a bunch of idle hands today, if you know what I mean."

Kirk lowered his voice. "We were actually discussing some business." He attempted to draw her by the elbow back out of the room. She stood firm, however. Kirk looked around. Everybody was still staring at them.

"Don't be rude, Jim," McCoy said.

"I'm afraid I'm the one who's being rude," Barbara said. "I'm sorry for interrupting—"

"You're not interrupting, Barbara." Kirk again tried to lower his voice and get the conversation down to just the two of them. "But maybe I could call you later."

"Wait a minute. Oh, my goodness. You're *all* going to Beta Prometheus!"

Kirk sighed, and let go of her elbow. Dr. McCoy grinned.

Uhura smiled. Scotty raised his glass. Mr. Spock raised one eyebrow.

"Why don't you come in," Kirk said in a tone of resignation. Then Chekov got up and offered her the armchair he was sitting in. She sat down. And waited.

"This isn't going to be a Starfleet assignment. This is a private trip. We're all retired. That's what retired people do, they travel. We're just going on a little cruise."

"To a stinking corner of the galaxy beyond Federation boundaries that features a primitive civilization whose best tourist spot is dilithium crystal mines? Fire your travel agent."

"All right. We might be able to help. We can't just sit here waiting."

"I can help. I've been recommended for a Starship mission. I'm just waiting for an opening."

"Then you'll get it. Be patient."

"I have some leave time coming. It's not a problem."

"We don't know what might happen. Deep space isn't always predictable. I can't be responsible for you."

"You wouldn't say that if we weren't lovers," Barbara said without embarrassment. But Kirk blushed. Barbara went on. "You were responsible for more than four hundred people on your precious *Enterprise*. I'm qualified, and I'm volunteering. It wouldn't be logical to turn down help. You might need some younger officers aboard. Deep-space navigation has changed a bit in the year since you left Starfleet."

Chekov looked insulted. Scotty looked depressed. Only Bones smiled.

"I'm sorry." She softened. "I didn't mean to insult anybody. I know that nobody knows a Starship like you do. But you've got to admit it. You could use me."

"I'm sure we could, Barbara. And I mean that. You're going to make an outstanding Fleet officer. Why, I'll bet you'll have your own command one day. I'm sure you can look forward to an extraordinary career. But our mission, our trip that is, has nothing to do with Starfleet. As a matter of fact, only today I inquired about going on active status for this emergency, and was politely rebuffed. So you can't go, because you are under orders from Starfleet. I can't be responsible for making you Absent Without Leave, can I? And suppose something were to happen? Suppose we were taken prisoner, or got into some sort of conflict with the captors? As a Starfleet officer, you are a representative of both the Fleet and the United Federation of Planets."

"Jim, I do have other clothes."

"It might be dangerous."

"That's my concern. Have the decency to let me weigh the danger and let me make my own judgment. Again, if we weren't lovers—"

Kirk sighed. "All right. I won't speak for you. But if you haven't been assigned yet, you can't just run off and head for deep space. Starfleet bureaucracy—"

"Has given me a leave of absence. I have to attend the funeral of my great-aunt."

"When did she die?"

"Any century now, I'm sure. I'm going to get started; she lives a long way from Earth."

Kirk sensed that he was losing ground when he heard the others chuckle.

"Frankly, Barbara, you're asking me to compromise both your career and your safety. Leaving aside our, uh, personal relationship, you are a very young officer. Hell, you were only a cadet until a few weeks ago."

"I can handle the job. You don't have a helmsperson. That was my training. You want to see my scores from the Academy?"

"Still—"

"Oh, and one more thing. This." She took a small silver disk out of her pocket.

"What is it?"

"The most recent holographic map of the city where the *Excelsior* crew is being held, on the first planet in the three-planet system Beta Prometheus. It's classified Top Secret, and there's no way any of you could get it without hacking into and illegally searching through the carefully guarded private files of Starfleet's Navigation Group. Which would take you a week at least."

Startled, Kirk reached for it. But Barbara O'Marla pulled it away.

"Think of it as my passport."

There was a long moment of silence. Kirk might never have filled it. But Bones spoke up.

"Sounds like we could use her, Jim. She's pretty resourceful."

Day Seven

BARBARA O'MARLA didn't sleep at all before her first journey to the stars. Growing up on Earth, the closest she had come to interstellar travel was on the Academy simulators. She was every bit as excited about that as she was about her companions for the journey: the most famous crew in the history of the Starfleet. *Will I measure up?* was her principal thought as she tossed and turned in her bed.

In his apartment Kirk, too, had been up all night, sitting in the chair that faced the big picture window, watching the port traffic come and go. *Is it a fool's errand? What can we do that the United Federation of Planets hasn't? And with a luxury tub that is probably not equipped with firepower of any kind?*

Uhura slept, though she tossed and turned continually, hearing in her dreams the harsh Promethean language. Chekov pored over the charts he had collected until long past midnight, then fell into a fitful sleep during which he still saw them floating in his mind.

McCoy sat with a fifth of Mercury bourbon and nursed it through the night, having reached that age when sleep was nearly unnecessary, and came in any case in short naps. *What in the universe is a doctor my age doing, going off into deep space again?*

Scotty paced his room, and sat for long minutes at his televiewport, through which he could see west to the edge of the city and the *Plush Princess* moored near the cliff. He grumbled about it continually, though in truth he was primarily concerned over its unique design and up-to-date power systems. *I've spent my entire professional life in the engine room of the* Enterprise *and its various progeny. What if, at this late stage, the complex engines of the younger designers should prove too complex for my ancient skills? I risk looking like an old fool.* Unwilling to go to bed, he slept an hour in a comfortable chair, then woke up and carefully packed his small cache of handheld analysis coders and equipment. Like the others, he packed his uniform, but did not wear it. They would be traveling as civilians, not representing Starfleet. Nor would they have the resources of Starfleet behind them.

It was this last idea that Spock mulled over for most of his evening. Using a Vulcan relaxation technique, he was able to sleep for a fair part of the night, but the political implications of their coming adventure were never far from his thoughts. Spock tried, logically enough, to project just what their actions would be once they reached Beta Prometheus. Should they check in with Starfleet or Federation officials at Starbase 499, just outside the star system?

None of the questions the crew pondered in the dark hours were answered for them, but the dawn broke and brought their initial enthusiasm back with it. All were up and ready in minutes. They left their rooms early, and separately made their way through the fog bound streets to Seacliff.

At 0500 hours Kirk and Scott went aboard the *Princess* and toured the facilities. Everything seemed tiny to them in comparison to the Constitution-class *Enterprise* that had been their last home.

Scotty learned how to program the coordinates in the sleek transporter panel. At 0555 he honed in on the grass only several hundred yards below them, and waited for a request.

The others arrived before the 0600 rendezvous. Spock was the last to arrive, at precisely 0559, strolling up with his silk duffel bag of personal articles. The others were talking quietly about the look of their transport. It featured a saucer module a fraction of the size of the *Enterprise*'s, perhaps as wide in diameter as fifty yards, and only two stories tall. Its twin engine nacelles were snug underneath the saucer, and the ports were broad and oval, though there were not many of them. (Kirk and Scotty had already discovered that the starship was built for interior privacy more than exterior visual evaluation.) There were no extensions or attached shuttles. It was a clean-lined starship of arching if impractical beauty.

When Spock arrived, Scotty beamed Kirk down to the grass below the starship.

"I see we're all here," Kirk said. "This mission—if you wish to call it that—is entirely unconventional, and has not been sanctioned in any way by either Starfleet Command or Federation bureaucracy, to which all of us still owe our allegiance, as officers, albeit decommissioned at the moment. Ms. O'Marla, in particular. You are a newly commissioned officer whose record will not be improved by an unauthorized trip to a tense and politically unstable star system. Let me ask each of you one more time if you wish to exempt yourself from this trip. It may be dangerous. It may even be illegal under Federation law. It will certainly at the least be uncomfortable," he said, glancing at the small star yacht. "Now is your last chance. I'm sure none of us would think the less of any others in any way should one of us decide to stay behind."

No one responded. Barbara O'Marla, having looked at Kirk without expression during his speech, simply looked away, and up at the star yacht.

"We're in, Jim. We're all in," McCoy said.

"All right then. Perhaps Ms. O'Marla, as the newest member of our crew, you would care to give the signal."

Barbara looked at Kirk uncertainly for a minute, then at once realized what he was offering. She smiled broadly. She glanced around to see that everyone was standing in a fairly tight circle. Then she touched the communicator on her breast, looked up at the star yacht, and said in a clear, young voice, "Beam us up, Scotty!"

The six travelers dematerialized.

When they found themselves on the small transporter platform in the stern of the *Plush Princess,* everyone began talking at once.

"Where do we stow our gear?"

"Where's the command bridge?"

"Is there a synthesizer? I forgot to eat breakfast!"

"Where will our first destination be?"

"Does this beauty have shields?"

"Gee, I hope we don't get this carpet dirty."

"Where'd you guys get this toy, anyway?"

"What's her top speed?"

"Where's the communications workstation?"

"All in good time," Kirk laughed. He led the way through the narrow corridor of the lower level. He raised his voice and cut through the hubbub.

"There are only four living quarters aboard the *Princess.* We'll have to share. On the other hand, they are all state-of-the-art staterooms, and I think you'll be pleased. Since there's seven of us, I've allotted this room"—he stopped in the corridor and nodded to an archway—"to Dr. McCoy on the basis of, uh, seniority."

"He means I'm the crabbiest, and no one wants to bunk with me. Thanks, Captain."

"You're welcome, Bones. Call me Jim. I think perhaps we're all in this little adventure together, and while we ought to run our ship along our usual lines of command and duty organization, there's no need to be overly formal." He walked on as the door slid open and Bones stepped gingerly into his small but well-appointed sanctum. "Now, on this side we have another stateroom with its own bathroom, so I have assigned that to Uhura and Barbara. Thus affording them a bit of privacy.

The ladies stepped into the room. Uhura looked at Barbara.

"Care which bunk is yours?"

"No, you go ahead."

Uhura threw her duffel on the bed. "All right. This looks like a pretty nice space. Small. But we'll get along."

"You must be used to larger quarters."

"The old *Enterprise* was pretty nice. Not so well cushioned, but larger. And the viewports for the senior officers stretched up to the ceiling."

"You must miss it."

"I guess I do. I suppose that's why I signed on to this mission. Do me a favor, will you?"

"Sure, anything."

"Stop me if I reminisce too much. I don't want to sound like one of those fat old admirals sitting around the Flag and Grog talking about the good old days. Heck, you're probably better trained than I ever was."

"I doubt it. Can I tell you something?"

"Of course—communications is my specialty."

"I'm just a little scared. I've been on some training missions, but never gone outside of the solar system. Never stepped foot on any planet except Earth. Traveling into deep space has always been a dream. A fantasy. Now that it's a reality, well . . ."

"I understand. It wasn't that long ago I was exactly the same. Came from a couple of local schools in Kenya. Read a lot of offworld literature, but never really dreamed I could become a Starfleet officer. I suppose I've never gotten over the thrill of being accepted into the Academy. Don't worry. You'll do swell. You couldn't ask for better mates on your first assignment. And there's no better navigator than Chekov."

Farther along the hall, Kirk had pointed at two adjoining staterooms, each featuring bunk beds. "These are ours," he said to the remaining three men. "We share the bathroom facilities here in between. We can divide up any way we want."

There was a pause, as the four of them stood awkwardly in the connecting general quarters to the two bedrooms. Kirk thought for a minute that for a crew that had traveled together for twenty-five years, they didn't appear to be very close. It crossed his mind that he probably hadn't shared many moments of nonofficial discussion with any of them. In fact, he couldn't think of one. Spock broke the silence, however.

"Captain, you and I can bunk in here, and leave that side to Mr. Chekov and Mr. Scott."

"Fine," Kirk said, and the little group broke up.

Everyone busied themselves stowing their gear. As they had brought only the bare necessities, this took little time. Kirk stepped out into the hall and climbed up the shiny circular staircase that threaded the narrow space and took him one flight up and onto the command deck. He found Bones already there.

"Jim, there's no medical quarters."

"No. Let's hope no one gets seriously ill. You can set up on that deck behind us, if you like."

"The aft space lounge? Looks like it's for owners who like to be pampered by their servants."

"At least you'll be comfortable. Although I'm afraid the ship didn't come with any servants."

The others arrived on the top deck one after the other. Kirk pointed out the amenities.

"Uhura, I think that corner over there can be yours. Most of the communications gear seems to be in that wall. We'll have to bring over a stool from the lounge. These three chairs here will be ours. I'll take this one in the center if that's all right. Mr. Chekov, that one will give you the easiest access to the ship's navigation terminal."

Chekov sat down at once and began loading information into his port from the disks he had brought.

"And this one is for our new helmswoman." Kirk was well aware that their relationship had taken a significant turn when she had signed on, but was unsure of just where things stood. "Congratulations on your first assignment, however unorthodox it may be. Please take the conn."

"Thank you," Barbara said quietly, and immediately sat down. For the next half an hour she hardly heard a thing going on around her, as she tried to familiarize herself with the main control and display panels of the small ship. She played her fingers over the sensor matrix and ran a program that tested her thrusters. Then she input several experimental warp-speed instructions and watched as the subspace information flew by. It all seemed quite like her hours of experience in the Academy simulators, and in a short time she felt comfortable. Then suddenly she realized that she would be responsible for boosting the ship right through the Earth's atmosphere and locking on to its first navigational target. Almost immediately thereafter she and the navigator would take the ship to warp speed. And it wouldn't be a simulation. A small sweat broke out on her forehead. She looked over at Chekov, who was delighting in the superspeed information displays the modern star yacht provided him. When he looked up, he smiled. He looked at her knowingly. He winked. She felt better already.

"There's no science station, as you can see, Mr. Spock," Kirk was saying. "But I thought you might be comfortable here"—Kirk touched a chair that had its own console—"where you could use this terminal to access whatever we have in the ship's memory banks. Also, Uhura can hook you into Memory Alpha, so you can access pretty much whatever you want."

"Thank you, Captain. This will be quite adequate." Spock had already logged on and began testing the ship's ability to sense atmospheric pressures, life signs, and gravitational pull.

"We do have shields, you'll all be happy to know. They wouldn't deflect a simple nuclear-powered missile from the earliest days of atomic warfare, but they'll keep our hull impervious to the traditional flotsam and jetsam of the galaxy. All right, then. Is everybody ready here?" There were silent nods from the command deck. "Scotty?"

"I think I've got the engines under control, Captain," came the familiar voice. "But power is limited, so don't ask me to strengthen her shields," he warned Kirk. "They're not designed for any kind of battle. They're good for keeping the hull shiny and new, but that's all. Also, we don't have any torpedoes at all."

"We're not going into battle, Scotty," Kirk said. "We're just going out there to take a look. Well then, Mister

O'Marla. She's all yours. Let's take her into planetary orbit at once. One-quarter thrust ahead."

Barbara's fingers flew over the panel. The ship tilted toward the outer atmosphere. Kirk watched Barbara as the ship moved gracefully away from the Bay and headed up at ever-increasing speeds. There was a jolt, and the ship lurched forward so quickly everyone was thrown back in their seats. By the time they straightened up, the ship was floating gracefully in the dark and eternal blackness of space.

"I'm sorry. She got away from me for a moment," Barbara said apologetically to everyone on the bridge.

"Considering that was your first nonsimulated launch in an unfamiliar ship, I think you did awfully well," Kirk said. And he began a short round of applause that brought both a blush of embarrassment and a deep swell of pride to the young helmsman. Of whom he found himself unnaturally proud as well. He kept his faced composed, however, even as he felt his heart beat for her.

Moments later the *Plush Princess* was streaking across the galaxy on a direct heading—supplied by Mr. Chekov from his research of the previous day—to Starbase 499, the nearest Federation base to the planetary star system known as Beta Prometheus.

Sulu regained consciousness slowly. He first felt the hard floor he was lying on, then the soft material under his head.

"Captain?" the ancient voice whispered. Then again, louder. "Captain?"

Sulu saw Dr. Bernard Hans on his knees on the floor next to him.

"Are you all right?" Hans said.

With an effort, Sulu lifted himself up to his elbows. He felt his joints crack.

"You were stunned," Hans said. "How do you feel?"

"Well," Sulu groaned, "that's how I feel. Where is everybody?"

"Right here. All the men, anyway. They took Ensign Violet Bays and Engineer Nora Schmidt away."

"I remember now. Where are we?"

"In a room of some sort. Don't worry, it's dark for all of us. There are no windows."

Sulu looked around. In the dimness he made out the figures of Lieutenant Roose, Cadet Spiros Focus, Chief Engineer Norquist Svenson, and the others. He climbed to his feet, several pairs of hands helping him.

"Actually," he lamented, "I think this hard floor was worse than the phaser shot. How long have I been unconscious on it?"

"Twelve to twenty-four hours. It's hard to say. There are no chronometers, and the little light doesn't ever seem to change in here."

"Any idea where we are?"

"Not really. Maldari returned with a bunch of Klingon soldiers—"

"Klingons!"

"Afraid so. He and another Beta Promethean who dresses all in black brought them. We were all hustled out of the shuttle and across a junkyard, and piled into a Klingon ship. A Bird-of-Prey. We carried you. We landed in some sort of freight and warehouse dock, but not a busy one. It was practically deserted. We're in one of the warehouses now. Some sort of room inside."

"Any way out?"

"You wouldn't have had to lie on a hard floor for a day and a night using my jacket as a pillow," Hans said as he picked up his jacket and shook it out, "if there were. The boys have been over every inch of the place. Even up there." He pointed at the ceiling. "Stood on each other's shoulders. Damn fine acrobatics went on, you should have seen it. But they found nothing. Our captors use the one door. Solid as a rock. Actually, harder, that's just an expression. Doesn't even have a handle on our side. They've given us some food from time to time, and this stuff to drink, but nothing else." Hans handed Sulu a cup of thick liquid. "It's not bad. You better drink some."

Sulu looked around him at each of the men.

"Everyone all right?" One at a time they nodded. "Spiros, your arm?"

"It's fine, Commander."

"Well then, here we are," Sulu said. Though all of his officers were brave men, and all of them had substantial training in survival techniques on alien and inhospitable planets, they were scientists, engineers, navigators. He didn't think they could last long under inhumane conditions. He felt entirely responsible for them. "And my fault, too," he added ruefully.

Everyone was quick to challenge him.

"No, no, not at all. You mustn't blame yourself," Hans said. "All part of the assignment." He looked around the dim room with a grim smile on his face.

"Why do you think we haven't been beamed out of here by now?" Lieutenant Roose said. "I mean, where the hell is Sencus and everyone?"

"Probably these bastards threatened to harm us if Sencus didn't withdraw," Hans said. "As for beaming, they took our communicators, and the *Excelsior* may have little idea where we are. They moved us just after Sven sent out our coordinates. Anyway, I'm afraid these walls might be transporter-proof. It seems a sensible thing for a prison. I'm sure Starfleet will be able to extricate us. Though we may have a fair amount of time to kill."

"I'll tell you what," Sulu said. "While we wait, why doesn't Swen lead us in some exercises?"

There were some groans from the less-fit members of the little group.

"Come on, everybody," Sulu said, uncomfortable in his necessary role of cheerleader. "It will help keep us fit. And exercise is essential to mental health."

"Clearly then," Dr. Hans said to Spiros as he joined the group assembling in the center of the room, "these heathen hosts of ours are out of shape."

Starbase 499

The artificial city floated in stationary orbit several parsecs from the Beta Prometheus star system. Its fifty floors of activity bustled in normal times. The addition of the response teams for the Prometheus incident made it virtually hectic, and so the arrival of the small star yacht the *Plush Princess* caused little notice. The spacedock commander wasn't even at the docking port when Uhura quietly requested permission to dock.

"This is the *Plush Princess,* requesting a spacedock," she called when they came within hailing distance of the starbase.

"What is the purpose of your visit?" the assistant docking officer said routinely. Uhura looked up at Kirk, who frowned.

"Vacation," she finally said lamely. There was another pause as the docking officer must have wondered what was worth visiting in this obscure part of the universe. Fortunately for Kirk and company, other, larger ships required his attention at the time.

"Permission granted," the voice came back. Seeing the size of the *Princess,* he assigned her an obscure berth in the corner, read out the coordinates, and subsequently forgot about her. But just before he did, he requested the name of the ship's captain.

"James Kirk," Uhura said. Then the yacht sped through the gate and headed for its assigned berth in the great spacedock. As it did, all of the crew, at their viewports, took note of the three huge Starship cruisers that were hanging in space near the entering port, armed and ready. Lights blazed from their ports, and activity was brisk and businesslike.

The *Plush Princess,* which had dropped to the use of only its thrusters just before entering the spacedock, glided to a smooth stop, and Kirk requested that all but the artificial-gravity and life-support systems be shut down.

"I think we should all thank and congratulate Cadet O'Marla on the completion of her first deep-space voyage," Mr. Spock said quietly from his seat in the rear of the control deck.

"Here, here," McCoy said as he came forward from his rear lounge.

"Well done," Kirk said quietly.

Barbara beamed inwardly. "Thank you," she said.

There was a pause, and then Uhura asked the question that was on everyone's mind.

"Well, now what?"

Kirk stood and saw them all gathered on the control deck. He announced the plan that had been formulating in his mind since their launch.

"Now I think we all deserve a drink," he said.

"Good idea," he heard McCoy and Scotty say.

"But Captain," Chekov said. "Ve've come such a long way. Aren't ve going to . . . I don't know . . . *do* something."

"We are," Kirk said. "Because just about everything that happens on a starbase is talked about on the rec deck. If we hang around there, we ought to hear all the gossip, which is as good a place to start as any. Keep your ears open, particularly for anything on the state of the negotiations for the hostages. I'm sure a number of minor diplomats will be holding court in the bar at any given time. That's where diplomats usually are. Let's plan to meet back here in, say, one hour."

The crew gathered on the transport deck, beamed over to 499, and wandered into the labyrinthine starbase, looking for all the world like a yachtload of tourists.

Kirk and his friends arrived late in the evening cycle of the starbase, and the rec deck was crowded with raucous humans and aliens. Kirk noted that a dance contest was in progress, though how the judges were going to pick a winner, given the variation in style and anatomy of the contestants, he couldn't guess. The music was old age, a twenty-first-century blend of synthesized sounds and harsh percussive beats revolving vaguely around a pentatonic scale. Although Kirk himself had no particular emotional response to the music—it sounded more like noise to him—apparently the young officers and aliens who mixed freely on the dance floor found in the music, for the moment at least, a mutual bonding that transcended their cultural differences.

The group from the *Plush Princess* split up. Kirk, Scotty, and Chekov were crossing the room when Scotty spotted someone he knew. Even with his back to them, Scotty recognized the broad girth and ginger hair of one of his oldest acquaintances from Academy days.

"Flanny, you old gin-swigger, you!" Scotty boomed as he slapped the man on the back. "I thought they had laid ye ta rest years ago."

The engineer turned around, and his pink face crinkled into a broad grin.

"Well, well, well, Montgomery Scott, the second best engineer-graduate from the class of 2241. I thought you retired this year. Wait a minute, where's your uniform?"

"In mothballs. I am temporarily off-duty, Flanny. And it's a pleasure, I can tell you. But I'm expectin' a new assignment any time now. Why, as soon as I get back, I bet they'll be offerin' me one of their latest ships of the line." He winked. "This is James Kirk and Pavel Chekov, my old shipmates." They shook hands all around. "Flanagan and I went to the Academy together, over 50 years ago. How about that?"

"Do ye have to mention the years, Scotty? We're becoming a couple of dinosaurs."

"Nonsense. Fit as a fiddle, both of us. These younger officers aren't going to have our experience, not for decades. Boys, Garth Flanagan. Will you let a reserve officer buy you and your friends a drink?"

"We would not let you leave without taking a round, now you know that." The jovial man's eyes twinkled. "Now, sit down, sit down, and tell us what brings you to this starbase in the back of beyond."

They sat down and Scotty waved for a round. He told the engineers that he and his friends had come to the starbase in search of some news about the Beta Promethean situation, as they had an old shipmate who was one of the hostages. The men at the table with Flanagan all turned out to be from the Starfleet Starships that had recently arrived.

"They're armed to the teeth, Scotty," Flanagan said confidentially. "They could turn the whole planet into an asteroid belt in minutes. And I believe that is exactly what the admiral would like to do."

"Admiral?" Scotty asked.

"The Starships are here under the direction of Admiral Julius Fesidas."

"Fesidas?" Kirk interrupted. "I know that name. He's an admiral I know in San Francisco. He's in charge?"

"This is his son."

"There's a coincidence," Kirk said.

"Probably not," Chekov said. "Even in Starfleet, the son also rises."

Everyone laughed.

"Anyway," Flanagan went on, "I got the feeling young Fesidas is champing at the bit to go in and get the hostages. He'd like to prove his mettle."

"And why hasn't he?" Scotty said.

"It's not up to him. It's up to the Federation Council. Only the president can order a full-scale military attack. But there's something else."

"What?" Kirk said.

"In my humble opinion——" Flanagan began.

"Your opinion wasn't humble in Academy classes," Scotty said.

"Perhaps not," Flanagan said in his quiet burr, his eyes twinkling. "In any case, our Starships could nae hide in a black hole. They'd be seen coming a galaxy away. And then what would happen to the hostages? Of course we could beam down an elite troop of soldiers, but then we'd lose our firepower advantage. In fact we'd be at a disadvantage, because the terrain around Archnos, where we assume the hostages are being kept, is particularly hostile. It's rocky, barren, and ice-cold this time o' their orbit. The pirates who've got your friend might be a bunch of primitive dunderheads, but they have the home field advantage, if you know the expression."

"Then you don't think there'll be an invasion?" Kirk said.

"Now, Captain, you know perfectly well the last people to know what's goin' on are the ones down in the engine room. That's only me own poor opinion," he said proudly, "formed as it has been from more than four decades serving the insignia." He tapped the Starfleet patch on his uniform.

"I don't know what will happen. But here we are, ready, willing and able to serve the Fleet. Aren't we, gents?" He raised his glass.

The other engineers said "Here, here" and raised their glasses. Scotty, Kirk, and Chekov joined in the toast. Then Kirk excused himself, and left the jovial group.

Mr. Spock reentered the turbolift and rose up to a less crowded level of the starbase, on the opposite side of the spacedock from the star yacht he had arrived on. He stood in front of a big viewport. Hanging in space just off to the side was the *U.S.S. Excelsior.* He walked to the nearby transporter room and encountered a young engineering officer.

"My name is Spock," he said quietly. "I am looking for a fellow Vulcan. His name is Sencus."

"He's aboard the *Excelsior,* sir. He's our commanding officer. In Captain Sulu's absence."

"I see. Permission to go aboard, then."

"Yes, sir. Just step up there, and I'll beam you up."

"Would you care for me to give you some proof of my identity? Aboard my old Starship, we did not let just anyone talk their way on board."

The young officer smiled. "Mr. Spock, your civilian clothes don't fool me. I recognize you. I only wish your friend Mr. Sulu were here to welcome you himself."

Spock nodded, and stepped up onto the transporter platform. Moments later he was surrounded by the familiar trappings of a Starfleet Starship, this one an Excelsior-class, even larger than his old ship.

The officer on duty at the transporter room must have been warned by the young man who sent him there.

"Good morning, Mr. Spock. Welcome aboard. I've told Captain Sencus about your arrival. He's waiting for you on the bridge now."

"Thank you." Spock nodded. He stepped off the ship's transporter platform and walked through the archway. Although he found himself walking through the familiar corridors of a Starship, he realized that this was not the *Enterprise,* and hesitated about which way to go.

"To your right, sir. Then the turbolift there will take you up. Top floor, of course."

"Thank you, officer," Spock said, and followed the directions.

Moments later he walked onto a bridge that, for all the world, reminded him of his old Starship. Realizing he had not been on a Federation Starship in over nine months, Spock immediately recognized his surroundings, as he stepped onto a bridge that was identical to his old one, and saw the uniforms he and his crew had worn for years. He glanced to one side, and saw a young female officer at the communications station. He saw the command chair on the other side, but it was empty. A few officers were at their stations, performing routine maintenance checks, but the helm and navigation chairs were empty.

At the science station, a Vulcan taller and thinner than Spock stood up. He came forward with his hand outstretched.

"Mr. Spock. We have never met, though Captain Sulu has told me a good deal about you. I am Sencus, science officer of the *Excelsior.*"

Spock and Sencus both raised their hands in the traditional Vulcan greeting, and said quietly, "Live long and prosper."

"You were the first Vulcan to graduate from Starfleet Academy," Sencus said. "In those days, among my friends at the Vulcan Science Academy, that was tantamount to running away and joining the circus. We all knew the legend."

"Did you? Interesting . . . Sencus," Spock continued, "I wonder if you could tell me what happened? So I might hear it firsthand."

"Of course." Sencus leaned in. "Seven days ago we received a distress call . . ." Sencus rapidly narrated the events for Spock. After the story, he sat back in his chair for the first time. "Then we were ordered back to starbase," he said. "Since then, there has been no activity of any significance. The stalemate in negotiations the Federation admits to is quite real. The Federation emissaries are extremely frustrated. And I am afraid that the number of different civilizations trading in this part of the universe makes it virtually impossible to impose any kind of serious embargo. Too many other civilizations feel it is not their problem, and do not want to stop trading."

"What do you think the Beta Prometheans really want?" Spock said. "Surely they do not think that the *Excelsior* was actually spying."

"The captain of the *Sundew,* a Beta Promethean named Maldari, attempted to extort some sort of ransom out of us. I had to refuse, because of our General Orders. After that, things went from bad to worse. It seems to be more a case of blundering in than planned strategy," Sencus theorized. "From what our diplomats can gather from various representatives of the Ruling Family, the taking of the hostages was not sanctioned by them to begin with, and was probably one mad act by Maldari."

"Then what do they want with them now?"

"It is not so much what they want with them, as how to get rid of them without losing prestige. The Shrewdest Ones are in a kind of campaign to convince the people that Starfleet and the Federation are the enemy." Sencus, some years older than Mr. Spock, went on, considering his words carefully. "From what we know about this civilization, the Shrewdest Ones control the Conclaves as their religious leaders, but the boundary between their belief system and the power structure is very gray, as it is in most religions. To keep the people in line, it is necessary to focus their energy and, in some cases, their anger, since both the Only Way and the Ruling Family control an inordinate proportion of their society's resources. The Federation is an easy target, which seems, in this case, to have fallen into their hands almost accidentally. And they are being somewhat manipulated in this by another group, who have apparently jumped in to use the hostages to their own advantage. This group is attempting to convince the Beta Prometheans that the Federation has been exploiting them."

"Who is this?" Spock said.

"The Klingons," Sencus answered. Spock's eyebrow went up.

"Klingons?"

"In fact, there is a rally scheduled for tonight in Archnos. We are worried that the hostages will be presented there. It could be dangerous."

"A rally?" Spock said. "To what purpose?"

"An anti-Federation gathering jointly sponsored by the Clerics and the Klingons. An antigovernment rally, in fact, possibly to put pressure on the Ruling Family."

"Have they always been political bedfellows?"

"Not at all. It is an unholy alliance, to be sure. But they seem to have found common ground this week. They are going to fan the flames of hatred."

"Thereby refocusing the attention of the People of Light away from their own domestic problems, particularly the unequal distribution of dilithium profits," Mr. Spock finished.

"Exactly," Sencus said. "We have not been able to get close enough to Archnos to identify the prison the officers are held in. One of our biggest problems is the monocultural nature of the Beta Prometheus system. We cannot just transport a man—and certainly not a woman—down there, because anyone who looked remotely like he was from a Federation society would stand out like a Melkotian at a Caitian festival. Otherwise Starfleet's Intelligence Section would have the place well filled with security teams by now. That includes Vulcans, of course."

Sencus was a full Vulcan, from whom Spock did not expect to see any display of emotion. Yet he could tell from the tone in which Sencus had outlined the situation that he was frustrated.

"You have tried?"

"An officer from the *Excelsior* volunteered. We beamed him down. Within five minutes he garnered so much attention we had to beam him back."

"But they must have visitors. From other civilizations, I mean."

"There are. They trade with Kaferian insectoids, Aurelians, a number of others. We have a few sources, but nothing has proved useful yet. And they conduct a lot of business with the Klingons, who have refused to participate in the Federation embargo."

"Naturally. That might be promising, however. Do you think that a Klingon could go into Archnos and investigate some of these buildings we suspect might hold our officers?"

"They do have a great deal of access, especially in the warehouse areas, where they appear to do a lot of trading. But what Klingon would work as a spy for the Federation?"

"I cannot think of one." Yet Mr. Spock seemed to be hatching some sort of plan.

"Then how would that help?"

"Perhaps if this person only resembled a Klingon . . ."

Sencus smiled. "You mean, send in someone who looked like a Klingon. I do not understand."

"It seems possible."

"Too bad we do not have a shapeshifter on board. Maybe we could send for one. I believe there is a race of Chameloids who can change their identity rather easily."

"Yes, but they are not very friendly. And decidedly untrustworthy. I can attest to that," Spock said, thinking of one who double-crossed Captain Kirk during their last assignment.

Spock spent another half hour on the bridge, talking with Sencus. Then he rose to leave.

"Mr. Spock," Sencus said. "Might I ask you something else? Of a personal nature?"

"Of course," Spock said.

"I have only been aboard the *Excelsior* for less than a year. But you spent almost three decades with Starfleet, most of it with the *Enterprise*. Was it worthwhile?"

Spock stopped in the doorway. He thought about the question.

"Worthwhile? I do not know, Mr. Sencus. I do not know the value of life itself. I do not know who does. So I cannot compare it to anything else. But I can tell you this," he said.

Sencus leaned in.

"Between you and I? It was never uninteresting." Then the customary stern visage returned. "Good afternoon," he said, and disappeared into the corridor.

* * *

Kirk spotted McCoy at a table of young female medical officers. He walked over to collect the doctor.

"And let me tell you," Kirk heard him saying as he approached, "when I saw pink blood, I knew I was in trouble."

"Doctor, excuse me," Kirk said before McCoy could begin another story, "but we're heading back to the ship. Sorry, ladies."

McCoy scowled at Kirk, sighed, then rose and bowed to his tablemates. He ambled after Kirk.

As they crossed the room, Kirk searched through the crowd for Barbara, but couldn't find her. He felt a twinge of concern. Had he done the right thing by letting her come on this voyage? Certainly she had proved herself a capable helmsman, though Kirk was well aware that piloting the little star yacht in safe and well-charted territory from the Earth to a starbase was hardly a difficult test. He had privately talked her performance over with Chekov, and found that Barbara had gained the navigator's confidence too, though not without the caveat that "it vas an unewentful trip, Captain. Ve must vait to see how she vill do in unusual situvations." Again he experienced the unnaturally proprietary feelings he had for her. While these thoughts were going through his mind, he looked around distractedly. McCoy broke into his consciousness.

"I haven't seen her, Jim."

"I didn't ask—"

"You were about to."

"Dr. McCoy, have you become a mind reader since our last journey together?"

"I've been observing your behavior toward her, and I saw the look on your face when you were searching the dance floor."

"I do feel responsible for her. Maybe I'd better—"

"It isn't necessary, Captain. She is obviously a strong-minded and capable officer. As for your relationship with her, which I must admit I envy, take it from an old pro in these things. Don't crowd her."

"I'm not in the habit of discussing my personal life with fellow Starfleet officers," Kirk said.

"Jim, you're not in the habit of discussing your personal life with anyone, including yourself. But you're a civilian now. The *Enterprise* is under someone else's command, I understand. Loosen up, before you become an old fart like me."

"Thanks for the advice. For the record, I don't think you're an old fart, Bones."

"Thanks."

"We'll have to take these little trips more often, Doctor. It seems to be cause for a good deal of honesty."

"This is my last," McCoy grumbled, and led the way out of the crowded bar.

The business of the Federation, even on Starbase 499, until now a backwater assignment on the very edge of the frontier, was round-the-clock. The arrival of three Federation Starships and a diplomatic team only added to a cacophony that was constant and multifarious. Any number of humans and aliens were coming and going at all hours.

In this spirit of activity it was not difficult for even a Promethean to wander the corridors, listening to gossip and making acquaintances. Thus Taras Tarquin sat in a shadowy corner of the rec deck and watched the comings and goings. His squat Promethean body seemed out of character with his reasonably humanoid face, his straight teeth, and his genuine smile. Though on any of the worlds of Beta Prometheus he was considered something of a mutant, and thus an outcast, here he was merely recognized as a virtual cauldron of breeds, some of which were assumed to be human.

When he spotted the crew from the *Plush Princess,* he made inquiries among his acquaintances on the starbase. Discovering that they were retired Starfleet officers who had come up to 499 because of a connection with one of the hostages, he waited until they had left the rec deck, and followed them to the spacedock, where he stood in front of the great viewport, admiring the *Plush Princess.*

While the crew of the *Plush Princess* was visiting the rec deck, Barbara O'Marla took the opportunity to casually separate herself from the others, and headed for the starbase library. There she found an idle monitor in the empty room. She turned it on, and navigated her way through the system until she found starbase communications. She entered a private password to gain access to a private mailbox. Then she spoke a simple, two-word message: "Arrived. Barbara." She coded it secure, then rose from her seat and headed back toward the *Princess.*

"There's one more thing," Scotty said. "I did manage to borrow a few supplies. The engineer was kind enough to lend me a couple of photon torpedoes and a mobile launcher. I've brought them aboard, and I think I can hook them into our energy circuits, and find enough power to fire them if necessary. Just in case we have to fire on someone. Though at this point, I cannot imagine who."

Kirk smiled. "Always resourceful, Mr. Scott. But let's try not to start an intergalactic war, shall we? After all, we were all kindly asked to stand down from active duty when we almost started one with the Klingons a year ago."

Six of the seven travelers had returned to the *Plush Princess,* and were gathered in the aft space lounge reporting on their various conversations. Kirk alone noticed that Barbara was late in returning.

"What next, Jim?" McCoy asked, drawing his attention.

"Well, that depends. An idea has been broached by Mr. Spock that may be worth a try. It appears that the only near-to-humanoid species that is a reasonably integral part of the population of Archnos is Klingon. Although right now as you know we have a shaky but holding treaty with them, they do not participate in the Federation. So they are ignoring the embargo and still doing a good deal of business. There are hundreds of them coming and going, some even living there, we believe. Mostly traders."

"What good is that?" McCoy asked. "We can't trust a Klingon to help us."

"No, we can't. But perhaps one of us could disguise himself as one."

"What?!" several of the crew said.

"It is Mr. Spock's idea," Kirk said lamely.

"I've heard of cosmetic enhancement," Barbara said, walking onto the bridge. "But is it reversible?"

"That was a primitive medical technique used a good deal in the twenty-first century, during a time of extreme vanity," McCoy said. "Even reversible cosmetic surgery is possible, but I don't have the proper equipment with me. And even if I did, I wouldn't make someone look like a Klingon."

"We were thinking more along the lines of a temporary situation. Theatrical makeup."

"Makeup?" said Uhura.

"Actually," Mr. Spock spoke up, "I have had some little experience with this. When I was part of a little theater group. As an actor."

"You were an actor?" Chekov said.

"It was a hobby for a short time. In any case, we once mounted a production of *Romeo and Juliet,* and a rather theatrical stage director who was somewhat more imaginative than logical"—they could tell that Spock was being polite—"decided that the Capulets would be Klingons. It was his . . . concept, shall we say. And so we spent weeks perfecting our Klingon makeup technique. It did not work."

"Well, if it didna work," Scotty said, "what good is it to us now?"

"I meant to say that the production did not work. The Klingons are not well regarded in most of the Federation, as you know, and that gave all of the audience's sympathy to the Montagues. Thus, the production divided the characters into heroes and villains which, I think you will agree, Shakespeare did not intend for that particular play. However, the makeup fooled everyone. Almost."

"What almost?" Kirk asked.

"The ears. We Vulcans have rather well defined ears. We had great difficulty disguising them."

"No problem," Kirk said. "You'll make me up. I'll go down to Beta Prometheus and attend this rally."

"I'll go with you," Barbara said. "One person won't be safe. There ought to be at least two, in case something happens."

166

"That is an excellent notion, Cadet O'Marla," Spock said. "And thank you for volunteering. Your commitment to our cause is most gratifying. However, we will need a helmsman to remain aboard, for the ship will be in danger of discovery within the Beta Prometheus star space."

"Well, then——" Uhura began, and stood up.

"And we'll need an excellent communications person to remain aboard as well," Spock said quickly. "Someone able to deal with the Beta Prometheus language if necessary."

Uhura sat down again.

"Then I'll go," Chekov said.

"I would much rather you remain as navigator. You and O'Marla will have to bring the *Princess* within transporter distance of Archnos, and that could be dangerous. We also cannot accept you, Mr. Scott," Spock said just as the chief engineer was about to speak. "We need your skills here, especially in the transport room. You will have to stand by to pull them out of there the moment anything goes wrong."

"Well, let's see." Dr. McCoy looked around. "That leaves . . . uh, that leaves . . . ." He realized everyone was looking at him. "Me?" McCoy stood up abruptly. "Wait a minute. The last time I went near a Klingon ship I was thrown in jail and froze my butt off."

McCoy looked around him, sighed, and sat back down. "I guess I volunteer," he said lamely.

"Then that," Kirk said, "will be our first step. Now, while Spock works on us, would you, Uhura, and you, Barbara, go back to the starbase and forage for some appropriate clothes."

"Sure," McCoy grumbled. "There ought to be a Klingon haberdashery somewhere about the galaxy."

Two hours later Kirk and McCoy came out of the bathroom. Kirk sported an enormous forehead with waves of ridges running down to the bridge of his nose. McCoy had three vertical ridges on an almost bald head. Both were darker, and McCoy had a sour-looking beard and mustache. They were clothed in dark tunics of leather and metal, and their thick boots made them inches taller. They climbed the access ladder back up to the control deck, and walked onto the bridge. Scotty shot out of his seat.

"Heavens awake! Will you look at them now," he said, smiling. "I've nae seen two more Klingon-looking Klingons. Why, General Chang himself could not smell the difference. I've never seen anythin' like it!" he crowed.

"I've never seen a Klingon in person," Barbara said, "but you look just like the holographs I've seen. Mr. Spock, you did an incredible job."

"Thank you," Spock said. "It was merely the careful application of the correct physiognomy and the patience of my two models. I believe they now stand a chance of fitting right in with the local population. At least in the high-traffic freight areas where Klingons are common."

"What about if someone talks to them?" Barbara asked.

"We have solved that problem too, I believe. We have hidden Universal Translators under their tunics. Anyone who speaks to them, they will hear in English. Anyone they speak to will hear them in Klingon. Just be careful not to talk very much," Spock warned them. "Your voices are not nearly as guttural, your lips won't be a perfect match for the words they'll hear, and you know little of their customs and culture."

"Right," said Kirk.

"I hope we don't run into anyone we know," McCoy said.

"In this corner of the galaxy, it is extremely doubtful. You are very unlikely to be recognized," Spock said. "Nevertheless, keep your communicators on at all times, and we will be monitoring your whereabouts."

"I was thinking more about the embarrassment than the safety," McCoy grumbled.

Chekov and Uhura came onto the control deck as Scotty climbed down to the engine room. Chekov stopped in his tracks, and Uhura let out a yelp of surprise.

"Don't worry, it's only us humans," McCoy said.

"You look incredible," Chekov said.

"Thank you, Mr. Chekov," Kirk said. "What news?"

"We've isolated the coordinates of the rally site using the data on Archnos which Barbara brought." His hands played over the console, and a street map of Archnos illuminated the monitor.

"Well, we might as well get started," Kirk said. "There ought to be several more hours of Promethean sunlight left." He sat in the command chair, but found everyone staring at him. "What's the matter?" he asked.

"Oh, nothing, Captain," Chekov said. "It's just that I never thought I vould see a Klingon sitting in the command seat of a Starfleet wessel. Even an unofficial one." He smiled and sat in his navigator's chair.

A few minutes later the *Princess* was in orbit near Beta Prometheus 1. Kirk jumped up out of his chair. "All right, Mr. Spock. The command is yours. Bones, let's go down there and take a look."

"Jim, suppose they recognize us as human beings?"

Kirk turned and took a good look at McCoy.

"Bones," he said. "I don't even recognize you as a human being. You look like a Klingon. You sound like a Klingon. In those clothes, you're beginning to smell like a Klingon. Believe me, the only danger we'll be in today will come from running into somebody who hates Klingons. Come on."

He and McCoy hurried to the transporter platform, where Scotty met them.

"Just a couple of Klingons, or I'm not my mother's son. All right, good luck," Scotty said as he worked the controls.

The two Klingons disappeared from his platform.

The city of Archnos

On Beta Prometheus 1 the air was crisp, the temperature cold, and the blue sun low in the sky by the time Kirk and McCoy arrived. The most modern buildings appeared to be nearly windowless, and made of a shiny metal. The streets themselves were not wide. They tried to take a direct path to the location of the rally, but many of the streets wound around in odd ways. Clearly the city had not been laid out by a master architect, but grown every which way over the centuries.

There were signs everywhere of the Only Way. They

exhorted citizens to appear daily at the Conclaves, to raise their children to the Higher Calling, to follow the Book of Muharbar. They called themselves the People of Light, though it seemed to McCoy, an inveterate grump where any kind of organized worship was concerned, that "Light" was an oxymoron when artificial belief systems were involved.

Prometheans scuttled back and forth on their squat, four-legged bodies. Other aliens also walked the streets. There were enough Klingons to give them some small feeling of security, though both men froze the first time they passed a group of them. Fortunately, Klingons appeared to be as unfriendly to each other as they were to humans, so Kirk and McCoy did not find it necessary to engage in a conversation.

"This way, I think," Kirk said and started off.

"Oh, great," McCoy grumbled, and shambled along after him. "A walking tour of the city."

They walked with purpose, tried to maintain an arrogant bearing, and looked like they knew where they were going. After a while they found themselves on a more fully populated street, walking in the same direction as many others. At last Kirk and McCoy made their way into a district of warehouses, docks, and shuttle fields. Signs of intergalactic trade were everywhere.

"There's the rally, in that big building straight ahead," Kirk said.

Eventually the crowd overflowed the sidewalk, and droves of people moved along the street in the same direction, carrying Kirk and McCoy with them. It was a good thing that other Klingons and two-legged aliens were in evidence, for the tide of Beta Prometheans moved three times as fast as the others with their four muscular legs and lower center of gravity. The Prometheans tended to scuttle out into the street and stream past the slower life-forms. As everyone got closer to their destination—by the last block it seemed as if the whole community was heading for the rally—the Prometheans brushed passed real Klingons, who were slower, and tended to remain arrogantly gaited and in their own world.

Kirk strode forward. Half a block away he said under his

breath, "Remember, keep your Translator off if we talk to each other, and on if you have to talk to someone else. But try not to talk at all."

There was hardly time to say more. As they came within twenty yards of the doors to the warehouse, the crowd became so intense that it would have been impossible to turn and change directions. The doors stood open, and a sign overhead said something indecipherable in alien script.

"What does that say?" McCoy asked.

"I don't know. I don't read Promethean," Kirk said. "Come on."

They stepped into a lobby with hundreds of others. There were several tables staffed by young Beta Prometheans, and the walls were coated with posters, which carried more slogans or announcements much like the one over the front door.

The young Beta Prometheans smiled and nodded, and several said "welcome" in Klingon. Kirk and McCoy nodded and passed through another set of double doors guarded by two Klingons who didn't smile but stamped their feet as Kirk and McCoy went by.

The interior space was enormous, and the large floor was filled with spectators. There were several hundred beings, including Prometheans, other aliens, and Klingons, all facing a high platform at the far end. On the platform several representatives of alien races were standing, and one Klingon was exhorting the crowd. His speech was punctuated continually by shouts and roars and applause from the crowd. Kirk and McCoy were separated by the milling mob. Kirk worked his way to the front of the hall, and stood just under the platform.

The rally featured a number of speakers who decried the Federation as imperialist aggressors, and used the hostages as examples of spies. Klingons warned their "fellow workers" that the Federation wanted to control the dilithium mines and would soon take them over, subjugating the Prometheans. The Clerics described a paganistic, morally lax Federation anxious to export their decadence throughout the galaxy.

After half a dozen speakers, the crowd worked itself up

into a frenzy, and Kirk found himself raising his right fist and extolling the purity of the Beta Promethean people and their friends the Klingons. He used the tumultuous activity to look around, and spotted McCoy in the front ranks near him.

Damn. If we get too far apart from each other I could lose Bones in the crowd. He worked his way over to McCoy and stood next to him.

"Furthermore," the Klingon was saying, "the Federation wishes to impose its regulations upon the entire universe! They wish to impose their culture upon the entire universe! They wish to subjugate all races which they consider alien! They are attempting to destroy all non-Federation societies and place themselves at the center of a Federation-only cosmos!"

A roar of agreement went up.

"They have sent their warships to the very edge of this system! They have sent spies to prepare for their attack! But we are not fooled!"

Another roar of agreement.

"We must be vigilant! This disease must be destroyed. We must build a galactic army that is capable of beating back these imperialist Federationists!"

A third great roar. Kirk began to feel a bit claustrophobic. The heavy makeup didn't help.

"My friends, listen to me," the Klingon orator went on. "Only days ago a dozen spies were sent in a Starfleet warship to prepare the way for an invasion." He turned and nodded, and several of his cohorts on the platform hurried down to the back door. They opened it, and Prometheans carrying weapons walked through. Sulu and his eight fellow officers were led onto the floor in front of the platform in single file.

The Klingon orator told the crowd to look and see for themselves how the Federation had sent spies into the Beta Promethean star system.

"Although we captured these spies, there are more gathering even as we speak, at a nearby starbase belonging to the Federation. Dozens of their warships are preparing to launch an attack on Beta Prometheus. Only the great

Klingon Defense Machine can stop them. Only when each Starfleet cruiser is matched with the more powerful Bird-of-Prey will the balance of power be restored. The Klingon treaty with the Federation must be denounced! The Klingons are your friends! They will stand shoulder to shoulder with you against the imperialist destroyers! Stand up for the Beta Promethean culture or it will be destroyed, just as surely as the Federation has destroyed or subjugated so many other alien races."

Kirk looked around. He didn't feel safe, but logic told him that he was. There were a number of Klingons in the crowd, and in any case the crowd was so turbulent and chaotic that no one was looking at them. He lowered his voice and said with as little emotion as possible, "Let's get closer." He moved forward, and McCoy followed.

Kirk worked his way through the crowd until he was only a few feet in front of Sulu. Sulu stood stoically, his head held up, his face without expression. He didn't look at Kirk.

"Federation spy," Kirk said to him without malice.

Sulu didn't flinch. But his face altered imperceptibly, and Kirk knew that he had heard the words in English, as Kirk had said them.

"Federation spy," Kirk went on in what he hoped sounded like a menacing growl in Klingon to those around him. "Your Starfleet comrades are coming. We will be ready for them. Do you understand?"

Sulu looked over the faces in front of him. But he saw only Prometheans, Klingons, and assorted riffraff from the galaxy. Kirk spoke again.

"In memory of General Chang, we of the true Klingon Empire will be triumphant." He raised his hand and indicated himself with his finger. Sulu looked right at him. Kirk nodded imperceptibly. He couldn't tell whether or not Sulu understood. The *Excelsior* commander showed no sign of recognition.

"We repeat. This is Beta Prometheus star traffic control. Identify yourself."

Aboard the *Plush Princess* everyone was sitting very still.

The voice transmission boomed in the small cabin for the second time.

Uhura hesitated. She looked up.

"What should I say, Mr. Spock?" Uhura asked.

"How about, 'We're the crew of the *Enterprise,* and we're going to blow you out of the skies if you don't return Mr. Sulu, you nasty little planet,'" Scotty suggested.

"Mr. Scott," Spock said sternly.

"Sorry," Scotty said.

The same voice came back. "Attention *Plush Princess.* You are trespassing in Beta Prometheus star space without prior permission. A Promethean ship will approach and scan you."

"Let me talk to them," Spock said.

Uhura ran her hands over the console and nodded.

"This is Spock, captain of the *Princess,*" Spock said in a whiny voice. "We are a pleasure yacht out of Talos. Did you say Beta Prometheus?"

"That is correct."

"I am afraid we have made a bad navigational error," Spock said apologetically. "We were headed for the Delta Triciatu system. For recreation."

"Stay where you are until our starship approaches and gives you permission to move," the voice growled.

"They could spot the two torpedoes I borrowed," Scotty whispered.

Spock looked at Scotty and one eyebrow rose.

"I told you," Scotty said. "I borrowed two torpedoes in case of an emergency. I've attached them to the underside of the saucer."

"We were just leaving," Spock said to Promethean control. "We did not mean to be any trouble. I believe we transposed a couple of coordinates by mistake."

"Do not leave your star space until—"

"Plush Princess out." Spock nodded to Barbara, who was watching him intently from her seat at the conn. She swiveled to the controls and quickly touched them. The *Princess* veered to its right and shot into space, leaving the leisurely orbit over Beta Prometheus. In distancing itself

from the Beta Prometheans, however, it went well beyond matter-energy transport distance for Kirk and McCoy on the planet below.

"Death to the Federation," the Klingon leader shouted above them.

"Death to the Federation!" the crowd answered.

"Death to the Imperialist aggressors!"

"Death to the Imperialist aggressors!" the crowd answered.

"Long live the Klingon Empire!"

"Long live the Klingon Empire!"

"So I ask you, friends of Klingons, what should we tell the Ruling Family? Do we want to lie down and roll over for the Federation, or do we want to fight them?"

"Fight them!" the roar answered.

"What should we do if the Ruling Family fails to stand up for the Beta Promethean people and all other nonhuman species in our galaxy?"

"Depose them!" the cry rose up.

"And what should be done with the Federation spies?"

"Kill them!" the roar went up, reverberating in the large hall.

"My friends, let us make this promise to the Federation Imperialists. The Federation must withdraw from this quadrant of the galaxy. For every day they remain, we will execute one of their spies." The crowd was shouting uncontrollably now, and the orator was building them to a frenzy.

The hall was a blur of noise. The Klingon orator was screaming into his address system. The crowd was surging forward, trapping Kirk and McCoy in the front. Kirk noticed that Beta Prometheans and not Klingons were guarding the nine men, but they were having greater and greater difficulty keeping the crowd back. One Beta Promethean who seemed to be their leader was shouting at his cohorts, but Kirk couldn't make out what he was saying in the noise.

"And let us," the Klingon orator screamed, "start today!" Before Kirk could react, the Klingon drew a disruptor from his holster and fired point blank at the back of the head of the nearest Starfleet officer on the floor beneath the platform. When the bolt hit him, the young man shook and crumpled forward.

Chaos followed. Kirk heard Sulu shout "Spiros!" and leap to help him. The Klingons on the platform began chanting, "Death to Federation spies! Death to the Federation!" The crowd around Kirk and McCoy erupted, and tried to rush the other officers. The Beta Promethean guards surrounded the Starfleet officers and began pushing them toward the exit. Kirk tried to catch up with Sulu, but couldn't get close enough in the crowd. He passed near the dead Starfleet officer, who was being spat upon by Beta Prometheans. Kirk noticed that the guards were being exhorted to get the hostages off the floor by a screaming Beta Promethean. *That must be Maldari,* he thought, *the pirate who started all this. He doesn't seem too happy.* Kirk tried to keep his eye on the officers as Maldari and another Beta Promethean grabbed Sulu and pushed him away from the body of the young officer. In the melee, Kirk lost Sulu, but saw the rear door open and the guards hustle the Starfleet officers through. Then the guards closed the door behind them. At once the Klingon orator exhorted the crowd. Kirk found himself surrounded by Klingons, Beta Prometheans and other aliens waving their arms and shouting. He joined them.

"Death to the Federation! Long live the Empire!" he shouted. McCoy frowned, but understood and quickly joined Kirk in the shouting.

They carried on this way for several long minutes. Finally the crowd seemed to calm down to a low turbulence, and began leaving the building.

When the hall had thinned out, though still one-third of the huge crowd milled around, Kirk stood next to McCoy, both pretending to read a poster tacked to the platform.

"They went out that door?" he said as quietly as he could, though he had turned his Universal Translator off and doubted if anyone near them spoke English.

"Yeah," McCoy nodded. "Let's get out of here, Jim."

Kirk and McCoy joined the tide of people heading toward

the exit doors. They waited until they were on the street and well away from the building and crowds before they spoke, contenting themselves with an occasional "Down with the Federation!" for the sake of anyone within hearing distance. They hurried around to the rear door of the building. There they saw the last of the Beta Promethean guards pushing the last of the Starfleet officers into a shuttle, and closing the hatch behind them. Almost immediately the small starship took off. It was suddenly quiet. The streets around them were deserted, shadows were starting to fall, and Kirk felt conspicuous.

"That poor kid," McCoy said. "We should have blasted their guards and gotten Sulu out of there. We've got our phasers."

"You may have noticed that they outnumbered us by about five hundred to two."

"The Klingons are in on this," McCoy said. "That's confirmed."

"Not officially, I'll bet. This is only the militant Klingon faction that hates the treaty. They would like to use this incident as a chance to break it. By getting the Promethean people on their side and starting a war, they'd have just what they want. Uh-oh, look who's coming."

Kirk and McCoy stared as the Klingon orator and two of his toadies who had been talking with the Beta Promethean pirates behind the prison building began walking straight toward them.

"They just want to be friendly," Kirk said. "We're Klingons, remember."

"Klingons aren't friendly, even to each other. They want to know who we are, and what we are doing here. What's the answer going to be?" McCoy said.

"I'll think of something," Kirk said, just as the three Klingons approached them directly. He remembered not to smile.

"Did you attend my speech?" the Klingon said.

"Oh yes," Kirk said, remembering that Klingons did not use salutations or greetings. "Outstanding."

"Lifted our spirits," McCoy added.

"You are not from the Bird-of-Prey *Krogshat?*"

"No, we're not," Kirk said, desperately trying to recall what little he knew of the Klingon syntax, so his words did not appear to be translations.

"Where are you from?" the Klingon said.

"Qo'nos," Kirk said.

Brilliant, thought McCoy.

"How did you get here?" the Klingon asked.

"Oh, we've been here a long time," Kirk said. "We're traders. Dilithium traders. We work here." Kirk nodded in the general direction of the warehouses.

"Dilithium trade is reserved for only certain Klingons," he said. "What ship do you work for?"

Kirk stared at him. "The *Kerla,*" he finally said.

There was a pause.

"I've never heard of the *Kerla,*" the Klingon said suspiciously.

"It's named after Brigadier Kerla. You must remember him. He died defending the greater glory of the Klingon Empire from those filthy assassins on the *Enterprise.*"

"It's not a ship of the line, then. It is not a Bird-of-Prey," the Klingon said harshly.

"No, it's . . . a trader. Carries freight. Nothing so glorious as a warship. Just a humble—" But Kirk's expanding eloquence was cut short.

"In that case," the Klingon shouted, "you are arrested for illegal trading in dilithium, which is reserved for members of the Dilithium Mining Corps. Seize them," he said to the two Klingons standing next to him.

Kirk thought it about time he and McCoy left the city of Archnos. He reached down and turned off his Translator. Then he touched his communicator. "Scotty, it's us," he said in a low voice. "Get us out of here," he said.

But nothing happened.

Too far from Beta Prometheus 1 to beam them up, the *Princess* banked into a sharp turn and came to a near-sudden stop. It hovered behind a large asteroid as the Promethean warship shot by.

"Outstanding at the helm," Scotty said from the engine

room. "It's a very good thing I was holding on to something, however."

"Sorry for turning so sharply, everyone," Barbara said. "I saw that asteroid at the last minute. Thought it would be a good place to hide. We weren't going to outrun them without going into warp speed, and I was worried about getting too far from Captain Kirk and the doctor."

"It was an admirable ruse," Mr. Spock said encouragingly, as he climbed back to his feet. "Let us just wait a moment for that ship to give up," he finished. They all sat quietly, as the ship hid behind the barren asteroid. Then Mr. Spock spoke up.

"Uhura?" he said simply.

"They've reported to base, sir. Said we've left their star space. Said they shot at us and we must have left the area at warp speed."

"Good. Mr. Chekov?"

"We're only about half a light-year away," he answered quickly. "But that's too far to hear them or pick them up."

"All right. We will go in and listen every fifteen minutes. If we get a signal we will pick them up. If we do not, we will withdraw again. We will simply have to play cat and mouse with this warship until we can get out of here."

Unfortunately they were several light-years away when the first call was sent up by Kirk.

McCoy sighed. He and Kirk were surrounded by Klingons, and being marched along the street.

"Great. Another Klingon jail. Maybe this time they should just skip the trial," McCoy said as the two of them were hustled along, Klingon disruptors prodding them in the back. "I don't think reasonable doubt is part of their judicial system anyway."

"*Princess,* do you read me?" Kirk said quietly. "Kirk and McCoy here. We are ready to be beamed out of here."

"They've left us and gone back to the starbase," McCoy whispered.

"Why would they do that?" Kirk said. "They wouldn't do that. Something's come up."

"Not us," McCoy said.

"Bones, when we get to that corner, I'm going to trip this overweight brute next to me. We'll go that way. Turn the corner at once, and run into the crowd on the street. Maybe they won't attempt to fire with so many Prometheans around."

"Relying on a Klingon's humanity. Excellent plan," McCoy groused. He felt increasingly irritated, not so much at their immediate jeopardy—having been in tight places with Kirk before and spent a season ministering to the complaints of Earthbound civilians, he preferred the former —but at the thought that he might have to spend another night in a foul Klingon jail.

"It's the best I can think of just now," Kirk whispered.

"All right. I'm with you," McCoy answered. A Klingon soldier shouted something and shoved him forward and he stumbled, but found his footing.

A few feet farther on, their leader stepped off the sidewalk. It was almost a one foot drop to the street, a distance the four-legged Prometheans had no trouble scuttling over. When they reached it, Kirk began to step down, then shot his foot out in front of the guard next to him. With the help of a strong push in the back, the big Klingon stumbled forward off the sidewalk and crashed into the leader. The two of them fell to the ground. At once Kirk and McCoy turned the corner. Momentarily shielded by the building, they sprinted several yards ahead and into a crowd of pedestrians.

"Scotty!" Kirk shouted, touching his communicator. "Where the hell are you?"

"Where the hell are we?" McCoy said, out of breath, as they hurried through the streets, keeping inside the crowds of Prometheans and other aliens on the thoroughfare. Even as the Prometheans scuttled about, Kirk and McCoy sprinted ahead of them, causing many to wonder about the two Klingons rushing past.

Guttural noises exploded behind them. McCoy looked over his shoulder.

"Here they come, Jim," he huffed. They heard a zing of disruptor fire. Kirk looked over his shoulder. The Klingons had their weapons up, and were pushing through the crowd. A Promethean's average height was shorter than the humans' and a good deal shorter than the Klingons', which gave the pursuers a fair range of vision.

"Duck!" Kirk shouted, demonstrating. He bent over at the waist and hurried forward. Another zing of phaser fire heated the air. A Promethean behind them was hit, and fell to the ground. McCoy took his sounds to be swearing. The crowd around them began to panic as the Klingon soldiers stormed through, firing ahead.

"So much for safety in numbers," McCoy said.

An intersection ahead was blocked with traffic. The crowd began to slow down, and pedestrians other than Kirk and McCoy began scattering to the sides. Kirk looked back again. Several Klingon soldiers were well within firing range. They raised their pistols on the run.

"Scotty, bring us in. Now would be a good time. Kirk and McCoy to Scotty. I said—"

Kirk felt the first tingle of the dematerialization process, and knew he would be back aboard the *Plush Princess* in seconds. Their pursuers pounded up the sidewalk to where they had last seen the suspicious-looking Klingons who claimed to be trafficking in dilithium. Prometheans stared out at them from behind street refuse, but gave them a wide berth. The Klingons stood in the center of the intersection, staring around them in frustration.

"That was another close one," McCoy said as he stepped off the transporter platform. "Where the hell have you been?" he said testily to Scotty.

"Sorry, gentlemen," Scotty said. "We were out of range. A little business with a Beta Promethean warship. We were just orbiting back in when we heard you talking to those real Klingons."

The three of them went immediately to the control deck where the others were waiting. Kirk and McCoy stood in the doorway.

"All right, everybody, back to spacedock at 499," Kirk said.

"Would you care to take your captain's chair back," Mr. Spock said.

"No, I'd like to get out of this outfit. Spock, come help us get these ridiculous faces off." He turned and led the way down to their cabin's bathroom.

On the control deck, Barbara held a brief conversation with Chekov, then announced an eminent departure. Her fingers flew over the consul and she put the *Princess* on a direct route to the spacedock.

"ETA for Starbase 499 should be about thirty minutes," Mr. Chekov announced.

"Did you know they were going to do that? Did you?!" Maldari screamed at Dramin.

"I did not," Dramin said solemnly.

"I don't believe you! You arranged this with the Klingons! The prisoners are mine! You and that fanatic had no right, no right at all!" Maldari's gray skin was black with rage.

Dramin shrugged. "Believe me, I had no idea they intended to execute one of the officers. But it is of little consequence. One disbeliever less in the galaxy."

Maldari tried to control his anger. He tried to think.

"No more rallies. The Klingons will not be allowed to use the prisoners again. Nor will the Clerics."

"What will you do with them?" Dramin said.

"I'll sell them. Just as I sold the women."

"You can't. They have little worth. Their real value is to the cause."

"What cause?" Maldari asked, suspicious. "What are you getting out of this?"

"Me? Nothing, of course. But Beta Prometheus must be ruled by the True Believers."

"Meaning the Shrewdest Ones," Maldari said.

"The Ruling Family does not have sufficient commitment to the Only Way."

"And you think the Klingons do?"

"The Klingons are merely of momentary usefulness. Once the Ruling Family is replaced, and Beta Prometheus is isolated from the influence of the Federation, the Shrewdest

Ones will be in control of our star system. The Klingons will be irrelevant."

"So that's it. You hope to overthrow the Ruling Family." Maldari wondered why he hadn't seen it from the beginning. "And you're using my hostages to do it."

"The hostages are prisoners of the state. They are Federation spies who should be brought to justice."

Maldari wanted to tell Dramin he could drop that kind of talk right now, but he saw the gleam in the fanatic's eyes, and knew it was useless. He merely sighed. Dramin watched him, then spoke up.

"You made a good profit on the women. Your crew is happy. Let me have the men and you can return to space and pursue your trading."

"I have nothing to trade! The Ruling Family has informed me through my freight master that I may not take dilithium off the planet until this little matter is cleared up. My holds are virtually empty, and I had to divide up the money I got for the women to keep the crew loyal. I don't even have a starship. And your temporary political bedfellows have just eliminated one-ninth of my only source of income."

"I'm sure that the Clerics would be able to give you enough to return to trading if you were able to prove your loyalty."

Maldari stared at Dramin. Then he said, "What do they want?"

"Give us the hostages."

"So you can shoot them one day at a time until you have caused a war with the Federation?"

"Give us the hostages, and we will see that you have permission to return to trading. With your holds filled with dilithium. What do you care what happens to the hostages?"

"Traders don't need a war. Your last holy war caused us to lose many fortunes."

"There will be no war. As soon as the Ruling Family is replaced, the Shrewdest Ones will apologize to the Federation, and return the remaining hostages."

"If there are any remaining."

"Again, that is of little concern."

"I'll think about it." Maldari walked away from Dramin without the typical Promethean salutation.

When the seven crew persons left the *Plush Princess* in spacedock and went aboard Starbase 499, they found that rumor of the hostage execution was already spreading. The three Federation Starships were lit with activity. The rec deck was noisy with conversation. The official response, a short statement condemning the action by the Federation, seemed absurdly shallow to Kirk, who had seen the handsome young officer murdered, and seen the body lying on the floor beneath his feet.

"They have promised to execute one hostage per day until the Federation withdraws from this sector of the galaxy," Kirk said grimly as he gave his friends a detailed account of the rally. "We have to believe them. That gives us less than twenty-four hours before another Starfleet officer is killed. We have to get those hostages back," Kirk said, slamming his hand on the table.

From a shadowy corner of the rec deck one Beta Promethean had been watching the group since they returned from Archnos, so the sudden outburst on Kirk's part didn't surprise him. Now he judged it was time to act. He had discovered who the travelers were—retired officers from the crew of the old *Enterprise,* where they had served with the hostage's captain—and felt that their being out of uniform made them a reasonable target for his proposal. He screwed up his courage, slipped off his chair, crossed the room, and stood next to the Vulcan.

"Pardon me, but I wonder if I might introduce myself," he began. "I'm a Beta Promethean trader. An honest one, I hasten to add."

The crew stared at him. Kirk looked suspicious.

"And you are the crew of the *Enterprise,* I presume," he continued.

"The *Plush Princess,*" Scotty said. "And we are not trading just now, so if you think you're going to sell us something here, you're wasting your time."

"I understand. I do have something to sell, and I am

guessing that you would in fact be interested. I wonder if I might—"

"Sit down," Spock said, surprising his companions.

"Actually, we're rather busy—" Kirk began, but Spock cut him off and spoke directly to the Beta Promethean trader.

"Since you have been shadowing us since we first arrived at Starbase 499, you know perfectly well who we are. I think it only fair that you tell us now who you are."

Kirk and the others, fascinated by Spock's explanation, watched the half-Promethean squat on an empty chair.

"I am Taras Tarquin," he said quietly. "And I can arrange for you to purchase the hostages."

The noise of the rec deck covered the startled exclamations of the group.

"Of course we'll go. But I'll go instead of Uhura," Kirk said, as soon as Taras Tarquin had left them alone to discuss the offer.

"Now, wait a minute, Captain." Uhura stood up. "He asked for Spock and me."

"It might be dangerous."

"Yes, it might. But it might be more dangerous to ignore their instructions."

Kirk sighed. Before he could frame a reply, however, Uhura went on.

"In any case, you said yourself there's no need to follow strict Starfleet regulations. So, since no one here is giving orders, I've been invited, and I'm going."

"In any case, Captain," Spock interrupted their discussion, "the risks in this situation will have to be accessed by each of us on our own, since we are all technically civilians at this time. And if Uhura wishes to accept this invitation—"

"I do," Uhura said quickly.

"—then I think that is how we must proceed." There was a pause, during which Kirk scowled. "On the other hand," Spock went on, "I do not believe we should take this question of independence too far. After all, every good expedition has a leader, and I think we can all agree that Captain Kirk is the best there is."

Kirk looked up at him, glad to have the initiative back.

"Therefore, I think perhaps if you truly have an objection, Captain, perhaps we should reconsider."

"No. I'm afraid you're right," Kirk sighed. "If he has asked for a meeting with Uhura, for whatever reason, I suppose we have to go along. Be careful."

"Over the years," Uhura said to Kirk, "I have been in more dangerous situations. Please don't worry."

"Are you saying I'm being too protective?"

"You are."

"All right. Just keep your communicator open. We'll be aboard the ship if you need us."

Resigned, Kirk promised himself not to worry. He rose and looked around. Tarquin was lingering on the edge of the room, watching them. Kirk nodded an agreement, and Tarquin turned and scuttled away. Kirk took Spock aside and spoke to him in a low voice.

"I could understand that this Maldari wants you to be a go-between. Vulcans have an exceptional reputation for being straightforward and trustworthy. But why do you think he wants Uhura?" Kirk said.

Spock shrugged. "Possibly he feels less threatened by a woman. Or perhaps he saw her on the dance floor earlier, and is intrigued."

Kirk and McCoy, Barbara, Chekov, and Scotty all watched Spock and Uhura leave the rec deck, then headed back for the *Plush Princess* to wait. As they did, Kirk found himself wondering for the umpteenth time if Mr. Spock didn't possess something of a human being's sense of humor after all.

Spock and Uhura took the turbolift to the spacedock floor. Following Tarquin's instructions, they found an ancient shuttle waiting on a deserted platform, a marked contrast to the busy docks around them.

Tarquin was standing near several freight sleds. His smile, even more than his unusually straight teeth, was a mark of his human ancestry.

"Mr. Spock, I'm so glad you have decided to negotiate. We will attempt to effect a speedy return of your fellow officers." He looked around. "You are alone?"

"As you requested. May I ask who you represent?"

"Oh, I do not wish to present myself so formally. I do not wish to mislead you. I am simply a Beta Promethean with the desire to see our two civilizations become closer. Or at least not drift dangerously apart."

"You do not represent the government?"

"The Ruling Family? Oh, no. One has to be born into that tribe to have an official position."

"Or the Clerics?"

"The Shrewdest Ones, we call them. At least that's the closest translation in your language. I'm afraid not. They are much too dogmatic for my tastes. For example, did you know"—he looked at Uhura—"that women do not have first names on Beta Prometheus? They are allowed only the last name of their fathers, and later their husbands. Don't you find it characteristic of religions that women are second-class citizens?"

"We Vulcans do not—"

"Of course. I mean on Earth. That is why I asked you to come, Miss Uhura. You will not be a threat to them."

"Them?" she asked.

"The ones I represent. Or perhaps that is too strong a word. I do not want you to think that I speak for them, only that I can speak to them, you see. Without me or someone like me, it is unlikely you will be able to do even that."

"Then you represent . . . ?"

"Yes. The pirates."

"Now we're getting somewhere," Uhura said enthusiastically.

"I would not say that. These Beta Prometheans are very different from Federation citizens. They are very independent."

"Taras, we Federation citizens, as you say, actually pride ourselves on our independence. We elect representatives to the Federation Council, and our rights are—"

"Of course. I did not mean to insult you. The Federation is the pride of the galaxy. I aspire to membership for my own planet, even while for reasons of self-interest some Prometheans do not. I meant to say that most Beta Prometheans, in this case the crew of the *Sundew* who have arrested your fellow officers, do not consider laws, rules, or regulations something which they need to follow, except as it benefits them. How best to explain this? With the exception of the Shrewdest Ones, to which the average Beta Promethean pays only the slightest lip service, there is no feeling that cooperation among the members of the community would lead to a better life for all. It's more along the lines of every man for himself."

"That is very plain," Spock said.

"These men had no idea that they would set off such an intergalactic furor when they captured the Federation officers."

"In other words," Spock pressed on, "these pirates are holding out for something they want."

"I suppose that's so."

"What? What do they want?"

"That is something they would like to tell you themselves."

"Good. Let us go at once."

"I'm afraid it is not quite that simple. Only one of you may go. Miss Uhura."

Spock frowned. "I can go alone if you like, or you can take us both, but I will not—"

"It is the Only Way. That is a Promethean expression, rich in meaning. It refers to our religion, as well as a host of other things we do, rather blindly if you ask me. In this case, you must take me literally. They will allow only one, and to be perfectly honest, they would be afraid of a Vulcan. They fear the powers of your mind, which to them seems almost mystical. They are a primitive people, as you may know, and have very little experience with sophisticated telepaths."

"We are not exactly telepaths."

"The famous Vulcan mind-meld. It frightens them. As I said, they are not sophisticated. Miss Uhura only, please. I will see that no harm comes to her."

There was a tick of silence. Taras looked around and,

apparently in an effort to give Spock time to think about this, made small talk.

"This dock is seldom used. It is too small for the containers and shuttles now being operated out of this starbase. Alas, my own transport is, as you can see, of a much more ancient vintage. It is serviceable, however, and perfectly safe."

"Uhura, you do not have to—" Spock began.

"It's all right, Mr. Spock. This is what we came for." She turned to Taras. "Which way do we go?"

"I must make a few small requests first. You will leave your phaser behind. I must assume you are carrying one, even though I cannot see it. I understand you were all part of the great Starfleet in years past."

Uhura took her phaser out from the folds of her civilian jumpsuit, and gave it to Spock.

"And your communicator."

"I must protest—" Spock began.

"I'm afraid they would insist. You will possibly be allowed directly into their sanctum, and could somehow transcribe that location over your communicator. Also this." He pointed at the Universal Translator on her tunic.

"This is my translator. I won't understand what the Prometheans are saying without it."

"I shall be your translator."

Uhura took it off and handed it to Spock.

"I suppose you will want my clothes next."

"No, thank you. It is true there are cultures out here so primitive their women are not allowed to wear any. In the case of Beta Prometheus, the opposite is true. Women must be well covered. Your modest dress will do. Shall we go?"

"Taras," Mr. Spock said sternly. "I'm going to hold you personally responsible for Uhura's safety. She is an emissary, and is not to become a hostage with the others. If anything should happen to her, I will blame you."

"That is uncharacteristically dramatic for a Vulcan, I believe. But then I understand you are part human."

"I mean what I say, Taras. Uhura is to be kept safe at all times, and returned in less than three hours, or I personally will come after you."

"I understand, Mr. Spock. I think perhaps we can trust the pirates to behave in their own self-interest, and in this case it is to communicate with you through Miss Uhura. I shall return her here as soon as I am able." He then led Uhura up a short platform, and Spock saw them disappear into the shuttle. After a few minutes, it rose up and glided across the spacedock toward the big bay doors, disappearing into the traffic of dozens of larger starships.

Uhura felt the sensation of spaceflight. She had no idea where she was, since there were no viewports in the shuttle. She sat stiffly, aware of the shuttle's increasing thrust, then its deceleration, and finally felt it settle straight down. She heard the low hum of the ancient engines fade away. Tarquin took her by the elbow and guided her back out the door and across a short space. Under her feet there was only hard rock, dust, and dirt. Finally she was led through a door.

The light was yellow and streaked inside the room. She was surrounded by half a dozen Beta Prometheans, and saw at once the difference between the full-blooded versions and Taras. The others had ugly, sharp, angular teeth jutting in different directions, and a mottled gray skin color, where his was pale. Clearly Taras was only a minor figure among these pirates, she observed, because he was now off to the side and not part of the leader's group. The leader and several of his cohorts were animatedly discussing her among themselves.

Then the Promethean who looked to be the leader came forward, and said something to her in a harsh, guttural language.

"He is introducing himself to you," Taras said from the side. "His name is Maldari, and he is—was—the captain of the *Sundew*. That's the starship that captured the officers."

More talk from the captain.

"He wants to know if you represent the Federation."

"Tell him I represent the *Plush Princess*. James T. Kirk, commanding."

The captain then spoke several long sentences.

"He says you probably want to know if your spies are all right. He wants you to know that they are. They are in a safe place, and all are healthy. He will release them, provided you agree to a number of things. Nod, smile, say yes."

Uhura did. "What do they want?" she said, getting abruptly to the point, feeling that she ought to match bad manners to bad manners.

Taras spoke aloud to Maldari in their language. Maldari answered, there were a few more exchanges, and Taras turned to Uhura.

"They want weapons. 'Powerful Starfleet weapons' is the way they put it."

"There is a Federation directive against selling or even giving away any weapons to nonmembers of the U.F.P."

"They claim the weapons they want are for trade. They deal in dilithium and odd goods most of the time, but the dilithium trading is tightly controlled by the Ruling Family, and their share of the profits is minor. They know they can get a fortune for Starfleet-type weapons, even hand phasers, throughout the galaxy."

"Not to mention using them themselves to kidnap more Starfleet officers."

Taras shrugged.

"Tell them I'll take their demands back to Captain Kirk."

Taras said a few words to Maldari.

"Now tell them that I have to see Captain Sulu and his crew."

There was a pause.

"They are not being held here," Taras said. "This is a fairly uninhabited moon on the far side of BP 1. The crew is in a prison in Archnos. It's quite a way from here."

"Tell them," she repeated.

Taras sighed. "All right," he said.

Then he rattled some more to Maldari. Maldari angrily shouted back. Taras patiently spoke some more. He nodded, indicating Uhura. Maldari stepped forward and came within a foot of Uhura. She could see his brown teeth and his smile, though what exactly a smile indicated among these people, she didn't know. She smelled a rancidness about him. Bathing, she thought, has got to be exported. But she held her ground. Maldari spoke directly to her.

"He says you should take his word for their safety. You cannot make any demands."

"It's not a demand. I want to see them, or I cannot report that they are safe. If I cannot report that they are safe, Captain Kirk will not take your offer seriously. How do we know you even have them?"

Taras hesitated before he translated. When he did, Maldari stared at Uhura.

"Now tell him that the Federation will never ransom the hostages, because it is the strict policy of the Federation not to encourage blackmail. But Captain Kirk has been known to bend the rules. Tell him he is staring with his beady eyes at the one person who might be able to do something to help him out of the spot he's got himself in, because eventually Starfleet will blast his ass into the cosmos, and everybody will lose. If he's a trader, he ought to understand. Leave out the beady eyes part."

Taras smiled, and ran off a series of rapid sentences. In response, Maldari frowned. But he turned and spoke to his men. They moved forward quickly. One of them took Uhura's arms and began to lead her away.

"Hey—"

"They have agreed. They will allow you to visit the hostages."

Uhura tried to remain calm.

"You will be transported to Archnos on Beta Prometheus 1. I'll wait for you here."

"You're not coming?"

"It is better if I do not. You may have understood by now that I am an outsider here. My impure blood makes me virtually an outcast. I have been useful to them as an intermediary, but they do not trust me, and I do not know where your friends are being held. Just do as they say." He spoke rapidly to Maldari. "They'll bring you back here shortly."

Uhura was walked across the room. She passed into a corridor, was led out of the building, across a short stretch of hard ground, and pushed into the shuttle. Half a dozen Beta Prometheans climbed aboard with her. The doors clanged shut. She felt the shuttle lift off, and she settled back as comfortably as she could.

Her heart was pounding in her chest. *I know I've been in dicier situations,* she thought. *But I can't remember any others just now.*

Uhura felt the shuttle land. There was an exchange of dialogue between the Prometheans in the shuttle, and the shuttle door opened. She blinked in the harsh sunshine. Before she could look around, her Promethean captors hustled her out of the shuttle and across a stretch of pavement. They plunged her into a dark building and slammed the door shut.

When her eyes adjusted, she found that they were standing in a huge warehouse piled with transport containers. They moved down a corridor of stacked cases, then turned a corner. It was almost a maze, since the transport containers were haphazardly placed. She tried to remember the twists and turns. First right, second left, first left . . . she thought. Finally they came to a door. Two Prometheans were standing guard. Her own guards turned to her and ran their hands all over her clothes and body, a little too enthusiastically, she thought. But she held her temper. Another exchange of the incomprehensible language, and the guards opened the door. Inside, in a low light, she saw a blaze of Starfleet uniforms. She was ushered inside, and the door was closed behind her. Eight Starfleet officers stared at her.

"Uhura!" she heard the voice of the former helmsman of the *Enterprise* shout, and Sulu came striding over, a big smile on his face. "What—? How—?" Then his smile faded. "Don't tell me you've been taken prisoner too," he asked.

"No, Sulu. I've been brought here to make sure you and your people are okay. It's good to see you."

"Can you tell us what is being done about this?" Dr. Hans asked.

"Let me introduce you," Sulu said quickly. "This is Uhura. We served together aboard the *Enterprise*. In spite of these clothes, she is a Starfleet commander."

"Inactive. In fact, I ought to warn you, I'm here unofficially."

"What does that mean?" a gray-haired but young officer asked.

"This is Lieutenant Roose, my communications officer. That's Dr. Hans, medical officer. This is our chief engineer . . ." Sulu quickly rattled off introductions to the eight officers that surrounded them.

"I wish I could answer all your questions. I'm afraid I don't have much to tell you. Basically, the Federation is negotiating with the Beta Promethean Ruling Family. But, in the words of the diplomats, it's going to take time. If they are making any progress, they're not making it public knowledge. But I'm sure they are," she added quickly. The faces around her appeared strained and tired, though she was glad to see that everyone appeared healthy. "Are they treating you all right?"

"We are all in good condition," Sulu said at once. "But they have already executed one officer. And taken the two women somewhere else," Sulu said grimly.

"We know about the officer," Uhura said. "I'm sorry. The women are safe. Sencus and the *Excelsior* crew were able to retrieve them. And we're going to get you out of here."

"What did you mean, you've come unofficially?" Sulu inquired.

"I'm not here on a Starfleet mission. Kirk—"

"Captain Kirk is here?"

"Kirk, Spock, McCoy. Scotty and Chekov. A young helmsman just out of the Academy. And me. We came up here on our own. Don't even have a Starfleet starship. Came in a luxury tub."

The room was quiet. The disappointment was palpable.

"There are three Starfleet Starships standing by, however," she added quickly.

"But the Federation prefers to avoid setting off an intergalactic conflagration," Dr. Hans said quietly. "And they are unwilling to negotiate with blackmailers. So they negotiate without negotiating. And we are caught in this lethargic process."

"I'm sure they're making some progress," Uhura said encouragingly.

Suddenly the door opened and four of the armed guards came in. They took Uhura by the arms and hustled her out.

"Say hello to Captain Kirk," Sulu said, as the door was slammed closed behind her.

Uhura's guards hustled her between the high-stacked transport containers. She counted the turns and memorized them as well as she could. Then she saw a door ahead, and it popped open. She saw a flash of light, and a round, dome-topped building on the horizon. She was hurried through the door and pushed immediately into the waiting shuttle. The hatch closed, and she felt the shuttle lift off.

A Beta Promethean voice spoke. Taras translated.

"He says to tell Captain Kirk that your friends are all right. But to tell him that they will be turned over to the Shrewdest Ones unless he supplies the merchandise we have discussed."

A ten-minute journey brought her back to the dock of the starbase. Taras helped her out onto the dock.

"Here we are," Taras said. Spock was sitting on an unused freight container. He rose and came right over to them.

"You are all right?" he said.

"Fine," she said. "They took me to see Sulu and the crew."

"Excellent news. How are they?"

"They all seem okay. Tired and very tense. Particularly since I couldn't give them much news."

"All right, there is not much more we can do here. We must report back to Captain Kirk. Taras, I want to thank you for making this contact for us. I wish I could say I knew what we shall do, but I do not as yet."

"I am at your service. I shall stay here on 499."

Together they walked across the empty hall and down the corridor. They got into the turbolift.

"Taras," Mr. Spock said. "You are part Beta Promethean. What do you think of all this?"

Taras's usually accommodating face went somber.

"That is difficult to say. These pirates have found themselves with a commodity that will be difficult to barter. They had certainly expected a quick trade of some sort, but they underestimated the position of the Federation. They are now as stuck as you are. If they simply release them, they will look like fools by the standards of a Promethean trader's code."

Spock thought about this. "And you?"

"Me?" Taras said.

"Where, if I may ask, are your allegiances?"

"I am no more than a middleman, Mr. Spock. I am fortunate enough to be able to speak to Maldari and his pirates. I would not say they trust me, but they will communicate with me out of necessity."

"Usually middlemen take a percentage of the profits," Spock said.

"Usually they do." Taras smiled. The door slid open. "Here is my level. Please let me know how you wish to proceed. I will be on the rec deck." And the door slid shut between them.

"Now we know he isn't in this out of loyalty to his human ancestry," Uhura said.

"No, he is not," Spock said. "I suspected that. I wanted to be clear on where we stand."

"And where is that?" Uhura asked.

"We cannot trust anyone," Spock said.

"There's one thing I didn't tell you, however, Mr. Spock," Uhura said as the crew of the *Plush Princess* gathered on the lounge deck. "I got a glimpse of the building. I didn't want to say so in front of Taras, because I wasn't sure he ought to know that."

"Excellent reasoning, Uhura. Do you think you could identify it?"

"If I saw that side of the building again, I might be able to recognize it. It depends on how many buildings look alike on Beta Prometheus. But there's a few other things. When I was going in, I managed to look up. The next highest building behind the warehouse had a domed roof of some sort."

"That's one of their Conclave Halls. They're religious buildings. There are quite a few of them. Still, that is useful."

"And coming out, I did the same thing. I tried to take a bearing. The only thing I could see was a tall tower."

"You mean, like a tall building, a skyscraper?" Kirk asked.

"No, some kind of communications tower. Very narrow, and only antennas at the top. It was the tallest thing by far on the horizon, facing that way. It was about thirty degrees to the left of straight ahead. That's all I saw, I'm afraid. It's not much."

"On the contrary," Spock said. "It could be a great deal, as any good navigator knows. Correct, Mr. Chekov?"

"Correct, Mr. Spock." Chekov smiled at Uhura. "Vith any two points, I ought to be able to plot the third. It is a simple question of geometry. I'd bet ve could now find the prison vhen ve need to."

"Many Klingons," Sencus said evenly, "certainly would like to see tensions escalate between the Federation and Beta Prometheus." Kirk and Spock sat quietly on the bridge of the *Excelsior,* listening to Sencus. "It is undoubtedly the same political faction which last year was behind the Gorkon assassination and against the peace process. The Clerics have a different agenda. They want to replace the Ruling Family and install a completely theocratic state, with themselves at the head. Anything that weakens the family could encourage this. Thus for the time being these two factions have found a common cause, much to the regret of the Ruling Family, which is under increasing pressure from the right. The family could mitigate the growing resentment by allowing more of the dilithium profits to filter through to society, but capitalism like that goes hand in hand with democracy and freedom, which could in turn seriously erode the Ruling Family's hold on power.

"Also, the Ruling Family doesn't know if they could force the pirates to behave without sending government troops in. That could push public opinion in favor of the Clerics. Thus the pirates find themselves in an untenable position. We cannot offer them the one thing they would like, because it would be giving in to blackmail. However, I think now that had I paid their ransom at once, a young cadet may not have been murdered under my command."

Sencus sank into silence. Kirk glanced around, but the *Excelsior* was in dock and the bridge was deserted but for the three of them.

"As I see it, then," Kirk said, "we have very little choice if we want to effect Sulu's release. We have to give them what they want."

"Selling or trading weapons is a direct violation of the Prime Directive, Captain," Spock said. "The Federation simply will not condone such a thing, under any conditions."

"That's right," Kirk said. "They won't. But we don't represent the Federation any longer." Kirk ironically touched his civilian clothes. "And I don't see that we have any choice. The Federation is paralyzed. Hell, the Beta Promethean Ruling Family is paralyzed. As long as war doesn't break out, these diplomats can pat themselves on the back and assure themselves that they're doing a good job. But our friend and his fellow officers can't stand a stalemate forever. I know we're breaking Federation regulations, but there's nothing else I can think of. Before we put our lives and those of the hostages in danger with a frontal assault, I'd like to try this. We'll get what they want—I have an idea about that—and we'll arrange for the exchange." Kirk rose and nodded to Sencus. Then he and Spock left the *Excelsior*.

"It, ah, won't take all of us, of course. I'd very much like you to stay on the starbase, Barbara." The conspirators were gathered in the aft space lounge.

Barbara looked up, surprised. "I'm in. I've always been in. I signed on for the voyage and I'm not bailing out on you now. Jim, this is just you trying to protect me because—"

"No, this is common sense. We're circumventing the Federation's negotiations and acting without authority from

Starfleet. The six of us have already had successful careers, which are behind us. We don't have nearly as much to lose as you do. We'll look like idiots if it fails. If it succeeds we'll probably be court-martialed. I suppose we'll deal with that when it happens. My guess is that at the very least we'll all be ignominiously thrown out of Starfleet. You, on the other hand, have your whole career ahead of you. You've been a big help, and we appreciate it, but we don't really need you for the rest, and I for one would feel much better if we parted ways now. You're asking me to ruin your career, and I don't think I'd like to do that."

It was very quiet when Kirk finished. He was uncomfortable, but he had to say it. Barbara stood up resolutely.

"I'll tell you what," she said. "If you'll sleep on it tonight, I'll go quietly in the morning, if you still want me to."

"Fair enough," Kirk said. "For now, I think Mr. Spock and Uhura ought to go and seek out Mr. Taras Tarquin, and arrange a specific time and place for the exchange. Make sure he understands that there is to be no publicity. I'll leave all that to you," Kirk finished, nodding at Mr. Spock and Uhura.

"All right, Captain," Spock said. He and Uhura rose to go and seek out their contact on the starbase.

Kirk turned to McCoy.

"Let's you and I go over to the starbase. We'll need to access the Memory Alpha library to find some weaponry these pirates will love."

"They're not gonna accept pictures and technical specifications, Jim," McCoy said, puzzled.

"No, but a bunch of high-ranking Starfleet officers like us ought to be able to commandeer whatever we need. What do you think, Mr. Scott?"

Scott, who had been listening from a comfortable chair, stirred. "It's very possible. But I suppose you don't want to walk right in to the chief of starbase operations and request a supply of powerful weapons for the purpose of creating a ransom for the hostages."

"I don't," Kirk said.

"Well, then," Scotty mused, "there's a lot of Starfleet

officers on 499. I'll just have to find one who'll help us out. And keep his mouth shut."

Scotty hurried away.

Shortly Kirk and Bones were rummaging through the starbase library. Kirk foraged in the depths of the information catalogues until he found what he was looking for, then followed that trail. Used to making command decisions but quite unused to the technical minutiae of the databanks— which for the most part he had always left up to his science officer, navigator, and helmsman—it took a good bit of investigation and discovery. Finally he appeared satisfied.

"I think I've found what I'm looking for," he said cautiously to McCoy, who had been watching over his shoulder for some time. "Look at these."

They flipped through screen after screen of futuristic weapons, from small handheld devices to large shoulder cannons that required backpacks as power sources. They had ranges up to hundreds of yards, and carried charges that would last for long periods of time. They had laser sights and customized grips, and looked as if they were made of impervious titanium. Numerous controls testified to the variety of their fire areas, and many featured built-in computer functions to access range, load, and power instantly and accurately in the field. Most were sleekly designed, and some strapped onto the user's arm for steadiness.

Bones studied the catalogue and smiled. "Perfect," he said. "You old horse trader you." Then he wandered off in idle search of something more interesting to read than weaponry catalogues. Kirk turned back to the screen and began copying notations into his personal tricorder. It took him almost half an hour to put together the specifications he wanted. After that he disconnected from Memory Alpha library, closed down the terminal, and went in search of McCoy, who had settled down to read an article he had found on the curative properties of some rare, alien vegetation.

Kirk looked over his shoulder for a moment, and saw fields of mushrooms in a golden sunlight.

"What's that stuff?" he asked. "Looks good."

"Toadstools. They're native to Cytrops 469, a planet in the Deuteronimous system."

"They look awfully tasty. I've always liked mushrooms. They're not poisonous, are they? I suppose if they're poisonous, the inhabitants of that planet have to stay away."

"They're not poisonous; they *are* the inhabitants of that planet. They have a fully developed sonar language of over a hundred and forty thousand words and conceptual ideas, as well as telepathic abilities. Starfleet has held several hyperspace conversations with them, and an exploratory voyage is planned for the next five years."

"Oh," Kirk said, looking at the squat mushroom plants he had gastronomically admired. "I don't think I'll order mushrooms for a while," he said.

Spock and Uhura found Taras Tarquin in a shadowy corner of the recreation deck and waved when they entered the room.

"Mr. Spock, what can I do for you?"

"We have decided to try to make a deal with this Maldari and his crew," Spock said quietly. "Where can we talk?"

Tarquin looked around the recreation room, where humans and aliens from that corner of the universe were coming and going.

"I doubt if anyone could eavesdrop on us here," he said.

"I would rather that too many people do not see us together. No offense meant."

Taras smiled. "Follow me." He led them out of the room and along the corridor until they came to a small turbolift. They rode it up to a high floor, got out, and followed a smaller corridor nearly to the end. He led them through an archway, and they found themselves in a forward observation lounge that was deserted.

"It is unlikely that we will be disturbed here, especially at this time of the evening cycle," Tarquin said as he indicated chairs for the two of them and sat on a stool.

"You seem to know all the quiet spots on the starbase, Mr. Tarquin," Spock said.

"I am here often. I trade throughout this section of the

galaxy. I like to come here sometimes, as it is usually deserted but the viewport is enormous. That is the Magellus cluster overhead. Isn't it beautiful? Well, what shall I tell them?"

"We are prepared to provide what they want in exchange for the eight Starfleet officers."

"Excellent," Tarquin said.

"But let me make this, as an Earth statesman once said, perfectly clear. This is not a Starfleet matter. I do not represent the Federation or the Starfleet in any way. They have no idea we are negotiating with you. We are not going to tell them, and if you or the people you represent do, the deal is off, for surely they would interfere. We are well aware that we are acting illegitimately, and so are you. This is a straight trade, from one private party to another. We will supply, shall we say, eight transport containers of the goods they have specified, and we will turn them over to them in exchange for the eight Starfleet officers they are holding."

"Nine containers."

"I think eight ought to be . . . oh, I see. I think we have stumbled upon your commission. I was wondering when we would come to that."

"Mr. Spock, please believe me, I have the best of intentions here. My mother was a citizen of your Federation. My loyalty is unquestioned. It is only that I have taken very large risks, and I am after all, by profession, a trader. I believe this is the simplest way to handle the small matter."

"All right. Nine. And the exchange must happen tomorrow morning. Speed is of the essence."

"That is very sudden. I have to contact—"

"You will do it. If you are worth your commission."

"Very well."

"We ought to make the exchange in a reasonably private place."

"I have a suggestion about that," Tarquin said. "There is a moon orbiting Beta Prometheus 3. No farther from here than the principal planet, but uninhabited, a windy and inhospitable place, and you can make the exchange there. I will give you the coordinates, and the exact time."

"Early tomorrow morning."

"As you wish. And may I say that I think you are doing the right thing, Mr. Spock. Only you must be careful."

"You do not have to warn me that Maldari is not an honorable man."

"Good. We know who we are dealing with. Yet they have no desire to hang on to the hostages, of that I am positive. For them it is becoming more and more like holding a Berengarian dragon by the tail. But you must understand: the Prometheans prize wheeling and dealing above all. And not honestly, as you say. If they can best you in a trade, they feel you are a fool. Caveat emptor, I believe you call it."

"Let the buyer beware."

"Something like that. I tell you, Mr. Spock, they have a saying. *Grog optoman, nokt ingo.* Roughly translated, it means, 'Fool an enemy, trick a fool.' They have a very different system of ethics, or morality, altogether. It is simply a cultural difference. They believe the people of the Federation planets, especially the Earth, are fools to attempt to trade value for value. I would recommend that you be sure they have the goods to supply before you proceed. Now, if you will excuse me, I have to get into contact with the other side. That is not always easy. Look for a message on your yacht within several hours." Taras Tarquin nodded politely at Uhura, and scuttled out of the observation deck.

Spock and Uhura waited a few minutes after he had gone, then left the room.

Kirk and McCoy met Scotty on level twenty-four, near the inner shaft of the starbase. It was a room devoted principally to one of the starbase synthesizers, but at this late hour it was closed. The doors were shut. Great diagonal stripes and the words AUTHORIZED STARFLEET PERSONNEL ONLY formed an intimidating barrier. When Kirk and McCoy rounded the corridor and arrived at the meeting place, Scotty was waiting with a familiar figure.

"You remember Garth Flanagan, James," Scott said. "And this is medical officer Leonard McCoy." Flanagan and McCoy shook hands. "Flanny just happens to be in charge of starbase supplies." Scotty smiled.

Flanagan pushed a flat card into a slot in the door, and it

swung open. They followed Flanagan into the synthesizer room, and he closed the door behind them.

"My friend has been kind enough to loan us the use of one of his synthesizers," Scott explained to Kirk and McCoy. "I've explained that we're on a private voyage on that little toy the *Plush Princess,* and got a bit far from our home port without realizing just how inadequate her provisions were. We dinna need much."

"Here it is," Flanagan said. "Make whatever use of it you like. There won't be a record, as I've shut off the data transmitter. I'll turn it on again when I come to work in the morning."

"You're a good lad, Flanny," Scott said. "You always were."

"Well, it's almost as good to see an old countryman as it would be to see the heather again."

"Aye, I've got plenty around my place. When you're finished playing the bureaucrat out here, you'll have ta come by. I'll owe you a drink."

"I'll be collecting, dinna you worry. I'll be leavin' now. Don't leave a mess. There's plenty of transport containers and if you use that antigravity sled over in the corner, you ought to be able to move your supplies out of here and back to your ship. As for me, I dinna see you tonight." He waved and went out the door. The three conspirators waited until the door shut firmly behind him.

"Scotty, you sly old dog," McCoy said.

"Comin' from you, Doctor, I take that as a compliment. You can travel the galaxy over, but there's nothing like a countryman for loyalty, I always say. Now, Captain, if you have the specifications for what you want, let's get started. It may take us several hours." His experienced hands flew over the panels on the face of the synthesizer, and the console's lights began to respond. "Where's your shopping list?" he said.

Some time after Mr. Spock and Uhura arrived back on the *Princess* and reported to the bridge, a message came to them on a private frequency.

"Mr. Spock," Uhura said from her station. "I have a set of

coordinates coming in from Taras Tarquin. No message, just the location."

"That probably means the exchange has been agreed to. Anything else?"

"Wait a minute. Here's a time . . . 0500 hours. That's all it says."

"All right. The time and the place. There is our confirmation. Let us hope we have something to trade when we get there."

An hour and a half later Scotty shut down the synthesizer, while Kirk and McCoy manipulated the last transport container onto the antigravity sled. The whole load looked like it would fill a good-sized shuttle, which was what they were going to need to transport it onto the *Princess*.

McCoy slipped the last transport container that was loaded with weapons into place, then stood back and brushed his hands together. "Now what, Jim?" he said. "Do we just walk out of here with all this stuff?"

Kirk maneuvered the antigravity sled over to the double doors. He smiled at McCoy.

"That's exactly what we do. Walk out with it all."

Scotty and McCoy smiled at Kirk. McCoy shook his head and laughed. "Okay, Jim," he said, and he moved ahead to open the double doors.

They walked the twenty-foot sled out of the synthesizer room, then waited while Scotty shut the doors behind them. Then he took up the lead.

"If I've got my directions right," Scotty said, "we ought to be goin' right up this corridor. There's a freight turbolift around the bend, which will take us right up to the spacedock freight port. There's plenty of shuttles there."

They maneuvered the huge sled into the corridor and nudged it along until they came to the big bay doors. At that late hour, few people came along, and those who did were uninterested in the three men pushing freight purposely through the corridors of 499. They were alone in the lift. But when they stepped onto the freight dock at the edge of the enormous, airy spacedock where the dozen Starfleet Starships and assorted smaller vessels floated, it was a different story. The twenty-four-hour spaceport was busy with activity. Shuttles flew back and forth across the big open area and out to the Starships. Though the evening-cycle crew was not as large as the day-cycle, it was just as busy. A number of Starfleet personnel were there. Kirk looked around and spotted a tall, young African in a Starfleet uniform who looked like he was in charge. He walked over to him.

"Excuse me, I'm James T. Kirk, from the—"

"*U.S.S. Enterprise.* This is a pleasure, Admiral. I'm Deck Officer B'huto."

"Actually, I'm not an admir—"

"If there's anything I can do for you, don't hesitate to ask. Sorry, what were you saying?"

"Uh, oh, nothing. I was just wondering if we could borrow a shuttle. Just for a few minutes. We've got some supplies to take over to our, ah, temporary transportation. My chief engineering officer is an outstanding shuttle man, so we wouldn't—"

"I wouldn't hear of it, sir."

"But—"

"We'll take it over. I'll have my men make it their highest priority."

"Oh. Well, thanks, but I wouldn't want you to go to that much trouble. It's only a load of, oh, this and that, you know. For the trip home. Nothing important, we can handle it. Got it all loaded on the antigravity sled and Scott is an outstanding shuttle pilot."

"The chief of operations here would kill me if I made you take that by yourselves. Is that it?"

"That's it. One sled. It's no problem, we could—"

"Here we are. Officers Handler and A'ron, the best shuttle pilots on 499. This is Admiral James T. Kirk. Please take him and his crew and their luggage over to their ship at once."

"Right this way, Admiral," one of the young men said.

"Thank you, Mr. B'huto, you've been very kind," Kirk said to the officer.

"Anytime. Anything I can do for you, sir, just let me know."

"Thanks. See you later," Kirk said, and followed the two shuttle pilots.

As they approached Scotty and McCoy, the men stood up nervously.

"Is this yours?" one of the pilots asked.

"Yes, yes it is. Everything on this sled. We're on the *Plush Princess,* it's that star yacht in the far corner of spacedock."

"All right. I'll get a shuttle." And he walked over to a parked shuttle at the edge of the floor that overhung the spacedock.

"I've got us a ride," Kirk said to Scotty and McCoy, who stared at him. "Very kind of them. Rolled out the red carpet for an old Starfleet admiral." He smiled at them. "Be on board in a minute."

Scotty looked at Kirk with wide eyes, but was speechless. McCoy kept glancing at the transport containers, but didn't say anything either. The pilots backed the shuttle up to the sled, stopping it only inches away. A back bay door opened. Kirk tipped the sled up and slid it into the shuttle. Then he climbed in after it. He waved at Scotty and McCoy, still standing on the deck.

Scotty and McCoy scrambled in and the back bay doors slid closed behind them. In moments they saw the *Princess* off the starboard viewport. Then they heard the pilot's voice.

"Princess, open your doors, please, we have a delivery."

They heard Chekov's voice make a response; then a door on the rear of the saucer slid open. The shuttle driver neatly turned the shuttle in a 180-degree arc, then backed up until they were just touching the *Princess.*

"There you are, Admiral. Hope that didn't take too long."

"Fine, thank you. Just fine." Kirk got out and pulled the sled with him. Scotty and McCoy jumped out behind it. The shuttle doors closed and the shuttle shot off across the spacedock, back to the freight deck. McCoy turned to Kirk.

"Admiral?" he said, his eyes opened wide.

"They had me confused with my former self. I didn't want to disappoint them. They probably don't get many real admirals on the freight deck."

"Or any phony ones either," Scotty said with a chuckle.

"Well, we've got weapons to trade. Let's go see if Mr. Spock is back."

"We've made contact with the crew of the *Sundew*," Barbara said quietly, as she sat with her back to the bar in a dark corner of the rec deck. The man facing her sat back in the shadows.

"You have?!" he said.

"Kirk plans to make a trade for the hostages. He's worried that another hostage will be executed tomorrow. And there's always the danger that the hostages could be moved, or security around them might be increased. He is not a patient man."

"Where? When?"

"I don't know yet. Early tomorrow, I would imagine."

"Will you be going?"

"Yes. Kirk doesn't want me to, but I'll talk him into it. I'll leave a message on your terminal. I'd better get back now, I don't want to be away too long or somebody will suspect something. Wait at least ten minutes before you leave."

After this confidential talk with her contact, Barbara made her way back to the *Princess*.

The crew held a short conference in the aft space lounge, and briefly checked the starship's equipment. Then the little group broke up for the night.

Spock was climbing the ladder to his upper berth when Barbara came into their cabin.

"Jim, I'd like to talk to you," she said quietly.

Spock looked down at her. He looked over at Kirk, who had been staring out the viewport.

"Perhaps I will go up to the lounge deck and discuss *the weather* with Dr. McCoy," he said. He climbed back down the ladder and headed out the hatchway.

"Mr. Spock, I may be new to deep space," Barbara said, "but as there isn't any atmosphere up here, there isn't any weather to speak of, is there?"

"No, I suppose that is true. On the other hand, Dr. McCoy is not very good at small talk, so I doubt it will matter. Good evening." He left the cabin.

Kirk hadn't been alone with Barbara since the trip had begun. He had consciously put his original feelings for her out of his mind. He had wanted to make sure that his judgment wasn't impaired by their relationship. He'd seen that happen too often with other officers. Heck, he'd had it happen to him on occasion, although only when under a chemical or biological influence engendered in him by some alien life force. He sensed that she, too, had kept her distance, both physically and psychologically.

Now there was nowhere for him to go in the small cabin. He inhaled her fragrance, remembering it clearly from their encounters in San Francisco. He didn't know what to say, so he waited cautiously for her to speak.

"Jim, you're going to need a good pilot. You don't have one, and you can't get one from Starfleet or Starbase 499 without tipping your hand. You've got to take me."

"Scotty is an excellent pilot."

"So is Chekov. He taught me a lot coming out here. But you need Scotty in the engine room and the transporter room. You can't have him running back and forth, not in such a delicate situation. Who knows what's going to happen when we get out to that moon? And you know that Chekov can't handle both duties at once, without wasting time. Time that might be precious."

"I've been on the helm before. I didn't always sit and give orders."

"I'm sure you were a hell of a pilot. Twenty-five years ago."

Kirk frowned.

"I'm sorry, Jim. I didn't mean that as an insult. But you haven't handled the helm directly in a long time, and you've never handled the *Princess.* Tomorrow's voyage isn't the time to get the feel of her. Why risk additional problems?"

"I understand how you feel, Barbara. And I greatly appreciate your loyalty. But I won't jeopardize your whole career. We'll manage." He looked out the viewport, unable to look directly at her.

"Tell me something," Barbara said quietly. "You said you have nothing to lose. But that's not true. If I have my future,

you have your past. Your reputation. You are an icon of
Starfleet, and yes, you have on occasion done things not
exactly by the book. You're the commander who stands for
self-reliance and quick thinking. You're the smart cadet who
beat the *Kobayashi Maru* scenario. But you and I both know
this is different. This might very well be seen as arrogant
self-interest. You could jeopardize the peace you helped
bring about yourself. And you're doing it for one man. A
man who knew when he signed on with the Starfleet
twenty-six years ago that he might risk his life someday. His
loyalty is to Starfleet. Where's yours? Why are you doing
this?"

Kirk thought about this for a very long time. Finally he
was ready to answer her.

"I have a great feeling for the Federation and the Starfleet.
I always will. I'm loyal to the concepts they stand for, the
democracy, the freedom, the greater good of the community. I served for over twenty-five years not just for the
adventure and the excitement, but because I wanted to help
create the very glory, the future glory, that our explorations
would lead to. But I have a greater loyalty, and that's to one
man. To my old helmsman. He stood by me for a lot of those
years, and I'm going to stand by him now. I can't think of
anything else. I suppose that's what this boils down to for
me. I was never a man for the big picture. I was a failure as
an admiral, I'd be a failure as a politician and a diplomat. I
know I'm hardheaded. I know I sometimes have narrow
vision. But that's me. Getting Sulu out of there is all I can
think of. It's the only road that makes sense to me. Sulu is
real, and the concept of the Federation losing one of its
carefully cultivated intergalactic relationships isn't real to
me. I can only take this one step at a time. I'll admit that I
came up here partially for the adventure of it. Maybe it was
the excuse I was looking for to get back at the conn of a
Starship, to get back into deep space. But today when I saw
him, without the broad smile I remembered so well, the
whole thing became so simple. I'm going to get him out, and
if I can't think of a way to do it legally, I'm going to do it
illegally."

Barbara looked at him.

"Thanks," she said.

"For what? You know I don't want you going with us."

"For being so honest. Now let me tell you about my reasons," she said. She moved away from him and sat on the bed.

"I've come this far. If I have to quit now, I'll be mortified. I can go back a disgrace, but I can't go back a failure. If I stay, I'm one of you. One of seven. If I go, I'm on my own. My fellow cadets will know that I bailed out. You talk about loyalty. Well, I don't want to be smart. I don't want to be political. I just want to be loyal, too. To you and to the mission. This is my first assignment, unauthorized as it is. It may be unorthodox. Hell, we know it's probably going to end up being downright illegal. But I piloted the *Princess* out here, and I want to pilot her back."

"I appreciate that, Barbara. I really do. I know you'll be disappointed, but I won't drag a young officer into a wild, renegade plan like this. You'll have to stay on Starbase 499 while we're gone."

Barbara leaned against the bulkhead. Kirk wondered if it was a purposefully provocative pose. Her next words convinced him that it was.

"If you dump me here, you won't see me again."

Kirk looked at her. "I'll be lost without you. But I have to put my feelings for you aside. You know that. It's just not good leadership."

Barbara sighed. She stood up and walked to the door. Then she turned around.

"Last shot. I'm sorry to have to do this to you, James." She looked straight at him and something about her expression changed. He saw a Barbara he hadn't seen before. "If you dump me, I'm going straight to Starfleet and tell them your plans. You know they'll interfere. There's not a chance in hell they'll let you move one inch without their supervision."

Kirk's jaw tightened. "You wouldn't do that."

"I would. I'm afraid I never told you everything about myself, Jim. I'm also strong-minded."

"This is blackmail."

"That's right. And the only way you can follow through

211

with your plans is in secret. So I'm your hostage. Take me with you, or don't go."

"Barbara—"

"No deals. What do you say?"

A cold air hung between them.

"I guess I have no choice," he finally said.

She smiled. "Good. And now that we've got that out of the way, we don't have to bring it up again. I'm in for the duration. The crew will think you caved, but don't worry, I won't brag." She turned and started out the hatchway. When she stopped and turned back, Kirk hadn't moved. He was still looking at her.

"Jim, I'm sorry. I guess I'm as strong-minded as you are. Maybe we're a bad match. I hope not."

She smiled, but he didn't return it. She turned away from his quizzical stare. As she disappeared into the corridor he heard her say, "By the way, as long as I'm going, I'll drive."

Day Eight

WHEN THE CREW ROSE the next morning, they gathered in the tiny galley of the yacht and ate a synthesized breakfast. None of the seven had much to say. The air was thick with tension, as they faced an unpredictable rendezvous and none of them had slept easily. In the dawn stillness they moved up to their places on the bridge without being asked.

"Engage thrusters," Kirk said to Barbara's back.

"Thrusters engaged," she said without looking over her shoulder. Barbara guided the star yacht to the rendezvous coordinates.

"Leaving warp drive, Captain," Barbara said after the short voyage.

"Ve have the Promethean moon vithin visual recognition, Captain," Chekov said a few seconds later.

"Put it up on the screen," Kirk said.

The image was like countless others the space travelers had seen. A dry round orb, pockmocked with craters. No clouds or vegetation, hardly even any shadows. The highest peaks of rock would hardly have put a star cruiser in the shade.

"Mr. Spock," Kirk said, "Report?"

"Captain, there is a breathable if thin atmosphere. The only sign of life-forms is low-level vegetation rooted deeply in the planet's crust, and one species of small mammal. The former are not poisonous and the latter not aggressive. They appear to hide during the day and forage for food in the darkness. No recognizable minerals or ore of any value. No dilithium, which accounts for the abandonment of this particular sphere in the Beta Promethean system. A close visual scanning indicates that there are footprints. As there is little wind or water, however, these marks might well last for weeks, even months, and thus could be very old. There are also signs of small-craft landings and launchings. I would suggest that this small moon, because its orbit keeps it on the least hospitable side of Beta Prometheus 3 and thus is seldom in visual range, has become something of a useful port for precisely what we are doing now. Those Promethean traders who wish to keep their transactions secret land here. A smugglers' cove, if you will."

"Thank you, Mr. Spock. Barbara, place us directly over the coordinates we were given, within beaming distance."

"Aye, Captain," she answered.

"Any sign of their ship?" Kirk said.

"Negative, Captain," Spock responded. Not in visual range.

"Uhura?" he asked.

"No, Captain," Uhura responded. "I've been monitoring all frequencies and subspace channels, but there hasn't been any communications yet at all."

"Very well. We'll wait."

"For how long, Jim?" Dr. McCoy said.

"Until our patience runs out, I suppose. Does anyone know what a Promethean's sense of time is? Perhaps we're unconscionably rude by being on time. Anyway, if we have not been sent on some sort of wild-goose chase—or worse—I assume they will want to make the exchange on the surface of the planet. Mr. Spock, if you and Dr. McCoy will accompany me down to the planet's surface, we will speak to this Maldari. I'll call for the transport containers if I think this will go smoothly. Scotty?"

"Aye, Captain?"

"In our absence you are acting captain of the ship."

"Aye, Captain."

"Don't send the containers down unless you hear directly from me."

"Aye, Captain."

"I think you know the drill. I would keep your shields up, weak as they might be, and watch out for any tricks. If you have to pull away for any reason, we'll attempt to rendez-vous at our original spot every hour on the hour."

"Got it, Captain."

After that the crew waited in silence for what seemed like a long time. In reality, not more than five or ten minutes had gone by when Uhura spoke.

"I'm getting something, Captain," she said quietly.

Everyone tensed.

"They have not identified themselves, but the coded frequencies match the ones that Tarquin gave us."

"What are they saying?"

"They're using a code of some sort, not a language. I don't recognize it, but I'll—wait a minute, it's Morse. I'll put it through the Translator. They are asking us to identify ourselves."

"Put me on the air, Uhura. On a coded low frequency that nobody else will overhear."

"Channel open."

"This is Captain James T. Kirk of the starship *Plush Princess*. We are carrying nine transport containers of freight, and would like to trade them for your . . . cargo."

"Do you have the proper coordinates on the moon's surface?" Maldari's voice said as Uhura slipped the coded signal through the voice-equivalent translator.

"We do," Kirk said.

"Beam the containers down there."

"Beam your payment down."

Silence. Finally Uhura whispered, "Nothing, Captain."

Kirk sat in the chill silence without moving a muscle. Finally it paid off. Maldari's guttural voice burst into the bridge.

"Beam yourselves down, Captain, and we will meet you there."

"Agreed." He jumped out of his chair and shot into the turbolift. Spock and McCoy were right behind him.

When the three arrived on the lower deck, Scotty had the transporter ready. They stepped onto the platform and he gave them a thumbs-up sign. A moment later they were standing on the dry rock surface of the lifeless moon, in the center of a valley ringed by low ridges.

They stood there alone for some minutes. McCoy took out a tricorder and aimed it in a circle, reading off its display.

"No signs of life," he said.

They stood in the chill air of the desolate moonscape, lit only by the reflective glow from Beta Prometheus 3 as it loomed in the sky nearby.

Then McCoy read off his tricorder display again. "Something over there." They all looked.

An ancient shuttle, rusted and dented from inferior metals, inferior shields, and too much use, flew down and landed on the far side of the flat area. For a while it just sat there.

Finally a shuttle door opened and several Beta Prometheans climbed out. Kirk and McCoy recognized some of them from the anti-Federation rally. The three watched as the Prometheans scuttled forward until they were only ten yards away. Kirk realized they had covered almost a mile in only a few minutes. *They can sure as hell run fast,* he thought. *It must be their lower center of gravity, and four muscular legs.*

"Kirk?" Maldari said.

"I'm Kirk."

Maldari looked at him. "So, you are the famous Captain Kirk of the *Starship Enterprise.* Your reputation precedes you."

"You must be Maldari. Of the *Sundew.* So does yours, I'm afraid. You have kidnapped Starfleet officers representing the United Federation of Planets. We're here to take them back."

"They were spying!" Maldari shouted. Kirk saw the

others nod their heads. "They were invading Beta Promethean territory in preparation for a full-scale attack on our civilization. This is the way the Federation behaves, everywhere it goes, as if—"

"Why don't we dispense with the propaganda you have picked up from the Klingons. I'm not here representing the Federation or Starfleet. We're here to trade, which is, I understand, your business. We have nine transport containers on our ship, each loaded with Starfleet weapons, and will be glad to beam them down as soon as you can provide eight Starfleet officers."

Maldari's heavily lidded eyes narrowed. But he didn't say anything. Kirk went on.

"I can assure you that Starfleet will not allow this situation to continue indefinitely. In a very short time, they'll send Starships that could force your planet into compliance. As men of vision"—Kirk hoped the shameless flattery wasn't overly obvious—"you and I ought to be able to avoid that. Where are the officers?"

Maldari turned to one of his aides, and nodded his head. The aide turned and scuttled back quickly to the shuttle. He leaned in and said something. Then everybody waited. Kirk and Maldari looked at each other. Spock and McCoy stood patiently.

Finally a second shuttle, slightly larger if just as ancient as the first, glided in and settled on the rocky ground behind the first one. The door opened and Starfleet officers climbed out. From the distance, Kirk counted eight.

Kirk touched his communicator. "Okay, Scotty, beam down the transport containers."

Kirk saw Maldari signal one of his men, and the two shuttles rolled toward them. The containers began materializing next to them. Maldari scuttled over to one of the boxes and opened the lid. He handled a few of the weapons, then turned to Kirk.

"These are very modern weapons."

"That's what you wanted."

"They are difficult to use. We—"

"Look, Maldari. They didn't come with an instruction

manual. And we don't give lessons. Each and every one of them is primed and loaded with liquid neutron energy. Look at them. You want them or not?"

Maldari's helpers had pulled several of them out already, and were admiring them. One sighted a large, complicated-looking gun back toward the Starfleet officers.

"Hey, watch it. These things aren't toys," McCoy shouted.

"Load them up," Maldari called to his aides.

The Prometheans put the weapons back in the transport containers and began maneuvering them into the open shuttles. There were no antigravity sleds, and they lifted each one by hand. But the Prometheans were strong, and the containers disappeared quickly into the shuttles.

Kirk began walking toward the Starfleet officers, Spock and McCoy right behind him. As they did, Kirk touched his communicator again.

"Scotty, prepare to beam up eight officers."

"Jim, there's something funny here," McCoy said. Kirk looked at him and found him studying the tricorder display. "Those officers . . ."

"What?"

"They don't register any life signs."

Kirk picked up the pace again until the three of them were running hard across the rocky moonscape. As they got closer, Kirk slowed down and cursed. "Damn."

He turned to look over his shoulder. The two shuttles were just loading the final containers. As he watched, they closed their doors and sped off, disappearing into the sky behind the moon.

"Robots," Spock said. "Primitive customized robots."

"Damn, damn, damn!" Kirk shouted. "We've been cheated."

"It would appear so," Spock said.

Kirk turned one around and lifted up the Starfleet tunic. He saw the small indentation in the imitation skin and pried out the panel. A tangle of chips and data input terminals was exposed. Kirk frowned. "I should never have trusted these Beta Prometheans. Too much time out of action, I suppose."

"Do not blame yourself, Captain," Spock said. "We did our best. From a mile away, they looked authentic."

"Come on, let's get out of here. And let's bring them along. They might come in handy. Scotty, if you still have a fix on our location, please beam us up. Beam up our eight friends here as well."

A moment later seven humans and eight robots were crowded into the star yacht's transporter room.

"Robots!" Scotty exclaimed. "I'll be damned. Robots."

"I'm afraid so, Mr. Scott." As the other crew members crowded into the hatchway to welcome the returning hostages, Kirk explained what happened on the moon's surface. "I feel like such a fool," he said.

There was a depressed silence, then the humans drifted out of the transport room and back up to the bridge.

"Now where am I going to put these things?" Scotty muttered.

"You know," Barbara said, lingering behind to examine the robots, "these uniforms are pretty authentic, even if the people wearing them are not."

Sulu and his officers sat around the large bare room in their underwear.

"If Starfleet is trying to bluff these pirates," Lieutenant Roose offered, "I wish it were not with strip poker."

"At home we are often naked in the snow," Norquist Svenson offered. Everyone looked at him. "After the sauna. It is most healthy." He shrugged.

Sulu glanced around the room. The officers were tired and tense, the result of their incarceration and the death of Spiros Focus. The lack of sunlight in the sealed room was disorienting, and although there were vents, through which the breathable atmosphere of the planet must have been pumped, the air was stale.

Sulu wished he could have cheered them up, but he had assumed from the beginning that their captors could monitor what they said in their prison. So he couldn't tell them that he had heard the voice of James T. Kirk when they were taken to the rally and displayed. He had looked into the face of a Klingon and seen an extraordinary likeness, in an odd way, to his old captain. He would have laughed at the ridiculous makeup, if he had not been worried it might expose Kirk. Then Uhura had confirmed his presence. He had no idea what the captain had in mind. But he was there on the planet. Something certainly was under way that might lead to their freedom. He wanted to tell the others, but couldn't figure out how under the circumstances. They needed to know that not all Klingons were enemies. That one might come along who was a friend in a foe's clothing.

Dramin arrived at the door to the unused warehouse moments after Maldari and part of his crew had left. He was accompanied by a cohort of Klingon soldiers.

"We're to see the prisoners," Dramin told the young Beta Promethean on guard.

"Shrewdest One," the nervous guard said, "Maldari is not here, and he has left instructions to allow no one near the hostages."

"No one but me, I'm sure you mean."

"In fact, he did not mention . . ."

"My name is Dramin. I was a member of the *Sundew*'s crew. I was the religious officer. It was I who captured the prisoners in the first place."

"Yes, but—"

"What is your name?"

"Mikali, Shrewdest One."

"And Mikali, to whom is your loyalty? To Maldari, or to your Conclave?"

"We are all loyal to the Only Way, of course."

"Then it can certainly do no harm to allow your Conclave leader to interview the prisoners."

"I suppose not." He stepped aside hesitantly and pounded a coded knock on the door. Another guard opened it from the inside.

"Barush, he wants to see the prisoners," Mikali told the inside guard.

"Take us to them at once," Dramin said. "We will not be long."

Mikali looked at the group of Klingons who crowded behind him. "Shrewdest One, aren't you going alone?"

"They are to come with me." Dramin scuttled past Mikali, and the Klingons strode in after him. Inside they were led to the prison room. The guard stood aside.

"Open it," Dramin said. "Did you think we have come to stare at their prison?"

The young Beta Promethean scuttled backwards. "There are eight of them. I am alone. Maldari specifically said—"

"Do you think these miserable disbelievers can escape past a cohort of Klingon soldiers?" Dramin said forcefully, indicating the Klingons that towered behind him. The Klingons brought their weapons up, as if on cue.

"I suppose, if you will take responsibility for them . . ."

"Of course. Open the door."

The Beta Promethean inserted a luminous rod into an almost hidden hole in the wall. Then he used his massive upper-body strength to lift off an iron bar. He pushed and the door swung open.

Though the warehouse was dimly lit, the prison room was nearly black, and the officers blinked at the light. Dramin scuttled in.

"The one who is called Sulu," he said to the men. "Come forward."

Sulu rose up from his seat on the floor.

"I am Captain Hikaru Sulu, of the *Starship Excelsior.*"

"You will come with us," Dramin said.

The other officers rapidly rose to their feet and moved forward, warning Sulu against going. The recent execution of their young cadet was fresh in all their minds. The Klingons, however, growled in their own harsh language, and pointedly waved their weapons.

"Dr. Hans. In my absence you are in charge," Sulu said as he walked forward. Dramin turned and led the way out of the room, and Sulu followed him. The Klingons backed out. The young Beta Promethean guard quickly shut the door behind them, then scuttled after the group.

"I don't think Maldari will like this," he whined. "You'll bring that human back, won't you?"

"Maldari has seven left," Dramin said. And he hurried Sulu out of the building and into a waiting shuttle.

* * *

The mug of thick, steaming liquid was placed in his hands. Sulu looked at it.

"Drink this," Dramin said. "You need nourishment." Sulu looked at the Beta Promethean dressed in black. He was different from the guards who came and went from their prison room. His mottled gray skin was slightly darker, but the principal distinction was his eyes. They shined brighter than the average Beta Promethean. And he blinked less. In fact, he hardly blinked at all. That was odd, Sulu thought.

"Go ahead," Dramin said. "This is cacoa, a drink native to Beta Prometheus. It's the same thing you've been drinking since you arrived here. Just a richer blend. You drink it, and relax. And here is a tunic for you to wear. Put it on. Then I want to talk to you about some political ideas. After all, you're a man of intelligence."

Sulu drank the stuff. It had the same brackish taste of the other Beta Promethean liquids they had been offered. This was richer, and tasted also of something else, though Sulu couldn't have described it precisely. His head felt suddenly lighter. *Alcohol,* he thought. *That's it, there's something in this drink that's an intoxicant.* But even as he thought he shouldn't drink any more if he wanted to maintain his equilibrium, a warm feeling flooded over him, and he took another sip. *It tastes fine, and it makes me feel good,* he thought. *I wonder what he means by political ideas.*

"Commander Sencus, I've got a transmission you'll want to hear." Lieutenant Rand had personally hurried through the *Excelsior* to the Vulcan's quarters. She fiddled with his console as he turned from his desk to look at his viewscreen. "I monitored it from Archnos. It's been translated into the Beta Promethean language, but I'll put it back into English." Static crackled in the room. The viewscreen flickered. Sulu's face appeared, expressionless. He was wearing an ill-fitting Promethean tunic of some sort. Hans and Rand watched as Sulu spoke in a monotone.

"Citizens of Beta Prometheus. I am Hikaru Sulu, commanding officer of the *U.S.S. Excelsior,* a Starfleet warship from the United Federation of Planets. Eight days ago my ship was engaged in scanning the Beta Prometheus star system for the purposes of planning an invasion—"

Sencus stood up sharply. The image on the screen drew him closer.

"—of Beta Prometheus in order to force it to become a subject of the Federation. We were well inside Beta Prometheus star space when we were caught by the *Sundew* and brought to Archnos. Our ship, however, escaped, and returned to Federation Starbase 499, from where a fleet of Starships is preparing to launch an assault. I see now that such actions are an abuse of the power of the Federation, and that our desire to impose our will and our culture on other civilizations is in imperious ignorance of the Creator's will and in contradiction to the Only Way. I renounce such actions as an attack on peace-loving civilizations throughout the galaxy. And I ask all Federation Planetary systems to do the same."

There was a crackle of static and Sulu disappeared from Sencus's monitor.

"Nonsense," Sencus said. "He is—"

But before he could finish, a Beta Promethean face replaced Sulu's and spoke.

"The Shrewdest Ones have announced that the human commander Sulu will be executed at two-thirds orbit today, unless the Federation Council agrees to an immediate lifting of the dilithium embargo, a restoration of the rights of Beta Promethean trading ships to travel throughout the galaxy, including within Federation territory, and a penalty of two hundred and fifty thousand kerns paid to the High Conclave in exchange for the return of the spies."

Static replaced the Beta Promethean face. Rand touched the monitor.

"That's all there was, Captain."

Sencus still stood facing the blank monitor.

"Can you translate two-thirds orbit?"

"Yes, sir . . . 1500 hours. Today," she added nervously.

Sencus glanced at the chronometer in the wall above the monitor. "Almost 1200," he said. He turned and stared out the viewport and across the dock to the lights in the starbase's outer shell. "Get me the starbase commander."

Rand's hands played over the console in Sencus's cabin. In a few minutes a deep voice came through.

"Sencus, we've heard their ultimatum."

"And . . . ?"

"And I'm afraid right now my hands are tied. Admiral Fesidas is here with me. The Federation Council has already seen the transmission, and they are preparing a response. But you have to understand, even Starfleet Security doesn't believe that an assault would secure the hostages. We don't even know where they are at this point."

"You just saw Sulu on subspace transmission."

"Yes. We've identified its origin as coming from their most powerful transmission tower. Clearly they wanted it to be monitored by other star systems. But we don't know if Sulu was at that location when he made the speech. Or if he is there now."

Sencus thought to request that the Federation just give the kidnappers what they wanted, but he couldn't. He knew the Federation could not accede to the demands.

"You realize that Captain Sulu could not have said those things unless he was coerced."

"Of course. No one is blaming him. No one believes the transmission."

"Beta Prometheans are going to believe it."

"The Ruling Family has assured the Federation Council that they are doing everything in their power to insure that there are no more executions of Federation citizens," the voice said.

"That transmission did not mention the Ruling Family. Sulu referred only to the Shrewdest Ones. Clearly the Conclaves have the hostages. Who is in charge over there?"

"I'm afraid we don't know, Sencus."

"Neither do they, I think," Sencus said abruptly. Then he slumped in the chair by his desk.

"You will let me know if there is anything we can do?" Sencus asked.

"At once, Commander." Sencus saw Lieutenant Rand adjust the console, and knew that the communication had ended. He stared out the viewport for some time. Rand didn't leave the cabin. Finally Sencus turned to her.

"You know, there is someone here who is not quite so helpless as we are. Perhaps we ought to let him know about this."

"I'll forward the transmission to the *Plush Princess* at once, sir."

Kirk sat alone in his commander's chair on the bridge of the *Princess* as they flew back to the starbase. In his mind he saw the drawn face of Sulu on the transmission. He looked at the chronometer on the wall. It was almost noon.

He wasn't aware of Spock entering the bridge, but when he felt the tall Vulcan move up next to him and gaze at the dark galaxy, he felt less alone. Finally Kirk spoke quietly.

"The idea of attempting to make another trade for Sulu does not appeal to me very much, Mr. Spock," Kirk said. "We can't trust them, and we can't keep raiding the starbase for valuable goods."

"I concur, Captain," Spock said. "And with your new plan as well."

"My new plan? I haven't quite got a new plan, Mr. Spock." Kirk looked up.

"Surely you are thinking the same thing that I am thinking," Spock said.

"An assault . . ."

"With only seven of us? Better to call it a . . . covert action."

Kirk sighed. "I have been thinking that. I suppose we all have. I'm worried that I lean toward it out of anger. I hate to be bested. That was an embarrassing moment on the moon. For Starfleet even if they didn't know it, for the whole crew of the old *Enterprise,* and for me. Especially for me," he added glumly. Having admitted that, Kirk smiled at Spock. "I guess one thing I haven't lost with age is my ego."

Spock looked at Kirk. "Perhaps just recognizing that makes you a better human being," he said. "In the past, I posit that you would have—"

"Oh, never mind the old days, Spock. What are we going to do today?"

"Let us put our heads together on that," Spock said earnestly. Kirk stepped back.

"You don't mean—"

"Oh, no. Nothing like that. It is just one of your expressions, I believe."

"All right," Kirk said, relieved. "Let's."

"What do you mean, one's missing?!" Maldari screamed at Barush. "You were guarding them!"

"Dramin came and said that—"

"Dramin! That fanatic! I might have known. And he promised me that no more of my prisoners—*my* prisoners —would be executed! Who has he taken?"

"Their leader."

"The captain? *Picades!* I have just bested the Federation traders in a swap. I have whetted their appetite and we are ready to sell the real officers for more goods or kerns. How can I tell them that while I was selling them phonies, one was being executed?"

"I believe he is still alive. The Conclave Declaration said only that—"

"Where is he?"

"The prisoner? I don't know. Dramin still has him. He brought a cohort of Klingons to guard the prisoner."

"Klingons," Maldari spat and scowled. His black eyes blazed. "Didn't I say that no good would come of doing business with Klingons? Didn't I?"

"Yes, Maldari, you did," Barush said, nodding.

"This is my own fault. I should never have accepted their transport to Archnos from the No Where. They stick their oversize heads in everywhere. The rest of the prisoners are inside?" Maldari tilted his dark gray head toward the barred door.

"Yes, Maldari. All seven."

"Go tell the others. We're moving the rest of the prisoners."

"Now?"

"Yes, now. We're moving them out of the reach of the Shrewdest Ones, and out of the reach of these Klingons too. Go get the rest of the guards, then bring the prisoners to the shuttle. It's in the back. I'll meet you there." Maldari scuttled off, thinking.

"Vith Uhura's descriptions, ve have isolated three buildings. Ve're pretty sure it's one of them," Chekov said, as he stepped to the navigator's console. He ran his hands over the controls and a map of Archnos came up on the main viewscreen. "Now look here." He stepped up to the map and pointed with his finger. "Here's the tallest building on Archnos, and it's a transmitter, just like Uhura thought. We are positive it's the one she saw. There are a lot of those domed conclaves around, but by figuring the angle—the conclave has to be on the opposite side of the building from the tower—and judging by Uhura's description, there's only a thirty-degree difference, or a one-hundred-and-fifty-degree angle between them, leaving exactly two hundred and ten for the other degree, if ve postulate that the varehouse is in the middle. So there are three buildings large enough to fit Uhura's description. One here"—he pointed —"one here"—he pointed again—"and one here. Anything else vouldn't compute."

"Does this mean, Jim, that I have to dress up once more like a goddam Klingon?" McCoy said. "In twenty-five years with you, I've been in a lot of predicaments. But I've seldom had to act like a soldier, and never a Klingon. I'm a doctor, not an actor."

"You could stay here and let Scotty go. Run the transporter for us."

"Not on your life, Captain," Scotty jumped in. "Not that I would not love to go down there with a phaser and have a shot at these damn Prometheans. But I cannot trust the doctor with my engines. They're delicate things, and we may need all the power I can coax out of them."

"I'd have to agree with Scotty," Kirk said. "The women and Mr. Spock can't disguise themselves as male Klingons. So it's the three of us," he said, nodding at Chekov and McCoy. "That is, on a volunteer basis, of course. I really mean it, this time. There's probably going to be fireworks. This time will be far more dangerous. And once again, we're not representing Starfleet. Frankly speaking, I'm well aware this trip started out for most of us on a note of more enthusiasm and enjoyment than seriousness. I for one wanted to get back on a starship and back into space. But now I think we all have to admit we're a crew of slightly overage and overgrown adventurers."

"Speak for yourself, Jim," McCoy said. "Chekov and I don't weigh a pound more than we did when we signed on, do we, Pavel?"

"No comment, Dr. McCoy," Chekov said in his thickest accent.

"You have managed to insult four of us in one short sentence, Doctor," Uhura said. "That may be a record, even for you."

"And on that note," Kirk said, trying to steer the conversation back into more productive channels, "each of us must search his or her own soul and decide, in the harsh glare of reality, whether or not he or she ought to go forward." Kirk was looking right at Barbara, who was looking back at him with a studied and stern expression. "So perhaps I ought to say that I don't expect anyone—"

"Oh, come on, Jim," McCoy said. "Enough of this palaver. Do you honestly think there is anyone here who is going to jump ship? Even though I will be the first to admit that it's certainly what each one of us ought to do. We haven't abandoned ship in the past, and we're not going to now. I know I can speak for all of us when I say that."

There was a round of nods and short statements of agreement. Kirk was secretly pleased.

"As for you," McCoy went on, "I think you're just trying to get off the hook for bringing us into this. Well, it won't happen. Each of us is going to blame you for the rest of our days for dragging us out of our comfortable if boring existence and back into trouble. Now, let's go over this plan of yours one more time."

Kirk was looking at Barbara, and she smiled. He felt an urgent desire to go back in time, to be back in his apartment with her, back in that stage of their relationship which, in the light of the last couple of days, was less complicated. Equality between men and women, he thought, was something like that old logger's game of balancing on a tree log that floated on the water. You both had to keep running at precisely the same speed. One hesitation and into the water you'd go.

"Kirk?" McCoy prompted again.

Kirk looked around him. "Yes, the plan. Feel free to suggest improvements and alterations, of course."

Kirk couldn't help but lower his voice, even though there was no one aboard the *Princess* but the seven of them. The conspirators leaned in, and they spent the rest of the trip going over the exact details. When Chekov announced that they were arriving at Starbase 499, the meeting broke up.

Sulu walked ahead of the Klingon guards in a trance. He felt good about the statement he had made. The Federation had a heavy-handed approach to its position in the galaxy. While claiming its mission to be exploration and research, its vast influence was actually based on the power of Starfleet. Moreover, the Federation's insistence on the rights of the individual over those of the state led to excessive behavior that failed to benefit the community in general. Leadership was a responsibility of which only certain individuals were capable, and all others must submit to the will of the leaders for their own benefit. Sulu wondered how he could have spent so many years failing to realize that individual will had to be subjugated to the will of the larger community if civilizations were to advance without leaving some members of the community behind. He thought about the cacophony of cultures he had left behind, even on his own planet. Then he thought about the concept of a monocultural civilization, and saw at once how it led to peace and harmony, with all members of society equal. Surely it was truly the Only Way.

When they arrived at the warehouse, Dramin held a heated conversation with a number of Klingons who had arrived before them, but Sulu didn't understand what they were saying. Eventually he was taken back to the prison room, where he was mildly surprised to find that the others were no longer there.

He had wanted to engage in a discussion with Dr. Bernard Hans on the points he had been thinking about. Surely someone of Dr. Hans's experience could see that the Shrewdest Ones had the good of the larger Beta Promethean society at heart, that it was they who protected the interests of the average Beta Promethean. Surely Dr. Hans would be one of the first to see the efficacy of the idea of the eradication of individual will in favor of the collective good. Dr. Hans would see at once that the clamor of competing belief systems in their own society was harming their forward progress. And when he did, probably the others would begin to understand as well. Sulu had looked forward to discussing the ideas to which he had been introduced with his officers. When he found the room empty, he was disappointed.

He felt too good to worry about them, nor did he wonder where they were. He sat and waited patiently for the opportunity to talk with them about his new ideas.

"Do the preflight check for me, would you, Mr. Chekov?" Barbara said. "We might not be returning here, and I want to see an old friend. I went to the Academy with him. I'll be back shortly."

"I vill take care of it," Chekov responded. "Ve're launching soon, Ms. O'Marla. I should varn you that Captain Kirk vould not vait for anyone."

"Don't worry. I wouldn't miss this trip for the world."

Barbara left the deck and headed for the transport room, where she was just asking Scotty if he would mind beaming her over to Starbase 499 when Kirk appeared.

"Where are you going, Barbara?" he asked politely.

"Oh, hello James. I'm just going over to see a friend before we go. I figured that if we got hold of the hostages, we'd head straight back to Federation star space, and I might not see her again."

"Your friend hasn't guessed what you're doing here, has she?"

"Oh, no. I explained that I was just on a vacation. With you, as a matter of fact. She bought that, because . . . I told her about us. No, I've been very careful not to give anything away."

"Still," Kirk said looking at her, "if you wouldn't mind,

I'd like to ask everyone to stay on the *Princess* from now on. We'll be leaving shortly, and I think we ought to stick together. You can apologize to your friend in a transmission when we're all safely back in San Francisco."

Barbara hesitated. Then she smiled. "All right, sure. If you think that's best."

"I do. Thanks."

Barbara nodded and headed back toward the cabin she shared with Uhura. Kirk watched her go. Scotty watched Kirk watch her.

"You think she has a friend on the starbase?" Scotty said quietly.

"Yes, I do. But I'm just beginning to wonder what civilization this friend is from."

"What is it you're thinking?" Scotty said.

"I have no idea, Mr. Scott," Kirk responded. "But she told us her friend was a she, while a minute ago she told Mr. Chekov it was a he." He looked at Scott, who didn't say anything. "I just happened to overhear her conversation. Don't you think," Kirk asked, "that her presence here is odd, in fact? I know she is an impatient girl, but as a graduate from the top of her class at the Academy, I believe she could have had a deep-space assignment within a few weeks, or a few months at the very least. Yet she insisted on coming along on our half-assed mission."

"I am not one to talk about personal affairs, Captain," Scotty said. "But I do not think she's here for the adventure. I think she's here because of her feelings for you. If you'll excuse me saying so."

Kirk was almost startled. "I hadn't thought of that," he said. "What an interesting notion. But a not altogether sound one, as Mr. Spock would say."

"You underestimate yourself, Captain," Scotty said.

"Thank you, Mr. Scott. Yet I have to wonder how it happened that we were cheated by Maldari and his pirates. I mean, how is it that Maldari had the courage to pull such a fast one? How did he know we weren't carrying a lot of firepower? Or that we didn't have backup from Starfleet?"

"He could have taken the chance. He's a pirate trader, after all."

Kirk shrugged. "Yes, I suppose he could have. Let's just hope he isn't way ahead of us today."

"Not likely. Your plan's too clever by half."

"Unless there is a leak."

"Nobody knows about this except the seven of us."

"Mr. Spock is telling Captain Sencus. We'll want the *Excelsior* to rendezvous with us for the trip home. If we succeed, he'll ask permission of Starfleet to leave Starbase 499 and meet us. But Mr. Spock believes Commander Sencus to be entirely trustworthy."

"Because he's a Vulcan? Remember Lieutenant Valeris."

"How could I forget her? No, because of Sencus's actions immediately after the hostages were taken, and because they have apparently engaged in some private conversations. Commander Sencus hasn't told his crew anything, however. Nor has Spock given Sencus any hint of our precise plans. Only that we hope to do something, and would the *Excelsior* stand by to help if necessary. We'll send them a transmission if we need them. I wouldn't ask them to engage in any battle, however. They're still under orders from Starfleet to stand by at 499. I've compromised one crew already. That's enough."

"Then as I said, only the seven of us know."

"I hope I'm not letting my feelings for Barbara obscure my judgment."

"If you want my opinion, Jim, it's the other way around. You've been a captain so much more than you've been a lover, I'd worry about letting your judgment cloud your feelings."

Kirk looked over at Scotty with a surprised expression.

"I hope I haven't spoken out of turn, Captain," Scotty said.

At first Kirk didn't answer, contenting himself with turning back toward the corridor and looking after the ghost of Barbara O'Marla. Finally he spoke to Scotty.

"On the contrary, Chief Engineer. I suspect you know me better than I do myself." Kirk smiled. Then he wandered back to the bridge.

* * *

"How are the robots coming?" Kirk asked when Scotty joined the rest of them on the bridge.

"I'll have them all up and running in time, Captain. They're not going to last long, but they ought to look convincing enough."

"How much are they going to be able to do?" Uhura asked.

"Not much. They're sturdy but stupid, I'm afraid."

"That's probably just what we need," Kirk responded.

He turned to Scotty. "Why don't you tell us what you've done with these dime store robots."

"Well, I've rebooted their power source by plugging them into the ship's electrical energy system," Scotty pointed out. "I've programmed them to a more aggressive behavior pattern. I've entered a prearranged series of commands, which, once activated, they'll follow until they've either been destroyed or run out of power. As you requested, they canna actually fire their weapons."

"Good. We don't want anybody hurt."

"I could probably get them to recognize Maldari and his crew."

"It won't be necessary, and I don't want to take the chance that an innocent civilian, even a Beta Promethean, gets hurt. We have to remember that the Federation is seen as one big monolith out here, and is going to take the blame for anything that might happen."

"Unlike once we get back to San Francisco," Scotty suggested.

"Where we'll all be court-martialed for operating without direct orders in a situation under the operational eye of the Federation. Is that what you're thinking," Kirk said.

"It had occurred to me. Understand, Captain, I do nae wish to go out in a blaze of glory. But I would prefer to avoid being run out of Starfleet in a uniform of tar and feathers. Or spending any time on a prison planet."

"Having second thoughts, Mr. Scott?"

"No. But as long as we're out on a limb up here anyway, I wouldna mind blasting a few of these damn pirates who got us into this predicament."

"I wouldn't either. I suppose that's why you and I wouldn't make very good bureaucrats. We might still get the chance, Scotty. But I'd prefer it to be a judgment in our hands, and not in the hands of these addlepated robots. Better their weapons are disarmed."

"Dinna forget I've managed to rig two torpedoes up to this pleasure palace."

"That's right. Let's hope they won't be necessary. What about power, Mr. Scott?"

"There's enough to fire them both."

"Good."

"Or put up the shields."

"I see."

"Or get her up to warp speed," Scott said, frowning. Everyone was looking at him.

"Dare I hope for two out of three?" Kirk said.

"Nary a chance, Captain. The torpedoes and the shields alone are well beyond the specifications of this luxury tub to begin with."

"I'll keep that in mind," Kirk said.

"You'd better," Bones echoed.

"That about does it, then," Kirk said.

Everyone nodded and rose. As Kirk left the room, he glanced at the lead robot. "You know, this one does look an awful lot like Sulu."

The little star yacht slid across the black sky on its way to an orbit over Archnos. Kirk had the main viewport opened, something he had seldom done in the past, and as they cruised toward what he knew would be their last desperate attempt to extricate Sulu and the others from their prison, he watched the scenery go by. *Billions of stars, uncountable planets,* he thought. *How many more to explore? Another five-year mission? It would take a lifetime. It took mine. And we barely scratched the surface. I don't mind leaving the task incomplete. No, but I mind leaving it to others. How selfish of me. As if there weren't enough star systems to go around.*

He asked Uhura to record a transmission in the ship's memory bank and mark it for automatic sending at a later date, top-secret priority to Starfleet Headquarters, in the event the *Princess* lost life-support systems for more than twelve hours. Then he spoke out loud, so that everyone aboard the *Princess* could hear him.

"Ship's Log. Stardate 9625.10. Captain James T. Kirk aboard the star yacht *Plush Princess*. This afternoon six members of the original crew of the *U.S.S. Enterprise* will attempt to extricate the eight Starfleet officers of the *Starship Excelsior* led by Captain Hikaru Sulu, who are being held in a prison on the surface of the planet Beta Prometheus 1, somewhere in the city of Archnos. We wish it to be known that we are acting entirely on our own, in direct violation of standing orders and regulations from Starfleet and the Council of the United Federation of Planets. We take this action in the full knowledge that it could jeopardize our standing as Starfleet officers. We have no choice, however. A fellow officer with whom we have served is in danger, and we have chosen loyalty to him over our duty to the Federation. Should something go wrong, Starfleet Headquarters will receive this message, by which we wish it to be known that we meant no disrespect to Starfleet, or to the United Federation of Planets."

Kirk signaled to Uhura, who put the transmission in the communicator's memory banks.

"That's about all for now, I suppose," he said quietly. "Well, there is one more thing. It's all happened quite fast. I don't think I ever got a chance to thank you all for your help," Kirk said quietly. Then he rose and headed for his bunk. As the others broke up, Uhura could be heard to say quietly, "You know, I think that was our first thanks in twenty-five years."

"Imagine," Chekov said to her, "how much it means."

When the *Plush Princess* arrived at the space coordinates Chekov had chosen as appropriately far enough away to avoid detection and close enough for a staging area, the ship glided to a stop and hung in space, its powerful engines quiet, and only intermittent thruster power keeping it in a stationary orbit automatically. Chekov, McCoy, and Kirk joined Spock in his cabin, and he began the laborious process of transforming them into Klingons. Scotty was down in the transport room making final programming adjustments to the robots. Uhura had gone downstairs to check on the small arms weapons they had aboard. Barbara was alone on the deck, monitoring the ship's geographical position. She scanned the skies around her, but there were no signs of any other starships nearby. She calculated the ship's reserve power systems.

Then she walked over to Uhura's station and looked around. With no one else on the bridge, she sat down, and quickly typed a message out. She sent it off, and then she erased it from the ship's memory bank.

She walked back to her own station. With nothing left to do but wait, she strolled up to the main viewscreen and gazed out across the skies to a tiny blip on the horizon that she knew to be Beta Prometheus 1. She called up a closer view. The large planet filled the screen. She ran a scan and saw the pattern of heavy populations clustered around only a few areas of the reputably inhospitable environment. She guessed which one was Archnos—the largest—and asked for an inset. She left the holographic reliefs on the screen and sat back in her chair, where she waited impatiently. She drummed her fingers on the side of the chair. Not unlike other conspirators with hidden loyalties, she was uncomfortable when given too much time to think about things.

She was deep in her own thoughts when someone tapped her on the shoulder. She jumped. She turned around, and jumped again. Three hard-visaged Klingons were standing in a semicircle around her.

"Well, do we pass?" she heard Kirk's distinctive voice coming from the one in the middle. "Come on, how do we look?"

"Good," she stammered out. "Great. You all look great. No one will ever suspect you're not Klingons. Isn't it awfully hot under all that?" Barbara ventured.

"Yes," McCoy said.

"I have used a viscous application that should allow the pores to breathe freely," Spock said. "In any case, it is often below freezing on the surface of the planet at this point in their orbit."

"It was hot as hell standing around that anti-Federation rally, I can tell you," Kirk said.

"That was your nerves," Scotty said, as he appeared behind them, having come up from the engine room for a look.

"How," Barbara asked, "did the six of you ever agree on anything during your twenty-five years together?"

"We seldom did," Kirk said equitably. "We were usually too busy for discussions, however. Stations, everyone."

Upstairs Barbara watched, marveling, as the three Klingons took their places around the small bridge.

"Mr. Chekov, coordinates for stage two please," he said when everyone was settled.

"On the screen," he answered. "Beaming distance."

"Barbara, proceed with full thrusters,"

"Proceeding, Captain."

The ship shot forward and in minutes was cruising high above Archnos. Kirk and McCoy studied the map. Then Kirk turned around.

"Scotty," he said. "Can you put us down about here?"

"Aye, Captain."

"Okay, Klingons," Kirk said. "Let's go."

"There's the tower," Kirk said under his breath to McCoy. "If Scotty has put us down near the first target, then we have to go down this street until we come to a warehouse, then try to find a door which lines up with a Conclave."

They found the first building, a ramshackle two-story monolith faced with shiny metal of some kind that seemed to match Uhura's description. There were doors of one kind or another on all sides. They walked around it until they found a door that lined up with the roof of a Conclave behind the building. They turned around, and saw the communications tower in the sky. The whole layout was worth investigating. They watched the door from across the street, and found that a number of Beta Prometheans went in and out. Many seemed to be carrying oversized bags, as if they were bringing supplies of clothes and food.

"This seems very promising," Kirk said.

"Now what?" McCoy said.

"We go inside, I think," Kirk said, and headed for the door. McCoy and Chekov followed.

As they had seen others do, they simply strode up to the door and opened it. They stepped inside, trying to appear as if they knew where they were going.

At once Kirk realized this was not where the hostages were being held.

They could see the entire inside space of the large building. It was open from one wall to the other, and illuminated by large skylights in the ceiling. The large wooden floor they stood on was filled with Beta Prometheans, and music boomed out of speakers. There were mirrors lining the far wall, and everyone was facing them. In the front of a group of at least fifty, a Beta Promethean was leading them all through an exercise routine.

Kirk and McCoy stood mesmerized at the sight of a herd of Beta Prometheans—all with the customary four legs—moving back and forth in unison to the beat of some sort of punktronic music.

"Holy cow, Jim. Would you look at this," McCoy said. "It's a dance school. Or an exercise class of some sort. If Sulu is here, he's in great shape."

Kirk turned and frowned at McCoy. "Uhura said there were stacks of transport containers just inside the door. That was only this morning, so they can't have moved all that. This can't be the building."

As they turned to go, a male Promethean scuttled up to them from behind a desk.

"Hello, you're early," the man called in a singsong voice. "This is the four-legged class. Two-legged alien aerobics isn't for another hour. But you can watch if you like."

"Exercise?" McCoy said.

"Thank you," Kirk said. "I think we'll come back."

"Do. It's awfully good for your heart. I understand the Klingon diet is terribly fatty."

"It's nails," McCoy said.

"I beg your pardon?" the Promethean said.

"Never mind. He's just grouchy," Kirk said quickly.

"Of course. Hardening of the arteries. Too much meat. Not enough exercise. Come back in an hour. You'll feel much better."

Kirk piloted McCoy out the door. McCoy had a difficult time tearing himself away from the sight of fifty Prometheans scuttling back and forth, their muscular arms swinging in rhythm.

Outside, Kirk walked swiftly away from the building. McCoy caught up with him.

"Couldn't be a front, I suppose?" he said.

"Unlikely, Bones. It would take too many Prometheans, and then there's the building. It didn't look like they could hide much inside. That's all right, we have two buildings left to check out."

He looked up at the buildings around them, tried to see himself on the holographic map they had studied.

The three artificial Klingons from the star yacht *Princess* walked through the shadows of the city of Archnos on Beta Prometheus 1. It was freezing on the planet, but as they walked along a prearranged route toward the second building they had identified as a possibility, they began passing more and more Beta Prometheans, as well as various aliens and not a small number of Klingons. Chekov nodded as he passed a group of three Klingons. Two paid no attention to him, but one scowled back. After they had passed on by half a block, Kirk spoke in a low voice.

"Mr. Chekov, Klingons aren't friendly. You don't have to say hello to anyone."

"I forgot."

They passed several militaristic-looking Klingons, but were not stopped. More suspicious were the Clerics, several groups of whom milled about the streets. *They seem to be permanently suspicious, however,* Kirk thought. *I think they look at everyone that way.* He saw the second warehouse up ahead. He led McCoy and Chekov around to the rear of the building. There was a door precisely as Uhura had described it. He glanced over his shoulder and saw the transmission tower at the correct angle. He saw the domed Conclave in the distance behind the door. Moreover, a number of armed Klingons stood in front of the door.

"This must be it," Kirk said.

Their makeup had fooled everyone so far, Kirk thought. Now they only had to get inside.

And out again.

He reached under his tunic and touched his communicator.

"Kirk to *Plush Princess*. I believe we have found it. It's the second building. We are going in."

Then without hesitation he led McCoy and Chekov directly up to the door. He flicked his Universal Translator on as they crossed the street. He walked directly up to the guard at the door.

"Do you have the prisoners?" Kirk said in an authoritative voice.

"Of course," the guard answered back.

"Are they well guarded?" Kirk asked.

"Of course they are," the Promethean said.

Kirk began to wonder if he could keep up this conversation for long without seeming like an awful fool. He decided he couldn't, and opted to try to get inside.

"We would like to see them," Kirk said, lowering his voice both for more authority and in the hope that not too many of the others overheard clearly.

The guard hesitated.

"That is not possible."

"Tell Maldari we are here. We are——" Kirk had prepared the idea but even so hesitated, wondering how it would translate. "——the Klingon Council for Military and Espionage Matters. We have an interest in the spies you have secured, and wish to interrogate them."

The guards looked Kirk and his crew over. Kirk looked straight back at the aliens, hoping to intimidate them.

Just open the door, Kirk thought.

Finally the older one nodded, and said to Kirk, "Wait here," then turned and pounded on the door. He shouted a few words, and it was opened from the inside by another

Klingon. They exchanged words, and he stepped inside as the inside guard started to close the door. *This is crucial,* Kirk thought. *I'll have to take the chance of getting shot right here.* He put his hand out and kept the door from closing.

Just a few more seconds, Kirk thought. "We need to see Maldari," he said. "We have come to interrogate the prisoners at the request of the Klingon High Council. We are the subcommittee for—"

He didn't have to ad-lib any longer. At that moment a wild look came over the face of the Klingon left guarding the door, and Kirk knew that Scotty had timed it just right. He turned around.

Eight uniformed Starfleet soldiers, all armed with phasers, had materialized in the street facing the warehouse.

Kirk was the first to shout. "Federation soldiers! Shoot them!" he yelled, which he hoped was a reasonable command in either Beta Promethean or Klingon. At his words Chekov and McCoy drew their phasers out from underneath their tunics and began firing on the Starfleet soldiers. None of them hit their intended mark, a fact which, at least for the moment, seemed not to impress itself upon the Klingon guards. The other, authentic Klingons and Prometheans milling in the street were unarmed, and took cover once they understood the situation.

The inside guard was pulling the door closed on Kirk when Kirk forcefully shouted "Attack them!" and wrenched the door open. At once the Klingon joined his comrade and both of them began firing on the Starfleet soldiers, who appeared to be firing back. None of the real Klingons taking cover behind the wall questioned the fact that the two Klingon guards seemed to be holding off the complete squadron themselves, with only single-shot, laser-driven assault weapons.

As he disappeared inside, Kirk saw a couple of his Starfleet soldiers get shot and stagger back, but the others strode resolutely forward, firing, without the slightest effect. Chekov ran past the two guards and caught up with Kirk inside the warehouse.

McCoy dove in last. He fired his phaser at one of the

guards without looking directly at him, and passed into the building. Stunned, the guard fell to the street, and the phalanx of remaining Starfleet soldiers moved inexorably forward to the door, though, curiously, not quickly. The remaining guard looked at his companion, then turned to fire again at the oncoming enemy.

Inside, Kirk slammed the door shut behind them. The three stood still for a second, their eyes adjusting to the dark. Kirk, looking at a picture in his mind Uhura had drawn for him, yelled "This way!" and headed along the corridor she had been led down earlier. He counted off the turns and exits. He stopped, turned left, and began running again. McCoy and Chekov were right behind him.

Suddenly a dozen Klingons were running toward them, their weapons at the ready. Behind them Kirk saw a Cleric. They looked confused at the sight of the three Klingons in the prison. Kirk didn't hesitate.

"There is a Starfleet war team outside, trying to get in! At least two dozen! Heavily armed!" he shouted over the explosions of gunfire outside. The Klingons stopped directly in front of them. "You've got to get the prisoners out of here before the soldiers break in!" Kirk went on hurriedly.

One of them turned and shouted several commands. The Klingons broke up; half of the group pushed past Kirk and his crew and headed toward the door. The Cleric turned with the others and ran back along the corridor. Kirk, Chekov, and McCoy ran behind them.

The motley group arrived at a door. Kirk could hardly contain his urgency. He forced himself to wait patiently behind the group as they hurriedly unlocked and opened the door. Then he followed them inside.

Only Sulu was there. The Cleric hurried over to Sulu and brought him forward.

"Where are the others?" Kirk shouted. No one answered. The Cleric was barking commands at the Klingon soldiers, and sending most of them back along the corridor toward the phaser fire.

"Where is Maldari?" Kirk tried again. "Where are the other prisoners?"

But the Cleric shouted more commands, and the remaining Klingons took Sulu and hurried him farther along the corridor, away from the prison. Kirk, McCoy, and Chekov ran after the fleeing Cleric and his Klingons, until they all arrived at another door on the far side of the warehouse. There they stopped. The Cleric barked something at one of the Klingons, and the Klingon opened the door cautiously. Then he threw it open wide and stepped out. It was dark outside, as the Promethean sun was in the sky only a few hours each day. There was no sign of Starfleet soldiers, and the Klingons stepped into the alley. The Cleric brought Sulu. Kirk and his team simply stepped through the door after them. Then Kirk spotted the shuttle parked in the shadows along the far wall. He saw the Cleric signal to the others, and the guards ran across the street toward their transportation.

"We'll take over from here," Kirk shouted as he came alongside the Cleric. The Shrewdest One's eyes blazed as he turned to Kirk. Kirk wondered for a moment whether he saw Kirk, or the Klingon disguise.

"I think we'll take better care of them than you will," Kirk said. It was unlikely, however, that the Cleric heard Kirk. Halfway through his explanation Kirk fired his phaser directly at the Promethean, who skidded backward and flopped to the ground. McCoy and Chekov fired their phasers within seconds, and the Klingon guards fell almost at once. Only one was quick-witted enough to raise his rifle, but he was standing near McCoy, who quickly slapped it down, and it fired uselessly at his feet. A second later Chekov shot him, and he joined his friends on the ground.

Suddenly the alley was quiet.

"Sulu, it's me. It's us. Look." Kirk tore off the carefully applied silicone material Spock had re-created his face with. McCoy and Chekov did the same.

"Captain Kirk! Dr. McCoy. Mr. Chekov. This is a surprise. But why have you shot my friends?"

Kirk could do nothing at first but stare at his old shipmate. Chekov frowned. McCoy stepped up beside them.

"I'll take over, Jim," he said. Then he pulled a medical

tricorder out of his bag and quickly ran it over Sulu. "Vital signs are healthy. Tell me, Captain Sulu, do you know who you are?"

"Why, you know me, Doctor. I'm Sulu."

"So far, so good. These"—McCoy nodded at the fallen Klingons and the Cleric at their feet—"Klingons are your kidnappers, isn't that right?"

"Oh, no, Doctor. They've been our hosts. You see, I have renounced the ways of the Federation in favor of the Only Way, which I must tell you is the only path to a better galaxy. Why, did you know that—"

"Tell you what, Sulu. How about if you come along with us, and tell us more about this? Right now we're a little pressed for time. Do you know where the others are?"

"I'm afraid not," Sulu responded. "But I'm sure they're in good hands."

Kirk, McCoy, and Chekov could only look at each other in bewilderment. McCoy turned his back on Mr. Sulu.

"Brainwashed," he said under his breath. "I can help him, but not until we get back to the ship."

Kirk touched his communicator. "Scotty, we've got Sulu. But the others have been taken away from the jail. Probably by Maldari and his crew, since they're nowhere around. You'd better transport us—"

"Wait a minute, Captain," Chekov interrupted. Kirk turned to see that he had his tricorder out and functioning. "I'm getting some signs of human life. Our normal body heat is slightly higher than the normal Beta Promethean's. Here on the ground I think I can register the difference. I think we can follow the *Excelsior* officers. This way." Chekov started off up the alley.

Kirk touched his communicator. "Scotty, never mind. Just beam up Captain Sulu. We're going to try and track the others. Stand by." He started off after Chekov as Sulu dematerialized.

On the other side of the building, several Klingon soldiers had joined their comrades in defensive positions. They knelt, firing at the Starfleet soldiers advancing in a semicircle toward them. One by one the eight men in red tunics went down. Round after round crackled out of the disruptors of the Klingons until all of the Starfleet officers lay on the ground, small sparks and some smoke drifting out from under their tunics.

The guards fired a few more rounds out of nerves, then stopped. Finally one of them looked around, called out to the others, and began to move cautiously forward, his gun at the ready. He stood over the inert figure, and looked directly down into the crystal eyes of a Starfleet soldier. The other guards crept cautiously forward and examined the downed mechanical robots. The leader bent down and looked closer. Then he rolled the man over roughly, and pulled up his tunic. A red warning light indicating severe malfunction was blinking. He uttered a loud exclamation. Then he looked around at the other defunct soldiers. Only then did he notice a lack of blood anywhere on the battlefield, though perhaps he was one of many Klingons with a severely limited knowledge of alien anatomy, and wasn't aware that humans spilled a good deal of blood when shot.

During the fierce battle, not one of the robots had fired a lethal shot from the weapons they carried, but it was unlikely that the Klingons were aware of this, given the noise and urgency of the engagement. The noise had come from prerecorded phaser fire and been emitted through speakers that were part of the robots' equipment. If Scotty had been able to see his small army do battle using nothing more dangerous than those sounds he had preprogrammed, he would have been quite proud of them. But he was on the lower deck of the *Plush Princess,* waiting patiently.

Chekov jogged through the streets, reading the tricorder. Kirk ran right behind him, his phaser ready. McCoy ran behind them. Once a Beta Promethean turned the corner and stopped to stare as the odd platoon of three humans in Klingon dress ran by, but he was unarmed, and none of the officers shot him.

"Mr. Chekov," Kirk said in spurts of breath, "are we going the right way?"

"I believe ve are, Commander," Chekov answered. "Humans have been through here. This vay, I think," Chekov said, and he pointed across a deserted field. They had left the last building behind them and were in the open.

"We're pretty badly exposed now," McCoy said as he looked around apprehensively. "You sure you know where we're going?"

"Look. There's some kind of an installation up ahead," Chekov shouted. "If I remember our maps correctly, ve are at the outskirts of the city."

Kirk slowed down. "It looks like an abandoned installation of some kind," he said. "Probably an old dilithium mine."

"According to my tricorder, that mine is not deserted," Chekov said.

The three of them jogged quickly across the flat field.

"And what are we going to do when we get there? Now that we've run out of robots, I mean," McCoy said as they sprinted along.

A few hundred yards later they stopped in front of a pair of six-foot-tall steel pyramids that stood on either side of a crumbling road. The objects marked an entrance of some kind. A moon had risen high in the dark sky by the time they arrived, and moonshadows flickered throughout collapsing, rusted structures that were spread over several acres. They clung to the shadows as they approached the entrance. There was no sign of anyone else in the area. They gathered in the shadow of an empty guard booth just outside the perimeter. Chekov aimed his tricorder up the pitted path.

"Ve are not the only warm-blooded animals on the premises," he said quietly.

"Where?" Kirk whispered.

"Inside. That direction," Chekov indicated.

"Maldari must have brought the hostages here," Kirk said under his breath. "My guess is he's hiding them from the Klingons. We ought to take off this crap now."

"Now, there's the best idea I've heard so far," McCoy said as he began peeling off the remaining latex attached to his face. Chekov did the same.

When they were done, they stood in the rough leather of their Klingon tunics and waited for Kirk's instructions. He led them in a wide arc around the principal road. They kept to the shadows, and eventually arrived at a towering gridwork of open-air catwalks that ranged over an acre of scarred ground. There was a hill in the center. Chekov took a look at his tricorder again.

"We're getting strong readings. They must be just beyond that hill."

The three of them spread out to arm's length and moved slowly through the steel pilings that supported the gridwork above. As the ground rose in front of them, Kirk got to his hands and knees, then lay prone on his belly. The others copied him, and they crawled forward. At the crest of the hill they stopped. Kirk inched farther forward until he could just see over the hill.

Amid the scaffolding of the abandoned mine, Kirk saw a knot of humans in Beta Promethean tunics. They were surrounded by more than a dozen Beta Promethean pirates. Other Beta Prometheans were opening the transport containers Kirk had supplied, and passing around the weapons Kirk had traded to them. He thought he could see Maldari giving orders.

Kirk crawled back down.

"I think everyone's here. They're just opening up the weapons we gave them." Kirk rubbed his hands together in the chilly night. "It must be below freezing," he whispered. Then he smiled. "Perfect."

They heard the crunch of gravel and turned to look toward the entrance. A shuttle slid by the pyramids guarding the entrance road and shot into the compound. Kirk and company crawled back down the low hill and disappeared into the shadows just as it went by them. They watched it pull up alongside the edge of the structure, and several Prometheans climbed out quickly and hurried in.

Again Kirk crawled up the hill. He heard the guttural Promethean shouting, and he saw Maldari talking animatedly to the new arrivals. Maldari glanced at his seven remaining prisoners, then spoke again to the messengers. It was clear to Kirk that Maldari wasn't sure what to do. Then Maldari barked out some orders and the additional Prometheans spread out and took up defensive positions around the perimeter of the hostages.

Kirk touched his communicator. "Kirk to *Princess*. Mr. Spock, are you still with us?"

Spock materialized next to him. "Right here, Captain," he said.

On the bridge, Barbara looked around. She and Uhura were alone.

"Uhura," Barbara said. "I think we'd better get a bit farther away from Archnos. We don't want to be seen. Can you monitor Kirk from back there?"

"I think I can keep them in range."

"All right. Scotty, you there?" she said.

"Yes, ma'am," came Scotty's smooth burr back over the intercom. "Where would I be, now?" he said with a flicker of amusement.

"Of course. I'm pulling the ship back to our outer-perimeter orbit. We won't draw any attention to ourselves out there."

"Very good, ma'am," he said. "I'm sure they'll be all right," he added, sensing her discomfort. "Kirk's been in worse spots, he has. We all have. Try not to worry too much."

"Thanks, Mr. Scott," Barbara said.

Of course, we were all on the same side in those days, Scotty thought. *I hope we are now.*

Kirk's expression lit up. "Mr. Spock, this is timely. We were just about to surround them. Would you care to join us?" Spock nodded and began to circle around the perimeter of the clearing. Kirk watched him disappear into the spidery catwalks of the ancient installation. When Kirk turned back, he nodded to Chekov, who hurried off in the other direction.

Kirk stood up. He walked up to the top of the hill. There he paused for a minute, then began walking down the shallow slope directly toward the waiting Beta Promethe-ans. After half a dozen yards they spotted him. Maldari stepped toward them, and all of their weapons were raised.

Kirk waved and smiled.

He crossed the one hundred yards of open space until they arrived at the bottom of the hill. He stood only yards from the Prometheans, and the *Excelsior* hostages were only yards beyond that. Kirk suppressed the urge to look up at the catwalks.

"Maldari, you crook. You cheated us. We gave you the weapons you wanted, and we got only robots in return. We've come for the others," Kirk said.

Maldari's mealy gray skin turned darker.

"The officers are here. Except for one, who was taken by that damn Cleric. You can have these. He raised his weapon. "For fifty thousand kerns."

"How much is that, exactly? Never mind, we don't carry that kind of cash on us anyway. Suppose you just hand over the officers on credit, eh?"

Maldari started to shout, but before he could, Mr. Spock dropped down from the catwalk above and landed at the edge of the group. He reached over and pinched the nearest Promethean at the base of his neck. The Promethean froze and slumped forward. His body fell with a thud, landing, as it happened, directly between Kirk and Maldari, just as their conversation had reached something of a standoff. Maldari looked down at the unconscious pirate at his feet. He immediately fired his weapon at Kirk but nothing happened.

"Oops," said Kirk.

At once a firefight broke out. Chekov appeared from the shadows on their right flank. McCoy appeared from the shadows behind Kirk. They all fired their phasers at the stunned Beta Promethean pirates. At least five·fell to the ground without getting a shot off. Others were able to shoulder their new weapons and begin firing back.

But nothing emanated from their weapons. Try as they might, the Prometheans could not coax one bullet, one flicker of laser light, one miniphoton or blast of phaser fire out of the barrels of their shiny new assault weapons. They pulled their triggers, they lined up their sights, they adjusted every dial and studied every gauge on the complicated panels of their guns, but nothing helped. Kirk watched with interest as Maldari attempted again and again to fire his shoulder-mounted assault pistol directly at Kirk. It had no effect.

"Frozen," Kirk said pleasantly. "The ammunition inside is frozen solid. Sorry we didn't send along the instruction manual. Won't fire a shot in below freezing temperatures. Must be pretty cold out here." Then Kirk raised his phaser and blasted the frustrated Maldari.

In a few short moments, the Beta Promethean pirates were either all knocked unconscious by the phaser fire that rapidly enveloped them, or they were in speedy retreat. Their ability to run forward at a hare's pace, Kirk noted, was matched by their ability to run backward. In just a few minutes, the area was cleared of standing Prometheans. In the sudden stillness of the cold night, a round, aged but robust-looking man walked over to Kirk.

"Captain! How good to meet you!" he enthused, pumping Kirk's hand.

"Dr. Hans, I believe," Kirk said. *"Excelsior* medical officer. I am James Kirk, and that is Dr. Leonard McCoy, medical officer for the *Enterprise.* Until last year."

"Dr. McCoy! Of course. Sulu has spoken of you. Then you are his old crewmates, the officers he served with for over two decades until he was given command of the *Excelsior."*

"That's correct, Doctor."

"This is most extraordinary. How did you get here?"

"We can tell you all about that in a short time," Kirk said. "Right now why don't we all step out from under these structures into the open over there? There's a number of us to be beamed up, and we have a rather small transporter platform aboard our ship."

The hostages followed Kirk to the top of the low hill, while Spock, Chekov, and McCoy flanked them, keeping a lookout for more Prometheans. None appeared, and they all arrived on the hill safely.

Kirk touched his communicator. "Landing party to *Princess*. We're all accounted for. Beam us up, please."

Nothing happened. Kirk looked at Dr. Hans. "Got a new helmsperson. You'll like her. She's a bit late. A woman's prerogative I suppose."

"Captain," Lieutenant Roose said. "I overheard you point out that the Beta Prometheans' weapons were energized by liquid that freezes at thirty-two degrees. What would have happened to you if the temperature hadn't dropped below freezing?"

"Oh, not much. We would have gotten a bit wet."

"Wet?" Chekov said. "But wouldn't liquid neutron energy be fatal if fired?"

"I have no idea. Far as I know, there's no such thing as liquid neutron energy. Might be something to look into, though. That isn't what those weapons are loaded with."

"What was the ammunition?" Lieutenant Roose said curiously.

"Water. Pure H-two-O. All of those weapons were carefully synthesized from a catalogue of water guns."

"Water guns?"

"Squirt guns featured in a toy catalogue from the late twentieth century. We found it in the historical research library. Amazing-looking things. They make our own phasers look downright harmless."

Then Kirk called the *Princess* again. Still there was no response.

The noise of the shuttle grinding across the rocky landscape attracted their attention. Several of the Prometheans who had escaped had come back when the officers had moved off, and commandeered the shuttle the messengers had come in. It shot off across the splintered landscape and disappeared quickly into the sky.

"We had better get going," Spock said to Kirk.

"Any minute now," Kirk said confidently. They stood for agonizing minutes in the chilly air. "Probably just getting a fix on us. Scotty, we're ready to be brought aboard."

Still nothing happened.

* * *

"I'm getting a call," Uhura said suddenly in the stillness of the *Princess* bridge. "We'd better go in closer, don't you think?"

Barbara turned to look at Uhura. "What kind of call?"

"From the captain, I think. It's hard to tell, we're so far away, but I believe they're ready for transport."

Scotty stood still in the engine room. He was listening to the conversation. He held his breath. A beat of silence ticked by, then he heard Barbara's voice.

"Full ahead, Mr. Scott. We're going in."

He touched the controls, then took a deep breath. *She's a fine girl,* he thought to himself, and couldn't wait to say so to Captain Kirk.

Chekov pointed to the road they had come up to gain the mine. "Something's coming," he said.

They all looked. A fleet of war tanks was rumbling along the road toward the mine. They could just see a Klingon standing up in each one.

"Apparently someone has managed to follow you here," Spock hypothesized.

"Maybe they're not after us," McCoy said cheerfully. "Maybe they've come for Maldari. He can't have made too many reliable friends during all this."

"They're going to see us pretty soon either vay," Chekov said. His prediction was confirmed when an explosion rocked the ground five yards to their right.

Exposed and without the firepower to disable the land vehicles, Kirk and company would have been in serious difficulty, had not they begun dematerializing just then.

". . . So when I thought about it, I was shocked at how simple it all is. That's probably how it came to be called the Only Way." Sulu smiled earnestly. "The Federation's complex and varying belief systems are so terribly inefficient."

"He's been talking to me like this ever since he arrived in my transport room," Scotty said.

Dr. McCoy ran his medical tricorder over Sulu while he spoke. Kirk saw him studying it.

"Sulu," McCoy said brightly. "This is all most interesting. I've often thought there must be a better way to run this damn society of ours. Why don't we go into the aft space lounge here, where I've got some comfortable chairs and a bit of my equipment, and you can tell me all about it?"

Sulu nodded in agreement and walked amicably off the control deck in the direction the doctor indicated.

"Bones, what the hell is wrong with him?" Kirk whispered.

"Fairly simple, I think. He has been fed some sort of drug which has made him susceptible to brainwashing. I doubt if I will ever discover the true properties of the thing. Probably indigenous to Beta Prometheus. But I think I can find an antidote, or at least flush it out of his system. He'll probably cooperate."

McCoy followed Sulu onto the rear deck.

"You won't mind if I give you a physical while we talk, will you?" McCoy smiled. "You've been through a heck of an ordeal, and I want to see that you're healthy. Go ahead, tell me all about this Only Way stuff. We'll just start with a simple injection, in case that Beta Promethean food didn't have an adequate supply of vitamins and minerals."

"It works like this," Sulu began. "Each member of the Conclave works for the good of the community. None of this individual gain for individual effort stuff. Everybody contributes what they earn to their Conclave, and the Shrewdest Ones decide how best to allocate the resources. Of course, right now they don't have complete control. The Ruling Family creates the laws. But they're an aristocratic and tradition-bound group that's on their way out. And many of the traders go their own way, up to a point. . . ." Sulu became drowsy. McCoy nodded his head, smiled. He ran his medical tricorder over Sulu, while appearing to listen to the explanation. When Sulu was asleep, McCoy rose, covered him with a blanket, and went back to the control deck, where he checked the physical condition of the other officers. When he returned, Sulu was just waking up.

"I must have dozed off," he said to McCoy. "I guess I was tired. Where was I?"

"You were telling me about the Only Way." McCoy said.

"The Only Way? What would we want to talk about that

corrupt system for? Those damn Shrewdest Ones almost killed me, for heaven's sake! They're hypocritical, totalitarian, and abusive! Even most of the Beta Prometheus population hates them. They're completely narrow-minded, there's no room on their planet for the least dissension. Why, where would we be without dissension, without debate? How colorless our lives would be without a variety of cultural backgrounds. How ridiculous to think that individuals should have any loyalty to a system in which they had no voice. . . ." Sulu would have gone on, for his fury at being incarcerated for a substantial period of time was in need of release, but McCoy just smiled and wandered off.

Uhura was chatting with the young Lieutenant Roose, McCoy was talking to Dr. Bernard Hans, and Chekov was showing off the navigational resources of the star yacht to the engineer Norquist Svenson. Kirk walked over to the captain's chair and sat down amid the noise and tumult of the happy gathering. Barbara looked back at him.

"Warp ahead, Cadet O'Marla. We'll rendezvous with the *Excelsior*. Uhura, tell Commander Sencus we're on our way. We'll have you back on your Starship in no time," Kirk said to Sulu, who had come onto the bridge.

But Uhura shouted over the noise. "Captain Kirk, I've got a warship rapidly approaching from the starboard quadrant."

"Identify."

"It's hard to say. Not so large as a heavy cruiser but much larger than we are."

"Mr. Spock?"

"Confirmed, Captain. My sensors say that she is heavily armed."

"A Bird-of-Prey?"

"No, Captain."

"Visuals."

The main view monitor came alive with the dark universe. In the far distance was a rapidly approaching dot of light.

"Close up," Kirk said quickly.

The screen flashed and a rusty warship sped into view.

"It looks like the *Sundew*," Sulu said, coming to stand behind Kirk. "But it can't be. Probably that pirate Maldari has got himself another ship."

"Evasive action, Captain?" Barbara asked without looking.

"We'll have to outrun them if we can," Kirk said. Scotty and Svenson hurried downstairs to the engine room.

"Commander, I've got another ship coming up rapidly," Uhura called. "This one from the port quadrant."

"Identify."

"This one is a Bird-of-Prey. The Klingons are on to us as well," Mr. Spock said.

"Full ahead warp speed," Kirk said.

Barbara's hands flew over the controls and the ship shot across the galaxy.

"Scotty, do we still have two torpedoes?"

"Aye, sir. They're small but I think they'll launch. That is, if we don't use the engines at the same time."

"What?" Kirk said.

"I told you, Captain. This little yacht has enough energy for one or the other, but not both."

"All right. Tell you what. Barbara, on my word, you shut her down. All engines. We'll fire one at the *Sundew* and one at the Klingon vessel, then we'll take off again. Everybody ready?"

"Aye, Captain."

"Ready here."

"Full stop," Kirk commanded.

The ship slowed and stopped in seconds. It hung in space.

"Fire," Kirk ordered.

The ship bucked as the two torpedoes fired simultaneously and headed for the warships.

"Now, warp ahead full. Let's get going," Kirk said.

Barbara touched the controls and the *Princess* shot forward and raced across the galaxy.

"That ought to give us a minute," Kirk said.

On the screen, the crew watched tensely as the torpedoes locked on to the larger ships. The ships raised their shields, but the explosions rocked them and they slowed visibly.

"Direct hits!" Chekov exulted.

"Yes," Mr. Spock said. "But both warships are fully enabled. They are still following us. In fact, they are gaining on us."

Everyone looked at the main viewscreen. Views of both warships were up, and they loomed larger and larger.

"Warp speed?" Kirk asked.

"Five," Barbara said.

"She canna go any faster, Captain," Scotty's voice came up from the engine room. "As it is I do nae have enough energy to get us home at this speed."

"How long until they close on us?" Kirk asked.

"Judging from our speed, their speed, and the distance between us, I would say we have less than five minutes' safety. After that they will have no difficulty scoring direct hits," Spock said tersely.

Just then Barbara jumped up from her seat and ran past Kirk.

"Barbara, don't leave your post," Kirk shouted.

Before he could stop her, however, she stood next to Uhura. She reached past the communications officer and ran her fingers over the console.

"Calling Starbase 499. This is a high-priority message for the C in C. Please note code name: Princess. Repeat, patch me through to the C in C at once. Code name: Princess."

"Barbara?" a voice came back quickly.

"Admiral, it's me. We're being chased by two warships, a Klingon vessel and a Promethean pirate. We have the hostages safely on board. But we are being attacked. We need a little help up here."

"I understand. Over and out."

When Barbara stood up, everyone was staring at her. She looked over at Kirk, who was looking at her curiously.

"An old family friend," she said lamely, then she went back to her station.

There wasn't time for anyone to question her.

"Distance is closing, Captain," Chekov said.

"Captain, two incoming torpedoes, port and starboard."

"Scotty, put our shields up," Kirk said.

"I canna put shields up and keep us at warp speed,"

came the familiar voice. "We do not have that much power on this luxury bucket."

"Torpedoes at half-distance," Uhura said, trying to keep her voice even. The bridge had gone deathly silent.

"Put the shields up, Scotty. Barbara, cut all engines." Barbara looked back at Kirk. "Do it now," he said strongly. "Scotty, I've given you every bit of power this yacht's got. Make those shields hold."

"I'll try, Captain."

For a moment no one spoke on the bridge. Then the little yacht was hit, and it rocked halfway on its side. The officers were thrown to the floor.

"She's breached on the left, Captain," Spock's voice said as he read off his console panel. He barely got the words out when a second explosion pounded the ship on the other side. Lights on the bridge flickered and sparked, then went out. Emergency lights glowed in the corners, and the eerie cabin was in half-shadow. Kirk stood by his chair. Barbara crawled back into hers. Mr. Chekov was trying to stand up by his navigation console. Smoke began filling the bridge.

"Another hit will blow us out of the skies," Kirk said. "Return power to engines, Scotty. Barbara, evasive action. Set us on a zigzag course at warp speed."

The ship bucked and rocked as it moved forward.

"Incoming," Uhura said.

"Another torpedo?" Kirk asked.

"Yes, sir," came the answer. "She's locked on to us."

"Brace yourselves, everyone," Kirk said quietly.

Just then the ship changed directions radically and the torpedo shot by.

"I can't do that very often," Barbara said as everyone breathed a sigh of relief. "It takes too much energy from the main propulsion system, and we don't have much left."

"Well, here comes another one," Uhura said. "A Klingon torpedo is locked on to us. Arrival in thirty seconds."

"Warp ahead ten," Kirk called.

"Fifteen seconds," Uhura announced.

"Warp ahead twelve," Kirk called.

"She's going as fast as she can, Captain," Barbara said.

Just then three Starfleet Starships shot into view.

"What the hell?" Kirk said.

One of the Starships passed the little star yacht and took up a position on its tail. The Klingon torpedo exploded harmlessly against its giant shields. The other two Starships surrounded the *Princess*. The Klingon Bird-of-Prey and the smaller Beta Promethean starship slowed, then stopped. The *Princess* and her escorts left them behind.

"Thank you, Starfleet," Kirk said to nobody in particular as the whole crew applauded. "Uhura, open a channel to those ships. I want to thank—"

"I wouldn't do that, Captain," Barbara said.

Kirk looked at her thoughtfully.

"I'm sorry, sir," she said, "but we're not supposed to be here, they're not supposed to be there, and none of this ever happened."

Kirk looked at the solemn face of the beautiful girl, who was looking directly into his eyes from her seat at the helm. Those on the bridge waited as the two looked at each other, Kirk with a curious expression, Barbara with a quiet one. Finally Kirk spoke, though not to Barbara.

"Uhura," Kirk said.

"Yes, Captain," she answered.

"Never mind."

For a few minutes the Starships kept their positions around the *Princess*. When it was evident that she was no longer being followed, the Starships stopped, presumably to return to Starbase 499. The star yacht was once again alone in the galaxy.

Ten minutes later Barbara dropped out of warp speed and they found themselves gliding along behind the *Excelsior*. Those of her crew who had been in prison for the last eight days whistled at the sight.

"There you are, Sulu," Kirk said. "I'd like to invite you to be our helmsperson, but as you witnessed yourself, we have an excellent one already." Barbara smiled. "And one with pretty good connections, it seems." Kirk looked at her suspiciously.

* * *

The two ships sat side by side in space for several hours, as Montgomery Scott and Norquist Svenson led a large team of *Excelsior* engineers in repairing the little *Princess*.

"That ought to get you back to Earth, Mr. Scott," Svenson said, when at last they laid down their equipment and all systems blinked green.

"I'm much obliged for your help," Scotty said. He looked around at the hastily patched engines, the blackened walls, and the barely functioning electronic systems. "I hope her owner is patriotic," he said, shaking his head, when finally they were finished. Scotty called up that the ship was ready, and the engineers walked into the transport room.

Kirk and his crew entered the transporter room with Sulu and his officers. Scotty went to the transporter controls and aligned them with the *Excelsior*.

Sulu turned to Kirk. "Where will you all go now?" he said.

Kirk looked around at his crew. "Us? Back to San Francisco, I suppose."

Sulu held out his hand to Uhura and she took it.

"Kwaheri," he said in Swahili.

"Kwaheri," she replied, smiling.

He turned to Scotty.

"Slán agat," he said in Gaelic.

"Slán agat," Scotty answered.

Sulu turned to Chekov.

"Dos Vidaniya," he said.

"Oudachy," Chekov answered.

He turned to McCoy.

"Bon voyage, Doctor," Sulu said with a smile.

"And you keep warm, old friend," Bones said softly.

Sulu turned to Mr. Spock. He raised his hand in the Vulcan salute.

"Live long and prosper, Mr. Spock."

"Peace and long life," Spock answered.

Finally Sulu turned to Kirk.

"Commander, I don't know what to say," Sulu said quietly.

"Nothing, Commander. After all, nothing happened here, remember? That's the way Starfleet wants it. So that's the way it will be. I always do things by the book. You know that."

"Your book," Sulu answered quietly. "One that is filled with courage and loyalty. You came a long way to help. You all risked your lives," Sulu said, shaking his head. Then he took Kirk's hand in both of his. "May the wind always be at your back, Captain," he said. They embraced; then Sulu stepped up onto the platform to join the last of his officers being beamed over to the *Excelsior*. He turned to Kirk and company and saluted.

"Until we meet again, old comrades," he said. "Until that day." Then he disappeared.

Aboard the *U.S.S. Excelsior* Sulu and the other hostages were welcomed back by their crew. As Sulu settled into the commander's chair, Lieutenant Roose stood behind him, waiting for instructions. But Sulu was silent, staring at the main viewscreen, where the little star yacht floated. Finally Lieutenant Roose cleared his throat and spoke up.

"Where are we headed for now, Captain?" he asked.

Sulu came out of his own thoughts and looked up at the young lieutenant. "Where? There will be a debriefing at Starfleet. And then onward, of course. As always. There is so much to explore."

"Yes, sir. Uh, might I suggest, however, that we return to the Mirage? You remember, that newly discovered planet we had catalogued just before we were taken hostage. The one with the ideal environment."

"I thought we had learned all we could from that planet, Lieutenant."

"Unless we were to explore the surface in person, sir."

"I see. Still hoping for a little R and R."

"For the crew, sir. They've all been under a great deal of strain lately, and, well, I just thought . . ."

"It's a good thought, Lieutenant. What do you think, Sencus?"

The science officer looked over from his console, where, as it turned out, he had been reworking the old problem of who had read the ship's memory banks without permission, and how.

"Captain, I now believe the inhabitants of that planet are, in fact, aware of our existence," he said. "The dolpheels, with their extraordinary telepathic powers, were probably observing us just as we were observing them. It would therefore not be a violation of our Prime Directive if we were to say hello in some way. However . . ." Whatever Sencus was thinking, the rest was lost to his concentration on his computer.

"Yes, Sencus?" Sulu said. "What is it?"

"I cannot seem to locate them again."

"That's funny. Navigator?"

Violet Bays looked up from her own panels. "I'm afraid I can't either, Captain," she said. "It's curious but, well, they're simply not there."

"Not there? That's an impossibility," Sulu said. He stood up and walked over to the navigator's station. "Do we still have their coordinates?"

"Of course, sir. I know precisely where they are *supposed* to be. We have graphed their orbit very carefully. But . . . they're just not there anymore."

"Perhaps their orbit has variations. Did you check—"

"I have scanned their entire solar system, Captain. As far as all our instruments show, there is simply no such planet."

Sulu sighed. "Well then, I'm afraid we won't be going there again. Nor will anyone else, for we'll look pretty foolish if we announce our discovery and can't prove it. Too bad. And I was thinking of asking the Federation to officially name it Sulu's Planet. Just another one of the eccentricities of deep space, I suppose. Any analysis, Sencus?"

"The planet seemed to function in a most subtle and tranquil fashion, Captain. Absolutely in harmony with itself. And their telepathic powers were extraordinary. Whether they are there or not, I might suggest that perhaps they have the power to be seen or not. And now that they are aware of the greater universe, and a number of its inhabitants . . ."

"Yes?"

"Perhaps they do not wish to participate in interplanetary intercourse just yet."

"You mean, we've been studied and found wanting?"

"Just that, Captain. They seem to have found a perfect peace for themselves and their environment. While the rest of us . . ." He let the officers on the bridge, all of whom were listening intently now, finish the sentence for themselves. "Can you blame them?" he added.

"I see what you mean. An interesting proposition, Sencus. I'll tell you what." Sulu brightened and raised his voice. "We'll find another plant for some R and R. I understand there's a sulfurous mud moon on the edge of the Beta Quadrant. Perhaps we could receive permission to——"

But the officers on the bridge all groaned and went back to their stations before Sulu could finish his sentence. They left only Sulu and Sencus on the floor.

"They do not like the idea, Captain," Sencus said, and, not for the first time, Sulu had to remind himself that irony was never a part of the Vulcan science officer's conversation.

"I guess not," he said, shrugging. Then he turned back to the main viewscreen. "We'll just have to keep looking. Anyway"—he looked at the great dark field in front of him ablaze with stars—"we won't run out of possibilities."

With the exit of the hostages, the little star yacht the *Plush Princess* seemed suddenly empty. The officers returned to their stations. Barbara waited for Kirk to give a command. When he didn't, she turned around. He was looking at the viewscreen, though nothing was on it but the gleaming *Starship Excelsior* in the infinity of the surrounding universe.

"Home, Captain?" she prompted.

"Hmmm? Oh. No. Not home. I don't think so."

She looked puzzled.

"To San Francisco, I think," Kirk said. "We started there. Ought to return this little yacht to its owner. You think he'll notice the giant holes in her side?" Everyone on the bridge chuckled. Barbara's fingers skidded over the console and the ship slid across the universe toward the planet Earth.

Then Barbara turned around again. "Isn't San Francisco your home, Captain Kirk?" she said, puzzled.

"No," he said quietly to her, though everyone on board heard him. "And Vulcan isn't Mr. Spock's, nor Africa

Uhura's. Chekov isn't from Leningrad any longer, and Dr. McCoy has left the Earth's metropolises far behind. Scotty will go back to the Highlands, but they aren't his home. Space is our home, Barbara. Space. And when we're anywhere else, we're out of town."

Barbara looked around at the crew, and they were all smiling at her.

One Week Later

In the Neutral Zone

SAREK, flanked by his aides, sat down at the table in his customary place. They waited the usual quarter-hour beyond the appointed time, and then the door opened and Kannish and his team walked in.

Sarek watched as Kannish squatted on the stool on the other side of the table. He bade him a pleasant good morning. Kannish grunted his usual salutation. Then, as was his custom, he slapped the table with his open hand and began forcefully.

"We have decided to release the prisoners," Kannish said disarmingly. "In fact, they have already been transferred back to a Starfleet vessel. I hope this shows our good faith in the pursuance of a treaty with the Federation."

Sarek's aides all smiled, but Sarek replied without hesitation.

"The Federation sincerely appreciates your actions. That this misunderstanding has not been allowed to stand in the way of the momentum of our current negotiations is most gratifying. For our part I can assure you that the Federation seeks only peace and prosperity throughout the universe, and renounces any attempt to enter your star system uninvited. You have our sincerest apologies for any inconvenience the incursion of our Starfleet officers into your star space has caused."

The two able negotiators went on to exchange mutual pledges of goodwill, then cautiously moved into areas of concern. Some four hours later, their positions had altered by a degree so imperceptible as to be understood only by the participants. Nevertheless, both left the table somewhat encouraged.

When Sarek and his aides were seated in their shuttle after the long session, the young woman asked if, now that the hostages had been returned, their negotiations would come to an end.

"Oh, no," Sarek said. "There is still a real treaty to hammer out. We need clearly defined boundaries, trading conditions, armament agreements. Pledges of mutual security. Eventually we'd like to see the Beta Prometheans send an observer to the Federation Council. Someday—if we can achieve assurances that the Beta Prometheans will respect all humanoid rights—they might even become full members."

"How long do you think all that could take?" the young woman said.

"That is hard to predict. Unlike the peoples of your Earth, many alien civilizations find it difficult to get along with one another. I have been working on a treaty with the Legarans for twenty-one years now, thought I hope my work will bear fruit soon."

The two young aides looked at each other.

Sarek smiled. "We must have patience," he said.

San Francisco

It was dark when Kirk walked alone through the heavy fog that blanketed his port city. He could feel the pull of authentic gravity. Or perhaps it was just the weight of his age. He saw the Flag and Grog in the distance, its yellow lantern burning off the fog in a tiny semicircle around the entrance. He had received an invitation to a private gathering via the press aide Marasco. *Maybe a bit of Saurian brandy will cheer me up,* he thought. But what he had really been thinking for most of the walk was, *Will she be there?*

He hadn't seen her in a week. Not since the *Plush Princess* was returned to its owner and the crew stepped onto terra firma.

Just as he was about to step up to the bar's door, she appeared out of the shadows.

Her coat was turned up against the damp. Her hands were deep in its pockets. She was looking at him with a bemused expression. He stopped, and looked at her. He could feel his heart race at her beauty.

"Hello, Jim," she said. "Can I buy you a drink?"

"Barbara. It's good to see you." Silence hung between them like a black hole in the sky. Then Kirk broke it with the first thing that came to his mind. "I never got a chance to thank you for all your help. Or even to say goodbye."

"I was embarrassed, I guess. I just went back to my quarters. You never called."

"No. No, I didn't. I suppose because I didn't want to know."

"What?"

"Barbara. You didn't happen to have any old family friends in high places. You were working for Starfleet all along. You were a spy among us. Weren't you?"

He waited for her to answer. She took her time.

"Yes. It was an assignment. The Federation couldn't be involved, Starfleet couldn't mount a mission like that. But they knew you would try something. They asked me to go along with you."

"I see. Well, you did your duty. Beautifully. And you're an excellent helmswoman. We couldn't have done it without you."

"Then you're not mad?"

"Mad? Of course not." Kirk stood in the fog and searched his own heart. "To tell the truth, I don't know what I am. It came as a bit of a shock that it was all a Starfleet assignment for you, that's all."

"It was a great assignment."

"Gee, thanks."

"Jim. Would you believe me if I told you that what happened between *us* wasn't part of the assignment?"

"No."

"It wasn't."

"Well, let's call it a bonus, then. For me, I mean."

"Don't hate me."

"Never. Hey, wait a minute. I'm the experienced old hand here, you're the cadet. You underestimate me. A girl in every solar system. Nobody breaks the commander's heart."

"Not seeing you again is going to break mine."

"Starfleet worried about what I'll do next?"

"That's cruel."

"Sorry."

"Do you think," Barbara began, "we could start over?"

Kirk hesitated for a long time. *When I was younger,* he thought, *I would have said no out of sheer bravado.*

"Maybe," he finally said. Then he turned and led the way into the Flag and Grog.

They climbed the stairs to the bar. It was noisy and crowded, as it had been the last time he had patronized the place. Cadets, officers, and aliens jammed the central room. This time Kirk walked past the long bar and turned into a narrow corridor in the corner. They passed under an archway with a sign overhead that read THE WIDOW'S WALK. BANQUET FACILITIES. A neon sign was turned on just underneath it that flashed the notice CLOSED FOR PRIVATE PARTY.

They climbed a steep flight of stairs and entered the private room. Kirk spotted the tall Mr. Spock first, talking with Admiral Caius Fesidas. There were other admirals and high-ranking officers there as well. Eventually he spotted Scotty, Bones, Uhura, and Chekov. He waved at each of them. Barbara disappeared toward some young officers. The press liaison Eugene Marasco came over to him.

"Captain Kirk," he said. "Welcome. Welcome to a very unofficial function."

"Marasco," Kirk said as he took a drink from a uniformed waiter. "I want to talk to you."

"Of course."

Kirk walked the man into a quiet corner of the party room, and lowered his voice.

"Off the record, just how much did Starfleet know about . . . my little mission?"

Marasco sipped from his drink.

"Everything," he said simply.

"Everything?" Kirk said, his eyebrows rising.

"Everything. You were monitored from the moment you began gathering your old crew together."

"But they didn't stop me?"

"Of course not. Kirk, don't be naive. I know you've spent your entire life in deep space, but you can't be entirely innocent of down-to-earth politics. The Federation couldn't do anything officially without upsetting the delicate balance of power in that part of the universe. They couldn't give in to the pirates and they didn't want to risk an official invasion by Starfleet that could touch off an intergalactic war. And then there's the dilithium. Our Starships couldn't explore the universe without it, and the Beta Prometheans keep the market in good supply. As soon as you began nosing around—here and at headquarters—a secret, top-level team of admirals and science officers convened and studied your long record, and your psychological profile, and realized—as one of the committee members who knew you said—that you were not going to be the problem this time. You were going to be the solution."

"I don't know whether I'm flattered or not."

"I'm rather proud of the fact that I tipped off Starfleet to you, as a matter of fact."

"You?"

"When you sat down with the admiral and me. It occurred to me that your interest in the *Excelsior* had to be something more than idle. The next day I checked the records, and saw your length of service with the commander who was taken hostage. So I contacted—"

"Wait a minute. You said 'the next day'?"

"That's right. The day after the night we met here I reported your interest to—"

"The next day. Then this committee didn't meet until then?"

"That's right."

"Then what happened later that night, it couldn't have been a setup?"

"Later that night? What do you mean?"

"Oh, uh, nothing. Tell me, how did Barbara O'Marla come to be a part of our mission?"

"That was something of a coincidence. A couple of days later she came to Starfleet Security with the same suspicions. She said she knew you, and she was worried that if you went up there really on your own, it might be dangerous. She said she thought she could get you to take her along. The committee decided that planting someone among your crew would be ideal, a much easier way to keep track of you. So we gave her the assignment."

"I see. But she came to you?"

"Yes."

"After the night you and I met downstairs."

"That's right. Why?"

"Oh, I just wanted to get the chronology straight in my mind."

Marasco looked past Kirk and over at Barbara, who was chatting with several high-ranking officers. "This is going to be a pretty strong start for a young cadet's career," he said. Kirk followed his look and saw Barbara chatting with the other officers. He thought he saw a poise and assurance she hadn't evidenced when they first met. She was flushed with the confidence of someone who had a significant accomplishment behind her. He stepped on the urge to go over to her. Just as she looked up and saw him staring at her, the president of the Federation walked in, and a number of Starfleet admirals hurried to greet him.

"Say, how did you know Barbara, by the way?" Marasco was saying to him.

"Barbara? Oh, you know, just from . . . around," Kirk said. "I heard she was at the top of her class as a helmsperson. And with Sulu on his own Starship now, I figured we might need one."

Elsewhere in the room, Mr. Spock was talking with a middle-aged senior officer from some department or other in the bowels of the Starfleet bureaucratic machinery.

"The hull took a number of hits. The outer shell structure ought to be replaced entirely. At least two of the support pylons are collapsed. The shields need to be strengthened. One of the warp propulsion units is burnt beyond regeneration. The navigational systems were compromised when the electrical sensors were blasted, they probably need a good going-over by—"

"Mr. Spock," the officer interrupted. "The *Plush Princess* isn't a Starfleet vessel. I can't procure the materials or the engineers to renovate a luxury yacht owned by a private and extremely wealthy businessman."

Spock frowned. "I gave Thaylor my word the ship would be returned in excellent condition. I cannot go back on my word."

"Thaylor loaned us the ship because he knew he could trust the reliability of Vulcans," Scotty said, joining them. "You'd be putting Mr. Spock in an awful light, and dinna forget his father is a member of the Council."

"It's a strict regulation that private businessmen may not be approached to contribute to Starfleet operations," the officer protested. "There's too much room for special interests with private causes to affect policy."

"And of course, if he had to be told the real reason for the mission, it would certainly get around. Thaylor is a man with friends in high places," Scotty finished.

"All right, all right. I suppose I can have our engineering section do the work, and then hide the paperwork somehow."

"That's right. You can call it Community Relations."

"Yes, yes, I'll take care of it."

"Thank you," Scotty said, then turned to Mr. Spock and winked. "Because I would nae want the good name of Montgomery Scott and Mr. Spock, holodocumentarians, to suffer!"

Everyone took seats at a large table, and the dinner got under way. The president was seated at one end, the C in C at the other, and the admirals and two dozen officers and the crew of the *Princess* spread out in between. Kirk found himself sitting diagonally across from Barbara.

There were speeches thanking the crew of the *Enterprise* for the "non-event." Kirk thanked Starfleet for its loyalty, but he was looking right at his old crewmates when he did it, and everyone knew what he meant. The Federation president got a good many laughs conferring an invisible "Citation for Bravery" on the six retired officers and one cadet, whose record of service during the ten days in question would read "on leave, whereabouts unknown."

"There's one thing I'd like to know," Admiral Fesidas said to Kirk. "About those weapons you traded to the Beta Promethean pirates. Have you been in the habit of ignoring General Orders throughout your career?"

There was a delicate silence at the table. Kirk smiled. "Absolutely not, Admiral. Didn't you hear? They were all water guns. I never actually intended to give them weapons, and the G.O. doesn't say anything about toys. Why, you know me. Everything by the book." The admiral smiled.

The evening was well under way when Marasco asked Chief Engineer Montgomery Scott, who was sitting across from him, if this "non-event" had been their most difficult and dangerous mission.

"Difficult?" Scotty thundered. "Dangerous? Why, laddie, let me tell you about the time we came across a huge, green hand in space. It grabbed the *Enterprise* and wouldn't let us go. Why, I thought we would have to stay on Pollux IV forever. Dangerous? You haven't heard anything yet . . ."

The dinner lasted long into the night. By the time Phylosian cognac and Cobanian cigars were passed around, a great many years had gone by in Scotty's stories, and old friends had laughed and cried over old times, amusing, and amazing, the younger officers present.

Kirk had been quiet. Finally he stood up.

"I'd like to propose a toast," he said finally, raising his glass. "To absent friends. To Captain Sulu, somewhere on the frontier."

"To Captain Sulu," his crewmates shouted.

"And to young Spiros Focus, of the *Excelsior,* who gave his life for Starfleet," Kirk said. "To fallen comrades."

"To fallen comrades," the officers all echoed. They drank in silence.

Finally the C in C stood up. He had been listening quietly most of the evening.

"To all the men and women of Starfleet, past, present, and still to come, who have demonstrated a loyalty unmatched in the history of human endeavor. A loyalty to the science of exploration, to the cause of peace, and to the Federation. And to Starfleet itself."

"To Starfleet," the officers shouted, and everyone drank.

"But most of all," he went on, "to the men and women of the *Starship Enterprise*—excuse me, of the *Plush Princess*" —everyone laughed—"who have demonstrated the greatest loyalty of all. *Semper Fidelis.*" He raised his glass.

Everyone raised their glasses, and Kirk, Scotty, Bones, Chekov, Uhura, and Spock toasted their neighbors with due humility, and secret pride.

Most of the officers were still enjoying each other's camaraderie when the spaceport beyond their window began to twinkle with the early-morning dawn. Kirk looked out and saw the gleaming white skins of the shuttlecrafts. He looked up at the lightening sky, and imagined the great Starships that waited in spacedock for their crews to take them to still uncharted quadrants of the universe. He wondered if he would be privileged to captain one again.

With the dawn the party began to break up. The old friends found themselves the last to leave. Finally McCoy walked over to Kirk.

"Bones? Back to ordinary patients?" Kirk said.

"Not me. Not exciting enough. As long as the treaty is holding, I thought I would open a practice devoted to Klingons. I'll get to explore those ridiculous physiognomies. I'll wear my disguise to make them feel comfortable." Everyone laughed.

"Well, I'm going to earn some real money with what Starfleet taught me," Uhura said. "I've got a senior management position with Inter-Galactic Systems to return to." She hugged Scotty, Chekov, McCoy, and Kirk in turn. Then she raised her hand in the Vulcan greeting to Mr. Spock.

"Mr. Spock, back to acting?" Kirk asked.

"No, no. Far too emotional for me. I am going back to Vulcan, however. There is much to study. Much to learn."

"The greatest quest of all," Kirk said to him.

They all drifted out the door. And back to their own lives, thought Kirk. He took a last look out the window, then went out of the room himself. He walked through the now deserted bar, went down the turbolift to the street, and turned toward his apartment.

Barbara was on the street, waiting for him.

"And what about you, Jim? Will you still live here in San Francisco?" she asked.

"Yes. Our voyage cured me of restlessness, I think. For the time being, anyway. How about you? Starfleet will surely offer you an important assignment after all you've done."

"I've been offered a helm position on a newly christened cruiser. It's leaving in a week."

"I didn't mean to be quite so cold before the party," Kirk said. "I was talking to Marasco and I realized . . ."

"Yes?"

"Oh, nothing. Just that I would like to see you again."

"How about right now?" Barbara said.

A smile came over her face that Kirk was sure he remembered from several weeks earlier.

"Of course, now that I know all about your history," she went on, "I have to be careful. I'd need some kind of commitment. I wouldn't want to be just another one of your women of the universe." She looked at him.

"I'm not the marrying kind," he said. "Too young."

They walked along in silence a little farther. Then he spoke again.

"How about a five-year mission?" he offered.

"I'll settle for that," she said, and wrapped her arm inside his.

They walked side by side along the fog-shrouded streets as the sidewalk began to glisten with the rising sun, the black sky that had been filled with stars disappeared, and an orange daylight broke over the city.

"Maybe we could even take a little trip together somewhere," she suggested, looking directly up at the last remaining stars just before the sun washed them all out of the sky.

About the Author

Denny Martin Flinn grew up in San Francisco, then journeyed to New York, where he spent twenty years in the American musical theatre as a dancer, choreographer and director before turning to writing. He is the author of *What They Did for Love*—the story of the making of the Broadway musical *A Chorus Line*—two mystery novels, *San Francisco Kills* and *Killer Finish,* featuring the grandson of Sherlock Holmes, and co-screenwriter of the motion picture *Star Trek VI: The Undiscovered Country.*